"YOU HAVE A LOVER!"

Her voice was sharp, accusing. Something in it made my stomach knot, my breath stop.

"I know, I know! You have a lover. Men are beasts!" she burst out venomously. "Those that walk with the beasts shall die like the beasts, Amberleigh."

She was advancing on me and I turned to run. A sudden flash of fire licked across my arm and my whole body shuddered.

A knife. She had a knife.

—CAROLE NELSON DOUGLAS—

A JOVE BOOK

First Jove edition published September 1980

10 9 8 7 6 5 4 3 2 1

Printed in the United States of America

Jove books are published by Jove Publications, Inc., 200 Madison Avenue, New York, NY 10016

For Garson Kanin,
one hell of a messenger

THE MINSTREL BOY

The minstrel boy to the war has gone,
In the ranks of death you'll find him,
His father's sword he has girded on,
And his wild harp slung behind him;

"Land of Song," said the warrior bard,
'Tho all the world betray thee,
One sword at least thy rights shall guard,
One faithful harp shall praise thee!"

The minstrel fell! but the foeman's chain
Could not bring his proud soul under,
The harp he loved ne'er spoke again,
For he tore its cords asunder.

And said, "No chains shall sully thee,
Thou soul of love and brav'ry!
Thy songs were made for the pure and free,
They shall never sound in slav'ry!"

—Thomas Moore

PROLOGUE

The Nightmare

THE MUSIC was harsh and jangling, more like an off-tune funeral dirge than the marital harmonies of Mendelssohn. But the bride advanced down the staircase steadily, a dream bride wafting along on layers and layers of tulle. Illusion, they call it.

Was it I, or someone else?

Her hair was the color of flame, her face pale. She cradled an infant, but she walked forwards without heeding its struggles, she marched formally ahead with that rapt expression so common to brides, so common to anyone playing a leading role in a ritual.

Was it I, or someone else?

An entire row of bridegrooms awaited her—black-shrouded shoulders receding into the dream distance, faces averted. They were three, standing quite still with their dark backs to the bride. Three.

She advanced upon them, the infant's mouth yawning in a silent howl, and her own bridal face as set and carved as a doll's. The first man turned slightly and had no face. The second glided past in a scarlet mask, as if someone had painted out his features with blood. The third pivoted, his countenance scar-crossed . . . The bride paused.

The music had changed, had shifted into the strains of an old song, a simple song. About three lads. One who left. One who haunted. One who loved.

9

"I see a lad that loves me
And I see a lad that leaves me
And a third lad,
A Shadow lad
And he's the lad that grieves me..."

The bride floated past the bridegrooms once more. One was faceless, one was fleshless, one was flawed.

She bowed her flower-crowned head as the dark high above, the dark lost in the distant church rafters, webbed into a veil and floated down upon her. The child in her arms squirmed fitfully, but the veil swallowed him whole and he was gone. The bridegrooms were gone; the black veil had netted and swept them into a pit at the bride's feet. Their three faces, pale and still unfeatured, lined the pit bottom.

But was it a pit? Or a dark oval that squared itself into a trench, then shrank to a six-foot-long slit in the earth? The bride bent and dipped a hand towards the hole. A hand as white and wide-fingered as hers stretched up from it, like a reflection from oiled, ebony water. Their fingers touched—the bride's pale face cracked, split into a scream. She drew back, back from the pit, away from the floating, vacant faces, far from the waxen hand glimmering corpse-candle-bright from the pit. It all whirled away, even the music, with the whine of a dozen severed catgut strings, of a savagely broken harp.

"It is real," some voice whispered. "It is real, this dream. Remember it. Remember it, remember..."

She turned and found a pale shrouded figure like her own facing her. "Elaine," she said, uncertain whether it was her own name she uttered, or another's. "Elaine..."

The music returned, cascading into an atunal climax, driving the dream voice away. The music became wind, became howling. The bride put both hands to her ears, and the fiery hair bright as flame flickered around her with the black veil, brushing her dead white face.

"I'll remember," she promised. "I will remember..."

Was it I? Or someone else?

CHAPTER ONE

Spring—1887

As ELAINE and I stood together on the platform, I could feel every eye in Miss Meachum's large drawing room upon me. Fifteen young voices trilled "God Save the Queen" (bless her black-bombazine-surrounded old heart) and I was finding it difficult to concentrate on countering Elaine's clear soprano.

My gaze wandered slowly from the smooth green lawns framed by the open French windows opposite me to the bobbing profile of Miss Priscilla pounding the melodeon with grim emphasis. My glance fell finally to the blur of pastel faces above pastel garden gowns and summer suits.

The audience. Proud parents and relations of the fifteen young ladies about to terminate their stay at Miss Meachum's School for Young Ladies. And we did look that, too. Even "Mousie" Arbuthnot seemed to have lost her lankiness, looking quite sedate in blue sprigged dimity.·

But Elaine, Elaine looked like an angel, I thought, catching a sidewise view of her fair, curl-framed profile. Elaine was all in white organdy and she was the only girl in the room with four ruffles on the hem of her skirt. But then, she'd always had the cream of everything. I thought I picked out a dashing nile green hat that could only belong to Elaine's stepmother, Lady Devora St. Clare, one of the most beautiful women in London, to hear tell. Beside me, Elaine's voice glided to a high "C" serenely. For a moment I wanted to slap her silent for being so carefree, for having an audience of elegant relations watching her with benign eyes.

Not that they weren't watching me, too.

Indeed, I was probably making quite a splash.

And between the murmured "Oh, your Letitia looks simply adorables" that stirred the assemblage like the hum of searching

11

bees, I fancied I heard the eyebrow-raised tones of "So *that's* the Dunne girl, next to Elaine St. Clare. You've heard, of course..."

Yes, they had heard, of course. Everyone had heard by now. I felt a tingle of red surge to my cheeks. But I also felt a bitter satisfaction in standing next to the others, seemingly as serenely unaware of everything as they, the only one who most certainly did not belong. Who had never really belonged.

The day I had first found out—had it really been only a month before? That day, I had so innocently gone down to Miss Meachum's parlour. It was just after dinner on a lovely spring evening.

"Hurry back," Elaine had said. "There's just time for a walk before last bell. Tell Old Prue that you promised to do my hair à la Greque tonight and I'll leave school and tell Papa never to send another sou if she keeps you too long!"

I laughed and tripped down the old mahogany staircase without the slightest sense of foreboding.

Miss Meachum's parlour always managed to look dusty and dank; no matter how bright the day it carried its own belljar with it, holding in the dust of years. The Black Hole, we students called it, and it was the scene of many painful remonstrances and unexpected confrontations with parents distraught about one thing or another.

On the last score, I had nothing to worry about. Father showed a merciful lack of interest in anything I did, or did not do, at the school.

As I knocked, Miss Meachum's barely audible "Come in" sounded from behind the double door. I always suspected her of using that low tone in hopes of someday catching an unfortunate entering before she had said it.

She was ensconced as usual behind her strangely delicate desk, her maroon gown blending into the dark crimson curtains at the window behind her. As I entered, a short stout man— but very Savile Row—sprang up like a bogey man from the shadow of a wing chair.

"Ah, yes, Amberleigh," said Miss Meachum in her usual dry tones.

"You wished to see me, Miss Meachum?"

"Yes." She paused for quite a while, another tactic to induce unease, I guessed. "Amberleigh, this is Mr. Harwood." She paused again. I resolved to say nothing and smiled sweetly at Mr. Harwood.

"... of Doyle, Martin and Chadwick," Mr. Harwood finally

added as a sort of clew. It meant nothing.

"Sit down, child." Miss Meachum's voice was almost bluff.

I slipped uneasily into the wing chair partnering Mr. Harwood's. I was beginning to sense that something momentous was in the air.

"Mr. Harwood is a solicitor, one associated with your, ah, father. He is here on rather urgent business." Another pause, and it was Mr. Harwood's turn to contribute to the staccato conversation taking place.

"Miss Dunne," he began rather nervously. "I'm afraid it is my sad duty to inform you that, ah, that your father has of late been plagued with large financial reverses, of which you are, or rather were, kept unaware."

"I see," I said, although I did not. "Am I to go home then? Is there no money to see me through here? Is Father . . ."

Mr. Harwood's plump hand, festooned with a masonic ring, patted the air hastily. "No, no, Miss Dunne. No worry about that. Your term here has been paid up in advance. It's not a question of that sort of thing at all."

How pitifully relieved he seemed to be able to reassure me about something.

"What is it a question of, then?" I said, trying to calm a growing tautness in my throat.

"It, ah, it . . . well, to be quite frank, Miss Dunne, it is a question of bankruptcy."

"Bankruptcy?" My tension collapsed into astonishment.

"Yes, bankruptcy." He seemed to savor the consonant roll of the word as only a barrister could. "That is what I'm here to tell you. There really is nothing left. Even household goods—furnishings, books, etcetera—they'll have to be sold off at public auction. The house in Eaton Square is yours no longer. It's a case of . . . total . . . bankruptcy."

"But why do you come to tell me this? Surely Father could have come. Or written . . ." Miss Meachum and Mr. Harwood exchanged a quick, cornered glance and I suddenly knew. "My father is . . ."

"Deceased," said Mr. Harwood.

I leaned back into the depths of the wing chair.

"It was quite sudden. Your father's affairs had been going badly for some time. The strain of regrouping a waning fortune—some men can't cope with it, especially at your father's age. And since there were no known relations to break the news. . . . It was suicide, actually."

I gripped the arms of the wing chair until I could feel my

fingernails digging into the stuffing. I wanted to laugh. How typical of Miss Meachum and Mr. Harwood and all people like them to give news of financial disaster first and mention death as an afterthought.

Grief? I felt none then. Father had always been too busy amassing the fortune that had left him so abruptly to dote upon me. I pictured him again—a tall, ginger-haired man, stooped over account books in his study, handing out erratic gifts of twenty pounds to his only daughter.

I had been reared by servants, servants who every so often would vanish to be replaced by new ones. Father had had few friends, only "business associates," and even those rarely came to the house. My only link with the past was Mrs. Bowers, the housekeeper. She had been with us since my parents' marriage and she remembered my mother. She never would tell me much about my mother. I suppose she thought it wasn't her place, but she was kind and never minded my tagging after her through the house. "Things used to be diff'rent," she'd insist whenever I'd ask her about the past, and she'd go no further.

Well, things were certainly "diff'rent" now. Bankruptcy. I'd known I was merely the daughter of a successful tradesman, that I wasn't to have the coming-out party the other girls at school regarded as the real beginning of life, that no Dunne, father or daughter, could buy social connections—but bankruptcy. The whole pattern of my life melted away, already slipping through my fingers before I'd even known about it. I wondered how Father had felt when he decided to die. I wondered whether he had thought of me at all. I wondered how he . . . did it. No, I really didn't want to know. A pistol? Yes, that was probably it. A pistol reverberating in the study, that study so familiar to me . . . a shot, and then a man crumpled on the red floral carpet. Father. Suddenly, I caught a word in Miss Meachum's fruity tones from the pair's murmured conference that pricked at my mind. ". . . scandal."

Scandal? Yes, that was another consideration. All my enemies here at school, the snide secure brats of the petite bourgeoisie, better than I merely because their families' wealth had been gathered one generation earlier, how they would enjoy discussing my plight in hushed groups in their rooms at night. Little circles gathered around illegal candles and smuggled sweets, they would have a field day. And the "nice," well-bred ones, not real friends but acquaintances, they would back off from me abruptly. Not maliciously, but because they simply wouldn't know how to treat me. Well, I didn't want to be "treated" at all, either badly or well-meaningly. I saw no point in worming my way into the hearts of girls with family crests on their stationery. Elaine was the only true friend I had. Oddly enough, her family was the most blue-blooded of the lot.

Poor Elaine. She would probably be more upset about this than I. Not noticeably bright, a little high-strung, more than a little vain, she was nonetheless my true friend, perhaps because she, too, didn't quite belong. The highest and the lowest in firm alliance. I would miss Elaine. I had expected to see her occasionally, shopping in London or to tea in Eaton Square during the season when her family opened their town house and abandoned their country manor in Ireland. But now . . .

"So you see, Miss Dunne, I have really done my utmost to tidy up a very messy affair." Mr. Harwood's voice oiled me back into the present.

"When is the, the . . ."

"Interment?" he asked delicately. "Tomorrow. Noon at St. Clement's."

I nodded absently.

"Perhaps you'd like to retire to your room now, Amberleigh." Miss Meachum's words were a command. She had no intention of allowing an overwrought, and bankrupt, girl to stay and cry upon her lavender-scented shoulder. She needn't have worried.

I stood and walked out mutely into the passageway.

It was Elaine who stabbed home the unhappiness of my situation when I fetched her to my room and told her the news.

"Amberleigh, this is awful!" she wailed. "I'm so sorry."

I paced the room, gathering the few things I would need for the trip to London. I would go to my father's . . . interment.

"Amberleigh, I just don't understand. It's so incredibly awful. How can you be so calm? Suicide. Oh, Amberleigh, I just couldn't bear it!"

I looked at Elaine. She was sitting on my bed, her hands picking at the counterpane embroidery. Her face was white with anguish and I could trace the fine blue veins in her high forehead even from across the room.

"It's all right, Elaine. You musn't upset yourself on my account. It's a fact, that's all."

Strange that I should be comforting her. Yet Elaine was like that, a walking Ouija board tuned to others' joys and sorrows almost more than her own. I think I was more touched by her concern than by my own bereavement.

"Where will you go now, Amberleigh, what will you do?"

"I'll go to London, for the funeral. There's enough money from Father's last cheque for that. And then . . . well, I suppose I could hire out as a governess or even be a schoolmistress here. At Miss Meachum's." How I loathed saying that! I did not want to be one of those "ladies of reduced circumstances" who were soon relegated to becoming meek, trodden-upon servants to the nobility's children.

"It's so unfair. I can't stand death. I can't stand funerals," said Elaine, her voice growing tight again.

"I know." I sighed wearily. "Elaine," I added, more to remove her mind from its present course than for any sense of proper attire, "can I borrow your black silk for the funeral? From when your great-aunt died? There isn't time, nor means, for me to . . ."

"Of course." Elaine jumped up, immediately diverted by the drama of the occasion. "It's packed already, but I'll knock it up. I think it's in the brass trunk."

She rooted in the trunk and finally emerged with the gown over her arm. I slipped out of my own and felt the silk rustle over my body like a cloud. Elaine hooked it; I could feel her icy fingers at my neck.

"It's a bit short," she fussed, kneeling to jerk at the hem nervously.

"Never mind. I'll stop at Corey's when I get to town and buy a mourning bonnet; I suppose it's only proper." I looked at my black-swathed figure in the mirror. "How I wish I were fair-haired as you are, Elaine. I look like a clown with my impossible hair in this black."

"Your hair's lovely. I wish I had red hair. It's so dramatic. You will be dignified and dramatic at the funeral. Perhaps some handsome gentleman will see you and be intrigued. And then you'll marry him and he's really a baronet and . . ."

"Handsome gentlemen haunt funerals only in American dime novels, Elaine, and you read too many!" Bless the girl— absurd, but the shock was already wearing off.

When I descended the familiar staircase to tell Miss Meachum I would go to London, I encountered a wall of maroon-wool resistance. It would have been one thing had I mentioned my desire earlier, she said, then I could have been escorted to town by Mr. Harwood. But he'd already left for the evening train to the city. Thoughtless as I'd been, it was perhaps understandable and she would arrange for Miss Priscilla to accompany me. I took some satisfaction in telling her that the remnants of Father's cheque would not accommodate two pas-

16

sages. She positively recoiled at the memory of my recent impecuniousness. It was not "the thing," she muttered, for a Young Lady, for "one of her girls," to travel unchaperoned. It was "unladylike." I wanted to point out that, by virtue of my newfound poverty, I hardly qualified as a "lady" any longer. Instead I promised solemnly to stay only for the noon ceremony and return by nightfall. I think she would have been glad had I announced my intention to not finish out term; she went so far as to ask me not to wear mourning as it would be "unpleasant" for the other girls. I replied that I could not afford to, in any case. It was a most disagreeable interview and I was glad to leave the seminary.

Travelling alone was a new experience, for Father had always sent his coachman and I had ridden home amid the swaying, creaking, strong-leather-smelling solitude of our old carriage. I wondered whose service it was in now.

Fortunately, Miss Meachum's was only a few miles from the city; I only had to endure an hour of curious side glances from the passengers on the train. It was harrowing to have to dig into one's reticule every few minutes to pay for tickets and cab fare. But the final harrowing of Amberleigh Dunne was standing at her father's graveside to watch him lowered into the ground in the shoddy casket the solicitors had allowed from the little left of his estate. Mr. Harwood was there, glancing at me nervously and licking his lips incessantly as the cemetery parson droned the service through barely moving lips. Except for Mrs. Bowers, who sniffled into a large white handkerchief, and the gravemen, we were the only persons there.

"Ashes to ashes..." and a bit of ground in a run-down cemetery were all the ceremony an Irish bankrupt could expect. I wished then that I had loved my father, that I could truly be a mourner, but the only tears that flowed behind my black veil were for the father I had never known, not for the man upon whose casket rained dry clumps of earth. Off in the distance I could hear the rumble of the city, where life and death went on so unceasingly. I felt a fleshy hand squeeze mine. "My dear Miss Dunne..." I raised my veil and looked at Mr. Harwood with leaden eyes. He backed away abruptly, murmuring something about returning to London. I do believe the man had designs on escorting me to a post-funereal luncheon and a bit of madeira in his offices! I turned to watch the dirt pile up on the casket. Mrs. Bowers edged over to me, her eyes and nose reddened, and tugged deferentially on Elaine's black silk sleeve.

17

"Miss Amberleigh?" It was as if she expected not to know me.

"Oh, Mrs. Bowers, it was so good of you to come." I turned to the dumpy woman who seemed to have the only real tears to shed for my father, the tears of a long-time servant.

"'Tis truly sorry I am, Miss Amberleigh. Mr. Dunne weren't a hard man to work for, quiet and always real polite to the staff."

"Where will you go now, Mrs. Bowers?"

"Aye, and it's not where I'll be goin' that's to worry about. I'm a housekeeper and that's all I ever were and all I'll be till they lower me into me grave, too. It's you to worry about, not bein' used to bein' on your own. When me husband died, and me but thirty, died he did, of workin' in the mines, I had no worry. Hired out I'd been since thirteen and able to do it again. But you, Miss Amberleigh, ever since you was a tiny thing, you was never brung up to have hard times."

"I'll be quite all right, Mrs. Bowers. I can always find employment as a governess or a schoolmistress." Cheers of victory to Miss Meachum.

"A fine girl, the likes a' you? It's a shame, that's what 'tis, but here, I'm forgettin' what I been wantin' to do." She pulled a small carved chest out of her capacious handbag and gave it to me tenderly.

"Looka here." Her full-bodied voice sank to a whisper as she pulled conspiratorily on my sleeve. "Like crows they were, them solicitors, all pickin' at the ruins. Took the linens off the beds, they did. Couldn't even leave the little rosewood piany, that you loved so. But I fooled them. 'Tis all I were able to keep their beaks out of. 'Tain't much, but I thought, 'Mary Bowers, it's something at least and I will do it!'"

I opened the box. Inside, on a torn blue silk lining, were about a dozen pieces of jewellery, old-fashioned and not very valuable.

"Don't you see, girl? Your own mother's. There's not too much. She died so young, poor lass, and your father wasn't much in the money in them days. Lived in a little house in Newcastle Street then, we did. Nice, but not toney. It's the opals especially I thought you'd be wantin'. You've got your mother's complexion for to wear 'em with."

I fingered the dusty filigree mountings. My only legacy. And what would Dunne, the humble governess, do with some modest bits of jewellery? Use them to buttress her pride? Wear a simple amethyst pin with her cheap black gabardines and

18

jerseys? I picked up a small but exquisitely carved cameo brooch.

"You must have this, Mrs. Bowers, for your kindness in thinking of me."

Her eyes lit up as if I had given her pearls beyond price as she took the cameo and clasped it to her ample bosom.

"It's a livin' shame, it is, and so kind you are."

I offered her a ride back to the city; it seemed she had driven out with someone who left. But before we departed there was one thing I wanted to do. I didn't care if it cost an extra pound for making the cabman wait. I walked past the other graves to the end of cemetery. Straight through the knee-high grass. The sun was hot and the warm April wind blew the veil back from my face. I picked a bunch of ditch daisies and wild flowers whose names I never knew. Nobody's flowers. Then I returned to the grave. The dirt was all filled in and the men had left, leaving a raw wound in the surrounding green. Mrs. Bowers was kneeling by the grave and hastily got up, crossing herself apologetically.

"I hoped you wouldn't be mindin', miss, me sayin' a few Cath'lic prayers for your father..."

"No, Mrs. Bowers, I don't mind." I laid the wild flowers on the fresh earth of my father's grave. It seemed right, somehow, to borrow blooms from nobody. It was one funeral expense the solicitors wouldn't have to quibble about. Mrs. Bowers and I rode back to London, silent, and after letting her off I drove straight to Victoria Station, the solemn clop of horses' hooves and the string of cabs and carriages forming an almost funeral procession to accompany my somber thoughts. Once a carriage pulled abreast of my cab and a glance out the window seemed to reveal an oddly familiar face, a bearded man who...but the carriage pulled away and I was left without having seen a single soul in London from the old days. Save for Mrs. Bowers.

I drifted the next few weeks at Miss Meachum's, living off a dead man's money. Miss Meachum, I suspect, would have been only too glad to have asked me to leave despite my being paid up for term, but I think she was afraid of Elaine. Or rather, of Elaine's stepmother, Lady St. Clare, an intimate of London society's best families. I had met her once or so at the academy; she illustrated perfectly what the French instructress meant when she said "Formidable!" Elaine's father never visited; I gathered he remained the entire year on the Irish holdings and was somewhat older than his beautiful wife. I'd always wondered why Elaine had been sent to a school like Miss Meachum's. Her relations could certainly afford governesses. It was strange they'd cart her off like this to associate with the tainted offspring of the lesser nobility and wealthy bourgeoisie. Still, I wasn't about to fault their eccentricities. Elaine was my true friend and I had never needed someone to look after more than I did now.

The last note of "God Save the Queen" was fading. As Miss Priscilla thumped the final chord with a final nod of her lace-capped head, a wave of gentle applause stirred the flowerlike faces swimming before my gaze. I discovered to my disgust that tears pooled in my eyes, and turned to march off. Elaine commandeered my elbow and pulled me out into the corridor.

"Hurry! Let's run up and fetch our garden hats. We can meet the others in the garden."

Our classmates had rushed off the platform to mingle with their families, despite Miss Meachum's dire orders for a dignified bow, exit and return, if you please, Young Ladies. The dark passageways were deserted as Elaine and I bolted up the stairs at a most un-Meachumly gallop.

She thrust me towards my room, ran down the corridor and returned with a huge white leghorn perched backwards on her head.

"Where's your hat, Amberleigh?" She was lost in joyously arranging her own on her long fair curls.

I took my yellow straw with its brimful of daisies from the cupboard and imagined it stripped of its frivolous flowers and much more suitable for an Independent Woman of No Means.

"I was thinking of not wearing it."

"Not wearing it? After the ridiculous porkpies we've had to wear all these years? Amberleigh, it's divine, and the first really sophisticated thing we've had a chance to own. You mustn't forget, we are Young Ladies now." Elaine glided about the room, her retroussé nose in the air, until her hat fell off and she collapsed on the bed in a fit of giggles. She seemed a bit too gay. "Listen! I want you to do my hair in a pompadour! It'll really surprise them." She tripped over to the dressing table and handed me the brush. "A really *magnifique* pompadour."

"Like your stepmother's?" I suggested, brushing through her gleaming hair.

"No," she said. "Different."

As I worked, I couldn't help looking at ourselves in the

mirror. Elaine, absorbed in straightening the crisp organdy ruffles that rose from her shoulders like white wings, and I. Elaine, so fair and golden, and I so dark and pale. It was all suddenly part of the past. She was going home, to Ireland for the summer, and on to a life of coming-out parties, teas, theatre parties, dinners, dances and balls. I was going on . . . where?

At first, after Father's death, Elaine had been full of plans for me. A position with one of the families she knew would be just the thing, perhaps one that kept a summer home near Carnhaven. But something was always wrong. The children were unmitigated beasts. Or the mistress would be demanding. Or the master would be demanding in his own way. Perhaps she hated the idea of my going into service as much as I did. But I think she really had no conception of what I was facing. Her hair had risen into a high smooth halo, and I combed one lock into a curl over her shoulder. Suddenly she looked up and met my eyes in the glass.

"Amberleigh, I'm frightened too."

I laid the brush down and fetched her hat from the bed.

"Why should you be frightened, Elaine?"

"I don't know." She watched me lower the sweeping brim onto her head. Her eyes were lost in its shadow and there was a tautness in her voice when she repeated, "I don't know. That's what's so frightening."

Ah, Elaine, I thought bitterly for a moment. You don't know what real fear is, that's why you can romanticize it. Real fear isn't something you don't know about, it's something you know only too well. Dear Elaine, could she help being sheltered and wealthy and loved?

"Come along, then," she cried suddenly and sprang to the door.

"I thought I'd stay up here awhile."

"Don't be a dolt! Devora's waiting. And I want you to meet Adrian, too. Don't look so down-at-the-mouth. It's all right."

"I wouldn't want to intrude . . ."

"I . . . I wish you'd come, Amberleigh." Elaine's voice took on a pleading quality. She seemed subdued and excited at the same instant; for a moment I believed that she wasn't merely being considerate of me, that she truly needed someone to walk with her down the wide expanse of cultured lawn to her family. But that was ridiculous.

"In a few minutes, then."

Elaine reluctantly turned and left. Outside I could hear the chatter of happy voices and I went over to the open shutters.

The garden was dotted with the pastel people I had seen in the drawing room. The ladies' wide hats nodded and bowed; here and there a parasol flitted above a flower-strewn leghorn like a butterfly over a blossom. I glimpsed Elaine's four organdy ruffles billowing down the slope to the nile green hat I'd seen before. So it had been Lady St. Clare. Devora, she was named. I ran my hands, suddenly moist, over the skirt of my own pale green gown, the last new frock I should have for some time. It seemed a frail imitation of the complex elegance that Lady St. Clare would be wearing.

I went over to the glass again. I looked quite nice that day. Not pretty, like Elaine, and delicate—but taller and more sensible, I'm afraid. I quickly pulled my dark red hair into a severe chignon. It did absolutely nothing for me. Yes, that is how I would look as the governess, Dunne. Sensible, severe and intolerably dull. What foul luck. I swept my hair into a loose pompadour and found a lovely octagonal brooch of amber in my mother's jewellery box. Amber. I wondered if my mother had loved its golden shine so much that she had named me for it. I had never cared for it, its murky color and spots; perhaps I could learn. The golden straw glided into place over my auburn hair.

Yes, Miss Amberleigh Dunne, I said to myself, this is your last chance to play the lady of the manor. Tomorrow it's the streets for you, girl. I laughed at my self-dramatization, made a music-hall seductive pout at my reflection in the glass (Miss Meachum would never guess what we girls picked up from the most unlikely sources) and sailed out the door in better spirits.

CHAPTER TWO

IT WAS six long years before the name of Carnhaven crossed my ears or eyes again. By then I was a world away from Miss Meachum and the concerns of that spring day on the well-trimmed lawns of England. I was six long years older . . . and wiser? No, I do not think I was very much wiser or I never would have grasped at Lady St. Clare's letter as I did that rainy twilight in Boston.

Her handwriting was surprisingly robust for a woman of

such delicate appearance—angular, rounded characters that lurched backwards. But her stationery had the St. Clare crest. I still felt a thrill of awe at it, despite five-years' well-worn service in that most unassuming arena, the well-to-do American family.

Governess I had predicted I would be before the school mirror, and governess I was. And well on my way... be honest, Amberleigh... arrived at, spinsterhood.

"My dear Amberleigh," Lady St. Clare wrote. "Friends have told me that you reside in Boston now. It's very odd, but Adrian Carstairs—I wonder do you remember Adrian?—was visiting there but a year ago and, in fact, met the Willoughbys, with whom, I understand, you are in service. (How I do ramble on!) At any rate, my dear, it made me think of you and those years when you and Elaine were so close."

So close. And letters, fast and furious at first, trickling down to nothing. I always had the impression that there was simply nothing to write about after a year or two. Elaine, bursting onto the London Season with all the youth, beauty and social entree of the St. Clare inheritance, merely became too... involved... with it all to spend time writing letters to her "poor American cousin," who was tending children's p's and q's and feeling very sorry for herself, indeed, at times.

And yet, there still came the sudden, melting bounty of Elaine's gifts from abroad. French chocolates, their elaborate boxes as sugared as their contents. A set of Dickens engravings sent piece by piece, like chessmen, so one always anticipated the next move. And only that single-word signature, "Elaine." It said nothing, and said it all. Perhaps if Elaine went beyond sending mute monuments to our school-day's friendship, she would overflow into the words I'd always sensed her holding back.

Not for her own sake. For mine, somehow. I remembered her abrupt, chilling anxiety on commencement day, when only safe sugar-plum ladies and gentlemen had awaited her on Miss Meachum's manicured lawns. She had wafted down the garden path towards them like a social butterfly to the flowers of British society, her four ruffles fluttering and I watching from the window above. I had wished to play butterfly to the world, too. Instead, I'd emerged from Miss Meachum's cocoon as a drab-winged moth. Dunne, the governess. Dunne, the bankrupt's daughter... No, it wasn't Elaine's fault, merely the nature of things.

I suddenly felt ashamed at the bitterness that the bleak Beacon Hill prospect of red brick, grey sky and stark branches outside my bedchamber window seemed to have stirred in me. Why did I blame the bright days for the dreary ones?

Lady St. Clare's letter seemed less like a challenge for self-accounting and more like what it was—a letter, plain and simple. Only months later I discovered that it wasn't plain at all and that if anything had been simple, it was I.

Elaine was the reason she wrote. Elaine had not been well. Really, she and Sir George were quite concerned. Thought it might do Elaine good to see a bit of someone to whom she felt close, someone like that Amberleigh Dunne from school. It was a good deal to ask, of course, but could not she, Amberleigh, take a leave of absence from her position and spend some time with Elaine at Carnhaven? My dear, certainly it would be understood that such time spent would be reimbursed, could we not regard it as a companionship position? Passage could be arranged through the Bank of Boston if one would be so kind to come. Really, Elaine was languishing and they feared it was lack of someone her own age to cheer her up a bit. Do come.

I suppose my hackles should have risen then at so bald an offer to buy my friendship. But the truth was my position was soon to end. Both my charges were shooting up past my time with them. The boy—bound for a military academy in Virginia. The girl—off to a seminary for young ladies. I must say, I found the American custom of sending their children to school with others early on better than the British practice of tying them to a succession of governesses' apron strings.

And frankly I was tiring of my lot in life. Harold Willoughby Junior was showing a revolting tendency to pull the wings off moths and lanky Emily was turning very reticent and giggly. My own girlhood was not so far behind me that I cared to relive it vicariously. A holiday in Ireland would do me acres of good. Besides, the easy equality I'd come to America to find, the famed democracy that would bridge the gap between my upbringing and my current position was not working out at all. My position was, if anything, more ambiguous than before. Wealthy American families, I discovered, were terribly eager to ape their British peers, as it were. And as for my marrying—any delusions in that direction quickly died.

The poor but ambitious clerks and salesmen who might not frown upon my position were caught up in a whirl of eligible, independent shopgirls and the newly born wielders of that formidable machine, the typewriter; not to mention the daughters of modest families who didn't have to seek employment and had courting time.

I was trapped in a rigid family setting, impaled between the idiot green grocer's boy who lurked in the kitchen to catch glimpses of my irresistible auburn locks and drove me to leaving notes to Cook, and the rare young bachelor of good family who came calling with Mama and barely noticed me as I ushered the children out of the parlour after they'd done their company tricks.

Oh, I was ready for an excursion to Darkest Africa as a respite. Ireland was even better. And that letter had been odd. What could possibly be wrong with Elaine? Lady St. Clare's words hinted at some sort of emotional upset. But what had Elaine to disturb her? Wealth? Breeding? Perhaps overbreeding. She'd always been a bit... well, excitable in a brittle, unhappy way. Odd that she hadn't married yet. After five, no six, London Seasons now. And some consolation. We were both the better side of eighteen, but my six "seasons" had been spent in more mundane pursuits than husband-hunting. Four-and-twenty spells spinster.

That decided me. I would be mouldering all too soon. Onward, to Ireland, to the fountainhead of genial Officer O'Rourke who strolled swinging his sturdy billyclub past the Willoughbys' each evening. Farewell Boston and its endless red brick, its gliding white gulls, its interminable seafood and its tight-lipped women who kept a sharp Yankee eye on me... at least I'm not too old for that yet. Into the trunk with my starched shirtwaists and my neat wool skirts and the lovely weekend frocks and suits I couldn't resist having made up out of my ample savings, the rakish straw hat I had never quite dared wear to Advent Episcopal Church with the family, my mother's jewellery. I was at last, in a way, going home.

The voyage was long. I was at first timorous about exploring the steamer decks, but I finally settled on a deck chair, a blanket to deter the Atlantic's spray kisses and a luxurious marathon of reading, walking and not thinking at all. Occasionally the vessel's roll would threaten my hard-won landman's equilibrium and tell me there was something not quite natural in bobbing about like a cork in a pond, but all in all it was a fine voyage, albeit solitary.

I landed in Queenstown, a messy rough settlement, once more made awkward by the dockside bustle, the reel of gulls that seemed to be screaming at me only: "Look, there she is. A woman travelling alone. No one to protect her. Guard her baggage, see her to the proper place..."

I clutched Lady St. Clare's latest letter with its directions to Carnhaven the way the black-shawled old ladies entering the wharfside church clung to their rosary beads. I was no Papist despite my half-Irish descent, but something must have worked. I, my trunk, bags and baggage arrived together at the Great Western Line train station, converged on the proper coach and began the long, rattling rail trip to County Clare.

Once out of the grimy port city, I was fascinated by the rolling hills of the Irish countryside. It *was* different from England. And green. I had known it would be green, as famous an Irish product as whiskey. But the actual real green of it dazzled me—with only meandering stone fences and cairns to distract the eye from an orgy of green that crept and twisted and wound itself over the entire horizon. I was charmed and for the first time in my journey, breathed a sigh of content. I was premature.

Arriving at Glennverran, my content was cast off like a cobweb dislodged by the broad broom of reality. The station-house was a mean little stone affair, with one attendant who spoke a dialect so thick it took me five minutes to determine that the "Greath Howse" was twelve miles distant and no one from it there to greet me.

I wormed Lady St. Clare's letter from my reticule. The date was correct. The time also. But there was simply no one there, no coachman to meet me, greet me and convey me to the "Greath Howse." Panic welled from the pit of my stomach and dripped, slowly, down through my arms. What good was it to stand there, among strangers who spoke no decent English that I could recognize and ask for explanations?

There must be some mistake. I would wait, I said, settling stiffly onto the hard wooden bench in the room's center—obvious, isolated and more uncomfortable than one quizzical old man should make me feel. I was, I considered, at least the picture of composure. My attire for this last day's journey, despite sitting up a night on the train, had been meticulously selected to resume as closely as possible my old status with the St. Clares. A smart skirt and short jacket of brown gabardine, edged with yellow bands along the flared hem and deliciously oversized leg-o'-mutton sleeves. The hat was brown, economically coloured for more than one ensemble, but lavishly tilted, feathered and draped with a truly elegant fave veil that tied in a bow at the back. It was my favourite and it had cost me dear at one of Boston's better milliner's. It was my gauntlet, if hat could ever substitute for glove, to Lady St. Clare and the minions of condescension I pictured surrounding her. It was the badge of self-respect that would let me enter Castle St. Clare with head high.

Soon my wait relieved me of the short yellow kid gloves that were another travel present to myself. Soon I was purusing the collection of Sheridan LeFanu ghost stories I had purchased to pass the time. An Irish author for an Ireland-bound traveller. Soon I could no longer lose myself in the adventure of "The Room at the Dragon Volant" and "Green Tea." Soon it was all too apparent that as far as Carnhaven's occupants were concerned, I was as good as one of LeFanu's ghostly visitors. I had been forgotten.

"Sir? I'm afraid that they've—overlooked my arrival. Would it be possible to . . ."

"Why, miss, don't ye be worryin' about sich a thing. I sent a boy a sluggard's hour ago to tell the House ye're here and sittin'. They'll be down to get ye in the flash of a cat's whisker."

That seemed simple enough and I returned to my bench for another hour, and then two, of reading and self-contemplation. Just as I was certain the oversight was deliberate and permanent, there was the clop of horses' hooves and the creak of a carriage outside.

I flew to the counter and the old man—now he was conversing with a scrawny boy who kept his eyes on me, and my marvelous hat, all the while he blathered to the station master in yet a worse version of dialect. Or brogue, as I was later to learn it was called.

"Ah, miss," intoned the station master with some reluctance. "It seems there's a hunt up to the House, and truly sorry they are, but no one was there to send for ye." I must have looked crestfallen, or at least my fine feathers must have drooped, for he went on quickly. "But there's not a thing to be worryin' about, Colleen. Young John McLaren is bound to deliver to the House today and will take a passenger gladly. Here, boy, take out the lady's trunks and bags"

The slender lad darted silently to my meagre pile of luggage, picked it up piece by piece until I thought baggage should carry boy rather than otherwise, and lumbered out with it. I followed him outside with some relief and drew up before a pair of plough horses hitched to the roughest dray wagon it had been my pleasure to see upon the streets of London or Boston.

"Here now, help the lady up," I heard the kindly station master at my elbow say, with a sudden realization that I was loath to leave what now seemed a haven.

And "Young John McLaren" grinned sheepishly to reveal several gaping holes in his teeth and extended a grimy hand for me. My yellow-kid-gloved hand reached up reluctantly and I was hoisted unceremoniously to the high seat beside him, fruitlessly catching up my skirts to avoid the inevitable snag on the rough wooden seat. My trunks were shortly slung up behind me by the boy. As I surveyed the alien countryside from my perch, it occurred to me that I was to enter Castle St. Clare in very high style indeed.

CHAPTER THREE

IT WAS a long, largely silent journey. "Young John McLaren" made a few feeble attempts at conversation in his abominable dialect. I politely yelled "What?" after each trial over the grinding clatter of the rough wheels and the multitudinous creaking of the team's much-mended harness.

Eventually we subsided into mutual silence and I surveyed the countryside. The hedged lane entrances that promised to lead nowhere, rough limestone outcroppings here and there in the distance, and—anxiously—my own baggage lurching unceremoniously behind me. Only God could have kept the road dust from encroaching on my smart travelling suit and He was about better things that day. I watched the dust's inexorable climb up my skirt. Brushing it off only raised puffs that sent me into paroxysms of coughing.

Finally I detected more civilized countryside ahead, and the towering of red brick chimneys beyond a beech grove.

"The house, that must be Carnhaven?"

"Aye," said my driver.

"It won't be long then?"

"Nay," said my driver.

There was a long curved drive on the left, but our outsized wagon kept to the straight road. I glimpsed the house, its graceful Georgian lines peeking at me through the hedges like a coquette's face through the slats of her fan. It seemed large. And elegant. It seemed stately. It seemed that I was to arrive by the back entrance.

28

We drew up behind the wing that housed the kitchen and faced the stables and outbuildings. The driver hopped off the high seat to sling my belongings to the paved court and left me to climb down over the giant wheels unaided. I turned toward the house—only to face the largest dog I had ever seen. A shaggy grey brute that eyed me levelly—I swear it was eye-to-eye, so tall was the beast. He stared at me gravely for a moment, then bent his mammoth head to snuffle disgustingly at my hem.

"Boru!" yelled a voice from near the house. "Boru, you rascal, you've got a way of sniffin' out the ladies for sure. Back, you hound!" A young but black-bearded man came loping up to collar and drag away the creature.

"He's gentle as a puppy, miss, and wouldn't lick the wings off a fly. Stay still, you shaggy beast, and mind your manners or ye'll show me up a liar entirely."

The young man whipped off his tweed cap belatedly, to reveal a head of jet hair as shaggy as his dog's. "You're for the House then, Miss—"

"Dunne. Yes, I'm a guest of Elaine's, or Lady St. Clare's really. But there was some—miscomprehension, and I was left at the station, so this gentleman was kind enough to bring me out." I pointed to Young John, who was now unloading sacks of something near an outbuilding.

"The hunt's up and they forgot you," my new acquaintance said with humiliating accuracy. "Sure, it happens often these days. Once old Sir George is ready to ride to the hounds, the world follows—or at least the world hereabouts—and to hell with everything else. It's all right, John, I'll see to the lady."

I pressed a half-crown into the driver's grimy hand. He grinned in his disconcerting way, touched the tip of his cap, climbed upon the wagon and turned the team around with a burst of raw commands and a sudden trail of dust.

"It's been drier than St. Bridget's Well hereabouts of late, otherwise your fine gown wouldn't be lookin' as though you'd marched through the wide Sahara. I'll take you up to the house and find you a spot. The servants can see to your baggage. Quade's the name, Devlin Patrick. What's yours?"

By now I was being piloted expertly houseward, my guide brushing off the worst dust from my skirt with his cap in a very familiar manner. But I was so startled by his infectious chatter and the big dog lumbering behind us that I began to take his presence as for granted as he did.

"Amberleigh," I answered bemusedly.

29

"Amberlee? Now what kind of a pagan name is that? Sure, no saint this side of paradise or the other would consent to a name the likes of that? No offense, girl, but with your good head of Irish hair—'tis a fine red—you should be a Molly. Or Kathleen. Or Sheilagh." And he broke into song, something about "dark Sheilagh" staring into the fire . . .

> "I see a lad that loves me
> And I see a lad that leaves me
> And a third lad,
> A Shadow lad
> And he's the lad that grieves me . . ."

It was a mournful melody and though his voice was a liquid tenor that I imagined would do quite well with some instrument to counter it, something about the tune ran against my grain. I shivered briefly in the sunlight and stopped walking.

"I'm grateful for the entertainment, I'm sure, but who are you and what is your—connection—here?"

"I've told you me name and as for me position, ma'am, I am but a humble Irish lad, as is allowed to come by and pay respects upon the great people at the House."

He made a formal little bow. I sensed that I had insulted him despite his constant barrage of good humour. It was then I spied a bicycle leaning against a low wall around the kitchen garden.

"You must live nearby," I said, nodding at the intricate machine.

"Yes, and a marvelous thing it is," he said, his face lighting up as we strolled toward the object of his pride. "It takes me up hill and down dale, with never a need for so much as a wisp of hay, has no teeth nor hooves with which to belabour me and needs a mere dustin' for a groomin'. A bit of work goes into the tyres, to be sure, but it don't take a blacksmith to put it aright again. Have you never taken a bit of a turn on one?"

"No. No, really, I couldn't. I don't even like horses. And I'm not dressed for it, you can see. But it is a fascinating machine. You're a neighbour of the St. Clares, then?"

"Still for puttin' me in my place, I see? Well, it's simple enough. I'm down from Trinity—College in Dublin," he added as my eyes looked blank—"where the St. Clares were generous enough to send me all these last years for—sentimental—reasons. So I'm a bit of a scholar and can prove it and I'm back in the County to preserve the lore and song hereabouts, that

30

the old folks will be lettin' out to the winds when they pass on, if someone don't stop 'em. And the St. Clares, well, sure I'm a bit of a disappointment, not readin' for the law on their charity but collectin' tunes . . . but I come and I go as I will with none to stop me, something no barrister could ever claim. With none to stop me save pretty Colleens in need of some steering, of course."

I felt my cheeks redden. I was not accustomed to so much attention, nor so extravagant an admirer. "Then hadn't you better steer me to the house?" I asked, and he immediately escorted me through a wide door and down some stone steps into the ample kitchen.

"Ah, Florence, me love, I've brought another worshipper at your altar for you. Though to you, me dear Am-ber-lee, she's *Mrs.* Featherstone or the inimitable "Cook," dispenser of the rare delights of table. And here's fair Sarah from Liverpool, and the dainty Rosie"—this to a housemaid who must have gone fourteen stone—"and Mary, mild Mary and doughty Timothy and Terrence O'Halloran himself."

The staff lounging in the kitchen was as startled as I to confront each other, I'm sure. I nodded all round and the girls giggled and trembled on the brink of curtseying, not at all certain where I stood in the household. But then, neither was I.

"Terry and Tim, see the lady's baggage to the upstairs front hall. They can decide whither they goest from there. Is any family about?"

"Just Miss Elaine. She never did care for the ridin' and less so now that she's back from London again," he was told promptly and without challenge.

"The very one we want. I'll take Miss Dunne to see her," he said, steering me rather quickly through the kitchen, up a short staircase, down a dark corridor and around a number of corners until we emerged suddenly into a lofty-ceilinged hall. A black-clothed butler skimmed into our path as if preternaturally alerted to our somewhat unconventional appearance there.

"Ah, Symes, just the boyo we need. This is Miss Dunne, Symes, Miss Amberlee Dunne, a guest of Lady St. Clare's that I found wanderin' the premises in search of a welcome mat. So I offered meself."

"I received the message of your arrival, miss," intoned Symes with unruffled formality, ignoring Devlin Quade as he would a fly that had settled on his nose, with the kind of

31

majesty that made things shrivel and die. Devlin Quade did not seem to shrivel.

"Miss Elaine is in the studio, miss, I believe. I can have one of the maids advise her of your arrival."

"Yes. I would like to see Elaine as soon as possible."

Symes withdrew, his ample chest preceding him from the room. I turned to inspect it. A graceful fanlight above the door admitted a wedge of lemon-pale sunlight. Otherwise, the room was as cool and shadowy as the grey marble tiles that lined the foyer floor. Beyond it, a sweep of white-painted and mahogany railing followed the wide stairs upwards to the second storey.

"I'll be leavin' now." Devlin's voice broke in on my general inspection. I found him already fading through the far door into the narrow passage beyond.

"Oh. Well, thank you then. I appreciate your trouble—"

"There's nothing to thank where none is given." He smiled, drawing the door shut and disappearing like the leprechaun of legend.

It was deadly quiet in the hall. Somewhere a clock ticked with a soft, steady beat, but I couldn't locate it. I stood there, my hands clasped before me like a child on company manners. I felt a bit like my baggage—something smuggled in by the back stairs and left to languish in the hall until someone else had decided what to do with it. I paced the hall a few times, listening to the hollow click of my heels on the hard floor. I made a game of looking for the clock and finally found it, high on its own shelf and painted to match the panelling. The ornate face read two-thirty. I had been en route to Carnhaven for six and a half hours.

There was a dim clatter high above me and I turned expectantly to the staircase. Around the curve Elaine hove into view, coming down with hasty deliberation, hand clinging to the railing, dark skirt billowing out below the full offices of a pink-striped smock. Her fair hair was carelessly pulled up and tendrils wafted around her pale face. I was momentarily shocked—as she came closer I saw the fine faint lines near her grey eyes, the price a fair complexion pays after six seasons. She seemed to have faded ever so slightly all over—still insubstantial, still airy but more so.

"Amberleigh! Amberleigh! Devora said you'd be arriving today but I was so wrapped up in my work upstairs I nearly forgot. Can you forgive me? Of course you can, we wouldn't be off to a good start if you didn't."

Elaine was wiping her hands repeatedly on her clay-caked smock, as if she really didn't quite want to touch me. As if she didn't quite believe I was real. She paused an instant before me and I froze also, uncertain that this vaguely rumpled creature was the fastidious Elaine I had known. Then she reached out to clasp each of my hands in hers.

"Why, Amberleigh, you've changed a great deal," she said, sweeping my hands wide and inspecting me. "You're so smart and imposing. I'm sure you must terrify your charges. It's very odd, but we left Miss Meachum's so...unfinished. And now we're different. I daresay it's almost as though we never knew each other."

"But, Elaine..." I stammered, surprised by the distance of her greeting. Before I could continue she swept me into a ladylike embrace, cheek to cheek, and strange because we'd never been effusive. She began chattering in the old, familiar way. I had the uneasy feeling that Elaine was like a long-unused child's rocking horse—stirred into life by the vibration of a familiar step but nevertheless long since put out to pasture in memory. Had I not a regiment of silk-covered French chocolate boxes, now humble repositories for hairpins and odd ribbons, had I not a quite costly set of Dickens' engravings rolled at the bottom of my most petticoat-stuffed trunk, I would have doubted that she even remembered me. Or cared to. Then I would intercept a terrified glint in her fugitive grey eyes, that seemed to sear mutely into mine and demand help. And I would know that we had been friends, had reason to remain so, despite the awkward intervention of the years, of the Atlantic Ocean, of Lady St. Clare. Of ourselves. We would have a future, because we had shared a past. And yet, yet...There was a clever, lancing suspicion in her. A watching, waiting. It was a feeling that returned often during the next few days as Elaine and I stumbled to renew a friendship I occasionally doubted had ever existed.

But at present Elaine escorted me to the bedchamber that was to be mine quite cordially. "It's right next to mine," she explained. "Devora wants us to be—together."

I sailed up the sweeping staircase behind her. The steps were shallow but many, and I was ready for the level when we reached it. Elaine led me down a wide hall.

"Here's my room," she announced, opening a door on a ruffled bower carpeted in Aubusson rugs. She tossed her smock clay-side down on a satin-covered settee before guiding me on down the corridor. "And here's yours. I daresay you shall even be able to hear me breathe from here," she noted, nodding to her adjacent room. There was hostility in her tone, but I hardly felt on firm enough ground to explore it.

"It's most comfortable, Elaine," I said with hedging honesty, for Oriental rugs and Queen Anne were not my idea of elegance, though all of it was very good, I'm sure.

"How was your voyage?" Elaine sat on the testered bed, for the first time looking familiar and at home—I suppose because it was a scene so common to our school days.

"Long. Uneventful. What else can one expect from an ocean voyage?"

"Peace," she said, with a strange note in her voice.

"Elaine, are you—well, quite all right? I came because—"

"I know why you came, Amberleigh. You came because *she* called you. They all come when she calls."

"I came because of you, Elaine. Because your stepmother said you weren't . . . happy. And because my post was running out and I had nowhere else to go," I added with a flash of self-honesty.

"It's true," said Elaine, with an odd speculation in her grave grey eyes. "You have nowhere to go. Now I, I have everywhere to go. I wish I could be you. Be free." She dropped her eyes then and ran her extraordinarily long fingers over the coverlet. I had forgotten what harpist's hands she had. I'd not remembered, really, what she'd been like at all. For a moment I recalled a day in my chamber at school when Elaine's grey eyes had grown charcoal with fear at the prospect of returning to where we both now stood. Or had that been fancy on my part? For here she was, a good six years later, still whole, still hale . . .

A knock at the door brought in a trail of boys bearing baggage under the direction of Symes, who barely favoured me with a glance.

"Ah, here are your things, Amberleigh. I'll send Henrietta in to help you unpack. She's my maid, but I'll share her with you." She paused at one of my battered trunks to finger the shipping label. "Boston. You must tell me about it sometime. To think that you have travelled so far . . ."

She was out the door, leaving me surrounded by a barrage of bags and the strong feeling that I had not yet touched the Elaine I used to know so well I could predict her conversation.

Alone in the room that was to be mine, I began unpacking my travel-worn baggage. Everything would have to be pressed again, I noticed with despair—starched shirtwaists, petticoats,

34

even the sturdy wool skirts, now creased from two weeks in the trunks. I laid my meagre wardrobe across the bed for sorting, puzzling more about Elaine and my oddly casual welcome to Carnhaven than the sad state of my clothing.

"Hullo."

I whirled to meet the sudden voice from the passageway, hardly the greeting of a well-trained maid. A woman was standing in the open doorway—leaning against the doorjamb really—regarding me with bright, curious eyes.

"Good afternoon," I said, at a loss. Was this Henrietta?

"You'll be staying here, then?" she said with an enquiring smile.

"Yes, for a time."

"Then we should be introduced, should we not? My name is Norah. Norah Chandler. I live here also. My, what pretties you have. However do you keep track of so many clothes? I couldn't be bothered with such clutter. I like to live free, like the Gypsies, you know. Be able to pick up and move on."

Before she had finished half of her remarkably familiar comments, her narrow bright brown eyes had inspected my wrinkled wardrobe, swept the room and come to rest on me expectantly.

"I imagine we should all like to live free," I answered rather stiffly, I'm afraid. "Only some of us can do it more readily than others. I'd never thought of my belongings as a burden—until I found them so in need of pressing," I added ruefully. "When I shall do them all I can't imagine."

Norah Chandler laughed, a throaty, almost taunting laugh that left me feeling at a loss again.

"Why, you goose." She laughed. "You'll never have to press your own clothes while staying at Carnhaven. This is a 'Greath Howse' that employs a proper legion of servants to do such things. When in Rome, you shall live like the Romans and, believe me, they did not press their own togas."

Norah's clothing, now that I noticed it, did not seem very pressed at all; I wondered how much she truly knew of the house's running and what her role was in it. Somehow I did not think she was on the staff.

"But," she said briskly, looking about once more and returning to the doorway's shadow, "you will probably need a guide to this...ruin...and I'm head archeologist when it comes to digging up skeletons. Call on me when you want an expert opinion. And you will."

She was gone and when I went to the door to look after her

she had vanished. I returned to my many-flounced bed and sat on the brocade coverlet. At that instant I felt as limp and out of place as my wrinkled clothing. Was coming to Carnhaven a mistake?

CHAPTER FOUR

ELAINE HAD unaccountably abandoned me after her Henrietta— a plucky little Cockney lady so starched she could hardly move—had finished separating my wardrobe into the wearable and the pressable. There was very little to choose from among the wearables; I compromised on a cerise waist overlaid with shirred black chiffon and a black wool skirt that looked only mildly wrinkled. Cerise had never been my colour, I thought, as I examined myself in the slightly scratched oval mirror that faced the foot of my bed. But it was fashionable this season. At least I would be smart if not pressed. I strung one of my mother's more innocuous cameos on a black satin ribbon, thinking of where Mrs. Bowers might be now, and picked my way downstairs.

Eight, Henrietta had said, for dinner. And dress. But no one had thought to tell me the way to the dining room. I loitered a bit at the bottom of the stairs. The hall had taken on the look of an old friend, so foreign was everything else. Left, right, ahead?

"Amberleigh, my dear, here you are!" A figure in coffee-coloured chiffon came whirling down the hall towards me, careening out of the dimly lit regions like one of Mr. Turner's painted locomotives out of the fog.

"I'm shattered, absolutely shattered that no one was here to meet you! But George would ride—and it was such a strain to organize things so at the last moment—but come along, you've hardly had an opportunity to meet our family circle."

She drew me alongside her towards the dining room—left, after all. Had Lady St. Clare always been this tall? I doubted it and credited the authoritative tap I heard from her heels with the difference. She seemed not to have aged at all—always poised on the brink of thirty-five. Or so. At the most. Six years hadn't had their way with her at all.

The dining room was ringed with awesome oils of scenes distant in both time and perspective. The small circle gathered at the somber landscapes' feet seemed somehow overbright and insignificant. Elaine was there, flashing me a nervous smile and toying with the lavalier she wore over her pale frock. And the woman who'd stopped in my room earlier—her hair still stuck at sixes and sevens, impaled in great hanks on half-protruding tortoise-shell hairpins.

And a man was there, a bulky man with an ample waistcoat pulling precariously at the buttons. "Well, Devora, is this the crew then? Gather round and let's get on with it," the man said gruffly.

"Perhaps you'd care to meet our guest first," said Devora calmly. "My husband"—oh, how that word stretched to a subtle kind of mockery—"Sir George St. Clare. Huntsman extraordinaire." She paused to smile over her impromptu rhyme.

"And my father," said Elaine suddenly. "You've never met my father before, Amberleigh."

"No," I responded, caught somehow between the two women. "I've never had the pleasure."

"How d'you do, girl," said Sir George, hardly casting me a glance as he flipped up his jacket skirt and sat.

We women stood frozen. I was not sure how to proceed when the gentleman seated himself first. But Devora waved me to a chair opposite Elaine, took the table's other end herself and we all sat. I glanced at the awkward fifth who shared my side of the board. Norah, I think she'd said her name was.

"Have you met our dear Cousin Norah, Amberleigh? Yes? Then here she is again. Now that we all know who we are perhaps dinner can begin."

Devora nodded regally to Symes and the slow procession of game, fish and greens that was dinner at the St. Clares' began to pass before us. Devlin Quade had been right. Mrs. Featherstone had a light hand with a sauce and a way with foods that turned the most predictable flavours into the most indefinable.

It was a fairly silent meal, I using my first opportunity to survey the household, to dart frequent glances at Sir George, who rather frightened me, and at Cousin Norah who simply puzzled me.

Sir George was a bulky man with white hair cut so close it stuck out in bristles, reminding me of eighteenth-century prints of gentlemen without their wigs. He seemed to have two topics of conversation, which he pulled out for general in-

37

spection at regular intervals and to which no one responded. One subject was hunts he had known, the other the disgraceful slovenliness of Irish servitors and the Irish race in general. In the next few days I would come to know the tenor of Sir George's temper better than I cared to.

"Damn clumsy wench," I would hear him bellow in the morning when Bridget, the maid who brought his breakfast, happened to clink cup against saucer. And God help the girl if, driven to shaking, she actually broke something. Then the invective pouring down the hall would be ear-shattering.

I was to find his behaviour at the evening meal—the only one he took with the family—predictable. His dinner repartee was often a mumbled criticism of the very servants who so silently brought and retrieved Mrs. Featherstone's culinary creations, including the inevitable array of potatoes prepared in every conceivable fashion but still unmistakably that humble vegetable.

"Supposed to have starved on these things!" Sir George would grumble. "Wouldn't know it the way they're spread all over the bloody plate like a pack that's lost the scent. If I never sight a damn potato again . . . here, girl, watch what you're doin' . . . These people by birth are the stupidest wretches, they've no sense of clean and they're clumsy as a newborn calf . . ."

This reminder of Sir George's country outlook would bestir the city-bred Devora. "Yes, dear, you're quite right. But I really don't know what to do about it. I bring as many servants from town as I dare each year, without leaving the town house deserted. And one simply must hire local help. Our ancestors managed with them for some hundred years—I daresay we can put up with it for a summer."

In the meantime, the servants would come and go like colourless shadows with no ears under the watchful eye of the British butler, Symes, who appeared to share his master's sentiments. I would cringe over my duck-and-kidney pie or beat my humble potatoes into a mashed version of the recipe.

It wasn't simply my half-Irish heritage that quailed under Sir George's open anti-Celtism. At times like these I recalled bitterly how I had patronized poor double-chinned Mrs. Willoughby back in Boston for dropping her voice every time a servant circled the dining table or entered the parlour. I had laughed at her inability to handle servants with the verve of those born to them. Nouveau riche, I'd intoned in my Miss Meachum's Academy French. I had considered the Willoughbys semibarbaric in their bourgeois timidity, their inability to live as if those who served them were as insensible a tool as their cutlery or hairbrush.

Now I wished for a dash of humanity to season the menu of prejudice served up nightly at the St. Clare table. I began to understand the Irish impetus for Home Rule. I even began to sympathize.

But that first night I was still too new a lamb to the fold to question its shepherds. I dutifully munched my greens and avoided the sweet. I sipped my one glass of wine lightly and answered quietly when spoken to. I was, in short, a model guest, while everyone about me behaved with astonishing eccentricity.

I was to unearth other eccentricities at Carnhaven during my stay. In my first few days there, Elaine and I explored the length and breadth of the estate, she eager to show me its marvels and I to puzzle out the change in her. Once away from the house, she slipped back into the girl I had known so well—giddy, a little shallow perhaps and always that hard core of suspicion, that startling, glossy cynicism I had noticed even during our most rosy-cheeked days at Miss Meachum's.

One Wednesday afternoon, Elaine had decided I couldn't go any longer without an outing on the lake and a look for the monster reputed to haunt its brakish depths.

"Oh, Elaine, I'm no water lover," I protested. "I swear, twelve days upon the Atlantic are enough for me this year . . ."

"Oh, do come! You'll like it. It's the only way to see the house and grounds properly, with all of Father's costly landscaping in perspective. There's a thought. You can bring your silly sketchbook and I'll row."

"Can we simply take a boat without asking?"

"Of course. We'll take the *Argonaut*. We always used to take it."

So, sketchbook and skimmer over my arm, I allowed Elaine to propel me to a spot along the lake shore where a small wooden dock jutted like a tongue into the gently licking waves. When I saw the *Argonaut*, I couldn't contain my laughter. Never had so small and battered a rowboat worn so regal a nomenclature. "How on earth did this unseaworthy—cork—get such a name?"

"I don't know," said Elaine, staring vaguely across the lake. "Get in, I'll row," she commanded. Her entire attitude seemed to have shifted. "We always called it that. Always," she said, rowing furiously, as good as her word.

I began to feel distinctly uneasy. It wasn't merely those dark, uncertain depths of water just a foot or two from my hand should I care to trail my fingers in it. It wasn't my instinctual fear of deep water. It was Elaine, remote and somehow alien to me. When my charges had been exceptionally bad, had done something utterly horrible, I would say that it must have been the Evil Twin who had done the unspeakable deed. And they would agree gravely that, yes, they thought that the Evil Twin had been just around the corner and, of course, they would get the blame. It was a way to make discipline separate from the relationship and it usually worked. I couldn't help thinking now that Elaine truly had an Evil Twin and that She was in the boat with me.

It took a long time to reach the lake's centre, from where, Elaine insisted, the best view of the countryside was available. I was surprised at her strength in rowing, but somehow I didn't want to ask her about it.

I dutifully sketched for a while. The sloping green hills cupped cottage and castle alike, fluffy white clouds scudded across a heavenly blue sky—everything was a clichéd ode to nature, but my heart wasn't in it. I ended by doing quick studies of Elaine, trying to catch the bitter, twisted expression that flitted across her pale face. I had almost convinced myself that I was indeed sketching the Evil Twin when Elaine suddenly turned her vacant gaze on me.

"Why, Amberleigh, you're drawing me! Let me see!" The boat rocked violently as she leaned towards my end.

"No!" I cried a little desperately, "you'll tip the boat!"

"You're not afraid?" Elaine laughed, the gay and girlish cast of her face overtaking that strange abstraction and combining with it in an expression of downright wickedness. "Really, it's quite safe." With that she put each hand on one rim of the boat and began rocking it roughly from side to side, all the while keeping a steady eye on my reaction.

"No, don't. It's not amusing."

"You said she wasn't seaworthy. Perhaps you're right, Amberleigh, she does bob back and forth a bit, doesn't she?"

Elaine began laughing then, that hard, harsh laugh that comes from the bottom of the chest, like a child who has the upper hand and knows it. It wasn't pleasant, that childish laugh with the lake wide and silent around us and the waves a good foot high and it a calm day. Suddenly, the shore was so far away; I sensed the great feet upon feet of water that welled beneath the fragile wooden vessel.

"Elaine!" Real fear tightened my throat. "Elaine!"

She stopped abruptly and went limp, staring down at the boat's bottom as if it were a crystal ball. "It was always a good boat. We called it *Argonaut*. You shouldn't have laughed, Amberleigh." And she wouldn't say another word to me, but sat there with her hands in her lap, weeping silent tears. I sensed that I had insulted the boat, that it was a live thing to her and I had hurt it.

"I'm sorry, Elaine," I said. And I rowed back, for she seemed as absent in presence from the boat as a spirit. Oh, it was clumsy rowing, laughable had any been there to see it. And I had to bathe my hands in olive oil and wrap them in flannel for three nights before the blisters began to heal. But after that, Elaine accepted me as she hadn't before.

"Come sketching with me today, Amberleigh," she invited a few days later at breakfast with real enthusiasm in her voice. We were late risers. I don't know whether it was because our bedchambers abutted and neither of us heard the other stirring so we both slumbered beyond the limits of industriousness; or whether the soporific country air had such an effect on my constitution that I slept long, exhausted by those lengthy after-dinner evenings in the drawing room.

So Elaine and I picked among the ravaged delights of the sideboard, usually cold ham and meat pies, potatoes and other hearty fare. I myself preferred croissants, but this Continental delicacy was no more than a few significant crumbs on a tray by the time I got there. I suspected Devora of forestalling my addiction. I tended to blame her for everything trying.

"You know you don't care to sketch, Elaine," I objected over the breakfast ham.

"But you do. And I like an excuse to go somewhere and sit in peace. Let's go out to the little lake today, or the pagoda, and keep away from the house. I'm lonely for the little lake, I think."

I needed no excuse to take up charcoal or pastels, welcoming the prospect of exploring the small artificial lake that nestled among green willows and the somewhat arch footbridges beyond the house's formal gardens. I had a passion for clever fripperies that tended to sentimentalize my artworks, according to the lean sallow lady who taught the subject at Miss Meachum's.

Elaine robbed the sideboard of a good supply of delicacies for later lunching, pointed me towards my art materials and pulled me out of the house through the gardens and down the quaint path that led to the water. She was like a puppy coaxing a somewhat staid master out for a romp on the heath. I hadn't seen her so, so vivacious since I had arrived. She was exactly as she had been at school—high-spirited, childlike, unrealistic. But that had been seven years ago.

"Oh, look, someone must have been here. I was afraid the pagoda would be locked so early in the spring, but it's open. How odd."

"This latticework looks as easy as an almond shell to crack, Elaine. Perhaps a poacher, or even a groundsman, broke in for some reason."

"Perhaps. At any rate, you can set up here on the outside bench and I'll settle inside and tell you all about Devora's house party."

"House party? Here?" I was surprised to learn of organized merriment at Carnhaven. It seemed as remote from the world as a convent, and I assumed it had always been so.

"Yes, she used to have quite a few. Until recently. I can't think why she should start up again like this, but Devora is never exactly predictable. Perhaps it's because you're here. I saw the letters on the salver ready to go out. She's having the Maxwells—he's a colonel and terribly stuffy in a funny sort of way, and she, well, she's so bombastic you'd need to invite half the House of Peers to balance her off. And Maisie (Martha) Dillingham, the Honourable, because she's no competition for me. And even Adrian. She asked Adrian Carstairs, can you imagine?"

"You sound as though you didn't like the idea of Adrian Carstairs coming. Isn't he a family friend? I remember meeting him—why, he even came up to Miss Meachum's for our commencement. Is he still unmarried?" I could imagine Elaine passing through six seasons unscathed; I couldn't imagine what I remembered of Adrian Carstairs managing it, not with London Mamas about.

"No, not married," said Elaine with a noncommital expression. Then her upturned nose wrinkled. "She was always throwing Adrian at me, you know. He's not really anybody, either. Except that his family has a distillery or something in the South and is very, very rich. But Devora never wants to go much into precisely what the money is from. Merely that they have it. I rather think she's hoping to have another go at Adrian and me. Devora never gives up. You should bear that in mind, Amberleigh."

Elaine's vague allusion irritated me. And the idea of sketch-

42

ing a lakeside scene so carefully prearranged as this artificial pond was like trying to execute a portrait of a portrait—unsatisfying. "How long has this been here?" I asked idly.

"More of Devora's work," she replied a bit fiercely. "It's new. They put it in after—after I was sent away to Miss Meachum's." There was something in her voice, some dissonant chord that made me turn to watch her through the lattice fretwork. She had thrust one finger into a square and was jamming it aimlessly against the wood. Her face was checkerboarded by the lattice, one eye only caught in a square of daylight. Its expression was vacant, far away.

"Elaine, you'll riddle yourself with splinters." I sounded like a governess.

"Will I?" she asked dreamily, pulling her hand back through the pierced wall between us and cradling it in her lap. "Sketching does bore me, you're right," she said suddenly. "I think I'll go for a walk."

She flounced off the bench and out the other side of the gazebo without a backward look, as if she were rather put out with me. I broke my chalk on the next stroke—half exasperation and half bad luck, I suppose—and decided to stay on, bending myself to the task of blending out the unfortunate smudge I'd made.

My sketch-pad lake wasn't coming along that well anyway. I had rather thought artificial lakes and expensive formal fripperies like pagodas and pavilions were somewhat outdated. But tastes at Carnhaven seemed varied and I supposed an eager bride—hard as it was to picture Devora in quite so vulnerable a position—would be anxious to make her mark on the new canvas that was hers.

"You really are quite talented, Amberleigh." It was the silken purr of Devora in full felinity. I'd been so absorbed in my reverie I hadn't heard her soft-footed approach. "No, don't shut your sketchbook, your work looks charming."

"Thank you, but I'm really only a dabbler; I've never done anything..."

"Nonsense." She sat beside me, setting her basket of cut flowers at our feet. She looked almost human, her shirtwaist sleeves rolled up and a long shears protruding from her lacy apron pocket. "You've a real ability, Amberleigh. I'd like to see it used. Did you know we had an old studio in the house? Oh, yes, it's on the third floor. They knocked out an entire portion of roof to create it. For one of George's dotty aunts, I believe. But I see no reason why someone not-so-dotty shouldn't have a try at it." She smiled.

"That's extremely kind of you, Lady St. Clare, but outdoor sketching is more to my style. I'm afraid there'd be very little inspiration to be seen through a skylight."

Devora cocked her curled brown head in the gesture she found effective with the male contingent and tilted my sketchpad toward herself contemplatively.

"What you require is a challenge. Something totally different from these schoolgirl attempts. Very good in their way, of course, but not— Oils. A large canvas. Why not a—yes, a portrait! The very thing. I've wanted one done and I think you would give it an unusual approach. Do try it, Amberleigh, you yourself might be surprised at the outcome."

For a moment Devora's enthusiasm almost made me forget her age and my station. For a moment she almost seemed like someone Elaine and I had known, and liked, at Miss Meachum's

"Yes, it would be so amusing, Amberleigh," she urged. "Elaine's already cooped up in the studio half the day sculpting and doing quite well at it. We three could retire up there for a day's work. And have Bridget bring up a picnic luncheon— what is it artists eat?—cold chicken and warm wine? And it might do Elaine good. I think she's already gotten, well, more down to earth since I encouraged her to work with clay. Oh . . ." She laughed, realizing her unintended pun.

What could I say? I was supposed to "companion" Elaine; my employer was essentially ordering me to take up my brushes and paint and the idea did sound tempting. I considered and agreed. Then, like Elaine before her, Lady St. Clare seemed suddenly to tire of my bench beside the gazebo. Her eyes narrowed towards the artificial lake that had been my subject and she stared at it as if she'd never set eyes on it before. Then she lengthened her long elegant neck and turned to me with that aloof look in her eyes once again.

"I'm glad you're to do my portrait, Amberleigh. I'm sure you'll find it very rewarding."

She stood, delicately shook out her walking skirt and wafted back to the house along the path as quietly as she had come, the basket of long-stemmed flowers bouncing rhythmically at her hip. She looked the picture of a Louis Sixteenth courtesan, I thought, all airy and countrified but still somehow decadently metropolitan. I sighed. I should never be escorted by admiring male eyes along pretty paths and down marble ballroom corridors. No one would ever mistake me for other than what I was—a boringly modern person in every respect. Unimaginative, that's what it was. Not at all fascinating and vapourish. At least Elaine was *interesting* if a trifle tiresome at times.

I packed up the pastels and wandered after Lady St. Clare, wondering if she had left any Essence d'Elegance in her wake which might settle on me. I had advanced to the large rhododendron stand near the terrace when I heard a sharp sticklike snap and stopped. A pointed little face peered at me through the rhododendrons, but a moment later only the quivering leaves proved a presence. I wondered briefly if one of the Little People were spying on me, but the face's owner shortly darted from around the bush and regarded me gravely.

She was a child of about nine, though she struck me as slight for her age—a ragamuffin, swarthy girl wearing tattered pinafore and dark stockings with great holes in them. Her thick black lashes swept her cheeks with shy regularity.

"Hullo," I said.

She didn't respond, but clasped an elbow behind her back and danced impishly in the path. She looked like a tinker's child and I speculated that such a family may have settled on the estate, perhaps to work as gardeners.

"Is your father, that is, does he work here?" I asked.

Her expression grew sullen.

"He's far, far away. But he's a bad man and I'm not to speak of him." I'd expected a lisping version of the local brogue. Instead, this child spoke the clearest Queen's English this side of Court.

"I see. And your mother, is she here then?"

"Of course she's *here*," the child answered, giggling and intrigued with the idea of a person being "here" but not precisely "here."

She puzzled me, this girl who seemed to have dropped from the overcast sky. There was something familiar about her, yet foreign. I noticed the soft brunette down along her forearms. She looked like some monkey god's changeling, perpetrated on a human race not quite ready for her. And yet, her dark skin had a golden cast, her eyes were tilted to an attractive slant; she might one day be a beauty.

"What is your name?"

"Opal."

"Opal. That's an interesting name. You must be an interesting girl."

"It means 'precious stone,'" she reported with some importance.

45

"Does it? I never knew that. But I have a bracelet of opals. Perhaps you'd like to see it sometime."

Her interest was piqued but she kept her distance. I had the oddest feeling that she knew who I was, and didn't like it. And still that familiar cast of face, even in the way she stood, weight on one foot, her arm twisted behind her back . . .

Norah. Substitute the fair-and-straw colouring of Norah Chandler for the tawny-and-black of this child and the features fell into place.

"You're Norah Chandler's daughter."

She nodded and darted back to the bush, rending a flowering branch from it. She pulled it through her circling hand, stripping the blossoms. They fell at her feet like pink pearls, unstrung. She held the denuded branch out to me, but when I extended my hand for it, she rapped me across the open palm, twittered and ran away. I pursued my course back to the house wrapped in a feeling of dread that I couldn't explain.

But by that afternoon, Lady St. Clare had had a voluminous painting smock sent to my room, with a note in her curious handwriting that she hoped I didn't mind if she wore something a bit more feminine to our sittings. Within days, Devora, Elaine and I had settled into a routine of withdrawing to our artists' garret (about the size of middling ballroom) at eleven each day and working away till teatime.

I loved the old attic studio. It was wide-open to the light and large, with only a few spare sawhorses, sculpting blocks, raw board tables and some lightweight abandoned chairs to share it with us. Elaine was curiously intent upon her work— a life-sized head whose features still hid in the hard clay. Devora would lean elegantly against one of the little chairs in an emerald silk and jet evening gown—so out of place in the attic's sun-filtered atmosphere—and I began my daily battle with oils that wouldn't mix, a palette that made my arm ache and a canvas so large I sometimes dreamt that I had to paint the whole world.

There was an entire new kit of paints, which surprised me. Somehow I had expected the dotty aunt's equipment to be lingering on; I actually relished the idea of taking up so eccentric a brush. But there was no excuse for me there; no way to claim a previous user had warped my expertise or that Greataunt Dotty's oddities had bewitched my hands.

The colours, the brushes, they were as raw as I was, but slowly a figure and face formed on the canvas.

"Oh, yours is coming along so well, Amberleigh," said

Elaine one day when we were working alone. She paused to dry her clay-caked hands before my canvas of her stepmother.

"Devora always looks so . . . right . . . in green. Like a garter snake." She said it absolutely without expression. I turned to make sure she hadn't been jesting but found her mouth drawn into the secret line it often took nowadays. "Devora is a snake, Amberleigh. I only tell you that so she doesn't bite you."

"Come back here, Elaine. You can't simply say leading things like that and march away. Why do you think Devora will bite me?"

"She already has." Her face was still in its seriousness.

I wandered over to watch her mold the never-finished head. Elaine's lackluster attempts at the sculpture had become almost ritualistic, a task she dutifully followed, a pacifying motion through which she went meekly. Was it simply because Devora had urged it upon her? Or more?

"Oh, Elaine, sometimes I—"

"Yes, Amberleigh?" She turned just her head, but her expression, the distant sideways glance of her eyes reminded me of the day in the boat. The remote, unhappy Evil Twin had emerged again from the Elaine I thought I knew. I half believed that she hated me at that moment.

"You've never tried painting, Elaine? It's quite exciting, really, to build the oils up, almost like sculpting in a way. Perhaps you'd like it." I was babbling and knew it. I didn't know how to talk to her when she became this new person. I began poking through some abandoned canvases in my effort to change the subject. "Why, Elaine, you have too painted. Here, isn't this yours?" I had glimpsed her name at the bottom of one dusty canvas and seized upon it to shape the conversation away from the vague, doom-saying prophetic turn Elaine could take of late.

But when I wrenched it free of its neighbours, I was sorry to have found it. It was poorly done—a flat, lifeless thing. It pictured a young man lying dead and floating among the lily pads.

"It's quite—intriguing. Elaine, you could try painting if you wanted something different to do."

"No," she said.

"But this one, what is it?"

She didn't even turn to see it. "King Arthur on his way to Avalon."

"But King Arthur was on a barge, wasn't he? I thought this might be, oh, I don't know—Narcissus, perhaps, drowning in his own image. Or..." Stupid, stupid make-talk.

"It's King Arthur on the way to Avalon, Amberleigh. That's who I said it was and it is. King Arthur on the way to Avalon."

Elaine's fair hair, shining in the filtered light that haloed us, glowed like a Rossetti madonna's. Her delicate profile, the bulky smock that mimicked a medieval gown—for an instant she reminded me of some lost Italian portrait, displaced and abandoned among dusty canvases as unreal as she.

Or Elaine. The late Lord Tennyson's Lady of Shalott. Her namesake Elaine, the lily maid of Astolat. Who "weaves by night and day, a magic web with colours gay" while pining for her lost Lancelot. I suddenly understood part of the change in Elaine that puzzled me. She was waiting. A passive creature, waiting, dreaming.

For whom was she waiting? Or for what?

CHAPTER FIVE

"IT'S ROSIE, isn't it? I've heard Henrietta speak of you. Where's the pantry? It's all right, I need some rags—for the oils—and Lady St. Clare said the kitchen might have them..."

The plain-faced kitchen maid looked surprised to be called upon to do personally for the gentry. She stuttered until her thick brogue tripped on its own missteps and she fell flat into silence.

Why hadn't I simply plunged into searching for the things myself? Surely one of these narrow, businesslike doors concealed a supply of well-worn dishrags and polishing mitts. Even an elderly petticoat would have sufficed. Where was Mrs. Featherstone—she'd set the tongue-tied Rosie on the scent in a moment.

"She wants the dust cloths, Rosie, in the pantry drawer."

The serving woman, middle-aged as she was, nodded dumbly like an obedient child and disappeared behind one of the doors I'd been considering.

"Thank you, Norah. I didn't know you were down here. She must like your accent better than mine."

"It's not that. No, poor Rosie's likes and dislikes have long since ceased to have anything to do with the way she lives. You're not familiar to her; she has a great need for the familiar."

"I didn't mean to put anybody out—" I started, feeling as though I'd invaded a land where any function I could perform would be listed under "Nuisance."

"Don't apologize. You apologize too much. I never apologize for anything if I can help it. No one pays any attention to one if one apologizes."

"I'm sorry," I retorted, half humourously and half antagonistically. I did not like to be lectured by one whose idea of manners was to cut convention with a butcher knife. Norah sighed, almost as one does with a naughty child who will not learn the elementaries.

"Here, Feather always keeps a kettle hot. Let's have some tea. I think Carnhaven is beginning to unravel you. Come on, sit down. I won't bite."

I slipped onto a chair at the long wooden table while Norah produced a pair of heavy white porcelain cups and a tea ball. I watched her rustle across the wide, stone-paved floor. She was wearing a fairly crisp grey-and-white-striped shirtwaist with an almost respectable skirt. The hem barely cleared her ankles, but then I'd noticed that Norah's single vanity was her feet—today slippered in neat and rather high-heeled pumps. Her great masses of ungoverned hair looked washed for once, though coarse and strawlike.

It must be frustrating to be a plain woman, destined to do everything wrong in the way of little touches—from her unkempt mop to the stick-spindly figure. She was a walking broomstick of a woman; no wonder she seemed more at home in the scullery than anywhere else in the great house.

"Ah, it's good and steaming. Nothing nicer than fresh hot English tea, is there? From Ceylon, of course." She laughed again, with the bitter edge sharpening any real mirth in her tones.

"It's a day for tea." I sighed noncommittally. "It's so dreary in the studio. I can't quite force myself to work as I should."

"Ah, yes. Painting the devious Devora. The deceiving Devora..."

"Why do you say that?"

"Don't you think so as well?"

"I don't know. I suppose it's easy for us to dislike Devora. After all, she has so much of what we never will."

"Does she? I refuse to credit that. Devora has nothing. That's why she's dangerous."

It was the second time in three days that I'd heard Devora described as dangerous. It sent a shiver down my spine despite the spicy aroma of tea clearing my head and sending new resolve down my limbs.

"Doesn't everyone overdramatize Devora?" I objected finally. "She's merely—unhappy, I imagine."

"Ah, but she can't say as much herself. Fancy Devora confessing that her glittering life was dull and empty and hemmed in by the hulk of Sir George—'Georgie, Porgie, puddin' and pie, Kissed the girls and made 'em cry'—I'll wager he did."

Norah's rich laughter rippled like cream over the teacups, tainting even my solemn cup with a reflected smile. Her brown eyes looked knowingly into mine. I dared not admit I didn't fully understand the source of her mockery. I had a feeling it would be callow of me.

"It must be hard for you here," I ventured. "You seem too much of an analyst for a country life."

"Yes, there's little in this house to catch me up. Not that there aren't other—oh, hello, darling. Come meet the new lady in the house."

Somehow I didn't want to tell her that I had previously encountered the waif who shyly lurked now by the pantry door. Neither did the waif, it seemed, for Opal edged over and steadfastly regarded my left shoe tip.

"Say hello to Miss Dunne, Opal, you can manage that, can't you, shrinking-violet Opal of mine?"

Opal twisted her hands deep into her pinafore pockets and bent even more attention on my fascinating feet. I was growing as embarrassed as the child and wished her mother would let us ignore each other in peace.

"All righty, little clam, back to collecting your butterflies. But I want you back for your lessons after supper."

The girl darted away with wood-nymph silence. She paused on the threshold to direct one almost malignantly knowing glance at me before she twisted the knob and snaked through the hardly open door.

"I can't imagine where she got her reticence," said Norah, a frown creasing her high forehead. She leaned her chair away from the table and folded one knee, draping an ankle over the other knee. It was a rude posture that set her skirts dipping between her legs like a washerwoman's apron.

I pushed away the cup with the few stray leaves washing against the bottom in a little lukewarm liquid. I noticed for the first time that the cup was cracked.

"I've got to go, too. There are things I've been meaning to do, and Devora's waiting in the studio."

"Yes, I as well," said Norah, standing up so we faced each other over the chair. "There are always things to do."

I nodded and briskly retraced my way to the front of the house, not taking the back stairs to the studio. I hadn't expected her to follow me.

She caught me up before I'd gone halfway up the stairs. "It's a hard house to find your way around in, isn't it?" she asked breathlessly. Her face broke into a smile that sent some of her homeliness spinning away. A tinge of overexcitement tinted her porridge complexion brighter. Here, away from the family or the drab kitchen, she seemed brighter, realer.

"But, listen, come up to my room. I've some very pretty pieces of material I brought back from abroad, the only jewels beside Opal worth taking from India. I'll show you."

Her words tugged me up the stairs behind her, the dust cloths still fluttering in my hand like a flag of surrender.

"If you like to bicycle, I've a pair of bloomers that might suit you," she added, swinging wide her chamber door.

The room was merely a few feet down the hall from Elaine's and mine. But it was a different world I entered. There were scraps of cloth in gaudy foreign colours strewn across every chest and dresser top; strange little carved figures leering from an open pigeon-holed desk jammed and burdened with an astonishing assortment of papers and portfolios.

Books leaned drunkenly, their worn bindings exposing yellowed and broken spines in places. The books marched across the top of the seven-foot-high wardrobe. They lay in precarious piles next to chairs and alongside the bed. There a cracked vase was used to prop them up, here a chamberpot, in plain sight.

I lurched across the threshold into the cluttered room, with the air slightly stuffy from things long hoarded and heavy with long-ago-burned incense.

"Take a seat," urged Norah, clearing a venerable stuffed chair of a pile of magazines and two pair of mismatched shoes. She kicked her own footwear off and jammed her feet into a heelless set of scuffed slippers that dragged across the floor with the dry scrape of a reptile when she walked.

"Well, what do you think of it?" she enquired, obviously proud of her *outré* corner of Carnhaven. It was a chore to tailor my response to the bright, particoloured shawl she held up for my inspection rather than the ruins around me. No wonder she referred to herself as an "archeologist."

"Very—lively," I answered in half a daze. "I mean, the pattern is very close. Does Opal sleep here, too?"

"Certainly. She's too young for her own quarters. I've a trundle bed I pull out. Then, how about this one? It's less vivid, perhaps more to your taste. More European; they've already gotten to the villagers and taught them the proper way to weave for Englishmen."

"That's very pretty, quite pretty, but really I don't require another shawl—"

"Take it! I've a dozen more. Here. The reason I really brought you up here is I've some pamphlets you might like to read. You ever seen anything by the Suffragists? I've got something by the Pankhursts—" She began paging through a pile of dislodged papers, impatiently pushing her hair from her eyes. The "lunatic fringe" she wore dipped toward her eyelashes. Norah suddenly slammed the pile of papers to the carpet at her feet.

"Bloody hair, I cannot stand it!" She reached into a sewing basket at the other side of the chair and fished out a sharp pair of shears. Snip went the blades and Norah carelessly hacked an inch of hair off against her forehead. The sharp silver points darted dangerously close to her eyes.

"Norah! For heaven's sake, do that with a glass—you'll blind yourself."

She shrugged in amusement. "I can't stand anything that fetters me. Never could. From Father to Him." She pulled her yellow hair straight out from her forehead and harvested it like a sheaf of wheat. The chaff scattered unhindered to the floor and across the papers at her feet. "I'm used to doing things my way. And as for a glass, what's to see in it but lies? Or do you still believe in reflected images, Amberleigh? I'd have thought a few weeks at Carnhaven would have cured you of that. Ah, but I'm being hard on you. You're new. You know so little. As I once was, you're a stranger from a strange land."

"Stranger from a—oh, you mean America. But from what strange land did you come?"

She brightened at my interest and clasped me proprietorily by the wrist to draw me out the door, down the hall, the stairs and to a settee on the landing. It was dim there, shaded by the dusky floral wallpaper and walnut woodwork. A trio of ferns on high stands shed their leafy shadows upon us.

"India." She said the word as if it were a magical spell. There she sat, Cousin Norah, her eyes laughing and her mouth taut with a suppressed smile. "Yes, India. I actually lived there, you know. Oh, yes, for seven years. It was where I met Him." Her tone intensified on the last word, but with what emotion I couldn't tell. "He wanted desperately to go to Oxford, of course, so it was natural my being from England should interest him. That and some other things."

"But why were you in India? I thought women didn't—"

"Go there? Oh, but they did if they were missionaries."

"A missionary?"

"Yes, don't I look it? Oh, I've tossed off all that blind nonsense now. But I was very idealistic then; thought I'd convert the world to the Lamb of God. Teach the filthy Indians to bathe and their children to ride rocking horses and be nice to their nannies, something like that." She slumped down suddenly on the settee, winding her shapeless maroon wool sweater around her bony arms and stretching her smartly clad feet before her. I noticed several white circles of flesh around her exposed ankles where the unmended stockings, odd partners for foot-proud shoes, were pulled to their limits. But perhaps I was too fastidious; one shouldn't judge on appearances.

"Haven't you ever been a True Believer? Perhaps you still are and don't want to hear my heresy. It might send you to Hell!" She threw her dark blonde head back and laughed wildly then, but I heard the bitter accents beneath that forced hilarity. Her enlightenment must have been a wrenching one.

"I'm not sure I believe in Heaven, but I know I don't put any stock in Hell," I answered. "Father never had any time for the Church. He called it 'an acolyte at Ireland's imprisonment' once," I remembered suddenly.

"Your father was an astute man," she said, serious again and sitting upright. "So he didn't pass on that filthy tommyrot about 'love thy neighbour' and 'leave thy riches to the rich' to you. Well, I believed it. I packed up and went to India because of it.

"And I simply loved the people. They were poor, really poor. After I left the Mission I moved into a hovel in Bombay. We ate on the floor, mind you, and with our fingers! Gruel and curry to keep from tasting the rot and little else. I had only two gowns the entire time I was there. But I like that. I like my life uncluttered. Is not all vanity?"

Had her voice not been ironic, I'd have suspected some lingering religious fanaticism. I could envision Cousin Norah with her narrow face, long jaw and sharp elbows lit from within and draped in rusty black, clutching a Book of Common Prayer on some foreign dais. I could see the brown faces arrayed before her like an army of enthusiastic ants.

"What made you go?"

It was an innocent question, but it started bitter embers glowing behind her brown eyes. For the first time I observed that Norah's hay-coloured hair sprang from a dark-brown part; for one who abhored fripperies, I found it odd that she should take to as shameful a practise as blonding her hair. And why bother, if she was bound to wind it upon her head in greasy hanks? Unappealing, but there was a shuttered eagerness in her for something. Perhaps it was understanding.

"Go? I had to go. I couldn't stay at home with Father any longer. A hateful man, an impossible man. Mean and small-minded. Yes, he's my father, but oh, Amberleigh, live with a man like that and you too might take to missionary work. It was a good way to leave home. It appalled Father, of course. A barrister's daughter, a well-situated barrister's daughter, abandoning hearth and all she held dear to ship to another part of the world, a wretched teeming place where people lived like and with animals . . . It was better than living with Father."

"I wouldn't know. My father died—early."

"You're judging me, I can see. But try being one of eight, all no more than asterisks to a father's dour youth. An—un-married—daughter home, past seven-and-twenty and no hope of luring some mush-mouthed young curate or even a country cousin for a husband. We were all a disappointing lot. And poor Meg at that awful place in Sussex, though nobody was to speak of that, how she—crawled—through her days in that institution. And my younger sister Katy—the pretty one he called her—run off with the soldier, another nobody for the barrister's family tree." She laughed again, deep from within her throat and chest.

"So I went. Packed my bag and went. Isn't that what you did, simply gathered up a few things and took ship? Only I had to find a Missionary Church to sponsor me. Church of the Beloved Brethren, it was. Not High Church, oh, my no, another blow to father's ambitions. Merely an earnest, almost unknown little sect looking for workers in the vineyard. But they paid my way to India. And set me up in a dusty little village five oxcart days from Calcutta. Have you ever seen a man with no legs begging from a wretched little wagon on the streets with flies on his eyes? Children wrestling dogs for refuse in the shadow of palaces as jewelled as a stained-glass window in

54

one of our safe home churches? It was like that. And worse."

"It must have been awful! How could you live like that?"

"Awful? Yes, it was awful." Norah said the word with a kind of reverence, an almost religious sense of fulfillment.

"I've thought that I had some difficulty when I left Miss Meachum's positionless," I said, recalling those agonizing days in Westaways' employment agency lobby before the American post had sprung up.

"I was born for problems. So are most women. And luckily for surmounting them."

"But when did you marry? You must have been there several years, Opal is . . ."

"Nine. Yes. Opal is nine. I—oh, you mustn't think me wicked, I didn't marry. I mean, marriage as an institution is one adverse by nature to women, you must have sensed that. I really don't believe in marriage. So I was quite content to live with him. He didn't believe in marriage either, oh, no. Then when it was evident I was to have Opal—well, he did a turn on me. Married, he said, we must be married. I never forgave him that."

"But, Norah, he must have meant well, have tried to do the—well, the right thing . . ." I stumbled, looking for the words that wouldn't indict my middle-class viewpoint and injure her already lacerated feelings.

"But the thing was he hadn't really been serious about marriage being all rot. He deceived me. And once married, the road to England was easier. Besides, he wanted Opal." Her voice was grim.

"It's only natural a father should have softer feelings towards . . ."

"It wasn't natural at all," she said, her hands clutching mine as her voice lowered. "He didn't believe in natural bonds, either. He thought that a father and a daughter could—once Opal was old enough, do you see?"

"See?" I felt vaguely I should understand her implications, but I didn't. "You mean, there was something unnatural—Norah, I'd like to help you, I'd like to understand, but—"

"Didn't teach you that at Miss Meachum's, did they?" She looked almost triumphant. "Incest. He wanted to lie with his own daughter. In the biblical sense." She sat back and watched me as realization flooded my stunned brain. I felt she fed in some way on my capacity for shock.

"That's what one gets when one marries a black man, that's

what dear Fath-uh would have said."

"Black? But wasn't he an Indian? I mean that's not exactly black."

"To some it is. Where do you think Opal gets her colouring? Not from my curds-and-whey complexion—no, it's his. The dark ruby of India in her blood. She's hairy, too, you know. All over her arms and back. I must show you sometime."

Another unnatural note—although that word would never have the same ramifications for me again—to describe her own daughter in such terms. Perhaps the poor woman secretly longed to disown her half-caste child.

"And how did you come back?"

"The Mission. They sent me, despite my having fallen away from their path. Good Christians, they were. They still send clothes for Opal. I left him, of course, though he tried to keep me. Once he stabbed a man twelve times. In a village brawl. Twelve times. It could have been I or Opal. He still might come, might follow. He won't give up Opal that easily. She's nine now, getting to the age. It's why I keep our whereabouts secret, why I'm in a bloody agony over whether we'll be discovered, why I'm worried to distraction half the time. If the St. Clares weren't here to hide me in their ample holdings— do you want to see a letter from him? Oh, yes, he can write, quite educated. To look at him, he's not unhandsome, to listen to him—well, you'd probably think he was quite charming. Quite charming."

She pulled a worn letter from her skirt pocket. It was thin foreign paper with slanted spidery handwriting across it. I almost shuddered to touch it, tainted as it had been by the monster she had described.

"He wants me back," she said with a tight smile as I glanced over his countercharges in the letter. "He says I'm foolish, do you see, foolish to worry about Opal, that he's doing well. You must remember that he impresses people at first. Men like him always do. If they don't know him well. And he writes well. It's between the lines one must read, one always must with men. What do you think?"

I folded the letter and returned it to her. "You're right, he does sound quite rational. He mentions something about your politics; what does he mean by that?"

"Oh, that? Yes, he finds it abnormal that my sentiments are with the United Irish and Home Rule. Says I'm only caught up in the glamour of the Cause. He loves to differ with me on politics; he believes it distracts me from other things. Men often do that, you know. Pretend to care what goes on in one's head."

"So when you were—disillusioned—in him, you took up the child and fled?"

"How biblically you put it! You can't have eluded all your lessons." Norah sent me a bright amused look. It lightened her entire face. She had pulled out a battered pince-nez when she handed me the letter to read. Now she scanned the writing once briefly through the spectacles before tucking away the much-folded missive again.

"Absolutely charming. At first," she mused, her eyes pursuing the faded ink with something like regret. "Like Bluebeard. And there are many like him." Her eyes flicked to me warningly. I couldn't help wondering if she always carried his letter with her. But that wasn't fair. It had been dated only a few months before.

"He still writes—?"

"Oh, yes, indeed. Wants me back. Wants us back. I live in constant anxiety that he'll not wait to coax us back. That he'll come over and get us. One way or the other."

"Aren't you being overworried by it? I hardly think he'd come all the way from India if you've left him for, what is it, seven years?"

"Eight," she said sharply, her voice almost a hiss of precision. As if every year had been weighed and found wanting. "If only I could be certain I were free of him. I was lucky to have relations to fall back upon, much as they resent it."

"Oh, I don't think the St. Clares—"

"They do. You mustn't give everybody the benefit of the doubt. I and Opal provide them with a certain amount of status in the philanthropic way, as do you. Carnhaven, home to Wayward or Mislaid Women, yes, I like that. And Devlin Quade, another charity. Only they'd never educate a woman, dear me, no. Precisely what women like us need more than bed and board."

"You're a cousin of Elaine's then?" I asked to change a subject she found bitter.

"Yes." Her brown lashes had sunk to half-mast below her heavy-lidded eyes. I felt that there was something more to Norah's history, something that I was missing...

"Don't you like living here?"

She sighed and sank deeper into the sofa, her ankles bending out awkwardly on the stair carpet and rolling it into little pleats.

"Have to. It's not where I'd choose to be. No—vitality, no

57

real life. Not if one's lived in Calcutta. And there's work to be done, work I can't do here, hiding away from that man. He'd kill us, you know. He really would. Oh, he's a bastard!" she burst out. "A vile, filthy, rotten bastard and he's got me utterly trapped. From seven thousand miles away."

I saw her then, mouldering along the back stairs, putrifying in the parlour, growing old, growing shrivelled—haunted always by the thought of what that man she had known years ago might do.

"Have you told the St. Clares, isn't there anything they can do?"

"Nothing. He hasn't done anything. The law can't look at him. We women have no recourse, you know. He is my husband still. I belong to him. And Opal does, too. If he came and dragged us off by our hair—the law would simply hand him a hairnet. It's a rotten way to live, at the beck and call of whatever man one's linked one's life to, particularly if he's a bastard."

I'd never thought of marriage as other than an ennobling institution, as my natural goal. The idea that I might not marry filled me with ice-water worry. Not that I minded so very much not marrying. It was the world knowing that no one thought me fit to marry. A matter of pride more than one of need. And spinsterhood—well, a lot of women lived through it. This woman next to me—that was the odd thing about Norah—her eccentricities, her slovenly dress, they were more the guise of an old maid than of a woman who had made a shocking marriage to a shocking man. Perhaps she was hiding now from all men. I'd never thought of that side of it. I'd only imagined beatific unions made in heaven and Mrs. Somebody's novels.

"It all sounds dreadful, Norah. But you speak like a Suffragist."

"Lord, no! There are greater things going on in the world than that! The Suffragists think merely by having the vote they can change events, make a better world, improve mankind, they'd call it, by improving the lot of womankind." Her voice had risen to a jeer. "They'll not only never succeed, but they haven't perceived the heart of it. Economics."

"Economics?"

"Yes. It's what makes the world go round. It's what keeps the Calcutta mobs salivating after garbage. It's what," she said, pressing the advantage her repulsive image had given her, "keeps England sitting down hard on Ireland. Money. Who has what's needed and who wants it and who can bring it from one point to another. You know the landlords wore out the Irish land. So now when it's finally being talked of the tenants buying it for themselves, it's naught but fallow earth. Worthless. All County Clare. But the English still won't give it up. Not as long as there's a drop of sweat—or blood—to be squeezed out of an Irish forehead. It's vicious. One wonders how people can sleep at night, knowing such atrocities are happening all around one."

"Surely you don't think that plain hatefulness motivates the entire British Empire? Isn't it merely ignor——"

"Shhhhh," Norah ordered imperiously. Her hand held my shoulder. I heard the vague footsteps above us stop as the feet began to tread the plush carpet leading down to our niche.

"Why, Amberleigh...Norah. Gracious, you startled me. I never expected to see a soul in this alcove." Devora, who'd materialized from the second floor, pressed a hand to her throat. I saw a nervous little flutter of her heavy lids as she dropped her eyes momentarily.

"I'm dreadfully sorry to have been so long about the painting rags, Lady St. Clare. Rosie couldn't find them at first. And then Norah came along and we brewed some tea—" I broke off, waving my cloths in explanation and feeling wretched. I'd kept her waiting so long at the sitting that she'd given up and come downstairs.

"Never mind, dear," she said almost meekly. "Really, I've ended up with a rather beastly headache. I thought I'd lie down awhile. Elaine's thumping away at that awful head of hers— not that I don't admire her for accomplishing something. I don't feel up to posing any longer today. I'm sure you'll understand. I'll see you at dinner." Devora smiled vacantly at us both and slowly made her way up again to the next turn in the stairs.

"Migraine," explained Norah tersely. "They've been getting worse. She never had them before she married Sir George. At least that's what she used to say. The pain drives her almost mad at times. It's the only time she's almost nice."

"How awful. I shouldn't have forgotten her, it was horrible of me—"

"Apologizing again?"

"It's simply that I've always thought Devora so, so arrogant, you know, and perhaps she was only in pain. I feel..."

"She is arrogant. There's one who's so arrogant she doesn't even know it." Norah smiled, thrusting her hands expressively into her haystack hair and pulling it back. "Now when I'm about to be arrogant, people will know it, believe me. I wouldn't waste being arrogant on the ignorant. No, I'd put my nose in the air and grind my heel into the victim." She laughed with real relish. "Everybody'd know *I'd* been arrogant." I burst into a laugh, even though it seemed at Devora's expense.

"But, seriously, Norah, why would marrying Sir George give Devora the migraine?"

"Marrying any man gives one a headache," retorted Norah wryly. "No, but you see"—her voice softened to a creamy sauce to spread over a morsel of gossip—"it's *after* she married him the headaches came. And perhaps because she was unable to produce another kind of pain for him."

The burning significance in Norah's eyes left me further confused.

"Oh, you're so thick sometimes!" she cried, her hands contracting on the folds of her skirt. "An heir! Devora couldn't produce an heir. It was especially galling because—well, that was ancient history and you're a modernist. But things were not blissful around here then, years ago. I'd come from abroad to fall back on Cousin George, and he was too absorbed in his own domestic drama to play audience to my foreign importation. Oh, they were troubled times, my mate, troubled times."

She burst into her mocking laugh. Carnhaven was not a good harbour for the homeless and troubled, that was what she was warning me about in her bitter manner. It had troubles enough of its own, too many to more than raise an eyebrow at the sorrows birds-of-passage like Norah and myself brought with them.

"And Elaine, surely you've noticed, what troubles Elaine?" I asked.

Norah's long laughing face grew veiled. "Elaine. I think her mind's going," she declared abruptly, almost unwillingly. "There's a man at the bottom of it. You mark me, Amberleigh, there's a man at the base of it." She stood abruptly, looking like a Cassandra dragged unwillingly from Troy to prophesy into the Irish wind. *"Cherchez l'homme,"* she advised cryptically, whirling away with her uneven skirts swinging like some scarecrow's jacket in the field. I shivered quickly once before I got up and slowly retraced my way to the studio. And Elaine.

CHAPTER SIX

SOMETIMES I wondered if Adrian Carstairs weren't the clew to Elaine's malaise. Certainly he was very much on Devora's mind. I remembered what I could of him from that brief meeting on commencement day so long before.

I conjured only a shadow figure in a summer suit and hat. A pale elegant form, tall but not too tall, broad but not too broad. Real, but not too real.

Elaine grew more and more withdrawn as the week of the house party came closer. She retired to the eternal clay head, punching its features around until they occasionally took on grotesque expressions. She became untidier than ever—sometimes I had difficulty telling her and Cousin Norah apart if I chanced to follow one or the other down the upstairs hall. She as much as lived in her paint-and-clay-dotted smocks and was becoming very absent-minded. But with me the old skeleton of our former relationship was resurrecting nicely. I was the only one to whom Elaine seemed to be growing closer. With the others, she was like a stationary object, rapidly receding into the past while they cannoned by her with their concerns and everydayness.

I began to find the third-storey studio oppressive. I began to escape it, leaving Elaine alone and my portrait of Devora untended, unfinished. The green gown still lay across the chair, like a snakeskin slipped out of and outgrown, so I could study it for detail. But the shimmer of silk, the highlights on the jet, no longer challenged me. I felt vaguely squeamish about sharing the garret with Elaine these days. Pastels from the terrace seemed more wholesome somehow.

"Hullo, here's one of the healthy country girls, now!" came a man's voice from the French windows into my musings one day. I turned from the landscape I halfheartedly sketched to face a couple teetering in the archway. She held his arm, although he was only a wisp of a man drowning in country tweeds and she was a flagship of the line, streamlined from her ample prow of a bosom to her taut but substantial hips. A mere ruffle of a sunshade supported her on the other side. I looked back at him again, with his salt-and-pepper mustaches in old-fashioned profusion and his contained friendliness. He had the most highly polished brogues of anyone I'd ever seen.

"Ask the young lady her name, Harold, since we've no one to do introductions," intoned the woman with a nudge at her mate. "So careless of Devora."

"Just so." He harrumphed a bit embarrassedly. "You wouldn't be Elaine now? No, she'd hardly have grown that tall and wasn't she a little fair wisp of a thing?"

"I'm Amberleigh Dunne, a school friend of Elaine's."

"Up for the weekend, too?" asked the woman.

"No, I'm staying—longer," I said, somehow loath to pinpoint my position in the household.

"Well, this is Colonel Maxwell," said the lady, advancing to the terrace, having satisfied herself that I was respectable and noncontaminating. "And I am Mrs. Maxwell, but you may call me Maude, if we're to get on like old friends. And we all should be like old friends at a house party, should we not?"

We three sat in awkward silence for a moment—the pair of them on the summer chairs, I on the steps and not sure it was polite to return to my sketch.

"Much rain here yet?" enquired the Colonel, his eyes surveying the countryside as if he expected to wring the answer from it.

"Off and on. Rain is always a threat in Ireland."

"I know what you mean, my dear," gushed Mrs. Maxwell. I seemed to have happened on a topic that caught her interest. "Nothing but rain, a fortnight of it, when we went to the Caldwells' last summer. I cannot understand why anyone would keep a house here when there's cunning little cottages at Deauville or the Riviera for the asking, though dear. Such primitive people, too, the Irish. It's the damp. It breeds freckles and surliness. I've never had a decent servant from Irish stock. Stick to the German or the French, that's what I always tell my closest friends; then you won't suffer any disappointments."

There was another pause while I weighed my chalk and the wisdom of responding.

Colonel Maxwell leaned his chin on his hands, which were clasped over his duck-headed cane. "Good shooting, though," he observed mournfully.

"Shooting! I daresay. It's well enough for you to go traipsing off with the men and leave us ladies to wither over cards. The only thing to do at these places is to take long walks, and they're always long, my dear, because there's very little *but* distance between one house and another in this uncivil land.

Well, at least Adrian isn't a great one for shooting and has the courtesy to spend some time with the fairer sex."

"Adrian Carstairs, you mean?" Here at last was something of which I could claim knowledge. I definitely knew about Adrian Carstairs. He did exist and was not a figment of Elaine's fevered imagination.

"Yes, most attentive fellow. Not the best family, but well-fixed and all that. You know, Devora has had great hopes for that boy and her step-gal all these several seasons. He's a wily one, though. Why marry when you can have the belles of London throwing themselves at you, as these girls are doing nowadays? Never would have been allowed in my time. We were docile, obedient, retiring girls in my day."

It was hard to imagine Maude Maxwell fitting any three of those words at any time of her life from the cradle onward. I couldn't help laughing.

"You see, it *is* silly, when you think of these young women hurling themselves into the marriage market willy-nilly and not waiting for their mamas to lead the way. It creates competition and all sorts of unhealthy urges. Well, we shan't have that here. I gather that Maisie Dillingham is coming up. Wise of Devora. No problem for Elaine there. Why, Maisie Dillingham must be going on seven-and-twenty and is quite, quite desperate. So Devora's Elaine should have a clear field. Now, Colonel, we should be settling into our rooms, so up and at it, old fellow."

The Colonel had been almost dozing on the head of his cane, but his eyes dutifully rolled up like a well-trained spaniel's and he rose to assist his wife from her wicker perch. They slowly sailed inside while I watched with a certain amount of amusement.

"You are a remarkably patient girl." Another voice, another interruption. I turned towards the garden to find a man sitting around the corner of the steps in the shade of a rather impressive stone urn filled with yellow-leaved geraniums.

It was strange that I'd been unable to remember what Adrian Carstairs was like. Now that I saw him he was instantly clear to me.

"I'm sorry I couldn't come forward and extract you from your conversation partners, but frightfully awkward considering I was the topic. You won't hold that against me, I hope?"

It was hard to imagine anyone holding anything against Adrian Carstairs and he knew it. "You remember me, don't you?" he went on.

"Barely," I said, resuming my sketching.

"Amberleigh." I looked up at my name. "I'd not be likely to forget a name like that. What have you been doing with yourself these many years, Amberleigh?" He'd come to sit beside me on the steps although I hadn't invited him by word or look.

"Very little," I said, the chalk positively flying.

"You've travelled."

"I went away to work, hardly travelling."

"The Willoughbys thought highly of you."

"I'm amazed my qualifications should become the topic of your social dialogues."

"Oooh," he groaned under his breath, shaking a hand as if stung.

I hardly dared look at him. I didn't know how he'd managed to get my back up in so short a time, save that he was paying that flattering kind of male attention to me and I resented it. As soon as Elaine or even the desperate Maisie came on the scene, he would be off to dance attendance on better prey. He was a womanizer, I suspected, observing his slightly bronzed face and buttery blond hair and mustache. He would be a charming dance partner, looking like a marzipan figure in black-and-white evening dress. He was used to turning women's heads and he should not turn mine. Not Adrian Carstairs, wealthy and fancy-free or not.

He was looking carelessly towards the house, planning his next victim, no doubt.

"I came up on the train with the Maxwells," he volunteered. "Quite a couple. Even the smoking car didn't deter her. I'm glad there shall be somebody more amenable here . . ." He left the sentence hanging for me to pick up but I kept sketching.

Suddenly he reached for my pad and the charcoal. "May I?" I acceded to his blue eyes, though they weren't as bright as Devlin's. He hastily scrawled something across the page's corner.

> There was a young lady named Dunn,
> Who frowned on the having of fun.
> She went round with a look
> As black as a rook
> So everyone took her for one.

It was a clever impromptu piece of doggerel and I smiled despite myself. "In America they call rooks crows, but they're still an unattractive bird," I pointed out, ignoring my misspelled surname. "I hardly think you'll win me over with such comparisons. What happened to the courtly poets?"

"The times, ma'am, are against such traditions," he said lightly. "But a limerick—we're only a few miles from the town of Limerick itself, did you know that?"

"Really? No, I didn't. It would be amusing to visit there—"

"Allow me to escort you."

"And we could have Mrs. Featherstone make up a picnic lunch and Elaine could come along and—"

"If you're going to play matchmaker," he said sternly, "I'll have to withdraw my offer."

I dropped my eyes. It was only natural that I include Elaine on such plans. After all, I was here to companion her, wasn't I? But had I most specifically mentioned her name because there was a stubborn little thought inside me that I didn't want her along at all? What was the use of fooling myself? Adrian Carstairs was merely exercising his charm to see it if held, as he must have done every day of his charmed life. I was a mere experiment that was bubbling along nicely. Oh, he was probably used to having all his experiments come out well. I could be nothing to him but a diversion; there was no status to be gained in winning over the hanger-on, the mere attendant. But perhaps I underestimated him. He was clever. Perhaps it was as wrong to be biased against someone because he was facile at social feints as it was to despise somebody who was clumsy and loutish.

"I'm sure Lady St. Clare didn't call her house party together to have the guests go careening off with the hired help," I said quietly. Strange, what I'd been so sensitive about confessing to the Maxwells I threw in Adrian Carstairs' face.

He drew back minutely and his features were still for a moment. Then I saw a shrewd look start in his eyes, as if he'd taken the measure of my mood and comprehended it all too well.

"I'll come back," he said softly, leaning towards me a little more closely than convention allowed, "when you're feeling more like a limerick and less like Il Penseroso." And he retrieved his coat from the bush over which he'd draped it to amble into the house.

I was hot with humiliation at my own bad manners and wracking my brains for what he meant by "Il Penseroso." And then it struck me. Milton. Adrian Carstairs had a nodding acquaintance with Milton, surely one of the dullest poets to clutter up the seventeenth century with blank verse. Well, it was hopeless, anyway. I had a great fancy for Coleridge and Tennyson. We were fated to disagree. I threw my chalk into the box with distaste. Where was Elaine? Had Elaine been here, Adrian couldn't have courted me in corners and whispered limericks in my ear. From now on I would be distant and unapproachable. Adrian could fashion rhymes till Milton rose again for all the good it would do him. So I packed up my things and went in search of Elaine.

The third-floor studio was deserted. I approached the featureless head on which she toiled to study it. It was as enigmatic as ever. I couldn't even tell whether it was meant to be a male or a female head. Or perhaps a bit of both. Why did Devora encourage her in this pastime? Why did Elaine grimly retire to the attic to shape the hard clay that fought her every attempt to form it? Why did Amberleigh Dunne coop herself up daily to paint a portrait of a woman she disliked?

I finally found Elaine in her room. The drapes were drawn and it was dim and remote there, despite the glitter of the bright day beyond the covered windows.

"Elaine, are you resting?"

"Yes, just resting, Amberleigh..." She was lying across the bed on her back, an arm thrown over her eyes.

"The guests are arriving. Perhaps we should be on hand to mingle, as we were taught in deportment class at Miss Meachum's, remember? 'Mingle, my girls, mingle. Do not plant your feet and take root, it is the first stage to becoming a wallflower.'"

"Miss Meachum's was so long ago, Amberleigh," said Elaine dreamily, her eyes still covered. "It was another world. I hated it!" she burst out suddenly, sitting up on her elbows. "I hated it more than anything in the world. If you hadn't been there—I should never have been sent away. Never. It's all her fault. Well, I don't care if she throws Adrian Carstairs at me day and night, I shan't have him."

"You've been coming up to your room lately, in the afternoons. Are you tired? Do you sleep? If you're not well—"

"I sleep sometimes. Sometimes I dream. Or merely think I do, perhaps. I dream of secret things... sometimes I'm not certain if they're real or not. Or merely dreams..." Elaine's voice was soft, sing-song. I shook her limp shoulders slightly.

"It's a glorious day outside. The funny colonel you told me about and his wife are here. Come down with me, please, Elaine. It'll be better somewhere else, I know it will."

It was not only for her own sake I wanted Elaine to shake the melancholy that enveloped her like a web; it was for my own. I had always thought everything was right in her world. Perhaps I'd even said to myself in my innermost heart—"If I were Elaine St. Clare, I'd have no troubles, I'd be rich and happy, I'd be happy..." She had to be what I thought she was, for my sake as well as hers. If there'd been no Elaine off whom to reflect my misfortunes, if she had vanished from my life, then I'd have to let the old life dissolve utterly, let it harden into the aspic of memory. The only life in it from the nudges and bumps I'd give it, and then it would ripple into disgusting quivering life. The quick and the dead.

I shivered suddenly in the sleepy bedchamber, aware for the first time since I came to Carnhaven that things were not what they seemed. That even I was not what I thought I was. Faithful friend? Or clinging parasite? Elaine's secret dreams must be contagious. And they must be nightmares.

The pall my introspection and Elaine's vacancy cast on the week glided over only the two of us. The others laughed, talked, played whist, ate, walked, took rows on the little artificial lake and in general behaved exactly as house-party guests should. Elaine and I clung to the terrace—I armored with my sketchpad, she sitting languidly in her loose gossamer summer frocks, looking more like a resident wood nymph than the marriageable daughter of the house. And acting even less like it.

"I'm off for the big lake," announced Adrian one unseasonably hot day, pausing beside the two of us. "Any lady I can interest in coming along?"

"Why yes, it'd be cooler on the lake. Wouldn't it, Elaine? Let's go." Adrian folded his ivory summer jacket over his arm restively. Playing nursemaid to an invalid of the spirit was not what he had had in mind.

"You go. I'm happy here. You're used to journeys over water. I think I'd only get seasick, Amberleigh." And Elaine loved the water, could row like a boy, as I'd seen when I first arrived. She gave me a sly upward glance from her glazed grey eyes. I wondered for an instant if she weren't throwing Adrian and myself together in hopes of fostering a courtship. But the lord of half the whiskey in Ireland didn't need a landless half-Irish governess as consort.

Adrian and I had started down the steps when Devora's voice from the French windows stopped us.

"If you're going to be in the sun, Amberleigh, you'd better

take a parasol. It's very bad for the complexion, you know; you'll freckle like a spotted bass." Devora was elegant in ivory lawn and lace, as pale as a winter moon. I flushed under the freckles the summer had so far bestowed on my nose and cheeks.

"Parasols are for elderly ladies on the Nile," laughed Adrian, clasping my hand and pulling me along. "We'll be back to tea, Devora, if we don't fall in or the monster doesn't sink us."

I rushed down the lawn after him, hatless, my sketchbook flapping. "Adrian, please, we needn't go so fast."

"We couldn't get away from there fast enough," he said, finally slowing to a walk past an outcropping of rhododendron. He released my hand and I felt suddenly shy. We ambled together toward the lake.

"I'm surprised Devora puts up with such, such . . ."

"Insolence?" He grinned insolently. "She'll put up with a good deal from me, you know."

"But not from me," I reminded him. I seemed compelled to put my position in the worst light possible when with Adrian.

A gust of wind whipped up my light skirt and whisked the sketchbook cover loose for a second. A number of drawings fluttered away and up in a little whirlwind.

"Oh, no!" I cried, running to retrieve them. Adrian joined me, pinioning the pages as they touched the ground with his hands and even his gaitered feet. Some lifted again just as we trapped them.

"Here, a heel print in the artificial lake gives it a sort of Lilliputian scale, don't you think? You can call it of the New School."

"Thank you. I imagine that's all of them, Adrian, and not too much the worse for wear." I had collapsed to the ground and Adrian sat back on his heels near me. "I really should wear a hat, you know," I said into the lengthening silence.

"I like freckles," he said.

"You seem to acquire a taste for everything Devora dislikes," I answered lightly, keeping my eyes glued to the familiar lines of my sketches as if they were new works by Old Masters.

"No, I simply have exquisite taste," he said.

"Well, I shall be grass-stained as well as freckled if I don't get up," I said, struggling to rise without stepping on half a yard of lace petticoat. "Then I'd really resemble a speckled bass." I said the last two words in overelegant tones and watched Adrian's eyes crinkle into amusement as he handed me up.

"You belong outdoors," he commented, watching me with warm blue eyes. "You smell like a grove."

It was a bold remark. Ladies weren't supposed to smell at all. Though half the world's whales died for their ambergris and all the perfumiers of Paris worked night and day to produce more elaborate and expensive scents, it was all for an effect that was supposed to go uncommented upon.

"I'm not wearing perfume," I said in some confusion.

"I know," he said softly.

I would have thought such words would set me blushing from stem to stern; instead I felt a sort of catch in my throat and a kind of tingle from my feet to my face. The world seemed to have slowed down, the birds' chirping was like a mechanical species unwinding. I would look up, I would respond, I wouldn't be intimidated by him. It was all skill, all practice. He meant nothing by it and I should not fall to pieces because of it.

"A connoisseur of common scents," I said mockingly and with a flair for flirtation that surprised myself. "If you are as good at steering boats as you are at steering the conversation, we should have a brisk turn around the lake."

We were face to face there in the quiet glade, so remote from the world you could hear a blade of grass shatter. I regarded him with a straightforward smile and a steady gaze into those deep blue dangerous pools. His eyes narrowed. He liked the game and the prey was worthy. "Come then," he said, taking my hand ever so lightly that I had only to let it drop back a bit and we would be mere path partners again instead of joined. I let my fingertips trail passively in his and together we made for the lake.

We burst through the last of the woods and onto the lakeside clearing.

"Blast," said Adrian under his breath, coming up short.

I saw the object of his concern strolling aimlessly back and forth in front of the dock. Maisie Dillingham, dutifully attired in an afternoon gown, complete with hat and sunshade, which she poked halfheartedly into the gravel shoreline. All in pink, she reminded me of some stately flamingo from Africa. If I was tall for a woman, Maisie was taller—a limber stalk of a female with pale skin that had no luster and lank weak-tea-coloured hair.

"Oh, Miss Dunne! Mr. Carstairs! How ripping! I was casting about for what to do and here you are. You wouldn't be planning a row on the lake—I would simply love a row on the lake, Mr. Carstairs, and I'm sure you'd do it beautifully."

Adrian was tall enough for me, but not for Maisie Dillingham. Even with her most studied slouch she had to cast her eyes down at him. Appeal does not work well from a height.

But he surrendered gracefully, handing us both into the boat—I seemed to require a good deal more handing—dropping his coat on one of the pillow-covered seats, and rowing smoothly around the shoreline.

"Oh, do take us out to the middle, Mr. Carstairs. It's ever so much more thrilling to be really out on the lake, don't you think?" What Adrian thought was a gentlemanly mystery.

"Well," she said when we had obediently been conveyed to the center and Adrian stopped to rest on his oars, "we don't seem to be a talkative party, do we?"

I caught Adrian's eye and smiled. Maisie was seated between us, and despite her nervous sniffing out of the situation, was opaque enough to deflect the wordless current that flowed between Adrian and myself since the interlude in the woods. Maisie Dillingham had unwittingly added piquancy to our game.

"You row so well, Mr. Carstairs," she trilled.

"Yes," I mocked subtly. "You row so well."

"I don't see how he does it, it must be ever so hard. I'm glad I'm a lady and needn't do things like row and trim my mustache."

"Yes, Maisie, there are a great many disagreeable things a gentleman must do," I agreed wickedly. I trailed my fingers in the water, as I had felt tempted to do with Elaine but had not quite dared. "It's cold," I said, surprised. "And deep," I added for Maisie Dillingham's benefit. "But I'm sure we're safe, Miss Dillingham, don't look alarmed. Mr. Carstairs is one gentleman with whom it is *very* safe to be out on the lake. Especially right now."

Adrian suddenly slapped an oar across the water and the splash sprinkled my sleeve. I withdrew my arm from the edge and couldn't help laughing.

"No, don't trifle with us like that, Mr. Carstairs. I was quite alarmed. There's said to be a monster in the lake, you know. Perhaps we'd better go back. Really, it looks as though it might rain."

Adrian complied once more, smoothly rowing the *Argonaut* to its lakeside berth. I spent the trip back discoursing on points of local interest, observed from my sketching expeditions, with Maisie Dillingham.

We disembarked and Maisie tripped gratefully toward the path. Adrian held the boat just far enough from the landing with his foot to keep me boat-bound, and froze in the midst of lifting me out. "You play a fast hand, Miss Dunne," he said softly into my ear. For a moment I feared I had truly offended him. I looked into his eyes, just a few inches from my own.

But I hadn't offended him, I had excited him. I'd never seen that look in a man's eyes before, but I knew it instinctively. Like Maisie Dillingham, I suddenly regretted raising the monster that lurked in the lake.

Monsters were said to devour unwary maidens.

CHAPTER SEVEN

"RIDE?" ASKED Adrian cryptically the next morning at breakfast. Only Elaine and I were there, raiding the sideboard. I suspected his invitation's abruptness signified an unwillingness to end as escort for Maisie Dillingham again.

"I suppose so," I said noncommittally, catching Elaine's eye.

"You go, Amberleigh," she said firmly. "You can take Lady Jane. She's my mare and gentle as a kitten."

"I haven't ridden since Miss Meachum's, Elaine, perhaps you'd better go too . . ."

"No, Amberleigh!" It was a flash of temper I'd rarely seen in her. "Adrian will take care of you, won't he?" Her appeal fell upon one well-versed in such sturdy Middle Class virtues as Taking Care of Women.

"I shall guide her as if she were an elderly abbess on a pilgrimage," Adrian promised solemnly.

"Very well. I surrender. Good-bye, Elaine, be it on your head." But she was abstracted and barely caught my melodramatics, finally giving a measured smile as I went out the door.

Adrian and I had agreed to meet in the front hall in half an hour. I retired to my room to confront the three still-dusty bags tucked at the back of the small dressing room. The habit was easy enough to unearth. But where were the blasted boots? And the heavy net snood? I snagged the snood on my third fishing jaunt through the bureau. The boots slouched in drunken disarray at the back of the armoire.

Luckily, the riding jacket still fit. Our riding instructress at Miss Meachum's had been a careless, beefy-shouldered woman whose armhole seams were always split and who tolerated no corsets on her "gels." She took one piercing look right through me the first time I was led out to the stableyard and assigned me Rocking Chair, the largest and most docile of the mounts. But I'd learned to sit my sidesaddle gracefully and to trot without looking as though I would bounce off every step of the way. Cantering was another matter. I suspected Rocking Chair didn't have the smoothest gaits this side of Steeple Downs. At any rate, I never took a good run across the moor without expecting to examine the flora at a very close range indeed in the next moment.

Adrian had produced a tan chamois riding jacket and jodhpurs from his mere visiting wardrobe. I would have to make do in formal black. Both stableboys and horses pricked up their ears at the unaccustomed pair's approach. I found that snap sizings-up were never so snappy as in a stableyard.

"Lady Jane for the lady," instructed Adrian. "And what have you for me?"

The lad gave Adrian that instant flick of the eyes that measures a rider forever. "There's Lowboy, sir—don't be lettin' the name fool ye; he's a goer. And Jester, a bit flashy and one that'll tug-o-war ye for the bit. But I'd be guessin' you'll find Gavotte to yer taste." He led out a solid and high-stepping sorel. "And he's a bit sweet on Lady Jane o'er there, so you won't have to worry about him wandering too much," he added with a wink.

I looked at Elaine's mare, a trim little horse with a blaze. She had a liquid brown eye I thought I could trust and a pretty way of butting her head up against my shoulder.

The stableboy helped hand me up and I once again surveyed the world from the only horsehair sofa in the world that moves. I patted Lady Jane's glossy neck and whispered that we would be friends.

We started down the shady drive while the stableboys watched.

"You sit her as if you'd ridden yesterday," Adrian commented.

I adjusted my derby rather grimly. "We're only walking," I pointed out.

"Then let's trot."

72

He gave Gavotte a jab in the ribs and the big sorel broke into a trot instantly. I hadn't decided whether to follow his example or not, but it seemed that was unnecessary. Lady Jane lifted her delicate ankles and minced after him. As my rib cage jarred up and down, for once I was grateful to that iron-spined woman and her hatred of corsetry. Had I been whaleboned I believe I would have ground myself to death with the jolting.

Adrian had mercy on me and pulled back down to a walk.

"Still with us?"

"Hat and heart," I said breathlessly. He turned Gavotte off the road. "No, Adrian. Really, the road is riding enough for me. It's been ages. I'd rather not leave it."

"We'll go slowly. And I want to take this way. It leads to the sea bluffs. The view should be spectacular. Unless you're afraid of heights as well?"

"Only when they come on four legs," I answered. There had been the taste of a challenge in his voice, as if he were testing me. He was sizing me up, I realized suddenly, as surely as the stableboy's eye swept us over. Testing my mettle, wasn't that the phrase? A low fire of resentment flared deep inside of me. I had never claimed to be Diana Daring, sportswoman and free spirit. I rather fancied that was what he was looking for. And had he mistaken my uncompromising acceptance of my position with the St. Clares, my natural resentment, for spirit, for dash? I feared so. Feared because he was wrong. I would never be that kind of woman pictured in the society pages back from an African hunt or on the way to Central America for a dig.

But I nudged Lady Jane and followed Adrian off the road, across the broad heath stretching before us, towards the limestone outcroppings jutting like monuments against the grey sky.

We rode in silence, I contemplating the insight I'd just had and Adrian glancing back at me from time to time. Finally he pulled up and waited for me.

"It's wider here. I want to go up that incline. Think you can manage it?"

"Of course," I replied, before I'd even measured it with my eyes.

So we wound our way upwards through narrow corridors of limestone. I turned once in my sidesaddle to view the way we'd come and was startled to see how elevated we were. The plain stretched below like a rumpled handkerchief of green. I could see some ruins yellow and sharp in a clearing, Carn-

73

haven's dull red chimneys looming through an emerald circle of growth, the Shallowford stream wandering through woodland and moor. Shallowford House, our nearest neighbour, was hidden.

Turning forward, I was stunned by the wildness of the world that lay before us. We had climbed gradually to the bluff top, like an ant to a saucer lip. A rocky headland jutted off for miles below towards the sea's silver sheen. It was flat enough ground where we were, with miles yawning before us should we care to ride the ridge in either direction.

"It is glorious." Adrian smiled at my praise for his pathfinding.

"Don't you feel you could be in wildest Africa? Or on some strange island where only wind and water shaped the scheme of things? Are you sorry you came?"

"No," I answered, meaning it. "Why didn't they build the houses up here? It's broad enough. And what a way to wake up every day!"

"It's a bit harsh for the kind of gentlemanly farming the gentry planned to do hereabouts," Adrian explained. "So they drew back from the coast to those cosy little hollows." He turned to survey the green land below us.

"What's beyond there? It looks fascinating, let's see." I gave Lady Jane a nudge and she picked her way across an uneven surface. We were just rounding a high jut of limestone, piled and striated like a wedding cake, when a voice burst out of the waste.

"Hey, man! Stop there! Are ye crazy or tryin' for it?" A man came scrambling down from on top the limestone outlook. "This is treacherous turf, fit for fools and their first cousins. Get the beasts off of here and yerselves wi' 'em if ye value yer skins."

"It looks solid enough to me," objected Adrian.

"Aye," said the man. "Too solid. There be sink holes drillin' down for eons. If once ye happen in 'em they be solid enough to serve for a sepulchre." He pointed beyond us. Adrian dismounted and led Gavotte over while I followed on Lady Jane. A shallow pit, ringed by limestone and some eight feet deep, broke suddenly upon the plateau.

"If ye don't like the looks o' that one, take a peer into this," said the man with a certain proprietory pride. This time I dismounted as well. Somehow the pit seemed less deep with my feet on solid ground. The man guided us around another rock face to show us a narrow hole in the ground, perhaps six feet across. We looked at him puzzled, for his voice had promised greater wonders. And greater warning.

"St. Bridget's Well, they call it. From time and before time. But ye'd go a ways to find water." He picked up a stone and dropped it into the black mouth below us. We never heard it hit bottom. "This place is riddled wi' 'em. I watch to make sure no goats, stupid beasts they be, decide to cast their lots wi' the pit. But 'tis no place for horses."

Adrian nodded and led us back to the place we'd come up. From the bridge of the bluffs it looked a steep and narrow way down. I clutched at my riding skirt while I gathered my nerve.

"If we came up, we can go down," Adrian said reassuringly. But when he helped me remount Lady Jane, the landscape lurched and I seemed to sit the back of a giant steed.

We started down after a friendly wave at our adviser. "A lucky chance we ran across him," I mentioned.

"Yes," said Adrian. "But I wonder how many goats really find their way up here."

I didn't ask for enlightenment on his remark. The path down seemed much steeper than our slow progress up. I leaned back against Lady Jane's ample derriere and hoped I wouldn't slide over her long lean neck and down the rough rocks that marked the way.

"That's the idea," said Adrian behind me. "Simply lean back. Are you sure you don't want me riding ahead?"

"It's rather late now. No, I'll merely rush headlong down the wee slope—one way or another."

My brave words fooled no one, least of all Lady Jane. She continued to pick her way downwards, her ears pricked back as the pull of the incline drew her along faster and faster. Obviously, she knew better what she was doing than I. I gave the horse her head—though what I could see of it was bent and below me—her back and neck forming one long slide into nothing. I blatantly clutched my saddle pommel and hung on.

At last I saw the land level off; finally there was the beginning of good green grass beneath Lady Jane's hooves. The limestone was passing behind us into a bad-dream landscape. Adrian was able to come abreast of me. His mouth was rather tight.

"That took a bit more doing than I anticipated. Are you all right, Amberleigh? You handled that well." There was a certain admiration in his voice there hadn't been before. "Here, perhaps we could dismount and walk awhile."

It wasn't until he lifted me down that I realized how taut

my muscles had been. My knees shook a little and I wondered if I could stand. But it didn't matter, for Adrian kept his arms around me. My derby tumbled off the back of my head in that rough descent from Lady Jane's saddle. "I don't seem to have come equipped for this," I remarked, feeling at sixes and sevens and grasping futilely at the derby.

"You come well enough equipped for me," said Adrian. I felt the tickle of his mustache as he leaned to press his lips against mine. His arm circled my uncorseted waist most appreciatively.

"I'm afraid," I said as I broke away—for this sort of thing mustn't continue—"that I did come equipped with a hat and should retrieve it." I was not certain what I should do if he ignored the hat and concentrated on its owner in the current manner.

"You come equipped with a great many inconveniences," he said in a low, teasing voice, running a forefinger down the long line of horn buttons on my jacket front. He bent to retrieve the derby while I gave his remark the blush it deserved.

It was horribly forward of him—that's probably why he was such a heartbreaker. He catered to the obvious. If clothes made the man, I reflected, on occasion at least they made the man behave. The seamstresses at Miss Meachum's who had sewn on those agonizingly lengthy rows of buttons had not been working in vain. Though what a spinster of four-and-twenty needed with such unnatural impediments escaped me.

We mounted again and rode back fairly quickly. Conversation turned on normal events. I began to wonder if anything had happened, if I had imagined the entire thing. We relinquished our horses at the stable and walked up to the house together.

"It was a ride I'll not forget for a while," I said lightly, dusting off my skirt and taking a step or two up the hall staircase as we parted inside the house. In the cool shadow of the deserted front hall our conversation finally ran into monosyllables.

"Nor I," responded Adrian as lightly. Or perhaps not as lightly. "I'm going South for a round," he announced suddenly.

"Are you?"

"Yes. But Devora's bound to have another fling at entertaining. Usually during the Holidays."

"The Holidays. Well, that's good to know. You might be back then and we can have another go at self-destruction on horseback."

The Holidays. Four months away. He didn't sound very eager . . . I linked my hands around the large finial on the newel post and leaned back. "So perhaps I shall see you at Christmas." I didn't quite look at him.

"I hope so. Shall you be glad?" His tone was light but his eyes were not.

"Glad? A family retainer is always glad to see a guest of her employers arrive." No, that is not what I meant to say at all. Why did I—

Adrian covered my hands with his. "Don't be so stiff-necked—" he began, leaning towards me so that his blue eyes struck me full on.

"Amberleigh! Amberleigh! When you're free, I should like to see you in my room."

Devora hung gracefully over the rail far above us, trailing violet chiffon—and a certain venom in her voice—over the balustrade to us. I stood to attention before I could stop myself, chagrined as she vanished without another word, leaving me feeling like a country girl caught at the garden gate with her beau.

"So should I," said Adrian wickedly under his breath, drawing even closer.

"What—oh," I said, catching his reference to the room. I slapped him lightly across the forearm and ran up the stairs.

It wasn't until I was in the upper hall that I dared think on what had happened. He'd flirted with me from the first, yes. But with that kind of persistence? Even gentlemen who trifle do not wrap their arms around ladies' waists or—or kiss them, I thought. It was the first time I'd ever been kissed. I had despaired of ever being kissed in my entire drab lifetime. And now it was all done with. I sat on the bed and tried to taste it over again. A mouth against a mouth, that's all there was to it. What was the mystery about? It hadn't been earth-shattering. And I supposed it was nice. It had made my heart beat like all the lady novelists had said it would, but that was merely expectation.

No. I mustn't trust Adrian. It was likely to be mere flirtation, that's all. No doubt he weaseled kisses out of more women than me. It might even be an avocation of his. I mustn't put too much stock in it. I mustn't lose my heart—or anything else permanent, I thought, as I unbuttoned the row of horn.

I almost hated to set aside my plain riding habit. Someone else would emerge when I was once more in gabardine and georgette day clothes. I certainly was a lot less interesting in the glass in my daily blues. But Devora was not so interested in my apparel.

I wondered why she'd called me so imperiously. Simply to lead me away from Adrian? Had the sight of us talking there at the newel post infuriated her, did she see Elaine's chances riding on the tilt of Adrian's fair head towards mine? I tucked my waist in as neatly as possible and whirled down the hall towards her door. I felt like spinning and didn't know why. I did skip a step or two, then worried that sober, watching eyes might see me, and pulled up short before Devora's door. It was shut.

CHAPTER EIGHT

LADY DEVORA ST. CLARE had never invited either Elaine or myself into her bed-sitting room. I stood uncertain outside the dark door, knocking finally in a casual manner that I hoped hid my nervousness.

"Enter," said Devora and I found myself in a rose and grey Georgian boudoir.

"Shut the door, Amberleigh. No, tightly. That's better. And come over here by the window. We're going to have to have a serious talk, so sit down."

I wished suddenly I had brought along a ladylike handkerchief to twist in my hands—something, anything that would let me do more than sit on the edge of Devora's rosepoint chair seat and straighten my skirt folds.

She was turned away from the little grey desk that faced the window and the dazzling light that poured through the tall glass spilled onto my face and almost blinded me.

"Don't look so alarmed, my dear," Devora said. "At least not yet." Her expression was hidden against the bright white light that haloed her. "It's about Elaine," she sighed finally. "You must have noticed. It's more than a young woman's decline at the prospect of spinsterhood. Or a touch of 'male de mere.' Meaning me, of course..." Her light laugh gave me time to see the jest. "Mal de mer," French for seasickness, translated to "male de mer," sick with evil mother. Or stepmother in Elaine's case.

"Yes, Elaine has little patience with me. I'm sure she's told you, Amberleigh. But I am not a wicked stepmother out of the fairy tales. And what I do is for Elaine, you must believe that. It's hard to come into a family with a girl but a few years younger than oneself waiting to resent one. I've done the best that I could.

"But it hasn't been enough." Devora rose, trailing her wrapper, and walked away. When she turned again, the full light of the window fell on her face. She looked strained.

"Amberleigh, Elaine is not... quite right, these days. So I suppose we mustn't blame her. I took all the precautions, Lord knows. I chaperoned her down to the simplest tea. I fretted over her seasons and did my duty till I grew wrinkles from it, I swear.

"There were many—no dozens—of eligible young men I paraded before her. Sometimes I even had to use myself to draw them to her. And still the girl had absolutely no interest in a single one of them. Not a one. She did nothing to encourage their attentions, she ignored their gallantries... so I can't understand why or how or who—oh, what's the use? What's the use of recounting history? Of breaking anything to you gently? Elaine is in the family way, Amberleigh. I thought you would have noticed by now. I thought all Glennverran would have noticed by now."

I think I stood up. At least I was on my feet and facing Lady St. Clare. There was no untruth showing on her fretful face. The bitter way one eyebrow arched higher than the other, the slight twist on her lips spoke of an unhappy reality accepted and digested.

"Elaine? Oh, Lady St. Clare—"

"There's no mistake, Amberleigh. I found out from her maid, Stone. She didn't even tell me herself. Stone thinks she doesn't even realize it herself."

"But, surely I would have noticed. I've been with her almost constantly..."

"Have you, Amberleigh?" Devora interrupted with an edge in her voice. I knew she meant Adrian but I wouldn't defend myself on that score. "She's seven months' gone, Amberleigh, seven months," she went on, returning to the desk and picking up an ivory letter opener. "We're fortunate she shows so little." She pulled the blade softly through her closed palm. "I did my best with a difficult situation. To find out who—I was after her half an hour. But every time one tries to pin the girl down, it's like trying to... to tie a bow out of fog." Her hands, thin and elegant, reached out in a helpless gesture, one of them tightening on the letter opener until she seemed to be holding it like a weapon.

She abruptly slapped the ivory dagger across her open palm. "Enough of senseless questions." Devora sat down and faced me once again across the window. "I've made arrangements for Elaine and you to take a holiday. A sketching jaunt to the North, we'll say. Actually, I've found a reliable doctor with a reliable nurse who is used to providing this sort of service with discretion. You and Elaine will go to them and stay until the . . . child . . . arrives. A family will be found for it and suitably reimbursed. Then you will return to Carnhaven and resume your lives here as before. Neither of you is to say anything—ever—about the matter.

"That's all, Amberleigh." She tossed the letter opener aside and started leafing through her correspondence. Audience over. Amberleigh Dunne, paid companion, had her instructions. Amberleigh Dunne, paid companion, could take her leave.

But Amberleigh Dunne was a friend as well. Was this a time to question a tone of voice, to quibble about how one's help was requested? It was needed. And badly. Elaine, how hard to imagine Elaine as, well, a Fallen Woman. Elaine, with child. I tried to picture her in some man's arms and my imagination balked. Especially since Lady St. Clare had revealed Elaine's utter disinterest in London bachelors.

I wasn't even that sure I knew much more than Elaine about how such—things—happened. How could I cope with it? All I knew was that strange tension between a man and a woman, that way they could let it dance between them and call it flirtation. All I knew was my own ignorance of what transpired beyond the "tender kisses" and "desperate embraces" that Mrs. Radcliffe and the other lady novelists went no further than. Elaine—of all people. Childlike, truly innocent Elaine. No wonder she'd been so unreachable, her moods so quicksilver. No wonder we'd all been baffled by her.

I was at her chamber door by then, not sure how I'd gotten there, only knowing I had raced down the hall as quickly as my thoughts had churned through my head.

The door was shut, the room empty.

"Elaine? Elaine?" Then I saw her, crumpled alongside her bed, huddled against the wall, her hands pulling the coverlet to the floor.

"Elaine."

"She wants me to go away, Amberleigh. She just said so.

I don't want to be sent away. Make her let me stay, Amberleigh. I don't want to go away. If I go away, I'll never see—someone, again. Make her, Amberleigh, make her." She was sobbing like a wild thing and holding onto both my arms. I helped her up, for the first time noticing the clumsiness of her body.

"Shhhh, Elaine. Here I'll bathe your face with some rosewater if you'll simply stop crying a bit. Elaine, stop crying. I'm going with you and we're coming back to Carnhaven again. Really, we are. I'll see to it. I'll take such good care of you. But why, oh why, didn't you tell me—perhaps I could have . . . done something?"

"If I go away, I'll never see him again. Never, never. That's why I was sent to school, you know. They pretended not, but I knew. Never, never."

She was subsiding into a fevered sorrow that wracked my heart. She was like a porcelain bird whose brittle feathers were chipping off one by one; before my eyes her mind was moulting inexorably and I was helpless to heal it.

"You'll stay with me, stay with me always? Because that's the only way I can be sure of coming back. I mustn't leave, they'll kill him, I know they'll kill him—"

"Elaine, who is 'he'? Tell me." Her face cleared into a blank mask.

"Why, what a strange question, Amberleigh. You know, I don't know. Sometimes I think I do, but then I don't. It's a far, faint thing, memory. But you'll go with me, I know you will. And we'll come back and we won't tell anyone. Promise you won't tell anyone. Not even that we're going. Promise, promise, promise."

"Elaine, of course I'll keep your secret. It'll be like at school, when we skipped deportment class, remember, and Miss Meachum had me up and was ever so angry and I never told her where we were or what we had been doing? And it was only to sail leaves on the pond on a beautiful autumn day. You know I won't tell."

I finally soothed her and left her clinging to the coverlet like a fretful child.

But I hadn't managed to soothe myself, so I slipped into my room, took a shawl and softly left the house by the servants' stairs. It wasn't until I was across the open lawn and bordering the informal garden that I let myself think about the last hour's revelations, so afraid I was that someone would somehow read my thoughts.

I sat on a stone bench, noticing the smooth clouds above me like a placid brow, the odd way the green about me took on an almost phosphorescent glow against the blue-grey skies.

The stone was cold, still damply wet from the morning fog and dew. But I liked its hard feel, its uncompromising firmness. It would help me think.

"Dark Sheilagh, dark Sheilagh, why stare you in the fire?"

I heard Devlin Quades's voice behind me.

> "For there's a lad that loves me
> An' a lad that leaves me
> An' a third lad,
> A Shadow lad,
> An' he's the lad that grieves me..."

He straddled the stone bench to face me while his song faded off. "And a Shadow lass, I think," he noted, catching the first reflection off my introspection.

"What are you doing here? It's almost raining."

"If rain were a thing to keep me from goin' anywhere I'd never leave me mother's peat fire," he said. "Nor would any Irishman accomplish so much as a good elbow bend, be it at plough or at pub. It nearly always is 'almost rainin' here, you know."

"I suppose I hadn't absorbed that fact yet," I rejoined, holding my shawl tighter around me.

"But what are *you* doin' here—warmin' a cold stone seat when the rest of 'em are in the Great House playing with their Ouija boards and correspondence."

He seemed to have a pretty accurate idea of how the gentry amused themselves on damp, dull days. "I gather all *you* need to entertain yourself is a spot of conversation..." I said pointedly.

"And a spot of something stronger on occasion," he noted with a wink. I tried to keep from looking disapproving, but failed. Devlin Quade seemed true enough of his kind to love the bottle more than the teacup. No wonder the Irish were always so argumentive.

"But why 'sit ye by the tide, lady,' when you could be up and puttin' a little rose in yer cheek? Let's walk."

Things always happened so naturally with Devlin. We were moving briskly along the lawn's edge and off towards the woods that wound their way toward the lake. Behind us Carnhaven loomed, etched like a cameo of carnelian stone against the smooth, darker grey skies. It was chilly but I seemed numbed to such considerations as mere discomfort. And Devlin, Devlin wore his threadbare jacket as if it were ermine.

I always tended towards the right path which led to a favourite woodsy clearing of mine I called the Fairy Circle, but Devlin's lead pulled me left. It was probably colder still under the moist overspreading beech arches, but it was quiet there and so peaceful. As if the cool wet air had a curative, smoothing effect. My emotions felt like a skein of yarn being unwound, my forehead like the sky being smoothed by a soft wind. Devlin hummed softly while we rustled through the thickest of the wood. "The Minstrel Boy" it was this time. I was beginning to recognize his repertoire.

"That other one was Scots, you know," I said.

"What?"

"The 'Why weep ye by the tide, lady?' That's 'Jock O'Hazeldean.'"

"And there's no law against the likin' of Scots' tunes, I hope?" He smiled.

"It's merely that you're so thoroughly Irish, I didn't expect you to march to a bagpipe."

"None of us'd have the need to be 'so thoroughly Irish' if we'd ever been given leave to be Irish at all. Don't ye see the wonder of it, that you should be ignorant of half your upbringin' for no good reason than it was unpopular?"

"I've never thought of it that way, Devlin. But what does it all matter? It's simply a case of names and places and who's calling whom master or servant. Why let it get to be such a muddle? There's sure to be ugly things coming of it."

"No, beautiful things, earnest Molly. We'll not hold still for it much longer. You know what Transubstantiation is? Of course not, you've never had your proper catechism. Well, a simple way to say it—it bein' a long, long time since I trailed Father McManus as altar boy—it's the part durin' the Holy Mass when the priest raises up the cup o' wine and the holy bread and wi' his words makes it the body and blood of Our Saviour Christ.

"Now, whether ye believe in it or not," he said impatiently, as my face mirrored Anglican horror of such assertions, "it's very like what's to happen to Ireland. She'll be changed forever, the same and not, do you see? The one real thing that time and the Lord always meant it to be. And it'll take blood, this Transubstantiation of ours. Miracles often do."

"But your blood, Devlin? You're with the United Irish, aren't you? Is it worth it? The troops know how to handle uprisings, they learned in South Africa, in India..."

"And right you are to compare Ireland to those poor lands. Colonies." The word slipped off his lips like spit. "That's all Ireland is now, a bloody colony. We're equal people. We're only just now beginnin' to find out that great books were bein' written down here while John Bull's ancestors were paintin' their foreheads blue."

We'd been descending another incline, Devlin taking my elbow lest I fall on the slippery moss and grass. Ahead of us lay an open space and the golden-grey ruins of a limestone building, the ruins I'd seen from the bluffs with Adrian that morning.

"But Dev——what's this? I've never seen it this close before. It's like discovering a currant cake in a coal bin. It's charming."

"Here, don't be goin' tumblin' down the hill, now. Haven't ye seen the old abbey? It's no wonder, no one cares about it much. It's what's left of one of those places where the goose quill served as our mother tongue when later it would be silenced in our heads. They used to come here from the House and picnic," he said bitterly, sitting on one of the rough stone staircases to the sky and little else.

"But they don't any longer? How odd. I should think it would be a spot hard to forget." I joined Devlin on the steps, sitting carefully around a small violet flower that bloomed between the stones.

"They haven't since they sent me off to Trinity, and even before that. Once Elaine was gone—it was she and Jason, you see, that held to the spot."

"Jason?"

"But that must have been ten years ago. I was just a boy then meself and not too familiar with the goings-on in the House. Though we'd play together when their fancy new step-mother wasn't lookin'. And just plain Deborah they called her in those days, if I remember right, what wi' goin' off to school and gettin' my head muddled with learnin' and other foolish pursuits. A line of Greek never did make a jot of difference to how many potatoes'll grow on a patch of barren ground or how many widows make up a fishing village. Now there's a calculus to stump the tutors, though it's knowledge they'd rather do without."

For some reason the name Jason worried at my memory. It was one I'd have sworn I'd never heard at Carnhaven before, but somehow I wasn't surprised to hear it. It fit in some vague way.

"Who was Jason? Now, Devlin, don't go off into another one of your political speeches. You've made me curious. Who is he?"

"The brother," he said, turning wide blue eyes upon me. "But surely you knew? Though they don't talk much about it. She must have told you. Off at that school of hers. There was a terrible dust-up when it happened. She came back from that school like a ghost and like a ghost she vaporized back to it. And I didn't set eyes upon Elaine again for all these years. She seemed to take it well after the first. I thought she'd gotten over it all or I'd have never—but there are secrets in that one it'd take more than Boru to sniff out. A strange, strange one . . ."

"Devlin! You still haven't explained anything. Are you saying Elaine had a brother? A brother who—?"

"Died? Aye, and in an ugly way. It's one reason Her Ladyship hates these bicycles you see about the countryside so. 'Twas an accident, so they say. Down where the little artificial lake is now. A horrible pile of twisted spokes and tormented boy. He lived a bit, you know. But he was dead by the time Elaine was hauled back from that school. They say she was wild as a banshee for a night and a day. But Devora shipped her off again and she seemed to have survived it."

"A bicycle? But there's only the lake there now—I see, it came later. And the boat, I see why the boat was named *Argonaut* . . . but have they all forgotten him, is that it? Why is he never mentioned? It doesn't seem . . . natural. And when I came to know Elaine at Miss Meachum's, well, it must have been after, but she never wore mourning, she never struck me as someone who'd lost a close family member—"

"It was more convenient for everyone to forget about him," said Devlin roughly. "For the new bride, though she'd not known then she was to be barren and Elaine would remain the heir. And Elaine, well, she always had a way of forgettin' what troubled her, from a thorn in her foot to bigger things. There were those as said it was convenient to all of them to forget. And convenient to have the brake fail."

"You can't mean—well, foul play?" Devlin laughed at my melodrama and I joined him. It was easy to believe the worst of things in the soggy air surrounding the long-abandoned abbey. Easy to imagine grey-cowled spirits flitting from pillar to half-tumbled pillar. I shivered a little and Devlin put his arm around my shoulders.

"Here." He laughed. "If I'd been wantin' to frighten you out of your chemise I'd have picked a more convenient spot in which to do it. No, Jason'd always been a reckless lad, ready for a dare or a lark, and half the time Elaine or I'd been ready to do it with him. But he was fifteen and gettin' more reckless. He seemed one born to do what others dare not even think of—swim among the rocks in the cove, take his horse over jumps the huntsman wouldn't try with a tail wind—no, Jason was aching for an overturn and he finally found the machine to do it for him. Now you won't be wantin' to take a turn on mine someday, I can see it in your eyes, you're thinkin'—'Devlin Quade, you want to do away with me, that's what you want, tellin' me I should be ridin' on one of those devilish bicycles—'"

"I'm not certain you don't have sinister intentions at all, sir," I said lightly, slipping out of the friendly circle of his arm. He was a man, for all his puppyish tricks and harmless banter, and it was best not to encourage too great an intimacy. "Anyway," I added, "you're not absolutely serious about 'gatherin' tunes,' as you put it? It's something of a camouflage for whatever political mischief—and I wish you'd tell me what instead of making vague speeches—you're up to? The music is merely a pretext, isn't it?"

"Music a mere pretext to an Irishman? Ah, it takes the English to boil the soul out of an Irishman born, and sure, yours is down to a wee wrinkled prune of a thing if you can ask that. Amberleigh, Amberleigh, don't you see the music all round you here in these rocks and rolling hills, don't you hear the brays and lows and barks, the wild cries of the sea birds—and the sea widows?

"The song of the sea and the soft warm wind all the way from Central America, the halloes of the hedges and cairns—it's in our language, our Gaelic, and we're finally findin' it again after centuries of silence and the British forbiddin' us to speak our own tongue.

"'Killarney,' over the hills, you know it? 'Killarney' you call it. But it was Cill Airne, the church of the berries, and that means more and says it better in our native Gaelic than all the Anglicizations in Christendom. And Bridget's Well, did ye know the Gaelic for 'well'? 'Domhnaigh.' Now there's a soft, whisperin' way of wailin' a word that belongs to not another language on earth. There's a circle of us fannin' across the oul' country, tryin' to gather her ways of speakin' before they drift out to the sea mists and the silkies forever. It's as big a battle as what you call 'politics' and maybe the better one. It's why I left Trinity—they were all for poundin' knowledge dry as dust into me skull when the real learnin' was out here waitin' for me..."

Devlin frowned, producing a very faint furrow on his young forehead but a sincere one. "But you don't understand me, perhaps someday you will, when you've done your share of learnin' in this wide wondrous world...but enough history. Smile for me and I'll tell you a story. What story would ye like?"

Devlin settled slowly back against the stone stairs and waited for me to call the tune, as good as his word. It was as if I had been granted a private audience with a leprechaun king, as if some gentle spirit had taken me by the hand into a land where trouble and weariness were barred. The problem of Elaine's unhappy situation still sat leadenly on the stone bench back at Carnhaven. It would wait for me there like a bad dream. But now I was in a lush green glade under an unworried sky and I could rest for a while.

Irish tales and St. Clare recent history dissolved from my mind when I dressed for dinner that evening.

For once I attended my own hair with as much care as I had lavished on Elaine's at special occasions during school days. I ended up with a lopsided pompadour of imposing proportions and aching arms. To this had Adrian Carstairs brought me.

"Oh, that's truly awful," said Elaine when she stuck her head around the door to collect me for dinner. Her frankness didn't ameliorate my mood.

"I don't know why you say that," I responded distantly, trying to swallow the rising realization that for once she was absoulutely right.

"Let me this time," she ordered like a nanny, extending a flat hand for the brush, on which I deposited it with a little more force than necessary.

"You needn't give me the back of your brush for being honest," Elaine protested. "A fine governess you must be. Turn away now, I want to work on the back."

I gave a last fluff to my lavender furbelows and ruching before reluctantly surrendering my coiffure to Elaine. Her hands fluttered above my head; I felt rather a multilevelled wedding cake or a church that must maintain its architectural dignity while its spire was being reapplied.

"I'll want a hairpin, I think," she muttered intently.

I riffled my fingers over the small carved jewel box Mrs. Bowers had tendered to me so long ago and finally found an amethyst-headed pin that Elaine snatched from my fingers to jab into my hair.

"Oh, that's caught me! Really, Elaine, it's a better thing entirely that I play ladies' maid to your mistress. I'm not a pin cushion, you know."

"Don't be nasty. You know you're merely nervous because things are going so well with you and Adrian."

"Don't be ridiculous, Elaine. There, that's enough fussing. If 'things' were going so well between me and Adrian, I daresay I wouldn't be nasty, as you call it."

"Oh, wouldn't you, though? But honestly, I'm so glad you've kept him out of my hair—now don't glare, it's merely an expression. I suppose he's an all-right sort, and quite a catch on top of it, but he isn't jolly much fun," she added almost wistfully. "All this strolling and chatting and bowing and boating drives me distracted. Sometimes I think I shall scream."

Elaine's quicksilver moodiness had glanced off mine and dived downward into her customary desultoriness. I could have shaken myself for letting my irritability crush the only real spirit she'd shown all week. And on top of this afternoon's revelation, which we both were carefully avoiding like a cat picking its way around a mud puddle.

"What shall I wear with this—I'm always at such a loss." Elaine invariably responded to being made a fashion arbiter. She joined me in pawing through my mother's jewellery.

"Well, you've a flower print in your gown, it's very pretty—by the bye, I've heard Devora say that men are absolute swooners for anything in lavender, and to think they used to use it for half-mourning—I'd take the green, the deep. Haven't you any ribbons that shade?"

We adjourned to the ribbon basket that hung in the wardrobe and finally unearthed a length of narrow ribbon as thickly green as the moss that ringed the great oak trunks of Carnhaven wood. It reminded me of the folk tales Devlin had unravelled for me that afternoon. Elaine tied it around my neck and fashioned a bow of the stuff for my hair.

"There, no jewels," she said, standing back. "Devora'll be oozing jewels. She always does ache to impress dinner guests.

And do try to flirt with Adrian a little, Amberleigh. It's the only way I shall survive another of these things. If I didn't forego breakfast and tea, I wouldn't dine at all." Both of our eyes dropped; I could well guess why she'd been avoiding breakfast and midmorning tea these last weeks.

I'd never quite looked at her, with all this overseeing of mirrors and ribbons and pompadours so regal they'd bring men to their knees. She was my friend, as she'd always been. Nothing Lady St. Clare could reveal in her shadowed boudoir could alter that. As I took one last glance in the glass—bless her, she *had* improved things—I saw her absorbed in straightening the ribbons behind me. My eyes slid secretly to her well-concealed waist, and withdrew, appalled at myself.

It was her secret. It could even be her stepmother's imagination. And it was so hard to tell with these well-stayed bodices we wore, with our swelling skirts and layers of guarding petticoats beneath.

"Seven months gone." How long was that? Should she resemble a trans-Channel ballon? Or hardly reveal her condition at all? I don't believe I'd ever seen a—pregnant—woman in my life. Or at least not knowingly. Mrs. Willoughby had had a sister in that delicate condition. But even in America she rarely went out and I certainly had seen neither bonnet nor bustle of her.

Yet Devora would hardly speak of packing us off to "ride it out" unless a storm of major proportions were gathering. It was so bewildering—Elaine had not a minute for a man as well-versed and charming to the feminine contingent as Adrian and yet I was to believe she'd—

"Why so pensive? Adrian isn't lions, though I don't care to be with him. Come down."

In the drawing room we all chatted stiffly while waiting for the summons to dinner.

"Lovely gown, m'dear," harrumphed the Colonel, his eyes twinkling at me as brilliantly as his perfectly polished dress shoe tips.

His lady pursed her lips. "Charming perhaps, but not the thing in my day. Well, you're fresh and you can 'scape censure, my dear, but half-mourning was a serious matter in my day. I don't know quite what these young things are thinking of. Soon they'll be offering their hands—or who knows what else?—to the young men instead of waiting nicely to be asked."

Maude Maxwell settled a darkly printed shawl over the very modest neckline of her dark blue gown and frowned in my direction. I kept my eyes steadfastly away from Adrian, whom I knew to be standing casually near the mantle, cosseting his sherry glass in the way of a man who's waiting for the brandy.

Lady St. Clare set her small-stemmed glass down sharply on the tray. "Nonsense, Maude. How can you continue to live in another age like that? Life in London wasn't as glittering and gay in your day, and I'd die before I'd return to hoop skirts and hooded bonnets. No, it's better now. I don't think this country has been so at rest and so able to provide the kind of life I'd like to live before in this century. Oh, I wish I were in London, George—" Devora turned impulsively to Sir George and her jewels clicked against each other in her motion. "This County Clare life is so dull!"

"I fancy it wouldn't be so dull if one were an Irishman."

All heads turned to the speaker, whose mild voice had fallen into their midst like an artillery shell.

It was Norah, coiled quietly in the lone wing chair and staring reflectively into her amber glass. It was the only jewel on her plain person and it seemed to rivet everyone else's attention as much as her own. A small smile played coyly at the corners of her small mouth. The candlelight fell softly on her hair, coiled neatly for once on her long, leonine head. She laughed as she held our blank gazes. "It was only a remark. Pay no mind to me." And she laughed again to herself, the mocking laugh of the observer.

Sir George, who'd looked gruff and hunched all evening in his dress clothes, leaned forward on the sofa and put down his empty sherry glass. The glass was dainty and toylike in his large lumpish hand. He looked like some clumsy adult replacing a dollhouse trinket in its proper place. I found it hard to think of him fathering anything so brittle as Elaine. Her eyes followed his gesture, too, and there was worry in them and a dull silver flame of resentment.

I looked at Adrian and almost started to find that he had anticipated me. Those cool blue eyes of his were a pleasure to plunge into after all the hot looks exchanged that evening. Adrian was one of the few men whom evening dress improved. All that stark stiff black cloth sheathed him like a scabbard slips over a sword. His gilded hair and mustache netted the night light and reflected it. Evening put shadows of resolve and refinement in his features that the daylight softened. I thought again that Adrian might be dangerous to me. He smiled at me slowly, without parting his lips. I smiled back.

"Dinner? Isn't it time, Devora?" Sir George sounded almost

querulous and the sherry glass hit the table too heavily and chipped. He was ready for wine in a constantly refilled glass, not this before-dinner effeteness. A frown clouded Devora's brow. The best crystal, I could see forming in her mind, the best crystal and the oaf I married must crack it.

She stood up rapidly and caught Symes' eye from the hall. She nodded once and we formed into procession, Adrian somehow materializing at my side. "We're uneven," announced Devora to no one in particular. "I'd asked our neighbour from Shallowford, but he had to decline. We would have been uneven at any rate," she went on, flashing a disdainful look across Norah, bringing up the rear. Devora looped up her train and trailed the Colonel toward the hall, with Elaine defiantly taking her father's other arm while Maude Maxwell marched on the first. Then came Adrian and I. Norah insisted on remaining an improper solitaire behind us. It made me nervous; when Adrian squeezed my hand as he placed it through his elbow, I stiffened and looked ahead, letting my hand rest on his sleeve as lightly as a cobweb. I didn't plan to companionably sway in yoke with him for anyone's secret amusement, behind me or ahead.

Dinner was a disaster. Even Mrs. Featherstone's sauciest way with the duck, her lightest touch on the sweet, her spiciest pinch of savoury couldn't redeem a dreary and sluggish gathering. Devora had bracketed herself with Colonel Maxwell and Adrian. I was exiled to Sir George, who barely spoke, and Norah, who smiled to herself a good deal. I was not certain which dinner partner was the more exasperating. Only once during the meal did an undercurrent surface to ripple across Devora, the Maxwells and Adrian's ruminations on London social life.

"I'll have to leave tomorrow, Devora," announced Adrian between the game and the salad. "It's unavoidable, and I hope you won't think ill of me."

I rather fancied he'd chosen the public route for his news to forestall Devora's certain protests. Elaine glanced up, catching her lower lip in her teeth and watching Devora like a cat. Devora remained as collected as that unflappable animal at this blatant desertion of her house party. And her matchmaking plans. Though how she expected Adrian to play docile mask for Elaine's condition, I don't know.

"If you must, Adrian. I'm sure we poor country mice have very little to offer a city cat like yourself."

Devora demure was more than even Adrian could bear.

"It's not that the hunting hasn't been good here at Carn-haven, Devora," he answered smoothly, lifting his wine glass in almost a toasting gesture. "It's that the prey has proved unexpectedly elusive. Retreat is called for, I think."

Elaine gasped, Norah began a long low chuckle in her throat that lasted longer than the silence and I kept my hands folded tightly in my lap and tried not to watch Devora. Like everyone else, I failed. Her pale complexion had turned a dull coarse red. But she lifted her glass also. "Then may you find better hunting elsewhere, Adrian. You know I wish you only the best. If only you would follow my wishes."

We all held our tongues after that; Symes was more con-versational directing the servants than we were at that dinner table. We filed out from the dining room in an aimless pattern, Adrian somehow managing to linger and brush past me. He caught me up in the doorway.

"If this were the Holidays," he teased softly, "there'd be more hanging from that arch than empty air."

"Do you think Devora will care to have you cross her door-step again no matter what the time of year and whether mis-tletoe or wolfbane hangs there?"

"The Holidays," said Adrian, running his fingers ever so lightly down my bare arm, "are a time of forgiveness. And reunion."

It was the last I saw of him, withdrawing into the library for Sir George's long-desired brandy, for cigar smoke and that disconnected kind of talk I imagined gentlemen went in for once freed from dinner-table volubility. Not that our dinner table had been a gay or talkative one.

I claimed headache after barely spending half an hour in the drawing room with the women. Elaine crept quietly upstairs with me.

"You didn't make much of your opportunity, Amberleigh," she taxed me halfheartedly at my door. "Sometimes I worry about you. If I don't see you settled, who will? But I don't want you leaving Carnhaven too quickly, I—I've no desire to see you go just yet." Her eyes dropped to her fingers laced together in their white gloves. "I haven't always been very gracious to you, Amberleigh. But I'm glad you've come. I'm so glad you've come."

She slipped away and through her bedchamber door without looking back at me once.

CHAPTER NINE

WE WERE wrapping up the work of packing to leave on our "sketching jaunt" North. That's what Devora was putting about to any ear that would hear her. And I'm sure her delicate mother-of-pearl pen was scratching that message on light little notes to half her acquaintanceship. Anything to forestall conjecture. My one ladies' skill did seem to have some usefulness after all.

But our hasty departure left no time for soulful retreat to the third-floor studio. And I was glad. Elaine went about as one sleepwalking. Those dreams of hers had been nightmares, after all. I abandoned Lady St. Clare's portrait gladly and, in the confusion of puzzling out Elaine's condition, didn't miss it at all. Just before we were to leave I found myself once more in the filtered summer light at the top of the house.

Elaine, docile through it all, had disappeared. Devora was furious; the carriage waited, passages were bought and many pounds had been paid to the accommodating souls who arranged this sort of thing.

I tried the attic as a last resort and there found Elaine, muffled deceivingly in a short grey travel coat, a little plum bonnet on her fair hair. She looked almost a Salvation Army crusader in her sober attire. When I entered the room and stopped, my skirts swayed on the floor for a moment and raised a flurry of dust motes that fluttered through the sun shafts like fairy dust. Elaine looked faded and dusty herself, someone retreating almost unnoticeably from the lively world around her. The lily maid of Astolat, who "took three paces thro' the room and turned to see the mirror crack from side to side..."

Her gloved hands were resting on the sculpted head almost caressingly and her chin on them. It was a dramatic stance.

"We've got to go." I saw no reason to be anything but plain with her. Shades of meaning glanced off her these days.

"Yes." She didn't move.

I crossed to her, feeling somehow loud and awkward in this silent, sun-shot place, and lifted her hands off the clay head. It was as unformed as ever. If it was her lover she sculpted, he had been a shadow lover, a ghost romance.

"Mine isn't done," she said plaintively.

"No, but you can finish it when you come back."

"I will come back this time, won't I, Amberleigh? I do so want to come back. But he'll be gone. As he was before. I want to say good-bye."

"Of course you do." It was useless questioning her, I'd learned that by now.

"Your work won't ever be finished either," she added, casting me a trial glance from her soft grey eyes that was somehow secretive.

"My work . . . ?"

"Yours. And hers." She nodded toward the easel and the little scarlet plumes trembled on her hat.

I turned to my canvas of Devora, for the first time noticing it had been set aside from where it usually stood.

"I think Devora has split her seams," said Elaine, with a little malicious laugh.

Moving to turn the canvas, I faced a series of jagged cuts that rent Devora's full-length figure into tattered remnants. It was irredeemable and irredeemably ugly in its complete destruction.

"Now there's a portrait that fits the subject," said Elaine, trailing to the door and waiting for me.

"Did you—?"

"Amberleigh, you know I'm not capable of doing anything *bad*," she said, half mockingly and half like a little girl affronted at an unjust accusation.

I threw down the canvas and followed her out. It didn't matter who had done it. I doubted any of us would have the heart to resume our artistic ménage-à-trois in the attic studio at any rate. I helped Elaine make her slow and steady progress down all the steps from the top of the house to the front hall, where Devora waited to see us safely handed into the carriage and en route.

"Good-bye, my dears," Devora trilled cheerily under the dubious gaze of Symes and the parlour maid. "Have a wonderful holiday and do just lots of sketching . . ." We rattled away to those false bell-like tones, Elaine giving a great sigh as Carnhaven caromed to our right, then rolled swiftly out of sight.

By the time we got to the little stone stationhouse, the local was ready and trembling on the tracks. Elaine and I and our baggage were hustled aboard like so much mail bound for

Ulster. Or dust to be swept under the rug, wasn't that more appropriate? She was so white and waxen—I hesitated to unburden my reservations on her. It was appalling the way Devora was treating her. But perhaps Elaine was used to it.

We clattered along the coast for several miles, I soothing my spirits by watching the rocky landscape meander to the sea that licked it into a thousand barren bays and inlets. Eventually, our track turned inland and even that grimly distracting view was gone.

We changed trains finally, to an even smaller local bound precisely for the coast we'd abandoned earlier. Here the white envelope Devora had entrusted to me before our departure was opened to unveil its humiliating surprise. Passages made in other names. Bates and Waterman. Plain, unattention-getting names that would slip off the official memory like a morning fog. Names of no note. Pseudonyms. Elaine barely noticed the "Miss Bates, Miss Waterman" the conductor extended us with our cancelled passages. It branded me to the bone.

Another grey Irish afternoon verging on evening, with rain always a threat or a promise. Here the seats were frayed and the line rough. Elaine's plumes trembled in the musty compartment air like a village elder's hand. It was dark when we disembarked on another lonely platform—was all Ireland nothing but these stone stationhouses and abandoned platforms, fit only for the feet of the transient, the careless, the homeless? A carriage and coachman awaited us. He muffled, the carriage nondescript. His unpolished masculine voice searched us out in the dark—"Misses Bates and Waterman?"—and drew us into our exile from the moral world for the next few weeks.

Twin Beeches, they called the place, I discovered later. That night it was merely a large cottage with banking fires in each spacious bedchamber and an ancient pair of fourposters that sent Elaine off to sleep immediately and me into a fevered tossing that mimicked our rail journey for half the night.

It had that queer damp smell common to less lordly Irish residences, I decided, when the clear cold morning light lanced my dilapidated pair of shutters. I slipped across the icy wooden floor in my bare feet to greet the place that would be home for Elaine and myself while she bore the consequences of a folly she wouldn't name.

There they were. The beeches, their smooth grey trunks twisted and clinging with a certain admirable tenacity to the limestone shoulders of the lonely road across the heath. Below them and stretching for windswept miles was the shoreline—

rocky, mist-wrapped and still managing to glitter somehow in the weak light of an overcast sky.

A grim place to house grim girls bundled away in the dark of night to hide their shame from the world, I thought. One would think these oughtn't-to-be mothers would take too fatal a liking to cliffside rocks, to pounding waves and misty stretches that looked as if a body could walk into them and halfway to another world without noticing.

I shivered and looked around for my baggage. There, huddled by the elderly chest with the crisp crochet-edged dresser scarf—I recognized the institutional sleight-of-hand familiar from Miss Meachum's. "Homey atmosphere for girls of delicate disposition," I could see them advertising on the basis of that one light linen touch.

Except I doubted they advertised quite that way, in tightly printed boxes at the bottom of the Little Magazines. No, one would hardly shout to the world that one's business was keeping whispers just that. I dressed quickly in the icy room, for the first time missing the choreographed servility that kept my bedchamber fire perpetually lighted, my clothing brushed and hung. It took three dives into the tightly packed trunk to find a warm woollen skirt and waist to match. I took a shawl for more protection against the house's inner climate and tried the hall.

Hall? It was merely a wooden balcony with a venerable railing leading down to one huge room below. Something about the place haunted me—perhaps it was the deer heads on the walls—their dumb eyes and uncompromising antlers somehow unnerving. Our voiceless fellow victims.

I crossed lightly through the large stone-floored main room. A pantry and kitchen brought up the house's rear, as I suspected. I stepped down a stone stoop into a low-ceilinged room rather pleasantly redolent of sausage and porridge and the friendly steam of cooking.

"Up is you? You'll be gettin' onto a country clock here soon enough, I guess. Well, sit if you're hungry and be about yer eatin'. Be you the girl who's breedin' or the friend? Not by that appetite, I'd wager. It's the friend then. Well, we'll want none of yer namby-pambyin' nonsense durin' the time, girl. We know our business."

I dropped the unconscionably large lump of bread I'd pulled off a round loaf at the speaker's invitation. She was a raw-boned woman in a pouchy flowered dress with a face as pink and broad and expressionless as a Dorset ham. Two fleshy arms akimbo on her upholstered hips looked like offspring of the face.

"Ratherskittle's the name, missy. And *Mrs.*, if y' don't mind. And don't be givin' me that city stare of yourn—mine's the onliest face you'll be seein' around here besides hers and what's in the glass for quite a while. Doctor won't be comin' down till she's nearer her time."

With that she turned back to a large black skillet in which something greasy sizzled. I felt my appetite wane by the second and turned to tearing my bread into smaller but untasted morsels.

A thump on the table before me brought my head up with a snap.

"Here. Have some grease for yer bread," said the woman named *Mrs.* Ratherskittle, whirling from her skillet long enough to plunk a pale slab of butter before me. It was fragrant and fresh and cheered me a bit, if her manner didn't.

"You seem experienced at this," I commented gingerly while buttering the rough-textured bread.

She cast her small, indeterminate-coloured eyes upward to where Elaine presumably slept.

"I've been midwife to more of them city lassies than you'd care to know about. Or the husbands they married later would. And 'fore that I was at Bellevue in London. Aye, many a wee one's first view of the world has been from between my hands as I slip 'im out into the light." She flexed her beefy fingers then. It was impossible to imagine those blunt instruments serving to aid infants to life. But she looked proud of her skill and I didn't doubt she had it.

"And there's been a time or two I've helped 'em out the other way, if you know what I mean," she added with a certain repellent intimacy. "If the alarm goes out early enough and the family is desperate enough. . . . Though the pay's never so good as for the blessed act of bringing a bairn into whatever world he'll grow in." Her dark hints started some leery suspicion growling at the back of my head, but I shook off these murky guesses and concentrated on what I could grasp. They'd done what they did many times before. "Doctor"—at least there was one—would come later.

"And what are we to do until—?"

"Do what you will!" she snorted. "It's you that's payin' for the privilege. All I ask is you stay outa my way at the birthin'. I've had them companions go yellow and fall in a faintin' fit. All they do is trip me up when I've work to do. You're the ones is payin'. I cook and clean and help Doctor at the time and get me five pounds a month. But I hope you've a good head, girl, 'cuz sometimes Doctor don't come in time and then—you think you can help?" I couldn't tell whether she meant it or was just baiting me.

"I think so," I managed to spit out between chews of the tough loaf.

"Don't look like that—it's not likely to be happenin' that way. This one looks to be a proper lamb. I saw her last night and these scrawny ones are made for it. Now, me, I'd had me times with mine." She laughed sharply and patted the swollen stomach that billowed out her gown. "Too old for it now, though. Good enough."

I escaped as soon as I'd swallowed an adequate amount of bread and retreated to Elaine's room. She was awake, her eyes fastened on the shutters.

"Here, I'll get this so you won't get chilblains from crossing the floor—you did bring slippers—oh, yes, here they are. Well, there's nothing to do but get up and find out about this place, is there?"

She didn't move, but I don't think she was feeling dispirited. The light fell across the foot of her bed and I was surprised to think that despite being as far along as she was, one would hardly know that she was pregnant.

"A boy," pronounced Mrs. Ratherskittle with one expert glance to Elaine's waist when I brought her, dressed, down to breakfast. "Can always tell a boy—they carry long and flat. Easier to keep 'tween you and me and the gatepost, eh, lassie?" Mrs. Ratherskittle's odious inferences were wasted on Elaine.

"A boy? I think I should like that, Amberleigh," she said dreamily to me, as if we were discussing the merits of Earl Grey versus Ming tea.

"Milky stuff, it'll keep your stomach settled," Mrs. Ratherskittle explained gruffly as she put a plate of porridge out-posted with currants before Elaine. At least the woman did seem to know what to feed her: Elaine downed it methodically without a demur.

And that's how all our days at Twin Beeches began. Each morning I would awaken before Elaine, draw her from the bed that threatened to become her quagmire and take her down to Mrs. Ratherskittle's noisy mercies.

It was a bitter damp place, with even less sun than slipped through the coastal cloak of clouds onto Carnhaven. We walked those first few days—down the lonely road, along the sea bluffs but not too close—our shawls clasped round us like talismen. Now the great arc of Elaine's pregnancy began to make itself felt. She leaned back in a peculiar way and took her shaky steps with me at her elbow. Finally our walks worried me and we spent many hours cooped up in the cottage, playing parlour games I used to despise, as if our lives depended on them.

"I have no patience with it!" Elaine said petulantly one day, throwing down the cards from the game whose name didn't reflect her current feelings.

I picked them up.

"And leave them there, Amberleigh—you're forever traipsing about after me as if I were ill. I'm not ill. I'm perfectly all right."

I glanced at her, stunned by the lancing shrillness in her voice.

"No, don't you—I'll get them," Elaine said contritely, dropping clumsily to her knees and gathering up the scattered pasteboards. She stopped in the midst of it.

"Amberleigh. I'm frightened. I'm so frightened." The tears started squeezing out from between her closed lids. I sat there helpless to do anything. Could I tell her it would be all right, that she would be all right? I didn't know. And Mrs. Ratherskittle didn't speak well to the safety of the enterprise upon which Elaine was now eight-and-a-half months embarked. "Had one breech," she'd tell me in harsh whispers when I'd come down to breakfast alone, "in Bellevue. Worst I ever seen. Baby bent like a hairpin. And hemorrhage. Lord, I thought that woman'd never stop. Hard to tell sometimes, whether they're whinin' for the sake of it or the fever's comin' for 'em. Sometimes the ones that looks the best, all pale and peaceful like, they're the ones that go, fast. And quiet. I guess I'd take a yeller, meself. You've not had any wee ones? No, a 'Miss' still like the other one, eh?" Here she laughed in a high wheezing way that almost made me grind my teeth. "Well, you'll have time for yer own, girl, just don't wait too long..."

Cold comfort. I wasn't sure I wanted to be like Elaine, ballooning before me in her cambric gown, crying useless tears down a face as thin and wrinkled as a dried peach. She looked awful, her colour gone, her hair thin and lifeless. And still at least two more weeks of this eternal waiting. At least. "Might be later, lots later." Another wise word from Mother Ratherskittle. "These first ones take their time. And why not? Would you or I want to slide out into this wicked world any faster than we had to?"

I should have stayed there to comfort Elaine in her tears and her terror. I should have held my hand out to her—but I was tired, weary with waiting for another woman's folly to reach its appointed end. I whirled up and out of the room. "I'm going for a walk," I threw behind me. I didn't think she heard me and I didn't care.

Sharp wind, cutting along the road and wresting my shawl away to drive cold airy shafts through to my body. I wound my fingers in its woollen depths but still they chilled. Grey. It was always grey here. No sudden shafts of sunlight like those that struck Carnhaven from time to time. No illuminating wafts of sun debuting behind the cloud curtain to footlight the fields and moors with vibrant, sparkling green.

It was hardly even green here. Only dun-coloured from the dirty grey and yellow mosses that clung like living things to barren rock reaching out to the sea. For what? Companionship? What was happening back at Carnhaven? Was Devora fluttering on some limpid lawn in her pale ivories and laces? Who danced attendance on her, some amorphous male figure in well-cut suit or country tweeds? Was it some citified suitor of married ladies? Or Adrian? Was Adrian Carstairs there, bending over the billiards table, his face ruddy and golden in the overhead lamps—no, why should Adrian be there? Why did I paste him into my mental picture book? Not till the Holidays, he'd said. And it was to me he'd promised return, not to Devora, leaning jealously over the bannister and calling me back to duty.

But her call had ended it, hadn't it? Elaine and I packed away for three dreary months, leaving Adrian open to other amusements, other pursuits, other women. Hadn't Devora said she'd played lure to Elaine's suitors before? Perhaps she was playing out her line to see if it still held.

It really wasn't anything Devora might do that I feared, but what Adrian might not do. He might not find me indispensable. He might not want to slide away from the easy supercilious society to which his grandfather's business judgement had so conveniently provided entree.

I sat on a bluff-top boulder and watched the waves ruffle against the rocks far off and below. So delicate they looked, those waves—lacy wristlets on an aristocratic hand. Cold hands, giant hands, that would rend the unwary limb from limb, like a dinner guest dismembering a particularly succulent squab. I felt tiny and brittle and cold, caught in the designs of someone larger than I. I looked out over sea and sky and for a rare moment experienced its vastness—a great expanse of hard rock that curved over the edge of the planet and faced out into an alien universe. I was the merest speck on that giant bauble. A movement too quick and I might hurtle off into that bubbling grey uncertainty above me. It was a wonder we hung on at all, with our insignificant shoe-clad feet to our barren planetary rockpile . . . but then, not everyone did.

I clutched my shawl tighter, getting no warmth from anything but the gesture. Did nothing but whiskey and water flow from these wet wastelands in the North? And wool, soggy wool it would be, wool not worth the weaving, wool tinged the melancholy hue of the sky, grey.

Soon I would be sunk in utter melancholia. But I wondered if that would be so terrible. There would be a kind of harmony here, to join mood to landscape and simply mindlessly let the thoughts crash on one's brain with the same brutal rhythm as waves pounding rocks—

"Amberleigh! Amberleigh! Please come back. You've gone so high. I can't come there."

Elaine's voice, wispy and wailing, drew me like an umbilical cord out of my watery wallowings. I turned to see her, wind-whipped and pinch-faced, a few feet below me on the rough path. Behind her was a gentle slope of rocks, the road and the grotesque Twin Beeches.

"Whatever are you doing up there?" she demanded.

CHAPTER TEN

"GROWING MORBID," I said with some bitterness and much truth. And it was Elaine I had fretted about heeding the surf's siren call. A poor tragic heroine I would make, to succumb to mooning by the sea at the drop of another person's guard!

"Come down then," Elaine commanded, with a little of the old imperiousness back in her voice. "I had to walk ever so far to find you and I'm feeling vapourish. I'm sorry about the silly cards. I don't know why I'm such a bear—"

"Here, you don't have to shout it to the world, I'm coming down, Elaine. And I wasn't angry with you at all, I was angry with me."

I half-slid my way down to her. Her skirts were curving

ludicrously under her swelling stomach—she looked a bit like Tweedledee or his twin—was it an Evil Twin, I wondered suddenly—from Mr. Carroll's amusing books, but I didn't tell her so. Or Humpty Dumpty, a giant egg perched on a precipice and about to break.

"You oughtn't to have come up here by yourself, Elaine." Snapping more than I meant to again, guilty no doubt that I'd occasioned her search.

"If you were gone, if you were angry with me, Amberleigh, I don't think I could face anything. For a moment I—I thought.... You wouldn't leave me, Amberleigh? Not now? I wouldn't be able to stand it, really, I—I couldn't go back to Devora alone. I don't know what I might do—I'd like to kill her. Haven't you ever wanted to take her by that long lean throat and twist it? I have. I've thought about her like that. I shouldn't perhaps, but I have. And especially lately. Why has it been especially lately, when my dreams have been so strange...?"

Elaine walked companionably beside me, leaning a little on my arm and whispering her words into my ear before the wind could net and whisk them away. Ugly words they were, but I thought it better she say them and banish them.

"Oh, I am tired. It was a long way. And I ran. I was afraid you'd gone. But that was stupid, where'd you have gone to? We're marooned here, you and I, quite like Robinson Crusoe. And Mrs. Ratherskittle is our Friday. I wonder if she eats people?"

"No! She's a kind lady, though a little odd. And she's been a good midwife or she wouldn't be here. You must believe that, Elaine."

"I dreamed—the other night, no I didn't tell you, you always worry so, really Amberleigh, you are such an old lady sometimes. I dreamed It"—her eyes fell to her protuberant belly with a virginly modesty that only in Elaine could I find sincere—"It had turned dry and crackled, all purple and blue, like a coloured peach pit. Isn't that odd? What do you think it means?"

I swallowed, repelled by the image she painted for me. Elaine lurching down the rocks of a dream landscape with a bloated, barren belly before her.

"And little hands came out of it, Amberleigh. Such clever little hands. Like an elf. And they were beckoning me...I thought about it the longest time before I went back to sleep..."

"It was merely a dream. Dreams don't mean anything. You know all that nonsense is for ladies who read tea leaves and play seance in the library."

"And then I dreamed of lambs, pretty fluffy lambs. Perhaps I'd been counting them to go back to sleep—but they played in a great green field and the sun shone and it was so happy there. The sun shone and they had golden fleece. Like the sun. Now what was that to mean?"

"Elaine, if you'd wanted an oracle you should have applied for one. I've only got the Misses Meachum's rather limited education behind me, you know. I'm sure I don't know what your dreams mean. But I'd say the happy one followed the—worrisome—one, so you mustn't fret."

"I don't worry. Sometimes I think I don't worry enough. But it's as if it were all happening to someone else, you understand? I wish I worried about things like you do, Amberleigh. I think that's safer, somehow."

"It's more time-consuming, I can tell you that . . . but, Elaine, don't you want to tell me—?"

"Tell you what, Amberleigh?" Her grey eyes impaled me on her innocence in asking the question. What else should I want to know but what every gossip in Glennverran would lust after if they knew: Who? I dropped my eyes to the hard and rocky path at our feet. It was an answer she had to be willing to give.

Elaine's fingers suddenly dug into my forearm with the intensity of a claw. "Elaine, what is it, your face is so . . ."

"Oh." She had stopped walking and shut her eyes, as if she feared the earth would waver. "It's gone now. It was such an—ache—it nearly took my breath away. Do hurry, Amberleigh. I think I'm going to be—unwell."

I piloted her back to the cottage with the speedy care of a tugboat pulling an ocean liner to sea—this was no time to wallow in shallows or run aground. Elaine grimaced and paused every few minutes while I stomped impatiently at her side and tugged her another few yards as her condition permitted.

"Mrs. Ratherskittle, Mrs. Ratherskittle!" My calls woke the old man who did chores about the place and brought the goat peering around the outbuilding corner. They could have summoned Davy Jones' mates from the amount of yell I put into them. But no Mrs. Ratherskittle. I steered Elaine around the cottage's back entry, still hailing my invisible saviour. "Mrs. Ratherskittle, come please. She's ill. I think—"

Her red raw face poked out the back door at last. "Weel, bless my soul, she's gettin' ready to birth, and early, too. Who'd a thought it?"

"Surely you should have," I snapped, easing Elaine onto a rude, rush-covered kitchen chair.

"How often are the pains?" Mrs. Ratherskittle asked bluntly, bending down to press Elaine's stomach indelicately.

"Every few minutes, but it just started."

"But her water hasn't broke yet—I can't understand it, that's always the surest sign..." Mrs. Ratherskittle frowned her narrow forehead and regarded Elaine as if she were a loaf of bread that had risen too soon.

"Water?" Elaine furrowed her forehead, too. "I think last night—it was awfully wet, but I didn't want to raise a fuss, you see..."

"Holy Lord and St. George! All right, girl, we'd better get her up and prepare for it. Doctor's not comin' for a week yet, so it's up to us."

"Up to us? But can't you wire—?"

"By the time he'd get here, girl, we'd have triplets on our hands and the first one a month old. Now grab an elbow, miss, and lend me a lever for our lady here."

Together we guided Elaine upstairs to her own fourposter, changing her into nightclothes and tucking her in like a sick child. Except that it was no child's task she was embarking on. She writhed with the pain more frequently now, in between murmuring to me to never leave her, to stay with her, to be there...

"Mrs. Ratherskittle." I had slipped away from Elaine to the beefy midwife, who was assembling a horrific collection of metal instruments in a basin. "How long will it be, what are we to do?" I hissed, but she disregarded me.

"You're to do what you're told, girl, and we'll come through this right smart. Hundreds of 'em I've done and lost no more than a third. So follow my bidding and don't go gettin' weak-kneed on me. That's all the Lord asks of a body and that's all I ask of you." She elbowed me out of the way and brought her—equipment—to the bed.

So I did as she said, my assistance coming down to wiping pearls of perspiration off Elaine's face and learning to steady myself when her moans sharpened in level and frequency as the hours passed. For once the heavy climate that afflicted this desolate cottage went unheeded. We waited, we two, as the hours wound their way around the spool of Elaine's confinement—an umbilical cord of time.

She didn't say much—I'd expected her to lean on me more than ever during these last hours. But she lay isolated from us, her pale hair flattened on the pillow like very fine flax, her eyes anchoring to something beyond the confines of the plain little room. Between the cries that came faster and faster, she lay spent, panting like a wild thing spied by human eyes and not daring to risk a run to freedom.

"Ah, I can see the little head now," Mrs. Ratherskittle croaked triumphantly, rolling up her blowsy sleeves. "Now's my time to work the little bastard out."

Anger surged to my throat—to say such a thing, here and now . . . But Elaine was beyond hearing, her head thrashing on the bedclothes, her hands wringing the cloth ties Mrs. Ratherskittle had roped around the headboard posts.

I lingered midway between Elaine and the red-faced woman who grunted with her at the bed's foot. I equivocated between observing the phenomenon and avoiding it. The midwife's beefy hands disappeared under the gown—surely she wasn't simply reaching in to pull out the infant?—and she bellowed from time to time like a top serjeant.

"Push, me girl, push with yer whole mind and yer whole soul if you want to see an end to it. I'll pull, but you've got to push."

I stood helpless and unhelping at the end, as Mrs. Ratherskittle coaxed and ordered Elaine's child into the musty late-evening air of the seaside cottage.

"A blanket!" she ordered finally, cradling a small blue-and-red mass of sputtering flesh and giving it a healthy shake after she sucked out its mouth and throat. Almost gagging, I took a fresh green wool square from the chest provided. Mrs. Ratherskittle wrapped the infant, squalling now like an angry cat, and placed it on Elaine's suddenly diminished stomach.

The midwife's beefy forearms, stained with blood, hung almost lifeless at her hips, like a side of dressed meat in the Carnhaven kitchen. Elaine's arms lifted weakly up around the baby as if to embrace it, then fell back. She seemed half dead, with no colour beyond two red spots in her cheeks. Feverish red spots.

"We'll wait for the other, then tidy up." Mrs. Ratherskittle nearly blew the words out, like a winded horse. "At least you didn't go vapourish on me," she conceded, eyeing me almost approvingly. "I'll wager you'll be in no haste to go and do likewise, as the parsons say," she said with a sharp nod to the bed and a short laugh.

I didn't bother to answer her.

Elaine finally fell asleep, her breath drawing softly through parted lips. The infant, less purple now but still coated with a white sort of film, slumbered too, in a rude wooden cradle lined with blankets.

I followed Mrs. Ratherskittle down to the kitchen blindly.

"Here, don't you be trippin' on the stairs now, girl, after all that and coming through right fine. Hard work, though— them men don't know what they're missing. If they did they'd fall flat on the floor as like, they would. I've got a wee bit of somethin' here, girl," she said, pulling a crockery jug from a cupboard and uncorking it as tenderly as she'd eased the babe from its mother. She tilted back her head, exposing the mottled red and white dewlaps that usually took refuge in her collar, and had a few good swallows.

"Have some of this, miss, it'll put the roses back in yer cheeks. And a few places else, it will. Then have a mug for it, if you're so choosy. You'll feel better for it."

I poured a bit into a mug; a thin clear stream splashed into the crockery.

"Don't go and spill it, child. Those citified hands of yourn will never make good work of anything. Too precious to spill, isn't it? And don't go tellin' Doctor when he comes. I take it easy and only after."

I sipped the brew, anticipating a sort of country beer. White fire seared my lips and I very nearly spat it out. "You need it, though you don't know it, so drink, miss, drink," came Mrs. Ratherskittle's urgings, so I did. It was as if the small fire up in Elaine's room ignited in my stomach and spread slowly through my limbs. I sat down at the table and sighed. My shoulders dropped and for the first time I noticed my hands had been clenched.

"That's right. Could have been a rough one. Not too untidy, though. Doctor'll come up to see the twain and then we'll get the wee one off to a new place. And the two of you can go back to where you came from."

"The baby. Where will you send it? To some poorhouse?"

"Wi' the money behind it the likes of your friend has got? No, he won't be workin' in a mine ten years hence, that boy. A nice up-and-comin' home we contract to send him to, with nice monthly pounds comin' in to keep him."

"Who would take somebody's unknown child?"

"Lots of folk. Them as can't have their own. They knows he's stock. At least half of him is, eh? For as many as 'ud give their lives not to have 'em, there're those that'd take lives to get 'em." She nodded knowingly and took a long pull from the jug. I shivered from merely watching that dose of fire strike her insides.

"Bellevue. We had a few hard times at Bellevue. 'Twas a woman who came with a mop and pail and washed the hallways and scrubbed on her knees so no one could see her face. Wanted a wee babe somethin' fierce. So fierce one day she walked into the ward and found young Jenny Matthews, havin' her first and early besides. Killed her, she did, behind the curtain, slit her throat and while the blood still spurted from the mother's neck cut the babe right out o' her. Lived, it did, too. The Bobbies found her, when the street said it was a baby gettin' murdered in her room and it only the poor babe bawlin' for milk, for the poor dumb woman didn't know how to feed it, though she managed as neat a surgery as I've seen from some of the doctors in their time . . ."

I pushed myself up by my hands and lurched away from the table. "I'm going to see to Elaine, I—" The main room was ahead of me and I took a deep breath of its somehow fresher air. Let her ramble and rave in the kitchen, I'd not listen. A thrill of fear washed through me like the gin with which she lit her gruesome memories. I'd sit by Elaine, by God, until we got out of this awful place. Away from that disgusting creature—back to a normal world. Back to Carnhaven.

CHAPTER ELEVEN

THE SEPTEMBER sun still warmed the bay when the carriage rounded the last curve and Carnhaven hove into our view.

"I'm back, Amberleigh," said Elaine, leaning her scarlet-plumed head out the window. "It's true. Oh, how I've missed Carnhaven."

She'd settled back beside me and nervously pulled her glove

fingers tauter. I could hear Devora's voice somewhere in the past nagging her into the gesture. Devora had her way, even with the willful. There'd been no question that Elaine's child should be quickly bundled and trundled off to the home that would have it. I wondered sometimes how Elaine had been able to do it, but she seemed to lack the maternal instinct I'd believed accompanied every childbirth. She regarded the child almost as she would have a butterfly that had landed on her during a summer's day—something strange and beautiful and alien and ugly that touched her once and made her shiver and then was gone.

I attended him more than she did during the few weeks before the tight-laced couple from the comfortable farm came to claim him. I was not above searching his snubby features for some resemblance to a father I might have known. But his ruddy little face defied detection of a paternal link. His blue eyes rolled vaguely and expressionlessly in the tiny lids.

Once I bent to put him in his cradle and caught the fleeting feeling of familiarity. My heart jumped as the moment suspended me and the infant in my arms in time. Then I smoothed the memory into its place—it had been the sculpted head of which I was reminded—with the indeterminate, always-changing features, the half-features that loomed out of the clay on one day and skulked back into the mass the next.

Would he remain like that to me forever, this abandoned heir, this boy? Soon to be shunted to another woman, another environment, with less knowledge of Carnhaven than the ground squirrels that scampered across its lawns?

Unnatural; I found the entire thing unnatural. But what was I to do? Nothing but consign Elaine's son to the anonymity Devora wished for his legacy. And even if Elaine were interested in raising a protest—I glanced over to her sleeping form lost in the ample linens—perhaps she was no mother to whom to entrust a seeking human soul; she had trouble enough finding her own.

"What will you call him, Elaine?" I had asked her once as she nursed him, his small face muffled in the lacy ruffles and ribbons on the bedjacket she wore modestly on such occasions.

"Call him?" She gazed down at her son's pale, rounded face. No suns had had their chance to follow it through careless days in an open world; his skin was as alabaster as Devora's powdered and protected complexion. He seemed an unreal person, a sketch untinted as yet that remained to be fleshed out and filled in. I wanted him to have a name. I would feel better about the entire affair if he had a name.

"Call him? We don't have to call him anything, do we, Amberleigh?" asked Elaine slowly, lifting her light grey eyes to mine in a way that sent chills down the back of my neck. "After all, he's to be somebody else's look-out soon—"

"Yes, I know. I'm—glad—you see that. But you've a right to name him."

"Very well, what about—" Some thought hovered at the edge of her tongue; only her silver eyes held it back. "I was thinking J—James, I was thinking. But no. It was Michaelmas he was born, wasn't it? Then it's Michael. I'll call him Michael."

But she never did. She never did call him by any name. I called him Michael. Even Mrs. Ratherskittle called him Michael. But not Elaine, not even on the day, weeks later, when the self-concious couple from further North came to claim him.

And it was I who relinquished him. Elaine had refused to come down to the cottage's main room and wait for the expected parents. I waited for them, cradling Michael on the crook of one arm. My fingers fluttered nervously against the narrow amber choker around my throat—the only jewellery I'd thought to take with me from Carnhaven and then only because I often wore it with the brandy-coloured travelling suit.

I remembered having been fascinated by the tiny necklace as a child rummaging through the very carved wooden treasure box Mrs. Bowers redeemed from the scavengers of Eaton Square.

"Baby beads," Mrs. Bowers had called them. Possibly my own dead mother's, placed round her infant throat to ward off childhood diseases. I'd worn them, Mrs. Bowers had guessed, though she'd not been there. And should save them for my own children, she'd said. Poor souls, they seemed as remote as the moon to me here at Twin Beeches.

I undid the delicate carved-amber clasp and slipped the slender string of beads, like hardened honey, through my cold hands. There was an oily richness to their feel, as if they were formed of something once warm and liquid, like blood. And they were; I'd heard that eons ago a resinous weeping from trees trapped insects in its flood and then froze to become this semiprecious substance.

It was pure impulse, but I slipped the bauble over Michael's head; he shouldn't go off into the wider world without something to call his own. As Mrs. Bowers had salvaged something for me, so should I for him. The necklace, tight enough to almost throttle me, hung to his baby chest. A good wish to banish croup and cough and pox. A good wish from a godmother—not a fairy one, perhaps, but all that was available.

And so I relinquished him, to that wife with her stiff, pathetically styled Sunday-best suit and the impossible hat with the hard red cherries bobbling along the brim. Good folk. Simple folk. Not-Devora folk. The husband bobbed his head at me and asked, "Have ye a name for him?" Irish folk.

"Michael."

The farmer nodded his grizzled head. He looked older, but I guessed him to be no more than four-and-thirty, with a skin baked and cracked by the wind and too many teeth missing accounting for the false impression. "Michael," he said, rolling it on his Irish tongue as if it were a blessing, and smiled. It was as if the sun broke from behind the clouds, the smile sending the lines of his face scudding away in my mind. "'Tis a good choice."

"We'll christen him that with pleasure," said the wife a bit breathlessly, cradling the shapeless bundle like her best Sunday pitcher and it cracked. Michael's light blue baby eyes seemed to roll once in my direction, or was it?

"It'll be a Cath'lic christening," added the man with a certain defiant deference. I nodded silently.

"Well, we'll be thankin' you, Miss—" He looked hesitant about what title to render me. It occurred to me that the pair thought me Michael's mother.

"Oh, he's not mine. But please, take good care of him. And I won't intrude on your privacy, but if I might know your name, where you're taking him—"

The couple exchanged a glance and she caught her bundle closer. Michael gurgled.

"Kelly. It's James Kelly from Tyrone."

They turned hastily, as if by naming themselves they'd spoken the word by which their gold would turn to straw, and left Twin Beeches.

We left soon after.

"It's time to get out, Amberleigh. It's Carnhaven. We're here. Whatever are you staring out at the woods for? The house is this way."

There was no Devora to greet us, only Symes skimming into our path, raising an admonishing eyebrow at a footman who clumsily dropped a bag behind us, and letting us sink into the cold hall beyond. Still hostile somehow.

"I'd almost think the hunt was up and they'd forgotten us," I remarked to Elaine, remembering my arrival here. Save for Devlin Quade peering around the hall door, the clock and the quiet seemed to toll the same time as months before.

"Are they hunting, Symes?"

"No, miss. The Lady St. Clare is in her chamber attending to correspondence, I believe, and your father is in London."

We glided upstairs alone, with only Elaine's Henrietta—"Stone," Devora more properly called her, in a voice as hard as—to welcome us back to Carnhaven. Henrietta flitted impartially between my room and Elaine's—shaking out clothes and dispersing gloves and stockings to their proper corners like some maternal sparrow cursed with twins.

"'Ere now, I'll take a 'and wi' that, Miss Elaine. You sit yerself down and get off o' yer feet—I been sittin' all day waitin' for the twos of you to come home," I heard trilled through the ajar door. A moment later Henrietta's unquenchable pointed little face rounded the door and she was at me.

It was "Sit, Miss Amber," and "Don't bother yerself, Miss Amber" (she never did master my name's third syllable) until I retreated to Elaine's chamber. We ended by having dinner brought up on a tray for us both. As darkness dampened the glisten of the great house, cloaking its white pediments in hostile shadow, all activity seemed to recede. And I myself had a vision of Elaine and me eating quietly like mice on the second floor in our lamp-lit room and nothing but darkness plunging below us, except in the fire-warmed kitchen where Mrs. Featherstone would still be grappling with tomorrow's menu and the kitchen maids.

It seemed such a giant shell to house so few and puny creatures.

But I was wrong—more than we two and the staff were busy that evening. Devora's maid came for me after dinner and I followed her formally back to Devora's suite. It seemed she had not forgotten us.

"Amberleigh. My Lord, you've thined. And paled. What kind of place was it?" Devora sat upon a chaise lounge buffing her nails with a silver-handled chamois buffer. Her hair was loose and made her look younger, like a schoolmate.

"Didn't you—that is, I rather expected you knew something about it when you sent us there."

"Lord, no! If you think I needed such a retreat in my day you're woefully mistaken. Not that there weren't those among the male contingent who would have been more than ecstatic to assist me—all that virtue, unnecessary after all..." Her words trailed off as she selected an elaborately engraved silver file and began sweeping its rasping length rhythmically across her nails. The sound marched ants up my back. Unnecessary virtue—of course, she never had any worth guarding. She was unable to bear children.

"No, my dear"—Devora shifted suddenly in her wrapper, catching the skirt up and hauling it somehow gracelessly over her knees—"I'd no preview of the place. Most of my erring friends, when I did hear of their disgraces, were sent to sanitariums in Switzerland. And that was done early on when the consequences could be—well, they didn't have to be borne..." Her light laugh joined the file in grinding on my nerves.

"It was a frightful place, Lady St. Clare," I said bluntly, sitting uninvited on the needlepointed side chair. "I'm sure I'm amazed Elaine and I came out of it at all. Much less the infant. The woman they had there was so—unfeeling. And the doctor didn't even arrive in time for the confinement. I shouldn't pay for it, if I were you."

"Not pay? My dear, I'd have to pay for it if it had been a pig sty on the edge of a puddle. Not paying means telling. And we wouldn't want that. Would you want Elaine cast out from the only society she's known, crossed off everyone's list? Not so much as a Monday-afternoon tea that would have her? I was told it was a respectable cottage by the sea. Well-located with balmy breezes and healthful air. A bit primitive, no doubt, to one used to American efficiency"—one delicately plucked eyebrow arched at my sensibilities before her eyes dropped once more to her glossy pale nails.

"Efficiency was hardly the question, Lady St. Clare. A little humanity was more to the point—"

"Yes, yes, I know you've both had a ragged time of it and I don't mean to belittle it, truly, Amberleigh. It's merely that these things are best forgotten. And if remembered at all, with a nice little dusting of amnesia over the—cruder—realities." She tossed aside the nail implements and trailed to the windows. Elaine had been right—there was something scrawny and strangle-able about that neck of hers. I wondered how Sir George avoided the temptation. But perhaps that was why their bedchambers bracketed the house, with rooms of buffer zone between them.

"I'm very pleased with the way you've handled this, Amberleigh. Very level-headed. No hysterics. I know it hasn't been easy for you, but perhaps your reward is in knowing that Elaine will most likely come out of the ordeal remembering little of it. She has a facility for forgetting things."

"Perhaps because so much of what has happened to her has been forgettable," I said, not without a malicious twinge.

Devora turned her delicate-featured face on that immobile arrogant neck of hers. "How much better for us then. And her. I am not unaware that it would have likely been a different story with Elaine if not for you, Amberleigh. For that I'm grateful. But don't mistake gratitude for licence."

Her soft warning pinned me to the needlepoint chair, my feet seeming to shrink until they dangled incompletely over the edge. I almost ducked my head like a child. Her tone had carved the resistance out of me as a sharp knife disgorges meat from a melon.

"Elaine seems well." She changed the subject with her attitude and came to hover over me. I was sorry I'd sat down; it made my position weak, like a child called in to face the schoolmistress.

"Very well. One would hardly know. It wasn't an easy time—"

"I'm sure I don't want details. Lord, Amberleigh, you must remember that ladies keep such things between themselves and the bedsheets." I blushed as she resumed her place on the chaise lounge. Her gesture to pull the wrapper over her knees made a rent in the flimsy material. "Does nothing last? Well, I wanted something more appropriate for the Continent next spring anyway. I shall simply have to go to Dublin and Alfred Manning. Perhaps I can find something smart for you there, hmmmm? Amberleigh, I've been thinking that I must do something to ease Elaine back into normal society. It wouldn't do to have her turn hermit, you know. Even this brief an absence is barely excusable. What do you think of a party?"

"A party? Isn't that rather too callous? After all, she's just left an infant son to the winds and waves of that awful North country—"

"Stop it! I won't have you putting it that way. That—boy— is well cared for. We've done our duty and met our obligations. And parties aren't so callous. You know how easy it is for Elaine to—sink. We must buoy her up. I'm depending upon you, Amberleigh, to keep her from drifting out with whatever tide ebbs and flows in her head. You know how delicate she is. I really can't tolerate one more of the unbelievable St.

Clares going strange on me. I spend enough time here as it is. Soon I'll be as good as alone. You shan't stay forever. Help me bring her back."

Her voice had grown resonant with real feeling. I appreciated the way she felt at sea with Elaine. Lord knows I did often enough. There were even times when Elaine's moods made me fear that she was fairy-touched—something fey unloosed on Carnhaven as a jest and left to wreak the kind of unintentional havoc that only someone out of her depth can. Or was it unintentional? Was Elaine altogether unaware that her disgrace had put two more fine lines into the planes of Devora's elegant face?

"You think a festivity would do her good, Lady St. Clare?"

"It would do us all good, I'm sure of it. I can even invite Adrian Carstairs." Her eyes measured me as those last five syllables caught me unawares.

"I'm sure whomever you invite will be capable of distracting Elaine, although I'm sure Adrian"—I deliberately omitted his surname—"could do it better than most. Don't you think?"

Pink tinged her cheeks. For a moment I was certain she had seen him during the time Elaine and I had been away. Seen him? All the jealousy in my bones shouted that it had most likely been much more than that. And now she was dangling him before me like a bone before slobbering old Boru, expecting me to gracelessly galumph after it, in Mr. Carroll's so-perfect word.

"I don't know how distracting Adrian can be of late. I haven't seen him since that house party before you girls left." It was a confession and a slicing little voice inside my head commented, "Not because you haven't tried, I'd wager."

"I'll try for a crowd for this party, I think, perhaps even some of the young officers from the barracks—not too many of the junior ones, of course, but Captain Mayfair will know whom to include. Do try to get her up for this, Amberleigh. I think a lot depends on it."

A lot depends on it.

Those words came back to me during the next few weeks as I watched Elaine half carelessly ready herself for the ball. Ball we called it, though the servants twittered in the linen closet about it. Calling it an "After the Fall" Ball. They were witty and earthy, these Bridgets and Marys and Kathleens, taking their own pound of flesh from those who tried to work the hides off them. The gavottes that guilt put the gentry through amused them. But none of their disdain seeemed aimed at Elaine and they kept their secrets to themselves and the linen closet. It was as if she were a mere bystander to her own disgrace. It was Devora's pretensions they ridiculed in the half-whispered conversations I chanced upon in dark landings and around odd corners. No one seemed to think of Elaine as a central character in her own tragedy. Somehow that realization disturbed me. It was as if she were beyond blame, removed from reproach, so other-worldly that no mere mortal considerations bound her.

But she was mortal enough to require a gown for this ball that was to resurrect her for polite society. Devora lent her own maid—an accomplished seamstress—who concocted a waterfall of dotted tulle and yellow satin for Elaine's now-slender figure.

Devora even took an interest in my wardrobe. At first she merely insisted that I wear one of her cast-off evening gowns. When I produced a green velvet gown of my own only three seasons old and quite respectable, she would have nothing but that her Etoile freshen it for me.

Somehow I was maneuvered into the swarthy little French-woman's wiry fingers. And my plain gown was frosted with black lace and jet. As if the threat of Etoile's needle tacking fripperies to my bosom weren't enough, Devora waltzed in during the fitting and declared that I had to wear a newer corset and lace it up tightly for once.

"Really, Amberleigh, you don't want to go around looking like some *German* princess, do you?" Her tone told me precisely where German princesses ranked on her ladder of elegance. Elaine, waiting patiently for her turn under Etoile's mercies, gave a slender smile at this remark—the first I'd seen since our return. I sighed and pulled in my middle while Etoile plied the long laces until my waist was whittled to a mere thread and my bosom and hips poured over the corset like so much lava. But Devora's instructions had their advantages. I had never looked so fashionable, so head-turning, as I did in the glass after Etoile left me and went to perform her duties for Elaine.

The green and black colour combination made me look ever so much more worldly. The tightly laced corsets gave me a silhouette that rounded my hips and bust. No handkerchiefs would be needed now to flesh out any deficiency. I smiled to remember the piles of snowy starched squares we girls used to stockpile in our fronts at Miss Meachum's, hoping against hope to produce something worth looking at—something that might not even disgrace Miss Lillian Russell. I saw now that sophisticated devices far beyond those lacy squares were required to make hourglasses of us all. I smoothed my hands over my waist and squeezed in one last breath. It made my lungs ache. Shallow would have to be my guiding rule tonight. Shallow breath, shallow steps—otherwise the heavy train would tangle my hopeless ankles and trip me.

And shallow hopes? I plunged a tortoiseshell comb studded with topaz into my piled-up hair. It was the first time I'd be seeing Adrian in more than three months. Supposedly I'd been travelling with Elaine, sketching. Did I look as though I'd done more than simmer on some primitive hearth in wild western Ireland? Perhaps that's why Devora supervised my appearance, to further the idea that we had indeed been travelling, that we'd seen Dublin... What was left of my stomach that wasn't squeezed into my ribcage churned at the idea of being quizzed about our whereabouts. I felt rather an imposter—was that what was turning my fingers to ice? Or was it Adrian? I suddenly wanted to see him again very much. It was as if he were a key to some secret part of myself I wanted very much to unlock.

A whimper from the chamber adjacent mine tore me away from my self-inspection.

"I don't want to go! Leave me alone!" Elaine was huddling on the dressing chair, turned away from me with her arms clasped tightly across her middle, as if she were in pain. Her corset was only half laced and the pink strings streamed down her back to the floor, where they lay like limp rat tails.

Henrietta stood looking exasperated, and frightened, her hands on her plump hips and strong words on the tip of her tongue.

"Now, Miss Elaine. Don't you be doin' any of that for 'Enrietta. You've got to be dressed and ready for 'Er Ladyship. Else she'll 'ave my position for it, she will. You don't want to see your 'Enrietta put out, now do you? See, 'ere's Miss Amber come along now. She'll put things to rights. I'll leave you to Miss Amber."

Henrietta exited gratefully, leaving me to the petticoat-littered room with the yellow satin gown almost standing on its own stiff power against the bed.

"Here, I'll help you finish. Was she lacing you up too tightly? I swear, I could use a respite myself. Devora probably wants to case us both like sausages and ship us off somewhere else."

I thought her instinctive dislike of her stepmother would shake Elaine out of herself, but she didn't move. Her huddled shoulders stretched the thin chemise so I could see her shoulder blades sharp against the fabric. She'd gotten so thin. All the new mothers I'd known were plump, comfortable creatures like Mrs. Willoughby who attributed every additional chin to each successive baby.

"Elaine, are you ill? Are you crying?" She shrugged my hands off her shoulders with a convulsive shudder.

"I won't go, it's her idea. She wants to humiliate me. I can't go. No tonight, Amberleigh. There are reasons. It all came back to me somehow."

She hurled herself at the window, almost like a domesticated bird instinctively beating itself against the light. The late Irish evening was dimming over Carnhaven grounds. The ball began at nine; by then dark would have settled and the guests could rattle up to the entrance in lamp-lit carriages and descend to the flicker of the great torches that flanked the doors.

But now light still caressed the horizon. The sky—blue just moments ago, darkened until only the stretches above the horizon still held their ultramarine glow—a deep, glassy incandescence from the last of the sun spilling over the rim of the world. It was a beautiful time, my favourite, but Elaine sensed some danger in it.

"You mustn't get hurt, Amberleigh!" she said, spinning suddenly and clutching my arms with strong fingers. "I won't see you hurt. I'm afraid—I remembered. Remembered it all. Why did I have to? It's usually gone, gone like a will-o'-the-wisp. I'm afraid for you, Amberleigh, afraid you might be hurt. What's that—" Her grey eyes fixed again on the view outside the window, the lawns and the dark, hunched shoulders of the distant trees. A figure skirted the clearing where the formal gardens ended, working its routine way round to the back of the house.

"Dear God, Amberleigh," said Elaine in a sort of silent scream, her face leaning unattractively toward the window and the vague figure, almost like a pack hound straining at the lines. "He's here. I knew he'd come. Most of the time he wears his everyday face, but you mustn't let that deceive you, Amberleigh. The other face is still there. The dead one. I haven't seen it for a long time. He's careful of that. He knows it would upset me. But tonight, I know he'll wear it tonight. I can't go, don't make me, I don't know what I'll do if you make me. You can't, you can't!"

She was sobbing and clinging to the curtains as if they were the skirt of a favourite nanny and she but a child of three.

I called Henrietta.

"Fetch Lady St. Clare," I said grimly and Henrietta skittered away down the hall, her brisk little heels tapping out urgency on the hardwood.

Devora loomed out of the half-light like some demonic queen, glittering in tulle and jet and a copper gown encrusted with ebony tissue.

"It's Elaine."

"I see," she said, merely glancing into the room and at Elaine's half-dressed form collapsed near the window. "Then leave Stone with her. She's used to it. If it must be this way, Amberleigh, it must be. I can't say I'm not disappointed, but there's no sense in forcing the girl—I've got to check on George. Lord, these St. Clares!"

She rustled away in the opposite direction. I had not offered to stay with Elaine, I noticed rather coldly as I walked slowly to my door and shut myself in my room. It had ocurred to me, but I had not offered. I didn't want to nurse Elaine tonight. I wanted to take myself and my refurbished green gown downstairs, to gather ices and punch, compliments and chatter, dance invitations and . . . perhaps even Adrian. Elaine would not begrudge me this moment, I thought, as I collected my black silk fan and blew the candles out. She owed me it.

CHAPTER TWELVE

STRANGE HOW fine feathers make one preen like a peahen. I swept my train into an arc behind me and steadfastly sailed across the drawing-room floor. I had not seen Adrian yet. I was most anxious to see Adrian. Searching the crowd of strangers, I sought his polished golden head.

They were rather like exotic birds, the guests, bowing and scratching and pecking in an elegant yard. The ladies' plumed headdresses rose and nodded above the sea of bodies like cockatoo crowns. The men in their uniform black-and-white were the drabber-garbed males of the bird kingdom—and truly hard it was to pick one from the other. Where was Adrian, why had I not seen him yet?

There, against the wall, trapped by the dowager in puce satin and peridot, surely that was he . . . no. I stopped. Suddenly I felt as I had on Miss Meachum's platform so many years before, the hissing rustle of the taffetas seemed an ugly whisper surging through the gathering of St. Clare friends, neighbours, acquaintances.

I paused to fan myself with the silken frippery dredged from among Devora's castoffs. I needed a caress of air across my burning cheeks. It was then I saw Adrian, in a knot of couples halfway across the floor. I recognized odious Sally Compton from school among them, she of the haughty airs and implacable self-assurance. Well, it couldn't be helped, so off I glided to see Adrian, my heart pounding as it surely shouldn't.

"Adrian."

He turned from the circle and recognized me with a flash of light in his eyes.

"Yes?" he enquired politely then. Too politely.

I stared at him, seeing him hedge with his eyes, watching the light that had dawned draw far away, down into some pit at the back of his bland blue eyes. There was no welcome, no reunion, for me there.

"I—I simply hadn't seen you since our holiday, Elaine's and mine. I wanted to tell you that the—sketching was really quite rewarding. I thought you'd be interested." I had to say something to the stranger I had tapped on the shoulder in hopes of something else besides the blank, frozen face turned upon me.

"Indeed I am," he said formally, as though talking to the dowager in puce. "I haven't been able to go in for much of that sort of thing myself lately. It wears on one after a while, don't you think?"

He glanced for support around the circle and I saw their silent eyes flick over me with, could it be, embarrassment? But Sally Compton wasn't embarrassed—her face was alive with a complacent contempt that swept me like cold April rain.

I backed away a step, immediately tangling myself in my train. I was forced to stand fixed.

"Hmf, we'd better go in to supper or Devora's likely to blame us for the smoked ham being cold, what?" said a portly man with a chest on him like a pigeon's pouf. He didn't quite include me in the glance he sent round the little group. Magically, they melted into couples and sauntered towards the dining room.

"Sally?" said Adrian, extending his arm. She didn't even

bother to send a triumphant look my way.

I was left standing, numbed, snared in my finery, alone by the wall and an empty bank of chairs. There were still a few stragglers in the room. I wandered over to the ruins of the punch table and poured myself a cup—there was no one to do it for me—even though the cherry-sweet taste was the last thing I needed to wash away the bitterness in my mouth.

"Aha! Molly Malone. All alone. In the room. Waiting for whom? No doubt this strapping Irish broth of a boy. No? How d'ye do this day, mum?"

I was in no mood for the antics of Devlin Quade, but I turned to find him fairly resplendent in borrowed black tie, if a bit confined-looking.

"Why, I hardly expected to see you here, Devlin."

"No, but I make meself useful about the place and the lords and ladies up to the house let me in on occasion."

"Like me."

"Like you. But look at you, all fripperied up, must be one of Her Ladyship's goin'-to-opera gowns. And green yet. Tell me, girl, didn't the wee slightest bit of green blood stir in your half-Irish veins when you donned this colour?"

"And sure, I hadn't thought of the choice of my gown as a patriotic gesture, Devlin." Nor had I meant to descend into my favourite defence, sarcasm, but there it was.

"I was merely about to point out that men have been hanged for wearin' that colour."

"And women hanged for not wearing it? You won't make a United Irisher of me, Devlin, my red hair to the contrary."

"Aye, contrary's the word. I simply thought you were sendin' us a message . . ." He shrugged with a certain wry charm that ordinarily would have won me over. Tonight it rasped on my nerves like Devora's file.

"You mean that even what I wear must be political? Well, what isn't in this infuriating country of yours? I had this gown made in Boston three years ago with no conception that I was espousing any cause this side of the Atlantic or any other. Green was very good that year. And Lady St. Clare was kind enough to lend me her own seamstress to make it à la mode. So I shall wear it and not worry my conscience a whit!"

"Yes, I see Her Ladyship has managed to turn a perfectly ordinarily constructed human bein' into a modish version of Old Dobbin," he said, surveying the fashionable swayback that had thrilled me when I checked my profile in the mirror. "It was most generous of her," he added so dryly that I could no longer ignore him.

My sides ached from the close embrace of Devora's demanding corsetry; the thin soles of my slippers were turning wood planking to embers under my feet. I had the beginning of a headache, the gala evening felt flat and I felt trussed-up and foolish. And I think my heart was breaking. Devlin Quade was a worthy target for my temper.

"And where, pray, Devlin Patrick, is the fabled Irish blarney, the silver tongue that makes every man a poet and every woman a queen? If you are any sample of it, I would suppose that it is in the same place as your manners—irretrievably lost!"

"Now wait a minute, girl." Devlin's voice had dropped low and coaxing and he caught my wrist as I was about to flick my fan into nervous motion. "I didn't mean to ruffle your feathers. And the joy of tweakin' them a bit wouldn't be there if you weren't a splendid sight altogether."

I didn't dare look up at him, finding that when I thought I was in anger I was instead on the verge of tears.

"Here now," he said, gently taking away my untasted punch cup and leading me over to the wall, far from the few scattered souls surrounding the table. "I think you're makin' a brave show of it and nobody who knows you truly blames you. So, hold that fine red head up and don't let any of these toney folk make you bow an inch."

I looked amazed into Devlin's face. His clear brow was slightly furrowed, his blue eyes kind, concerned, solicitous—so unlike the teasing, superficial Devlin I knew that I was suddenly embarrassed by his honest gaze—I felt I'd crossed some path I was not meant to.

"Devlin, what do you mean? Of course, I'm a bit nervous about such a gala, what country mouse wouldn't be? But there's no cause for me to ... to flaunt myself. I don't understand."

"Amberleigh." He so seldom called me Amberleigh that I had to listen with redoubled seriousness. "Amberleigh, they can't help but know. And now you'll be findin' out who your friends are. You can't have thought it'd take a bloomin' genius to figure out why the sudden journey North, when no one in his right mind'd go dallying off there to paint at this time o' year or any other. And there was little to guess about why you turned up so suddenly here from America ... or why you buried yerself in that studio day after day. It was brave of you to come back now and face it out and kind of the St. Clares to shelter you, though they're not known for it. You've got the spirit Ireland needs. If you worked with us, really worked, you wouldn't have to stay here, we could send you to a new district, where no one knew. But it don't matter to me." He drew himself up after making this uncustomarily serious speech. "I'm not supposed to be intrudin' myself for the supper, so I'll be goin'. But think about it."

Devlin patted my velvet shoulder awkwardly and left. I heard his heavy boots ring across the polished floors and blessed him for being down-to-earth, for being real, for caring and for telling me what I had been too stupid to see myself.

They all—the guests, neighbours, villagers, family members, even Adrian—they all believed it was I whose indiscretion had caused the retreat North for three months. I, who divested of my illegitimate...issue...had returned to Carnhaven to attend balls and pretend nothing had happened. I, not Elaine. Elaine was safe. Behind a wall of my flesh.

I felt suddenly ill and sought the coolness of the French doors and the terrace beyond. My train, once my pride, dragged brutally across the flagstones. I felt it catch and rip with a certain satisfaction. I wanted to hear destruction, perhaps at that moment I wanted to be destroyed a little.

No wonder Adrian had so tastefully extricated himself from any suggestion of friendship with me! No wonder he now paid court at the side of Sally Compton. Would he write notes in her sketchpad? Would he even miss me? Had there been so little of substance between us? I sat on a stone bench and raked my palm across it suddenly while I bit back the anger. It hurt. Something still hurt, it was not all numbing, empty, useless...For Adrian not to know better, not to trust me at all—

"I beg your pardon, ma'am, are you in some distress?"

The voice originated from the French doors. I turned to see a man in formal dress silhouetted against the light behind them.

"No. I'm not—ill. I, I damaged my gown, I'm rather afraid. On the bench. I shall have to fix it."

He stepped further onto the terrace and I was forced to look up at him. The faint light from the drawing room fell upon my face.

"Oh, it's you." I thought his tone was cold.

"Have we met?"

"Hugh Davenant. Neighbour. From Shallowford." He gestured into the night vaguely in the direction of the Fairy Circle. How nice it must be to be from somewhere else, I thought.

"You're the Dunne girl, aren't you? Are you sure you're quite all right?"

He extended a hand to help me up and I rose, pulling on some unsuspected source to hold my head high as Devlin had urged.

"Here, you've hurt yourself." He looked at my scraped palm and then at me. He was tall, but not too tall for the window light to sweep across his face. I saw he was one of those lean muscular men one often finds riding a horse or leading a regiment. Or sitting on the bench in judgement. A curious scar angled along his left cheekbone; I fancied I had been right about the regiment. He lifted my hand to the light between us and examined it.

"A scratch, but one hard to come by. I'd attend to it, were I you." I turned to go but he held my hand.

"Perhaps you've been overdoing," he said, regarding me with a speculation I imagined reserved for brood mares, a look I imagined I was to receive again. His eyes, whatever colour they were in the half-light, swept me up and down in a way that I believed revealed even the tears on the bottom of my train. He looked at me as if I were a piece of Waterford, something etched and brittle that he could decide whether to break or not.

"What is your name?"

"Amberleigh," I answered, forced by convention to be polite.

"Well, Amberleigh, I'd take care of that hand right away."

"I daresay there's no great hurry," I said, wrenching my hand away although he held my wrist so tightly the skin burned as I freed it. "I doubt it's the kind of thing to scar."

I had picked the only weapon equal to the one he aimed at me. A gentleman so handsome would find disfigurement as bitter a burden to bear as a ruined reputation. At the word "scar" his eyes glittered in the dark and sent a twinge of regret through me for my hasty retort to a stranger.

"No," he agreed then. "Till we meet again, Miss Dunne." And I turned and rustled back into the deserted drawing room, through the foyer and up the great curving stairs. The house was empty except for the muffled ring of cutlery and murmuring voices from the dining room and the soft echo of Hugh Davenant's shoes as he crossed the hard wooden floor to join them.

Once in my room I stood ripped and ragged at its center, a Cinderella returned to her ashes. Then I tore the finery off, carelessly, as one who never expects to don it again. My night-dress drifted over me like a shroud. Bed. I stood by it and knew sleep wouldn't come easily. No, there was something I must know. Something only she—without a lamp I felt my way into Elaine's chamber next door.

I had counted on moonlight to guide me, but what there was that night was ringed with clouds as curly and innocent as lamb's wool. From Elaine's window I watched the moon glow behind them like a candle through a milky globe. It was dark below, with only the treetops gleaming in the filtered illumination. I heard Elaine's steady, almost inaudible, breathing.

No, I couldn't sleep. For the moment I resented her. To sleep like that, like a babe, after all she'd been through—and I, bearing the burden of her misstep, I tossing upon a bed of needle-sharp regrets, upon a mattress of thorny rebellion against injustice, bound up in the bedsheets of my own nobility and delivered over to the slanderer.

"Elaine." It took my saying her name twice and shaking her to break through that heavy slumber.

"What?" she asked, unalarmed at being wakened in the dead of the night. She had no fear in her, that was her trouble.

"It's I, Elaine. Amberleigh. I—couldn't sleep. I want to know, I've got to know, truly I do, or there'll be no sleep for me ever. If I'm going to go down for it, and I don't mind, I don't wish to see you . . . Elaine, if I'm going to be blamed for it, I've a right, don't you see?"

"A right? What are you talking about—?"

"To know. Who. Who the—father—is. I can't imagine who you'd . . . who is he, Elaine, I've a right to the entire secret."

"Father? Amberleigh, is there something wrong with Father? Is he all right—?"

"Not *your* father, Elaine." I held her down, almost weeping in exasperation. "Your father's perfectly safe. No, it's the father of your baby, the little Michael. I feel I've got to know."

"My baby—I had a baby once, all wrapped in a long lace gown. But we gave it away when I got older. To someone in the village, I think. A little girl who didn't have a doll. That was before Devora came, of course. I called her Jonathena. If I'd had one later I wouldn't have named her after a boy."

I recognized Elaine's sweet reasonable tones of unreason. And sighed.

"Your baby, Elaine, the little one you cradled at Twin Beeches, don't you remember? I do hope you remember. If

124

you don't I might as well simply give up."

"Oh, don't give up, Amberleigh. One must never do that. You've had a hard life. Remember when your father, well, did that thing? And you wore my dress. I've other gowns if you wish to wear them. I'll help you always, Amberleigh. You are my true friend."

Again I sighed and sank back on my heels at her bedside.

"But, Amberleigh," she said then and there was something clear and cutting to her voice I'd never heard before. "You must never ask me to remember things I don't. Never."

I stood up and drew away from the fourposter. I didn't like the way the curtains leaned in towards me. My feet were cold. Of course I hadn't put on slippers. Her fire was no more than embers. It must be late. I should get back to my own warm bed. I was cold. I do not think I had ever been so cold before. I found my way to the door and cracked it open, so a shaft of hall light fell upon the room and sliced it like an apple.

"Good night, Amberleigh," said Elaine quietly from the dark side of the moon.

CHAPTER THIRTEEN

IN THE morning, my green velvet gown was lying where I had cast it off the night before—in a heap on the carpeting, some discarded shell whose owner had crawled out and left it behind as a benchmark.

So I had finally slept after all. There was no brightness billowing in at the window; it must be late.

I felt slightly ill, sated. I remembered my tears, the muffled sobs in the pillow. The many unfairnesses of my position, that I had enumerated over and over to myself. And I remembered the many imaginary conversations with Adrian.

"So you see, Adrian, I can't explain anything, but you have not understood..."

"I understand only too well, Miss Dunne..."

"Adrian, you must believe me, there is nothing for which I must apologize in my recent behaviour..."

"My dear Amberleigh, I have been a fool, forgive me..."

My dear Amberleigh indeed. No, it was all past undoing.

Should I even ever be free to explain my predicament to him, should he apologize manfully and follow it up by declaring his undying love, it was all too late. That icy snub last night, that calculated withdrawal belonged to no man to whom I had any business handing my heart. He was shallow and I had half known it. And still, still I was disconsolate.

By the time I'd dressed and applied a bracing dash of rose-water to my ravaged face, the clock confirmed my awakening guess—well past noon. I picked up the "braw green gown" Devlin Quade had taxed me for wearing. The velvet was mossy to my touch and lay across my hands like a living thing. Like a vivid green snake. There were said to be no snakes in Ireland. Except...

"Devora is a snake, Amberleigh." I heard Elaine's soft steady voice again. That day in the studio, Elaine had said that Devora had already bit me. And I'd thought she'd been wandering again! I flung the gown away and rushed into the hall, almost colliding with Cousin Norah.

"'Morning, Norah." I brushed by, eager not to be sucked into her maelstrom of enthusiasms, to avoid the whirlpools of her avid curiosity. In that bitter morning, I suspected that her intellectuality hid a major thirst for gossip. And I would be nectar for that yearning.

"Was it a nice party, Amberleigh?" she flung after me down the hall, but I was far enough away to ignore her.

I knocked boldly at Devora's door, knowing if I stemmed my impetus now, I'd fade back into my room and a refuge of helpless tears. There was something I had to know. If I were going to go down for it, I had a right to know why.

"Amberleigh. Come in. La, my dear, you look a sight. Oh, now that wasn't tactful of me. But I swear it takes a day for our heads to clear after a do like last night's.

"Norah says you weren't down for breakfast yet. And no supper last night. I distinctly remember remarking that you never did come in to supper. Lord Hugh thought you might have damaged your gown, but Sally Compton said she thought it looked perfectly ripping...ah, not amusing? I'm sorry you missed Adrian. He insisted on leaving the first thing this morning, said he had something vital in London, but then these men always do. And it does leave me a man short for the rest of the week, most inconsiderate of him. I shall have to fill in with Bobby Howard. Or possibly Hugh if I can cajole him into it.

"Well, sit, my dear, and don't look so absolutely...grim. What is it?"

Devora continued her elaborate toilet, all the while chattering to me as if we were simply discussing a lovely but rather late party in which we both had an equal interest. Something in the way she arched her eyebrow while she sketched it in with a pencil cut through any shyness I might have felt.

"It seems there's been a rather serious misapprehension, Lady St. Clare. People seem to believe that the holiday North was taken for my benefit."

"Well, let them. What does it matter if they think your health is fragile..."

"It's not a matter of that kind of health, Lady St. Clare. They seemed to have guessed it all, only they believe that I and not Elaine found it necessary to have a private confinement. I suppose they even think that's why I left America and came here."

"Frankly, I don't see why they should think either one of you was in the family way. There's no indiscretion on the Galway end—oh, my dear, no, and quite a few pounds it took to ensure that.

"If the blame has fallen on you, it's unfortunate, Amberleigh, but I really don't see what I can do about it. Save announce to the world Elaine's folly. Is that what you want? Because if you do, I not only won't do it, but I'll see to it that there is no question whatsoever about who went North for what reason."

She stopped rouging her cheeks with a hare's foot and regarded me calmly over that creature's severed limb. I adjusted my position on the rosepoint chair and thought how I should like to see her shaken for once.

"It's no surprise to you, is it, Lady St. Clare? I imagine it should have been obvious to me from the first. Elaine is the local girl, I the exile. No one would believe misconduct of Elaine, but a stranger—come from America, a girl nobody knows... why, I believe the entire invitation was a—a mask, for what was actually going on. You lured me here out of concern for Elaine and left me as a diversion for the local gossips."

"You have been well paid. You can leave. I'll even help you find another post, where no one need know what Glennverran country gossip says."

"But that sort of thing has a way of following one. And what of the people I know here, who think this of me, who believe..."

"Ah, Adrian, you mean? Yes, I think Adrian was a bit

disappointed, poor boy. But then, you never had any serious hopes there, did you, Amberleigh? Because really, he will marry some well-dowered girl of, forgive me, suitable family. Like Elaine. You should have know that."

"Perhaps. But if I had known everything I 'should have known,' I'd have been no use to you."

"Amberleigh, what can I say—you will have it that I'm some sort of schemer who tricked you here into, well, substituting for Elaine? How could I have guessed what people would think? How could I have planned it all? Really, you credit me with rather more brains than my most ardent beaux. If you feel you must vindicate yourself, tell your friends the truth. Tell them." Her clear eyes regarded me with absolutely no expression. Behind them, and in the tone of her voice, I knew that she had read her victim well. I could never tell anyone anything because I could never expose Elaine to what I faced now.

Devora laughed as she read my conclusion in my face.

"So serious, so somber, Amberleigh. Yes, we must find you a lively post near London where country concerns are soon forgotten—would you like that?"

"I believe it would be best for me to leave," I agreed stiffly. "I'll let you know when I can make plans." And I got up and left without another word. Her eyes didn't even follow me to the door. I could hear the snap of the brush through her thick brown hair before I'd even taken two steps away from her.

So that was how it was to be. Swept out the servants' entrance while no one was looking. Of course. The portrait, the long afternoons we spent smocked in the studio. Not merely to hide and divert Elaine, but to yoke me with her, to conceal me from those who would never believe that I was to have the child . . .

And worse. It was to be worse. It was to be Adrian forever scurrying to London in the first blush of morning. It was to be that man in the French windows last night saying, "Oh, it's you" in a way that meant only one thing. It was to be forever stripped of pretensions, of hopes for eluding the fate for which Father's death and Miss Meachum's ministrations had so perfectly prepared me. "Dunne, the Governess."

Back in my room, I hastily pulled out the heavy cream paper I used for stationery. It was unengraved. There was little point in blazoning it with an address when my own shifted so often. I immediately drafted a note to the Willoughbys, explaining that my position with the St. Clares was about to end and requesting a secondary reference from them. No need to tell that innocent Boston couple that they were to be my primary reference; I'd take no favours from Lady Devora St. Clare. I copied the letter in my best hand and ran down to leave it on the hall salver for Symes to have posted.

Halfway up the stairs I met Cousin Norah coming down, hugging the wall with her usual sidelong gait. Sometimes she reminded me of a crab, or a spider—with her lean sharp limbs and rounded body.

"Quite a party, wasn't it?" she said with an almost pretty smile. It occurred to me that Cousin Norah would not be so unattractive if she simply went about her toilette with a little care. I had seen her around the fringes of the room last evening, I recalled, done up in some strangely figured long skirt and clutching her shawl. I even recalled seeing Devlin dancing with her, but then he had a kind heart and perhaps a little too much punch, if truth be told, and I was not surprised to picture him having mercy on the woman. He had even had mercy for me.

"Yes, it was quite an affair," I said lightly, determined not to let the slightest remark become salt for my wounds.

"That was a pretty gown you wore," she said, almost shyly. "I didn't have anything suitable, so I made do with some cloth I'd gotten in India."

It was the first occasion I'd ever heard her take an interest in dress. She seemed to want to gossip with me about the affair, like two friends reliving an exciting evening. I might even have obliged her, save that last night was still too near a thing to me.

"It looked very nice," I lied with a cooler tone in my voice. But she missed my dismissal and her eyes narrowed as she leaned closer to me. I smelled the musty odor with which she always seemed permeated, as if she went to bed at night in a drawer wrapped in camphor.

"You did quite right," she whispered conspiratorially, with the ghost of an encouraging smile about her lips. "I like people who can face things out. No creeping around in corners. I can't tolerate people who won't come right out with it."

Something in the admiring way she looked at me, as if I were some kind of heroine for supposedly cutting across society's grain, sickened me. She was avid for my scandal; in some paradoxical way it elevated me in her eyes. But I did not care for the view.

"That's kind of you to say, Norah—well, I've got to get

129

along. I haven't reported to Elaine yet." I brushed by her and took the stairs with energy; it would not do to let her know that her remarks had disheartened me, had almost made her "defiant scoffer at convention" want to sink in a heap on the stairs and give up the charade.

CHAPTER FOURTEEN

> After the ball is over,
> After the night is done
> Many the heart that is aching,
> After the ball . . .

IT WAS a tune very popular in America during my stay. And its light little melody waltzed me mechanically through the week following the great Carnhaven Ball.

A malaise seemed to settle on the entire household after the frantic preparations for the festivity. Even Devora grew lazy and took to lounging over coffee in the morning room overlooking the terrace. The terrace became my bête noire. I avoided it. It had been a private stage for my own version of "Romeo and Juliet." It was there I'd met Adrian. There he'd plied me with his 'crostic mind and caustic sweet nothings.

What was the word he'd written once on my sketchpad? The strange soft syllables that he said I was? E-phem-er-al. That was it. I had run to the giant Unabridged in the library to decipher it later. Transitory. A Greek derivative meaning a transitory thing.

How right he had been. I had flitted from one continent to another, from a secure cocoon at home and at Miss Meachum's to an anchorless existence in a world that had no new niche to offer me. Moth. It was a good comparison. A literary comparison even Mr. Carstairs might appreciate wherever he had gone. An unfrilly creature, useful in its way to consume pests others find annoying. But a twilight thing. A creature, perhaps, drawn to flames. Adrian had burned for me. And now he was gone and I was left to fan the embers with my dull, duncoloured wings and hope for another flame.

Well, I wouldn't do it. My life was already spending its little span. I would be four-and-twenty in October. Was my life to be shadowed because a man I'd half-known wasn't worth my devotion had proved it? I would shake this humiliation, the deep conviction that if Adrian were not of his circle, his time, he might have dared risk more for me than a mild flirtation. There was Elaine still on the mend with whom to concern myself. And leaving. Leaving as soon as I saw her settled, as soon as I could. Starting a new life, moving—mothlike—to a new place—oh, the rumours would hound me. Devora had marked me for life when she cast her nets wide for a scapegoat and pulled me in. But in my position even that would fade. Nobody really cared that much about a governess' past if she seemed—tamed—at the moment.

I clung to the house in those weeks following the ball and thought these sober thoughts. I clung to Carnhaven like a marooned sailor to his raft. There were hunts those chill, grey-green days—days in which Carnhaven seemed like an image under the cold clear curve of a cloudy crystal ball. Sometimes I peered down from the second-storey windows on the mounted hunt party prancing in the yard. Neighbours, they were, who came to Carnhaven to ride the ridges and take the fences and pursue a living thing to its last panting stand before the pack. Sir George was out there on the pavement, tilting his stirrup cup to the sky, his face as flushed as his pinks—'D'ye ken Sir George at the break of day, d'ye ken Sir George in his coat so gay, d'ye ken Sir George, wi' his cup all raised, d'ye ken this is how he'll end his days?"

Elaine never rode, which gave me company of a sort for rattling around the house. Devora rode, though, looking city-smart in her black jacket and newly fashionable ankle-length skirt, her brown hair gathered up into a snood at the back of her long, supple neck. The neighbour, Davenant, would be there. He was barely recognizable from my windowed perch, but somehow I always managed to pick out the white of a scar, I thought. His high sleek horse of black often rubbed flanks with Devora's mannered bay. And the Squire was there, as lean and shrewd as Sir George was round and lazy. And two maiden ladies from a very old area family, their grizzled grey hair slopping out from under the brim of their moth-eaten derbies. But they were behind the huntsman and the hounds, those two, whenever the party started off. And Sir George declared at dinner that they were always there for the kill.

So I floated on the fringe of what passed for winter social life at Carnhaven. Once the Maxwells came up for some shooting and we played listless cards in the evenings together. But they reminded me of what I would not be reminded—sometimes I wanted to look beyond the Colonel's velvet-lapeled shoulder to search for someone suave and gilded against the mantle, cosseting a cordial.

I concentrated on winning the game at hand and forgot about looking for phantoms of the firelight.

But the letter. I awaited the letter. From America. The letter that would take me on now, to something—well, different. To freedom from Devora's interference. If only it would come, but I had to allow two months for the two slow Atlantic mail crossings. And more weeks, for Mrs. Willoughby to closet herself in her bed-sitting room and embark upon that most hated of chores—correspondence. Then, too, as weeks dragged on through days of sudden snowfall and as sudden melting followed by hard cold and then a respite, I had to remind myself that the Willoughbys had often talked of wintering in the South some time. Perhaps this was their year for the long-withheld plum, and my letter reclined on a silver salver in Boston, muffled by unanswered invitations and commercial circulars.

Patience. Elaine still seemed in need of support. I was there, perhaps that was enough for her. But as spring came, her restlessness grew green along with mine. We watched the brown recede and the great green mantle of moss and grass wax emerald and with it my restlessness to be off.

But as I faltered, in some strange way Elaine seemed to gather vitality. Winter waned into spring, and Elaine—like a child recovering from a fever—demanded entertainment.

"Amberleigh!" I recognized that petulant tone and controlled the irritation it raised in me of late. "I want to *do* something. You only sit with that frightful sketchbook on your lap and draw rowers on the lake. You shall get halfway to Africa in that book if you don't stop soon."

It was an unreasonably hot April day, ripe with sun.

"What should you like to do?" I closed the sketchbook quickly. I *had* had a penchant for lake scenes of late.

"If we had more we should be able to get up a game of croquet."

"Croquet? I haven't played for years! What about lawn tennis—isn't there a net we could use?"

"Oh, yes, but that's so active, Amberleigh. One gets so moist doing it. Besides, I don't think I should—" Elaine cast me a veiled glance and stood up. I had forgotten she might still feel too unwell to dart about the lawn and could have strangled myself for reminding her about the past.

"Very well. But we two can't just play. Whoever else can we get?"

Elaine thought a moment. "Symes?" She giggled maliciously. "I should love to see Symes roqueted halfway to the Hebrides. It would be fun to make him play."

"We can't ask him to do it, though you're right, I'd like to see him chasing balls across the lawn. Look, there's Devlin, coming along on his bicycle. I've hardly seen him all winter. He'll play with us."

Elaine put her hand up to her eyes to pick out the small figure peddling along the service road, probably on his way to pay court to Mrs. Featherstone, who kept him well-fed, I suspected, in return for his keeping her well-flattered. They both had a special way of basting things—one with sauce and one with sauciness.

"All right," said Elaine suddenly, as if she'd just made a major decision instead of selected a playing partner. I had to run across half the yard to get within hailing distance. Devlin cast a reluctant eye kitchenward, but agreeably enough dismounted his machine and, walking beside it, came over with me to Elaine.

"Devora would have your head if she saw you running that thing over Carnhaven lawn." The wheels left their unmistakable ruts along the path of shortly clipped grass.

"Devora never gets angry with me." Devlin grinned. "Though she should."

"I think you could bridle a banshee, Devlin Quade, if you wanted to."

"I haven't had much luck with you," he retorted. "Still wearing your Orangeman's colours and complacent about it."

"One man's meat may be another man's poison," I replied rather unoriginally.

"It's when all the meat is rank you'll have people turning their plates back at you, though," he said. I avoided pursuing the subject. These talks of ours never moved either of us a centimeter.

Elaine had already sent a gardener's boy to look up the croquet set. The three of us adjourned to a long level lawn near the boxwood maze. The boy was already pounding down the wickets. It was to be an awesome field of play, with the boxwood on one side as a natural boundary and the beginning of the wild garden on the other.

"We're odd," I said suddenly.

"So observant of you," said Devlin.

"No"—I groaned—"I mean we can hardly play partners with three. Unless one of us switches from side to side. I wish we had a full set." I took an exploratory swing with my mallet at one of the bright balls. It rolled smartly across the turf and into the boxwood hedge.

"Now you've done it, Amberleigh." Elaine laughed. "If you strike like that it won't matter how many play, we shall soon be out of balls to play with."

But my ball was not forever lost. It came docilely out of the hedge in the hand of a man who'd been taking a turn with Devora in the maze.

"May I return this to the owner of the mighty mallet?" he enquired, moving towards Devlin.

"It's mine," I was forced to confess, feeling overheated and as unladylike as a pugilist. He dropped it into my hand, looking as if he didn't quite believe I had sent it so far from home.

"Lord Hugh and Devora can play!" said Elaine so quickly and so inspiredly that there was no way for anyone to tastefully withdraw, not even Devora. She shifted her sunshade restlessly and eyed her delicate lace dress dubiously.

"Unlike these girls, I'm hardly dressed for exertion..."
Lord Hugh had picked up a mallet and was sighting down the handle for warpage. "I haven't played in years," he remarked. That was enough for Devora. Any man in her field of interest expressing one of his own would be steadfastly obliged if she could help it.

Devlin tossed off his worn tweed jacket and we chose out colours. I got red, Elaine yellow, Devora green, Lord Hugh orange and Devlin was left to take the blue. "That's auspicious," he noted. "The colours have fallen out most appropriately."

"I rather thought you fancied the green yourself, Quade," said Lord Hugh, folding his light jacket meticulously over the empty carrier.

"That I do, that I do. And the only greater pleasure I take in it is to see a lady benefitting from it." And he bowed to Devora but he looked at me with his blue eyes twinkling.

"How are we going to play this?" asked Elaine. "We're still odd. We're only five. Unless someone should sit out ... we can't have three and two to a side."

"I'm ambidextrous, I'll trade off," Devlin volunteered.

"Follow the biblical advice to not let your left hand know what your right hand is doing, eh, Quade?" Lord Hugh was

134

casually swinging a mallet, grazing the short grass with a sharp slice.

Devlin flushed a bit and seemed about to answer, but Elaine blurted out, oblivious to the tension forming on the lawn— "Oh, don't talk circles! Let's simply settle it and play."

"I don't object to playing on a side of two," said Lord Hugh. "You three play as a side and Devora and I'll do the best we can."

The three of us exchanged glances, clearly thinking the same thing. Devora could as likely throw a barn down a well as send a ball though a wicket. Lord Hugh would be as good as playing single-handed against all three of us. Elaine, as I recalled, swung an indifferent mallet. But I had been rather good at it and I didn't intend to go bad now.

Devora was first and made Lord Hugh hold her sunshade over her while she endeavoured to hit the pole and make ready for going through the first pair of wickets.

"There!" she squealed. "I've missed the pole and shall have to come back. This is the most—annoying—diversion."

I was next and skimmed through the double hoop with finesse and the luxury of a look at Devora, my confidence high with the lucky beginning. I then cleared the first single hoop, accompanied by a hoot of surprise and admiration from Devlin, which tribute I accepted with a mallet wave. My next shot was a long, hard drive to the middle hoop. I calculated that if the ground lay as it looked to, if my arms were still as strong as at Miss Meachum's, and if luck rode my shoulder, I could get through in one stroke. I took a position perfectly behind where I wished to go and swung the mallet, gentlemen's style, directly in front of me. The ball gave a tremendous thwunk and began rolling merrily away, its bright red wobble a thing of gaiety on the green lawn.

But it began slowing sooner than I expected; the course was rougher than I had known. The ball barely brushed by the side of the wicket and came to rest just past it. We all strolled over to judge its lie, gathering round it as if it were a treasure someone had unearthed.

"It's through!" That was Devlin, sounding triumphant.

"Is it?" Devora, sounding dubious.

"Of course it is!" Elaine, mildly rebellious.

"Good." Lord Hugh, being authoritative.

"May I take my next shot?" I asked demurely, waltzing up to the ball with an appalling satisfaction at so small a triumph. Pride went, for my swing caught the ball on the side instead of square and it wobbled off for a few feet before stopping.

Lord Hugh returned the sunshade to Devora gravely, hit his orange sharply at the mallet, tunnelled through the two wickets and took two long strokes towards the first hoop. He went through on the second shot and advanced to the next, passing my red. The rest of us waited in a fever of impatience; we might all well be left at the gate without a race to run.

But he stalled at the next wicket, landing awkwardly to the side of the wood, unable to get through in one clean sweep.

Elaine started out next and surprisingly strongly. She overshot the first hoop but came back in good position. Devlin was last. I could see the glint in his blue eyes even from down the field as he smartly rapped the pole, pulled through the double hoops, made the first single wire and elected to position himself for the middle wicket.

Devora was forced to retreat back to the pole for her next try and leave the rest of us arrayed at our respective wickets. Lord Hugh was too far down field to be called upon to hold her parasol. She sullenly set it on the ground before picking up her mallet. This time she missed the pole by a good six inches.

"I shan't even have this part over and you'll all be coming back," she wailed helplessly. I was sure if a gentleman had offered to show her the rudiments of the game she would be willing to learn. But the gentlemen here were intently surveying the greensward and squinting their eyes at the next wicket. And I had a chance of going ahead of them all.

I hit my ball cleanly through the next wicket, then stroked mightily to set it in position for a straight try at the double hoops at the course's end. It rolled beautifully into perfect position and I couldn't resist a triumphant gaze at my competition trailing behind me.

Lord Hugh smiled tightly at me down field, picked up his mallet and studied the wicket closely. It was an impossible shot. I was certain he'd miss it and then my next threat would be Devlin, still three turns away. But Lord Hugh tapped his orange ball lightly and it skimmed the wire, stopping just through the wicket by a few inches. Far enough that this time there was no rush to determine its lie. It was still a long drive to the next hoop and the angle was impossible. I waited patiently by my ball.

Suddenly the orange came bowling across the green towards me at such a clip that I jumped back a good foot to evade it.

But it rolled to a stop sooner than it seemed—again the ground doing its part to confuse the game—and stopped with the slightest kiss of a click directly upon my ball.

"Something wrong, Miss Dunne?" Lord Hugh asked amiably as he ambled over to check his ball. I tried to look unconcerned.

"Oh, Amberleigh, he'll roquet you for certain," said Elaine, peering at the two balls lying cradled in the same hollow of grass. I wished she hadn't mentioned that he had the option to send my ball away; perhaps it hadn't occurred to him. But he put one expensively shod foot atop his orange ball, saying— "Red and orange don't quite go together well, do they?"—and rammed his mallet into the ball with a knock that started the birds out of the boxwood behind us. My red ball careened over the ground like the flash of a fox tail before the hounds, rolling out of sight in the underbrush.

"It's over the line, it's over the line!" screamed Elaine, openly jubilant. "You forfeit your turn, you forfeit it!" Lord Hugh looked a bit chagrined; he'd merely meant to put me out of the game a turn. Now he was mired almost as deeply as I, stalled like a beached whale.

Elaine danced back to take her turn, went through the middle hoop but overshot the critical wicket and came to rest near Lord Hugh's becalmed orange ball. Devlin took up his mallet with a determined air and a wicked gleam in his eyes. It was child's play to put him through; he'd stopped right where he ought to have the previous play. Once through, Devlin studied the field with great deliberation, swung his mallet thoughtfully, then struck the blue ball with a certain precise power that sent it flawlessly to pair with the orange. Without a pause he held his sturdy brogue down on the blue ball and sent the orange caroming to blazes and the boundary. It stopped just inside the natural line of lawn that separated croquet field from woodland.

"That gives me two turns, I believe," Devlin said, clipping his ball handily back towards the wicket, whisking through and on his way to the double hoop at the midpoint. I traipsed to the border to find my ball much more gracefully than I would have a moment earlier, for I'd seen Devlin wink at me as he bent to go through the wicket and I'd rather have him winning than Lord Hugh.

Lord Hugh had gone to retrieve his ball as well and found it easily placed. Mine was not so evident.

"Do you recall exactly where you dispatched my ball?" I

finally enquired, being tired of fighting underbrush and gnats in the shadow of the woods. He took my implication and trotted over to search for it.

"I don't actually enjoy roqueting people, you know."

"Why ever not, it's part of the game," I answered, swearing to myself that I'd send his orange to Hades and back should I get the opportunity.

"I can see why you'd say that. You play to win, Miss Dunne." He used the word "Miss" with a certain disinclination, as if it offended his sensibilities to so address one of whom he knew what he thought he did.

"Doesn't everybody?"

"It rather depends on the game, don't you think?"

"No. There's only one set of rules and either one does everything by them or one must reconcile oneself to being— disqualified."

"Oh, I can't imagine you qualifying for disqualification under any circumstance," he noted obliquely, turning up my ball in a pile of pine needles. "One of the benefits of being a martyr," he added, handing it to me, "is that *you* are allowed to place it a yard in and to your liking. *I* shall have play mine from the spot to which young Quade conveyed it."

I took my red ball with little pleasure. Even spotting it as advantageously as possible it was a long drive. Devlin was exactly opposite me already. Even Elaine was on the halfway post. But I gave it all the impetus I could and it cracked across the lawn, putting me a turn away from finally making the wicket and moving ahead. The orange came cracking towards me again, this time stopping discreetly away. We ran through the order once more, Devora bringing up the rear with less and less grace.

I easily passed Elaine, with Lord Hugh hot upon my mallet swing, and finally caught up Devlin, who was making for the goal with all possible haste. We paired off on the final wicket before goal, a tacit agreement in our eyes to keep Lord Hugh, sole flagbearer for his "side," in abeyance. But the orange clung to us as the moon circles the earth; this time it silently rolled up and embraced the blue. Lord Hugh sauntered up without looking at either of us and sent Devlin and his ball off to the edge of the boxwood, but within bounds. He could have as easily roqueted me again. I don't know whether his sense of gentlemanliness held him back or whether he merely had diagnosed Devlin as a greater threat.

"You play to win," I noted with some irony as he addressed himself to his ball while Devlin went to retrieve his vanquished colours.

"Imitation is the sincerest form of flattery," he reminded me. I couldn't discern whether he meant that he was imitating my philosophy for winning or my mimicking of his earlier words. But it was with no mere imitation of skill that he swung through the hoop in one stroke and positioned himself perfectly for a straight try at the pole.

I brushed my hands lightly on my dark wool skirt, hot for such a day but excellent for absorbing fears. Going through was child's play and I hit the ball hard enough so I should be closer to the double arches that stood between me and victory. The angle was sharp. I thought that from where my ball had landed I could make one hoop and then come back for the second of the pair.

But the bright orange globe lay temptingly near on the grass. It was a shorter, a straighter shot. I would dearly love to spin my ball up to Lord Hugh's and give him a roquet he would remember. Save that I had never been too skilled at roquet, at sending my opponent's ball to blue blazes. Whether it was a soft heart or the soft shoes that women wore that didn't give them enough purchase on the ball, I didn't know. Then, too, if I went for the orange and missed, I'd be a perfect victim. He could tap me at his leisure, gain two strokes for it and win without a whimper.

I picked up the mallet, noticing then that everyone had gathered round to watch, aware that here the game was decided. Lord Hugh was more aloof than them all, indeed, though his fate rode on my mallet swing. I recalled the tone of his voice when he had said, "It's you," the night of the ball, lifted my mallet and swung it briskly—my eye burning into the hoop for which I aimed. The red ball rolled gracefully along and through the first hoop, stopping a bit farther past it than I'd planned. It would take another narrow shot through an angled hoop to stay in this game.

I took the shot carefully, but the ball ticked off the wire and stopped, lolling into place in the no-man's-land between the two wires. Lord Hugh advanced to his orange and sent it thundering truly past my hampered red to thwack the post and end the competition.

"Hugh! That was well played. You must show me how to do it so cleverly."

"You have someone closer to home who could show you a swing or two," he commented, retrieving his coat and donning it with some relief.

"Amberleigh? Well, one never knows what talents our dear Miss Meachum imparted to her charges, but I'm sure croquet wasn't meant to be among them. It's such work! But I wouldn't mind learning those clever little taps one gives the ball. It reminds one of billiards without all the cigar smoke."

Devlin came trudging up to deposit his ball.

"Ye'll be needin' more, I'm afraid. Fairly cracked this one, m'Lord," he said, facing Lord Hugh with an expression that meant more than his words.

"Perhaps I don't know my own strength," Lord Hugh replied, turning the chipped blue ball slowly in his fingers.

"If you don't, there's others as would care to know," said Devlin levelly.

"We shall have to have another game then," said Lord Hugh, tossing the ball suddenly to Devlin. He caught it and a white smile flashed across his country-tanned young face. "Aye, m'Lord," Devlin said, with the brogue mimicking the voices of the field men who still pulled their forelocks to the master.

Lord Hugh gathered up Devora and her parasol and they retreated to the house for tea, leaving the three of us hot and dusty and somehow left out of things.

CHAPTER FIFTEEN

ELAINE SEEMED restless again.

"I'm going to lie down, Amberleigh," she said finally, keeping her grey eyes on the ground as if she'd lost something there. "I'll see you later."

Devlin seemed about to say something, but Elaine's fugitive glance caught his eyes as she turned away. He stopped abruptly. She ran up the lawn like a startled fawn while Devlin and I stared silently after her.

"Madam, will you walk?" he said then. I couldn't think of a good reason for refusing, except perhaps Devora's watching eyes from the terrace, where I could see two tiny figures fluttering now and again like white moths.

We started along the border to the woods.

"Devlin!" He laughed as I clutched his arm at the sight of a lean grey shadow that detached itself from a beech stand to lope towards us.

"Only Boru. Look at the beast loll out his long red tongue. You wouldn't know he had a tooth in his head."

The huge dog ambled up to Devlin and sat before him, leaning his shaggy head adoringly along Devlin's hip. I tried a tentative pat on the brute's head. He just tolerated such intimacy.

"How long had he been there, Devlin?"

"All the afternoon. These beasts have more sense than to spend unguarded afternoons following coloured balls around the ground in the noonday sun. Only mad dogs and Englishmen. Boru's not mad. Only enough to tear His Lordship limb from limb if he'd won too handily."

"You don't like Lord Hugh."

Devlin shrugged. "He's an Englishman."

"So am I."

"Not at all. You merely think you are. But the Almighty doesn't shower those snaky green eyes and that burnin' bush of a head on those too dull-witted to recognize their motherland when they see it."

"They're closer to blue," I snapped.

"Sometimes," said Devlin, leaning to peer under my low-ered lids, "but right now there's a Galway Bay green storm blowing up. It's not my comparin' you to a snake that's set you off? They're said to be very wise creatures. Perhaps that's why we're still yoked to the Orange; all our wisdom was driven out with the snakes by St. Pat's rod."

"I do object to your saying such nonsense, Devlin. You seem bound to slather the—blarney, I've heard the stableboys call it—on the nearest possible object. And you're bent on finding everything about me Irish or politically significant. The Vikings had red hair as well as the Celts, you know. Perhaps I'm the long-lost great-great-granddaughter of Eric the Red. Should I then move to Norway and start a revolution?"

"The Vikings. Now there was a bloody lot. Puttin' the coasts to blood and fire. Aye, red was a fine banner for 'em. And it'll serve us well before we're done." His voice sounded an ancient hostility that reminded me of heads on pikes and other eldritch horrors. I was sorry I'd mentioned anything so warlike as Norsemen.

"What of Elaine?" I asked more lightly. "She is English and

141

yet you like her. You do, don't you?"

He turned his blazing eyes fully upon me with a very curious look; it seemed to shiver through me. He frowned.

"Elaine," he said slowly. "The little heiress. Yes, I like her. But I'd keep my eyes to her, if you're her friend. There's a deep trouble in her."

We walked silently for a moment. Then Devlin went on, almost as if chanting an old tale of the sea or the fairies.

"We were friends, as true friends as the young lady and lord of the manor can be with a tenant's son, Jason, Elaine and I, and it might surprise you to learn how the young ones make friends in this auld land . . . Then Jason was gone and the candle went out. Elaine was off to her school and I to mine. The St. Clares insisted, or rather Her Ladyship did. I was the new bride's first act of village charity. And the last. Perhaps I turned out badly. It's as well. Trinity wasn't for me. It was cruelty rather than kindness to send me there—luckily I'd a thick Irish skin and enough wit to keep me warm those years—

"When I came back to Glennverran, Elaine was already in London, playin' the debutante. Going through her 'Season,' like a horse through the show ring. She was always too fine for that, too temperamental for the bit. I knew it'd show up sooner or later."

"Sometimes I don't know what to make of her, Devlin," I confessed. "Sometimes she even frightens me and I feel so at a loss—"

He nodded, a gust of wind smoothing back his rough hair and making him look older, more serious, like a churchyard brass of a young dead knight.

"Elaine." Devlin sighed. "First Jason gone. And now Elaine as good as. But she was never one meant to lie down in Labasheeda."

"Laba——what?" I'm afraid I looked puzzled again, for Devlin's serious face suddenly widened into a grin.

"La-be-shee-da. A place right here in County Clare. 'Bed of silk,' it translates to. She was never one born to lie on silk, her way was briars through and through." His blue eyes brimmed into my bewildered ones. He put out his hand and tousled the hair on my head as if I were Boru. "But, come along, you've promised to have a go at my machine. What better time than now?" He was not-so-subtly leading me back to the infernal thing, leaning perilously against a sturdy oak trunk.

"Devlin, no! I'm not dressed for it—"

"You're fine. Sure, you've spent half the afternoon swelterin' on the lawn—a turn in the shade couldn't do yer dressin' more harm."

He lifted the bicycle away from the tree and took a quick run down the drive that circled off towards the house. "See. There's no more to it than ridin' a mare. Or old Boru here."

I looked dubiously at our shaggy shadow. No, I wouldn't care to sit his broad grey back, though I guessed he could nearly support me. "I don't care for horses that much, Devlin, and ride them only when I must. But, all right. You probably think I can't do it. Hand me the machine . . . oh, it's heavier than it looks. And what do I do with my skirts, pray? No, I don't want to hear—I'll manage it."

I contrived to mount the thing, my petticoats caught up in the middle and flowing awkwardly to either side. "Now, I merely keep my feet moving up and down on these things . . ."

"Pedals. And you steer with the handles. You've got to move the wheel a bit from side to side or over ye'll go like a turnip cart."

"A lovely thought, Devlin. I can't get hurt, can I?"

"No, no, I've never seen anyone do more than scrape a knee—but wi' those petticoats that seems a remote possibility. I'd better walk along with you for now—"

With a last silent hope that disaster didn't attend me, I pressed down on the footpedals and felt the bicycle lurch into motion . . .

"Don't stop now! Keep peddling, I'm holding it up but you've got to keep the blamed thing movin' . . ." The front wheel veered wildly from side to side despite Devlin's efforts to steady it. I realized with a twist of fear that if getting on with grace were difficult, getting off at all would be more like disgrace.

"I can't do it, I can't. Stop! Devlin, let me off—"

"But you're doin' it. Look, I'm only balancin' you now. You'll get the feel of it." The wheel trembled back and forth abruptly under my hands, bobbling brutally when the tyre hit a stone in the road. I found myself moving along rather rhythmically now; then grasped the fact that Devlin had drifted behind me.

"Devlin," I shouted, turning my head to see him. The wheel turned with my look and I felt the whole world shift violently to the side—the bicycle spun away from me and we both landed lopsidedly on the dusty road. One of the wheels turned still. I was shocked for a moment, and felt the most demanding urge to bawl since I'd cracked my head on the dark back stairs in Eaton Square. Mrs. Bowers had given me tartlets and pudding for days to make up for my spill. Now all I got was Devlin rushing up, his face torn between concern and laughter.

"St. Ambrose protect us! Lord, Amberleigh, you're a fantastical sight! But are you all right?"

"Ye-es," I said, biting back my childish impulses. "No, I don't want to get up for a moment. I want to make certain I'm still all here." Devlin's blue eyes held mine, probing for signs of mortal wounding, then the laughter began pouring out of his eyes and mouth.

"Ye should have seen yourself—like a cloud in collision with a flyin' machine. Poof! Ye must have gone five feet in the air. But you're all right now? You're not angry?" He picked me up, dusted me off and squeezed my reluctant shoulders. I was indeed angry and couldn't decide whether Devlin or his machine deserved my wrath more. "I suppose you'll never be within five miles of such a contraption again," said Devlin matter-of-factly.

It was that assumption that settled me.

"Why not, pray? I'll have another try at it right now if your filthy machine has survived the dust-up."

Devlin seemed surprised, but he righted the thing and spun the wheels mysteriously a few times while making vague noises. Finally he announced it satisfactory. I straddled the thing with purpose, perched once again on the uncomfortable leather seat and we started off down the lane at a wobbly rate. This time I seemed to catch the rhythm of it more quickly and when Devlin peeled off I didn't turn so much as an eyelash towards him. The little machine spun merrily down the road. I found a carriage-wheel rut and kept to it. The going was getting smoother.

"But how do I stop?" I shouted back at Devlin as a gruesome thought occurred to me.

"The hand brakes, squeeze them to the handles," he yelled back.

I tried it and the bicycle slowed as obediently as Lady Jane to a pull on the rein. It was great fun, there was a feeling of flying and freedom to the wind riffling my hair.

"Make a circle," instructed Devlin, his voice a way off by now.

"How?"

"Turn the wheel to the left slowly but steadily till you're turned."

144

I very nearly went over again but after tracing an ungainly orbit on the road I was faced once more towards Carnhaven and Devlin loping along the lane after me. I was surprised at how far I'd come. I started back, spying the small black bulk of an open carriage moving towards me. Devora out for a turn with her beau probably. It was unnerving to have something coming at one, to have to peddle into the face of it. But I kept my eyes to the road and the wheel steady.

Devora was driving a new pair of chestnut mares. I remembered then the rig she'd been so excited about—a pretty little trimly painted rig with reins like ribbons and two dainty horses to pull it with.

I was aware of the horses' snappy rhythm, the way their delicate ankles flicked the road dust behind them like a cat walking through milk. Devora sat as delicately on the leather seat, playing with the fluttering reins. Lord Hugh lounged beside her with the air of a lazy panther watching a kitten frolic.

I kept my feet moving and my eyes mostly to the road. Devlin was coming abreast on the road's other side, but the carriage passed between us first. It was then that the nearest chestnut lifted her muscled neck and rolled one eye at me. The other broke stride and they brushed polished bellies and made guttural whinnies. My own mechanical steed began wavering. One of the horses lifted its forelegs a bit in a halfhearted rear; enough to send me wholeheartedly steering away from the trouble. The tyre veered towards the grassy roadside, then down a small incline.

"Jump off, jump off, Amberleigh!" cried Devlin from somewhere behind me. I heard a woman's shriek and let the machine run on without me. There was a rip of petticoat and a jarring crash to the ground. I wasn't too dazed this time to see Devlin's bicycle course straight for a venerable oak and crumple at its feet.

There was no laughter in Devlin's eyes now as he rushed over to me.

"Saints preserve us, Amberleigh, are ye still breathin'?"

I must have been breathing, for I don't think my heart would have pounded so without it. Devlin knelt by me and pulled me up to a sitting position. "Did you hurt your hands?" he asked, checking them finger by finger ... "your head?"

"I'm quite all right, Devlin. Truly I am. But your bicycle is what you should inspect. I don't think it'll take a turn again without great persuading." My voice was breathless, shaking with something close to laughter but very different from it.

"Damn the bicycle," said Devlin, looking so alarmed I nearly forgot the waves of fear smashing into my stomach.

"No, go and fetch the thing or you're bound to lose something vital from it. And leave me to retrieve my own scattered parts." I began searching the ground for my vanished hairpins and the white trail of my vanquished petticoats.

Lord Hugh stood in the shade above on the crest of the road and surveyed the scene.

"Can she stand up?" he asked. Devlin's hand was on my elbow and I shook it loose.

"Of course I can," I said, lurching to my feet with the customary dignity and grace I had displayed in the last half an hour. My ravaged petticoat dust ruffle dipped round my feet like a flag of surrender, my hair lay across my neck in total disarray. I was hot and cold with fear at the same time. And up on the road, Devora waited tight-lipped while the chestnuts sidestepped impatiently.

Devlin began brushing me off, though what good it did when I was hair to foot dust and grass I don't know.

"Leave me be!" I said pettishly, startled by the fervour in my own voice. Devlin was startled, too. For he dropped back like a licked puppy and watched me from lowered lids. I was hot and humiliated. Devora would crab at me about my appearance and cluck in that light slashing voice of hers and Lord Hugh would look down on me in that lordly way of his . . . Devlin still lingered, not turned aside to attend to the bicycle, but held back on an invisible leash. I suddenly realized that at least a portion of my discomfiture before the polished pair from the House—and I wasn't thinking of the horses—was being found so friendly with a landless Irish lad. I had always pretended to more.

I held out my hand to Devlin. "But if you'd help me up the hill I'd be most grateful." He wagged to my side like Boru, drawing me up the incline as if I were a teacup.

Devora waited, still standing in the new rig, her parasol lolling over her shoulder in a drunken sort of way. Her face was white as newly tatted lace and somehow as crackled. There were narrow white lines of tension along the furrow between her eyebrows—her only concession to wrinkling—and along two new lines from her nose to her mouth.

"I won't have it! You're not to—to mount that foul contraption ever again. Do you understand me? I won't have it." The parasol ruffle trembled with her words.

"Lady St. Clare, 'tis not Amberleigh's fault, 'twas my machine did the damage..."

"Amberleigh, is it?" Her white words veered to lash Devlin's half-formed defence of me. "Perhaps you're in the market for a cast-off companion, young man." Devora's thin pale hands spun the sunshade on her shoulder, the gay pattern glazed her face with carnival colours there in the hot road. Devlin's mouth moved but for once a retort didn't pass his lips.

"It's hardly a case for the Assizes, Devora," interjected Lord Hugh, "a mere country collision. I'm sure the girl meant no harm—"

"I could have been killed. Killed. It's happened before. The reins were like cobwebs, I couldn't hold them—we could have all been killed. You're not to ride that thing again, Amberleigh. Not if you wish to call Carnhaven home. That's all."

She sat stiffly. Hugh Davenant shrugged and exchanged a glance with Devlin, then mounted the carriage and took the driver's seat. The pair started out smartly, long past the panic that had been my downfall, and turned round in the road. The carriage wheels creaked and rolled past us again, back to the House. Soon the outfit was a small black speck in the distance again.

"She's as frustrated as a horsefly in a henhouse," said Devlin, "itching for flesh to sting and naught but feathers before her."

"Yes," I said, turning because I feared I was going to cry and didn't want him to see. I picked my way down the slope to the ruins of his magnificent flying machine. At least it had sent me flying. And almost packing.

"She didn't mean it, she's all pepper and very little salt. So take her with a grain of it."

"She meant the other things she said—" My throat tautened and I decided further discussions of the scene were the last thing I wanted. "Can you salvage anything?"

"That I don't know. And won't till I've had some of the lads take a look at it. I'm not much for keepin' the thing hummin', you know. Never had a head for nuts and bolts." Devlin sighed and idly picked up a spare portion of his once-whole bicycle.

"I feel almost a murderer." I ruefully overlooked the ruin I'd caused.

"Oh, for God's sake, Amberleigh. And all the saints, too, if you're going to look at me that way for a little name-takin' in vain. She'll settle. And it wasn't your fault. It's hers for

147

playin' at horsewoman, if you want my opinion. If Davenant had been handling the reins it would have never happened. Look, I'll walk you back to the house and you have a rest or whatever it is you ladies do when you've had a turn, and everybody'll have forgotten it by suppertime."

"And would one of your rebel Irish ladies take a rest after she'd had a turn?"

"I'm sure of it." He smiled.

We strolled up the lawn, arm in arm, and for once I felt the need of leaning on someone. I did need a rest. I felt I'd escaped two very near things that afternoon and I wanted to put them behind me.

We were veering to go around to the house's rear when I felt an urgent sense of surveillance. I turned to run my eyes back down the road—deserted and still as if no foot or hoof had ever crossed it. I glanced at the terrace—quiet, without a flutter of curtain or sleeve. My eyes arrowed upwards for some reason, to a strange reflection against one of the second-floor windows. A pattern in the mullion, like leaves casting light and shadow on the glass. But there were no trees there to create the illusion. Before my gaze, the anomaly resolved into a chalk-white face hollowed here and there for features—like the moon's visage on a clear night. Like a death's head. I blinked to see better and the vision melted from my sight, leaving only the black blank stare of a vacant window.

"Amberleigh?" Devlin's voice was so concerned that the window apparition sank into the deep blue pool of his eyes as I turned to him.

"It's all right," I said, eager to dispel any lingering worry.

He slipped my hand out of his arm and patted it. "Don't dream of bicycles," he said before taking his way, on foot, down the road.

But I did. And the woman who rode it had a white, pinched face and a tall pointed hat. She rode like the wind and she promised to make me pay.

CHAPTER SIXTEEN

THE SUN was just slanting across the dew-drenched turf and the birds were up and about with their early-morning chatter. For the first time since I had arrived at Carnhaven, I was off doing something *I* wanted to do for no other reason than I wanted to do it. I felt useful, at least to myself, even adventuresome. I'd always wanted to try watercolour from life—a challenge beyond the silly drawing-room pastel imaginings we were taught in school. And now I had accepted that challenge, forced myself awake at an untoward hour, armed myself with sketchpad, paints and brushes and was swinging down the little dirt lane by the estate's cow pastures. The air was mortal chilly, but my light wool-plaid shawl—a gift from one of the Willoughbys' Canadian jaunts—kept the Irish air out. The pale morning sunlight lit the landscape with a lemon-yellow freshness. The tempers and temperament and tantrums of the last few days seemed rinsed away.

The object of my outing was what my overactive imagination had dubbed the "Fairy Circle" from the first time I had seen it during one of my rambles with Elaine. It was a clearing off the road with an eminently suitable truncated log for a seat and a tall ancient-looking pine set somewhat into the clearing to tower over the firs around it. I had been fascinated by this tree and its red-brown bark. Its height was stunning, almost preternatural. I fancied that some hoary Druid, last remnant of a moribund dynasty, had changed himself by sorcery into this tree to watch the modern world cut its roads and carry on its petty commerce before it. And all the while the wise old tree reserved judgement for a time when it would rule once more. A fancy fit for the schoolroom, yes. But mine own. I had enquired about the tree several times—of Elaine, Devlin, even the locals—no one seemed to know or care which one I meant, which was strange, for one would think such an outstanding growth would surely be a local monument.

All these ruminations played round in my head as I set to washing bands of colour on my pristine white pad. Lay in sky blue first, then ground. I slashed in a bold vertical for my tree trunk, then looked at the hodge-podge flowing from my brush. Watercolour was not as easy as the result looked. My sky blue and grass green flowed into each other at the horizon line and merged into a dirty blue thundercloud shade, hardly an accurate reflection of the glorious day a-dawning.

I sighed and gazed around the clearing with a critical eye. Sketching was one thing. It would be easy for me to charcoal in the undergrowth, the rough barks, even the delicate grass stalks. But how was one to make these shapeless blobs of colour look anything like the real scene? Why, that flash of white there—I couldn't even tell if it were a wildflower or a giant mushroom or... I walked over in no good temper for an artist's eye view of the thing.

But it wasn't a natural phenomenon after all. It was a man's hand. And from the way the fingers curled, I knew instinctively that there was something very wrong with the man behind it, his body half hidden by the undergrowth.

There was a strange clutching in my stomach as I delicately parted the branches for a closer look. He was lying face down, dressed in a dark sweater and trousers. I touched his hand and found it still warm. In a moment I'd run back to the log to fetch the covered jar Mrs. Featherstone had given me for carrying water. I had some idea of bringing him to consciousness, if he were still alive, with a painting rag dipped in water.

But when I turned him over, taking both arms to shift the dead weight, two things stunned me into inaction—the bloody stain that saturated his sweater front and the fact that it was Devlin Quade.

It was infinitely worse now that I knew him. It if had been a stranger, I wouldn't have been so panicky. I drew back in a queasy sort of panic, afraid to touch him, terrified that he might die even as I sat there helpless on my heels. "Oh, my God," I said softly and deliberately under my breath, and the measure of saying something so forbidden as taking the Lord's name in vain was strangely reassuring.

"Think," I ordered myself, breathing unsteadily into the hands that I had clapped over my mouth. The wound. Gunshot? Must be. Devlin Quade. Gunshot wound. Oh, Devlin... Think. My clearing. Dawn. Yes, it must be something to do with the underground, with the United Irish. British bullet? Irish bullet? Doesn't matter. Not near his heart. Stomach wound. Bad? Where did I read... Kipling?... Pressure. Apply pressure. It had been done to me as a child, I had used it to stop the small bleedings my charges had incurred. I began ripping the fine Canadian shawl into wide strips, until my fingers burned from the friction as I strained to part well-woven wool from wool. Once knotted, I labouriously wound my make-do bandage around Devlin's chest, and that done, sat back on my heels again and tried to think clearly once more.

Absently, I followed my first impulse and dabbed at his forehead with my wet rag, not expecting any response. But his eyelids fluttered and I saw a pale glimmer of the famous blue Quade eyes. I doubt he even focused on me, or that he even knew where he was. His face contorted with effort and he whispered in a horrible hoarse way—"They're coming..." Then he was unconscious again and I was left racking my brains.

"Oh, Devlin," I said almost angrily, looking down at his pale face and chewing brutally on my thumbnail. "They're coming," he had said. Who? What? Why? When? Where? "They" must be coming after him. The hunt was up, the fox was run to earth and here was the housecat left to face the hounds. I looked desperately around the clearing. What had seemed so deserted, so safe and charming five minutes before was now alive with sinister rustles, sudden silences and an imagined array of dangerous men.

I shivered, as much from undiluted fear as from the sacrifice of my shawl. If I could hide him... My eye scanned the landscape one last time. At one side of the clearing, the ground broke upwards abruptly to form a small steep hillock thick with underbrush and trees. If I could get Devlin up there—they would never suspect a wounded man could climb such a rise—I could hide him there until I got help. What kind I didn't know, but I could worry about that later. Perhaps moving him would be fatal, but so was staying at the clearing edge.

I began dragging him across the ground, stumbling frequently as I hooked my heel on the back of my skirt. It wasn't so hard at first. I gripped him under the arms and launched myself backwards at the base of the little hillock. Then, with a wiliness that pleased my self-esteem, I covered traces of our passing by fluffing the grasses over his heel marks. Going upwards was different. My hem was torn to rags as I slipped again and again on my skirt while I struggled up the terrain. My shirtwaist seams strained and then split under my arms and along my back. My memory idiotically dredged up a picture of my riding instructress at Miss Meachum's, she of the open armhole seams. A most unladylike sweat dripped onto my eyelids, and when I paused to wipe my forehead with the back

151

of my hand, it came away streaked with dirt. Once a small stalk whipped across the corner of my open eye and I had to stop, blinded, while tears washed down my cheek.

After an interminable struggle, I paused to gauge my progress. Ten feet up the incline. High enough to avoid casual view, but no shelter from the searching gaze of pursuers. I gathered myself and again began to drag Devlin along as gently as I could. I was tiring greatly, but found I could goad myself along by muttering forbidden words under my breath. I began to understand why men would not give up their cursing despite the ardent pleas of both women and church. "Sweet Jesus," I muttered in tribute to one of the stableboy's more inspired moments. "Demn it t'Hell," I grunted in remembrance of one of Sir George's louder expostulations to poor Bridget. I was nearly to the top of the grade, almost in tears and certainly in an agony of effort, when I hissed "Bloody bastards!" with some satisfaction and heaved Devlin over the last rise. "Bloody bastards" was of my own creation, being the two worst expressions upon which my maidenly ears had ever chanced.

I turned, unable to straighten from my crouch, and was face to face with the slender black leg of what I judged to be a rather fine horse, standing the bridle trail behind me as quietly as his owner sat him. I looked up into the impassive features of Lord Hugh.

My heart went into a gallop that left me shaken. "They're coming," Devlin'd said. This was not a "they." But "they" could become one by separating. Lord Hugh dismounted and I instinctively stepped between him and Devlin—still unconscious, perhaps dead by now—on the ground. Lord Hugh seemed surprised at my interference. He looked at me steadily, then spoke in quite normal tones.

"Do you always take your morning constitutional this early, Miss Dunne? If you'll excuse me—" He set me aside deliberately and knelt down to examine Devlin, expertly lifting an eyelid, feeling for a pulse, finding and checking the wound.

"This man should get to a doctor immediately," he said, rising and dusting his hands off with an unconscious fastidious gesture that made me shudder for some reason. "I'll take him with me. Help me get him up on Blackbriar." He had already laced one of Devlin's arms around his neck and held him upright. The sudden vertical position brought a blossom of fresh red to flare on my strips of sober-coloured shawl and I stepped back, overcome by a conviction that Devlin would die.

152

But I heard myself say, "A doctor? No. He can't go to a doctor..."

Lord Hugh's eyebrows lifted but his expression never changed. For an instant I saw a pleased look shift across his handsome face and bury itself in the horrible scar at his left eye. I was thankful I didn't know what he was thinking.

"No, of course not," he said softly. "Help me," he ordered crisply and together we lifted and pulled Devlin into the saddle. Lord Hugh mounted swiftly behind him. "I'd advise you to return to your 'constitutional.' Say nothing of this."

Blackbriar slowly made his way along the narrow path and disappeared. I sank to my knees and thought awhile until I was breathing normally again. I was weary and dazed and stumbled down the incline to my watercolours without sensing much of anything.

"Weeel, an' what Colleen 'ave we found 'ere, mates?" It was a British voice, in a low London dialect, and I wheeled to see a ring of British soldiers fan out from the trees. I thought I knew now who "they" were.

"Faith an' begorra," said another in rude imitation of the Irish brogue, "but surrrely no dacent woman would be abroad at this hour?"

"Not 'less she'd been up to indacent things," retorted the first voice as a stocky man with sly eyes and a florid face advanced upon me.

"What could she 'ave been doin', lads?" he asked the others with a thespian sort of attitude. "Berry-pickin'?" he jeered, catching at my skirt to exhibit my tattered hem. I spun away from him and into the arms of a lanky man who pinioned me expertly and then sallied back at the first—"Look, 'ere, Baskins, the lydy prefers me, don't you, Red? The lydies never 'ad much tyme for the Liverpool boys, it's us blokes from Lydgate that knows 'ow to please the lydies." He squeezed me harder until I thought my ribs if not my corset bones would crack.

I had not yet spoken. Obviously they thought me a local, an Irish ally of the underground and fair game. Alone, and at this hour, I was indeed vulnerable. I knew my travel-weary accent blended British and American into a sort of meld, but I called upon the highest Mayfairian British my memory could recall and burst into speech.

"Gentlemen!" I drawled in such upper-crust tones that the man holding me dropped me like a hot scone. "I really don't quite know what your business is upon these grounds. But you should know that this is St. Clare estate—not open grange for whomsoever choose to wander through it. If you're on official business," I added, coolly taking in their uniforms, "then I'm sure you should apply for permission to Sir George at the House later this morning."

The first man, Baskins, frowned and shifted from foot to foot. Despite my appearance, the British class system had bred instant respect for cultivated voices into the crudely-spoken lower classes who served as enlisted men.

"It's enough," I went on, gathering up my watercolour equipment, "that I've been led in a fruitless chase through bramble and briar after a squirrel that took a fancy to my morning croissant, but I absolutely refuse to be accosted in my own meadow, even by the Queen's army!"

I strolled down the road, without a backward glance and with my knees trembling at every step.

It took me till luncheon to calm and straighten myself. I haunted the kitchen, knowing that rumours of captured underground members would surface here first. There were no whispers that day, no intimation even that anything was afoot.

Elaine wheedled me into a jaunt in the small dogcart and I agreed, eager for any news of the broader world. Lord Hugh had made no promises to keep Devlin's condition secret. Stunned as I had been, I had extracted none. For all I knew Devlin might be rotting in the barracks prison by now. Or be dead. I still couldn't reconcile the lighthearted young man who had flitted about the St. Clare household these last months with the pale, silent person abandoned in the underbrush. Life wasn't all that serious. That grim. Everyone did not have secret causes and surreptitious missions to carry out. Perhaps he deserved capture. Perhaps he'd done something awful. Killed someone. All for the holy cause of Mother Ireland. Perhaps I should have left him there, to bleed to death or face the cruel circle of British soldiers on his trail. But that was specious argument and spurious emotion. I was overwhelmingly anxious about him. Everywhere I went, I saw places that reminded me of him. I constantly carried his portrait in my mind's eye— laughing and teasing Elaine and me in that lovely brogue of his, embodying everything I'd heard of Irish charm. And then I superimposed the image of his white face and the horrible wound over what I knew of him and was swept with anxiety again. Lord Hugh couldn't be trusted, that I knew. If I didn't hear anything by tomorrow, I must find out. I couldn't go on like this.

By midmorning the next day I was, if anything, more distraught than before. I had heard nothing. I had slept little. I was taut with worry and resolved that I would have Lady Jane saddled, would ride over the Shallowford and demand an accounting from Lord Hugh himself.

But Lady Jane was out. And so it was Jester, the gelding with a wicked gleam in his velvet brown eye, that I was compelled to have saddled and mount. The stableboys watched me take my seat with open anticipation. But I kept the rein short and Jester and I trotted out to the road in fair harmony.

Shallowford was reached by exactly that—a small arched stone bridge over a shallow stream with a current so fast the reeds along the bottom flowed horizontally rather than upright. Jester nickered at the unfamiliar direction, but gave me no more trouble than a blister on my rein finger from keeping him so tightly in check. Shallowford House was newer than I had expected; I guessed it had been constructed within the last seventy years, faithfully following the relatively recent and dramatic Gothic style of architecture. While it couldn't even touch Carnhaven for venerability, Shallowford appeared ten times more ancient, imposing and mysterious than Elaine's Georgian home. I entered under a shadowy portico covered with vines so profuse it was as if they'd been there since the Crusades. A stableboy ran up to take Jester and tie him near the yard. I boldly rang at the door with its arched, stained-glass window. The man who admitted me seemed totally unsurprised at my visit—but then all good butlers seem as incapable of surprise as a steamed trout.

"If you will wait here, miss. I will inform His Lordship that you have called." He returned shortly. "His Lordship can see you now. If you would be so kind as to step this way. His Lordship is in the upstairs sitting room."

And there His Lordship was indeed, attired in a tapestry robe of Oriental design with a mauve cravat, reading the *Times*, and sipping coffee from a Minton cup. I waited until the man had bowed himself out and shut the door.

"I'm sorry to disturb your morning meditation, but I really must know what you've done with Devlin Quade."

Lord Hugh wearily folded the newspaper, as if someone tiresome had called on him to discuss the national economy.

"It was really rather unwise of you to come here, Miss

155

Dunne. Enquiries have already started in the village and I rather suspect even the Great Houses shan't be sacrosanct this time. Your friend was up to something knotty for the authorities, I gather."

"Perhaps it was more unwise of me to have let you take him in the first place! But it was necessary. The soldiers were in the clearing already when I went down."

He raised his right eyebrow, which shouldn't have but did remind me of the scar near his left. "But you handled them, no doubt, with your usual finesse." I was about to protest but he waved me silent.

"Your, er, fellow conspirator, is right enough. At least he's alive, which is more than a good number of these crazed Irish rebels can claim. I don't care for the Cause and I don't care for its adherents," he said, eyeing me coldly. "But neither do I care to see helpless men snared too easily. A Davenant failing, I understand, going back to the Civil War. Your soldiers would not have treated him gently had they caught him."

His man, a middle-aged, wiry fellow with a humourous eye, emerged from an adjacent room just then. Lord Hugh turned on him with an air of relief.

"Ah, Hemlock, Show the lady that our catch is well cared for. I think that is all that concerns her. Hemlock served as orderly in India—he's as able at tending everything from gangrene to cobra bite as he is at easing the pangs of Bacchus after a night spent in worship of that deity."

A drunken orgy, you mean, sniffed the moralist in me, but I held my tongue and followed Hemlock into a small dressing room where Devlin lay upon a cot.

"He'll be quite all right, miss. In a couple or more days we can move him somewhere safer. Until then, what he needs is rest and to keep the bleeding down," said Hemlock in a surprisingly cultured baritone, when I'd half expected him to talk like Serjeant-on-Parade from one of Mr. Kipling's poems.

I looked at Devlin. He was as pale as I'd seen him last. Sleeping, I think, but I was at a loss as to say whether he was any worse or better than before. I sighed.

"He'll be all right, miss," said Hemlock, almost dropping one of his carefully schooled "h's" in his anxiety to reassure me. I looked closely at him and in that look believed him. This man with the well-pressed crinkles around his eyes and the neat salt-and-pepper mustache was the best of all that was typically British. He knew his place but he had a heart. *He* would still drink tea and not coffee with his morning meal.

"You'll keep him a bit?" I asked Lord Hugh on returning to the sitting room.

"Well, I can't very well throw him back. Yes, I'll keep the young fool until he's well enough to go down to the village. Doubtless Father McManus will know to whom to remand him. These priests are usually involved in this village intrigue up to their Roman collars. But I'd take it kindly if you not tell him where he spent the first few days of his convalescence, after he's recovered. I doubt he'll remember much of it and I really don't think a collaboration charge is a suitable reward for my . . . neighbourliness."

"M'Lord," said Hemlock discreetly from the window, where he'd been laying out his master's clothes for the day. Lord Hugh was at the curtain as quick as a civet. "The Captain and his aide. Well, well, well. I thought the Great Houses wouldn't 'scape a polite enquiry this time, Hemlock. We'd better get her out the servants' stairs."

Hemlock had me by the elbow and was ushering me out when Lord Hugh cursed and stopped us. "No, there's her horse, plain as day and twice as high. That won't do at all."

Hemlock and I stood stock still in the room's center. I glanced desperately to the little room that concealed Devlin, but Hemlock shook his head. We all stood darting our eyes about as though playing hide-and-seek. Suddenly Lord Hugh narrowed his hazel eyes in a sort of calculating amusement that made my heart sink.

"There's only one thing to do, considering my reputation— and yours," he shot at me, grabbing my wrist, tossing my derby and crop on a nearby chaise lounge and pulling me into the next room. "Hemlock, you will let them enter without knocking first," he ordered.

Hemlock paled at this deliberate dereliction of duty. *His* reputation came as cheaply as mine, I noted bitterly.

The next room was obviously Lord Hugh's bedchamber.

Testered bed, chinoiserie chests and such gave the place an air of Oriental opulence that, though I knew it to be fashionable, struck me as the very depth of decadence.

"Take off your jacket," he ordered, moving about the room to put the stage properties in order for our little drama.

"No," I protested. It was enough to have borne the blame for Elaine's indiscretion. But she was my old and dear friend. There really had been very little choice. Now, I was supposed to sacrifice my reputation again. It was becoming a habit. "Let Amberleigh do it." Let them eat cake. Oh, Lord Hugh was getting a sly kind of amusement out of it, the snake. No doubt he thought it served me right and was small price to pay for aid to Devlin.

"Such devotion," said Lord Hugh, arranging himself like a caliph on a Récamier sofa and patting the cushion next to him. "No? Perhaps we can arrange something less artistic but more casual."

He came up to me, and when I turned away, embraced me from behind and began undoing the buttons of my jacket and nibbling at the nape of my neck like a melodrama villian.

It infuriated me to be forced to let him toy with me, but I only struggled halfheartedly, knowing that for Devlin's sake I had to play the game out. Engravings titled "The Rake's Progress" flashed through my mind. I knew we looked as if we were playing a lover's game of rebuff and relent. I also noted, almost detachedly, that Lord Hugh was adept enough to keep the scarred side of his face away when he was making love to a woman. His attentive lips were wandering closer to my mouth, but I kept my face turned away so fiercely I thought my neck would snap. Absolutely odious. But oddly enough, I was aware of a certain elemental charm. Although I resisted his advances, although I wasn't attracted to him, was, in fact, repelled, it was as if an invisible net of some force he possessed was being slipped over me.

It was very disconcerting to be the sole object of that much concentrated attention. I wished to be rescued from standing as still as a china cat while he surrounded me with a counterfeit of intimacies, tangled his fingers in my hair and generally behaved as if I had been put on earth for his amusement. He was aware of how uncomfortable this charade made me feel, I knew that. But the more I tried to ignore or resist the feeling, the stronger it got. It was a battle of wills beyond expediency, as if he expected me to react in a certain manner, and being cheated of it, strove to force me to it. I gathered myself to break away in earnest—let Devlin face his own devils—

"Captain Mayfair, m'Lord," came the blessed baritone of Hemlock.

I sprang about a yard away from Lord Hugh, like a rabbit released from a trap, and gazed into the stunned pale blue eyes of a very proper, very British, very young military man. I felt a furious blush surge to my face. The baby fat still plumped out my witness' astonished face and made the mustache seem a ludicrous afterthought.

"C-Captain Thaddeus Mayf-fair, at your service, m-m-m'Lord," he said with a bow. I wondered if he always stuttered or if my disgrace had contributed to his lingual difficulties. Lord Hugh was perfectly at ease, of course. Why shouldn't he be?

"Delighted, Captain," he said, extending his hand. "You've caught me at an awkward moment." This comment caught everyone looking startledly at everyone else. Lord Hugh led us leisurely back to the sitting room. "Breakfast, I mean," he explained with a wave of his hand to the silver tray.

"Of course," agreed Captain Mayfair too vigorously.

"But then," went on Lord Hugh, "who is to suspect the British militia will be up and about at this hour? Hemlock, some coffee, perhaps, for the Captain. Or tea? No? Then permit me to ask your business."

"M-m-m-my business," repeated Captain Mayfair dully, as if he had completely forgotten it. He looked uncertainly at me, then to Hemlock who was standing just inside the door and looking martyred. And then, being fairly young and new to these things, he cleared his throat and began.

I drifted over to the window, hardly listening to his narrative of the fugitive abroad for the last two days. Or to his apologies for disturbing Lord Hugh's—h-hem—household. Or his assurances that no one in command seriously believed that any of the local gentry would shelter one of these rabid "Home Rulers." I was thinking instead of what Captain Mayfair would say when he was back among his peers and settled with a whiskey and soda. "Quite a shock, you know. There plain as day. The Dunne girl that's up to Carnhaven. Of course I'd heard about the trip North, what? But I say, I was absolutely flabbergasted. Damned bad show. What could I do? Asked my questions and beat a hasty retreat, what? Damned bad show."

I sent a sidelong glance to Hemlock, suffering manfully by the door. I noticed he had placed himself so that the dressing room door seemed almost invisible. I hadn't heard so much as a rustle from his direction. But then discretion would be a cardinal virtue for a valet to Lord Hugh.

Captain Mayfair enquired politely if Lord Hugh would object to the questioning of his household about the fugitive. Lord Hugh replied that he did object, but would allow the enquiry to absolve his staff. Captain Mayfair then asked, quite routinely, you understand, if Lord Hugh knew anything of the fellow's whereabouts. Lord Hugh denied it with aplomb. Captain Mayfair asked me if I knew anything of the event. I denied it. Captain Mayfair took his leave to make the rounds of the staff.

I kept my back to the room and my eyes on the courtyard below while Captain Mayfair's exit was sounded by the door's click, the rustle of regimentals and a subsequent crackling of newspaper. For a moment I allowed myself the luxury of letting these sounds wash over me like a dreamy distant wave that had nothing to do with me. It was a nice feeling, that detachment, after the leading role I'd had to play a moment before...

I turned from the window to discover Hemlock waiting apprehensively by the door and Lord Hugh reinstalled behind the *Times* and the pungent odor of coffee. I crossed the room briskly to retrieve my derby and crop from the chaise, hoping only for a quick escape.

"You're misbuttoned," came a sauve voice from behind the "Financial Outlook" page. I glanced down to see the hillock of fabric made by the errant button and tossed my hat down to wrest the aggravating horn buttons from their fastenings and into proper order. I would not leave this room in a manner to give anyone else cause for speculation. Captain Mayfair was bad enough. But then I likely would never see him again. Unless...I stopped buttoning, heartsick. Unless I remained at Carnhaven long enough for another of Devora's balls. Then he'd be there in his dress sword, ready to sip sherry and stab me with little offhand remarks. "That one, yes, I've seen that one before. Not exactly met, if you take my meaning. I'd stay away from her, my boy, unless you can handle a quiet dalliance in the boxwood, what?" This remark my imaginary captain extended to the handsome young subaltern who'd been considering asking me to dance...But I didn't need to concoct scenes to understand how utterly gossip could cling to one. And this, this scene, had made things even worse than Devora had managed in her heartless attempt to save Elaine at anyone's expense.

I gathered my belongings and sailed to the door where Hemlock waited like a cuffed spaniel. The dressing-room door caught my eye. "He'd better live," I vowed to no one in particular and swept out the open door. Hemlock trotted along the hall behind me until I found a vacant mirror and stopped to apply my derby before it.

"I'm sorry, miss," he said very softly and as though it cost

160

him an effort. "His Lordship is usually quite the gentleman—"

"Quite the savage, you mean." I'd not mince words with either of them.

"It was the only solution to the predicament, miss, you see that."

"Perhaps. But he didn't have to enjoy it. Reputations are hard to come by—for servants as well as women. Once lost—" Hemlock's eyes had flicked upon me when I allied our respective positions in life—and he nodded seriously.

"I apologize for my master," he said. "It was a mean sort of game to play. I can only excuse him by guessing that his ignorance of how much can depend on the world's good opinion comes with his station in life."

Hemlock was not the sort of servant to speak personally about those he served. I realized that he had been as deeply embarrassed as I. His words now were as much an ointment to my wounded feelings as his medical skills were life to Devlin. I would be stupid to reject any verbal emergency treatment he could give me.

"Thank you, Hemlock. I'm glad you understand me. How can you stay with him?" I asked as we resumed our descent of the back stairs. Something closed in his face that had been very open a moment before. A wall of reserve sprung up. "His Lordship is a very good master, miss." He spoke the words by formula.

I stopped in my descent to confront him, certain that the man who'd started down the hall with me was entirely different from the careful creature who'd phrased that last sentence.

"Hemlock? You're not going to tell me next that he's a gentleman and a scholar and gives ten pounds a year to the home for indigent financiers?"

"It's twenty pounds. For the Society for the Preservation of Indigent Charwomen."

"Yes, I imagine he'd be rather good at subsidizing the dependent classes. Well, we shall just have to remain independent, shan't we, Hemlock?"

"If you say so, miss," said Hemlock demurely, seeing me out a side door into the courtyard and safely up on Jester's broad back. I hooked my boot firmly into the stirrup and gathered my skirts over the pommel, giving Jester a brisk slap with the crop. We trotted out of the yard in perfect harmony, both our backs very straight, should any eyes be observing us over a Minton cup rim from the windows above us.

Once on the road, I paid dearly for my gesture. Jester,

161

having tasted more than a sedate amble, longed for a canter. It took all the muscle in my arms to hold his hard mouth down to the jolting trot that saw us back to Carnhaven stables and the unflattering astonishment of the stableboys.

CHAPTER SEVENTEEN

AND SO the days settled into routine after the fright in the Fairy Circle. It was odd to carry yet another secret that no one else suspected. And odder still that circumstances at Carnhaven revolved in their steady domestic orbit, unshaken by the life-and-death drama waged not far from the Great House's classical doorstep.

No one questioned Devlin's absence. Or noted it. He was wont to ebb and flow like a will-o'-the-wisp anyway. Only I fretted over him; only I expected to be confronted by my complicity in his disappearance.

Oh, Sir George grumbled at the "demn cheek of that pipsqueak" that night at dinner, following Captain Mayfair's formal interrogation of the staff. I never saw a trace of that enquiry; perhaps I had not been included in the general questioning because I had already answered for myself at Shallowford. That fact bespoke some delicacy, some restraint on Captain Mayfair's part. The thought of my compromising position that morning in Lord Hugh's chambers sent a shiver through me.

"You'd think someone had walked over your grave, Amberleigh." It was Norah Chandler's observant brown eyes drilling me across the white linen the evening of that grim day.

"Oh, she's probably merely picked up a chill from all those early-morning sketching jaunts. You really must take better care of yourself, my dear." Devora sounding solicitous was a Devora of whom to be wary.

"But there's so little happening here," interjected Elaine in my defence, "one must take up something."

"Why not a cause?" Norah challenged. A silence extended itself over the long table until the scrape of cutlery was the only comment anyone would make. But Captain Mayfair had been forgotten.

As I had predicted, we all had abandoned artistic endeavours in the attic studio after Elaine's and my return from the North. Devora because she no longer needed to cloak reality in smocks. Elaine because stepdaughterly duty rather than desire had brought her there; and perhaps because the face that had haunted her during her—condition—had eased out of her mind with the child delivered out of her body.

And I—I because I was bitter about my folly, my easy surrender to Devora's duplicity. I hadn't been to the attic since the day Elaine and I had left on that too-transparent journey North and I had found Devora ripped to shreds, at least in her portrait.

But I was restless and perhaps a bit nervous those days following Devlin's wounding. I wandered up for solace to the only room in all Carnhaven House that seemed peaceful in and of itself. Surprised, I found Elaine there, too, staring out the small round window overlooking the gardens below. She started as my step made a board bend and utter protest.

"Amberleigh." Her cheeks turned as pink as a watercolour sunset. "I was seeing if there were anything I shouldn't leave up here." Her grey eyes skipped around the room as if she didn't want to see all its contents while at the same time searching for a pretext. They did not rest, I noticed, on either the slashed portrait of Devora or the clay head Elaine had laboured over so long the previous summer. Did she know, I wondered, that all this Devora-encouraged "artistic expression" was a ruse to hide her disgrace? Elaine had warned me of Devora, but then, Elaine was prone to utter vague warnings. I had walked over to the clay head and stroked a thumb along a rough place on the unfinished brow. Elaine half-stepped away from the window in alarm, her hand reaching out imperiously to stop me.

Then she caught up to her impulsive gesture and was walking calmly forward, talking to me. The disturbed girl of an instant ago had dissolved into the muted daylight behind her. Like Alice on the other side of the looking-glass, moving from one distorted world to another.

"I'm really sick of that head," she said, her voice shaking so slightly I almost didn't detect it. "I don't think I'll—finish it." Her lips almost pouted as she watched me after making that statement, defying me to argue with her. I didn't. "You've been so good to me, Amberleigh," she burst out then, as if aware that she was pushing me too far. "Really, I'm grateful. But you mustn't be—serious, with me. It makes me frightfully nervous, don't you see? Let's go down. I don't like this place—it's haunted, I've always felt that."

A place more sunny, warm and dry—a place almost sifted in the air with light and lack of clutter, with no shadows to fall anywhere—would be hard to imagine. But I would not be "serious," as she called it, and debate her.

Elaine paused before we shut the door.

"You know," she began, turning to close the white-painted door like the cover of a book she had decided not to read, "I've been thinking I haven't seen much of Devlin lately." She was introducing a new topic, some daily discourse to distract me. "Have you?"

Now it was my turn to temporize.

"Devlin? Why, no, I imagine not. Well, you know Devlin. He's probably off scouring the back roads and uncharted heaths in search of unspeakable ballads from the old days. How he can transcribe that gibberish I can't imagine."

Elaine nodded, satisfied.

I was the first to see Devlin again, a fortnight later, in an obvious enough place—Mrs. Featherstone's kitchen. It wasn't sufficient that the St. Clares served breakfast from eight till ten, copious morning tea at eleven, luncheon at one, high tea at four and dinner at eight. No, my girlish appetite insisted on gratifying itself at odd hours as well.

I'd taken to slipping down to Feather's domain to unearth some post-or-pre-tea sweet. Today voices wafted up conversationally from the bottom of the stairs where only baking smells and brisk directions usually emanated.

I rounded the last turn in the stairs to find the door uncharacteristically closed. I listened a moment before breeching it.

"Devlin! I thought I heard your blarniferous voice. Why, you—" Mrs. Featherstone sent me a worried and cautionary frown, leaning her sturdy hands on the rolling pin with which she'd been lightly admonishing a round of dough.

Devlin sat at the worktable on a stool he'd drawn up. A bit stiffly he sat, I noticed.

"Kath-leeeen Ma-vourrrr-neen, the grey dawn is breaaaaaking . . ." He broke into exaggerated song at my arrival and Mrs. Featherstone clutched her forehead in despair.

"Hush, my boy. I suppose you want the entire household, the entire neighbourhood in to ask where have you been and what have you been doing? You can sing to the girl in every glade in Clare if you wish, but not in my kitchen."

164

"Besides, Devlin, dawn has long since broken," I noted, joining the pair of them. I was happy to see him. And Feather was happy to see him. She was never so happy as when she was snappish.

"If you're feeding outlanders, Feather, have you anything for me?"

"Between you, him and Miss Blowsy, I'm feeding half the regiment," she growled, dusting off her floury hands with a sharp clap and producing a chipped floral plate heaped with currant scones. "Rosie'll be fair unmanagable if I hand away her after-dusting treat, a whole plate of 'em, she wants, does that girl. But I think the twain of you need them more."

I used the scone-passing ceremonies as cover for taking a long look at Devlin. He seemed diminished, as if he were sitting a few feet farther away than he actually was. A harsh charcoal grey sweater didn't help counter the pallor that pooled over his face and hands.

"Well, I don't need it, I fancy," I responded, sinking my teeth ravenously nevertheless into the crumbly delicacy.

"Neither does Miss Norah, for that matter," answered Feather tartly, picking up her pin and whirling it into action again. The dough flattened under it as if it had a life of its own and a need to stretch itself thin. Mrs. Featherstone liked people to come and go through her kitchen. It made her feel at home. Only Norah, Devlin and I besides the servants showed any tendency to linger in the large, flagstoned room heated by a behemoth of a wood-and-charcoal stove along one wall. But Feather gave off her own rough warmth that people like Devora and even Elaine were perhaps too thin-blooded to share.

"It's not that I don't like to see me cooking appreciated," Feather added of Norah's appetite. "But she's turning into a regular dumpling, that one. Something you could use a bit of, my lad."

Devlin shrugged under her sharp eye, stuffed a few scones into his jacket pockets and rudely replied with his mouth full.

"Don't know, Feather, 'bout that. Got to keep lean for the chase, you know." He winked. "Come along, Amberleigh, I want a walk with you."

"I've no shawl," I protested.

"Take this," said Devlin, casually sweeping a plaid one from a chair back.

"But—" I said, the shawl trailing me and I trailing Devlin out the rear door. Devlin invariably inspired "buts" from me. It was one reason he was so charming, I suppose.

165

"Can you walk far?" I asked abruptly as we broke into the courtyard and Devlin escorted me around the stable walk. He moved gingerly somehow and a flashing image of him crumpled on the Fairy Circle ground lit up in my head. "Devlin, are you—well, no one can hear us now—are you all right?"

"Perfectly," he replied, hauling out a scone and munching while regarding the branches above us.

"Well, then what are you doing hauling me away from the house like this? I'd not take a walk on such a soggy morning merely to pass the time of day. You misled me into thinking you're an invalid and you're healthy as a horse," I challenged.

"Aye, for sure," said Devlin with a grin that changed into a grimace. We veered for the abbey. I watched the path, and Devlin, narrowly. I'd expected to see him again, but not so unexpectedly. And so—what? Was it the pale-parchment, stretched look to his skin? The way the blue of his eyes was watered down? As if he'd been a County Clare apron scrubbed on the washboard and hung out on the nearest thornbush to dry . . .

"Devlin. Are you really well yet? Isn't it too soon—? Well, you don't look well at all to me. Why did you want me to come all the way out here? You look exhausted."

"And I soon will be if I try to answer all your questions," he said, with a pale pretence at the old raillery. He led me around a half-tumbled wall and to our familiar lounging place on the abbey steps to the sky. He sat on a limestone riser, one exactly level with him, I noticed, and looked relieved.

"I shouldn't be hangin' about the House overmuch. It's been given about that I'd taken a trip back to Trinity before the episode in the woods and there planned to stay awhile. To excuse my absence. The wheels of deception grind exceeding fast around Glennverran, ye'll be noticin'."

"But I am glad to see you, Devlin, to know you're all right. Even if you are overdoing."

"It's your doing that got me to this eminence, lady," he said with a wince as he shifted on the damp stone steps of the abbey. "Father McManus told me all about it. How you dragged me from the teeth of the pack and went to find help—"

I'd not expected him to know about that. Lord Hugh and Hemlock needn't have passed on my role in the rescue when they'd handed Devlin over to the village priest. I wondered why they had.

"Well, you were cluttering up a perfectly good landscape— I couldn't hope to get any sketching done until I'd cleared the area of superfluous bodies... But you don't look well yet, Devlin. I wish you'd settle back to whatever hole you're hiding in and rest."

"I had other business in the vicinity. Had to come out anyway. So I thought I'd look you up myself to tell you I'm not ready for six brawny men and a burial yet."

"Business? At Carnhaven? With whom?"

"Ach, it's sharp ye are and me still muddle-headed enough to give you more answer than I should. You wish to stay out of our petty political proceedin's, so you're out, except for some spare rescue and rehabilitation work, thank you, mum."

It was hardly fair to tax Devlin now, much as his allusion to Irish sympathizers at Carnhaven had set me twitching. I left off questioning him with a sigh.

"But there is something very strange about that night, that I was out in the woods."

"Strange! You were nearly killed—I wouldn't call that merely strange!"

"But there was an entire party of British on my trail, don't you see? If one or two of 'em had run across me and taken a shot or so, well, 'twould have been the natural thing. But an entire party. It makes me wonder if I'd been betrayed."

"But what were you doing out there? I've a right to know now."

"The only right you have now, girl, is to expect my gratitude," said Devlin with a smile that brought some depth back to his blue eyes. "You'll have to earn the right to our secrets. Even after cartin' Mrs. Quade's boy over a good patch of countryside by yourself and him as usual a lumpish unhelpful sort of fellow."

"Devlin." I put my hand on his arm and stopped him. "It's nothing to jest about. And I've a secret I can give you if you'll simply tell me a bit about the whole affair."

"Secret? What secret could you have?"

"I didn't drag you single-handed to Father McManus' vestry door, you know, Devlin. It was Lord Hugh and his man Hemlock who helped me with you. At Shallowford."

"Damn! I'll be damned and I'm not exaggeratin'. Now that's a bloody surprise. I'd have thought it certain that Black Hugh would've bound me up and over to the soldier boyos. There's some reason in it for him, you mark me." Speculation brought his blue eyes to a boil. I feared I'd started more trains of thought for him than any I could reserve space on for myself.

"Now, Devlin, I've been honest with you. You tell me. It

must have been predawn when you were dancing about the vicinity. What were you doing lurking about Carnhaven?"

"'Twasn't Carnhaven, m'darlin'. 'Twas the lough."

"The lake?"

"An' that's all I'll be tellin' you, Colleen, so don't glitter your emerald eyes at me. 'Tisn't fair, I'm a wounded man." He held up his hands for mercy and I relented.

"Really, it's ridiculous to speak of Carnhaven as a rebel center, anyway," I said, as much to convince myself as Devlin. "County Clare is as far from any commerce center, as removed from traffic and trickery as—as Outer Mongolia." I gestured widely to the empty grey sky above us.

"P'raps that's the point, my should-be Molly."

I flashed him an annoyed glance. Ill or not, Devlin Quade took too many liberties with my heritage. Or lack of it, as he would say.

"I see that raillery is my only reward for services rendered, sir. I don't understand what you mean and I'm certain you'll do nothing to enlighten me, for you always use more words to say less than you mean."

"Or mean less than I say," retorted Devlin as mysteriously as ever.

"But why should Carnhaven be a center of anything? You must admit a sleepier, less secret, country place could hardly be found."

"For one thing, it's here the entire mess started, centuries ago. Oh, not precisely here, but near enough," Devlin added to cool my amazed gaze. "But don't you know the story of the first de Clares, that have trickled down so ingloriously to the last o' them, Sir George?"

"I have an inkling that I soon will," I commented acidly.

Devlin leaned into the stairs and narrowed his eyes, staring vacantly at a three-foot-thick window-slit opening onto empty meadow and tumbled stones. I saw I was in for a one-sided conversational siege and settled my back against the wall. Devlin began his story, his lyrical voice rising and falling with some invisible rhythm that seemed like the slow, steady shhhhhhh of the sea on a calm night.

"Ah, yes, the St. Clares are an exceedingly ancient Anglo-Irish family, though how the 'St.' got tacked on there I'll never know. Scions of Richard de Clare, the first English brute to set boot on Ireland, all the St. Clares are—down to the cousins thrice-removed though it's seven centuries' water under the bridge. But don't ye know the story?"

I smiled to give him leave to continue.

"Aye. I'm sorry to begin the tale with the confession that it was an Irishman first sold the island out. Dermot Mac-Murrough, King of Leinster that's but a county east of here. He was a brave man, a warrior with but one weakness. Her name," he went on with a wink, "was Devoragilla and she was wife to Tiernan O'Ruirc, a proud man and a feisty fellow as well as a king in his own right. Or wrong.

"There are women like that, I'm told, with a face or manner to set kings at each other's throats. I've never seen one who could bring a whole nation to ruin, beggin' your pardon, but sure they must exist or the poets would be out of work.

"It was the middle of the twelfth century and a rough time besides. Dermot would have her and the lady, well, as often as not the ladies are not against the havin'. So Dermot and a stout band of men raided O'Ruirc's stronghold and came home to Leinster wi' Devoragilla. Of course he gave her back, within a year, and with one hundred ounces of gold for Tiernan O'Ruirc to stop the smartin'.

"But gold and Devoragilla weren't enough for O'Ruirc. He gathered the clans and battered at Leinster and Dermot MacMurrough and smashed them back halfway to the sea. And then came the moment that Ireland has paid for ever since. MacMurrough, beaten and not likin' it, went bowin' and scrapin' to Henry II at London. 'Henry of Anjou' the history books call him—himself but a few generations removed from the Norman hordes that conquered Britain under William. And Henry II turned our country over to Richard de Clare, Earl of Pembroke, but a soldier of fortune nonetheless, as they all were in those days. Richard gathered a motley force of fortune-seekers and joined MacMurrough to drive the Irish to the edge of the island and beyond. For his trouble, Richard de Clare was given MacMurrough's beautiful daughter—such daughters are always beautiful in the tales, are they not?—anyway, he was given Aoife as his bride.

"So a woman began it and a woman ended it. What you might call poetic justice and mayhap why there are so many poets in Ireland, since that's the only way we get any justice at all." Devlin's eyes slid from the misty distance to rest with amused cynicism on mine.

"And the St. Clares are descendants of that Richard de Clare? And Aoife? It's a romantic story, Devlin, and I'm sure true to the military part at least. But Devoragilla? Really, you can't expect me to swallow that coincidence—"

"Ah, our own Devora, you mean? I'd be willin' to wager me mother's soul that God made her a Deborah, plain and simple. Or at least that's the name given her in sight of God and the congregation at her christening. But she must have heard snatches of the tale and rechristened herself more to her likin' not too far distant. She has a great sense of drama, that lady. And not one to miss pressin' an advantage."

"And do you think that I've rechristened myself also?"

"Now I don't say ye took another name, Colleen, only that the one given ye doesn't suit ye in the least. Who'd want to be called after a little yellow-brown stone, when you could be a Glenna or a Mavis or—"

"But those are names of things, too, Devlin. A bird or a place, a glen. It's merely that they're Irish things, that's all. No, I'll keep my name, thank you. It may be odd, but I'm used to it. And it's one of the few things that my mother gave me that I still have."

"Well, you still have your mother wits about you, if I'm not mistaken," Devlin replied with a grin.

"Sometimes I wonder." I sighed. I was feeling so close to Devlin as we sat there in the hazy daylight and told tales. I almost wished I could unburden a part of my own tale upon him. I glanced over. He was leaning forwards, his arms akimbo on his knees, peeling a long blade of grass absently. He looked young in the soft light, almost like someone's younger brother back from school, his black beard a declaration of independence that wasn't quite signed. True, he played dangerous games with the rebels, but was it any more than a game with him? Somehow I felt I should save my confiding for someone old, hoary and wise. It was not the last mistake I was to make at Carnhaven.

Devlin got up stiffly and I offered him an arm for the walk back. Instead, he made me take his. Always the gesture, the white plume, for him. We wandered back towards the house.

"De Clare," I said finally, playing with the sound of it. "Is that why so many of the names hereabouts—I've often wondered why..."

"Why there's so many Frenchy names in the district? On the landed families? Such as—"

"St. Clare, for one. And—and—" I searched for another example and my mind came up blank. Except for—"Davenant."

Devlin threw the mangled blade away and regarded me with bright amused blue eyes. "Yes, that too. There's a lot of French

170

in a lot of the English. I only wish they'd go East instead of West when lookin' for lands."

"They tried that, too, you know, but didn't do very well at it."

"They're not doin' too well at Ireland, either," said Devlin grimly, bending down to gather and hand me a large three-leafed clover he'd found in the long grasses. "Just you remember that Devora's only a Deborah at heart." He grinned. "And you're Irish."

CHAPTER EIGHTEEN

DEVLIN SAW me to the edge of the lawn, then tipped his cap and vanished back into the lush green. I went inside with a jig in my step—it was such a relief to know that he was all right. All the time the last few days I'd borne the burden of clandestine worry and was glad to throw it off.

Elaine flung herself out of her room and at me as I came to the top of the stairs, almost as if she'd been lying in wait for me there.

"Amberleigh," she entreated, drawing me into her room, "you must take this for me. And put it in the boat. You know, the *Argonaut*. There's a crack between the seat and the side. On the right facing the bow. It's been there for ages. Simply leave it there. But please do this for me, please."

"Elaine, what are you about now? I'll try to help you but you must tell me what you're up to."

"I can't. I—can't. I saw. I remember. Perhaps he will, too. Oh, don't ask me. Amberleigh, if you only knew, you'd help me without my having to beg you. But I can't tell you. You are my friend? You don't hate me because . . . of what I did. You do! Everyone does . . ." She broke off in sobs. I felt sorry for her and angry with myself for my weakness.

It was tea time before I had a chance to slip away towards the artificial lake and the path through the woods to the Big Lake on my fool's errand. As ill luck chanced it, I almost walked directly into Devora as she and Lord Hugh, of course, were taking a turn through the boxwood maze—a favourite

171

occupation of theirs evidently and more reason to distrust them both. The note in my left hand slipped quickly into a fold of skirt at my side.

"Lord, Amberleigh! You take five years off my life, far too much of a loss at my age. How you young things have a way of careening around corners these days!"

"My dear," said Lord Hugh smoothly to Devora, not even acknowledging my presence or that he knew me, "at your age or any age, the loss or gain of five years would not make a whit's difference in the essential charm of your character." Devora looked pleased as a cat with its whiskers dripping cream at this gallantry and laughed deep in her throat and looked intimately at Lord Hugh. But knowing him, I was not too sure that an optimistic interpretation should be put on his words.

I was about to slip away when Lord Hugh shot out a hand and detained me by the wrist. The left wrist.

"But you're right," he said to Lady St. Clare, "these, ah, children do whisk about, rather too roughly for the wearing of heirlooms, I'd think. Such a charming bracelet," he said, raising and inspecting my wrist and the bangle on it with a too-casual eye. I'd forgotten my mother's opal filigree band that I had donned that morning. Whoever said opals were unlucky was accurate.

"Yes." I found my voice husky. "My mother's. She left it to me." Or rather Mrs. Bowers' services did. I resisted as Lord Hugh tried to turn my hand over on the pretext of examining the bracelet more closely. He knew I carried a message. He began to force my wrist, but I tightened my grip on the note.

"Such fine filigree work . . . craftsmanship like that will never happen by again," he purred, all the while tightening the odious grasp upon my wrist. I felt my fingers slackening and the tears start up in my eyes.

"Hugh. You do go on about a silly bracelet," interrupted Devora with a puzzled glance in my direction. "Come, let the girl get on with her walk. As long as she doesn't ride one of those beastly machines I don't care what she does. Let us take tea—it's almost four."

"Very well," he agreed, almost casting away my wrist. Without a backward glance, they both strolled away. It was far too risky to take the message to the boat now, I decided. Nightfall it would have to be.

It was base superstition, but I returned to my room and removed the unlucky opal bracelet for the day. If I were still to go on Elaine's errand after my disastrous false start today,

172

I'd need all the favourable omens I could manage.

I went to find Elaine and finally came upon her in the greenhouse, a south-facing glassed-in area added to the house but recently. Elaine was sitting docilely in the humid bright light and pulling leaves from the bases of long-stemmed roses gathered from the gardens.

"Gracious, Elaine, I had no idea horticulture was one of your interests."

"It isn't," she answered intensely, pulling off a leafy stalk so suddenly she raked a thick thorn across her thumb. "Oh! How dreadful." Elaine sucked her thumb rebelliously and warned me away with a look.

"Oh, see, Devora, now I've gone and cut myself on a thorn. Are you certain you want these silly things in vases? I think they should be caged."

Devora peered from behind a tall stand of exotic greens that grew so well in this moist climate. A sprightly apron covered her silk gown and she brandished an intimidatingly long pair of garden shears. Lord Hugh, I gathered, had not remained for tea.

"Really, Elaine, I'd thought you could be of some use to me. The roses are at their peak now, and I've not had any inside all summer. The frost will wither them soon—yes, I see it is a nasty rake," she said, as Elaine carelessly let a ruby drop of blood fall to her dainty wrist ruffle. "I swear, you'll remain a child all your mortal life." Devora set down the shears on the table before us fretfully and laid an armful of roses on the potting table. "Well, go find Stone then, and she'll tend to it. Amberleigh can help me with the rest."

I watched Elaine, with whom I'd hoped to have a quiet chat, vanish while I was left to arrange flowers with Devora. I toyed with the idea of scratching myself so I too could withdraw gracefully, but instead gave myself up to my fate and dispersing the roses to Devora's satisfaction.

Then I went to flush Elaine.

She was in the dim and rarely used library. A room musty with unturned pages and slowly rotting leather.

Must I deliver the note, I asked her. It seemed a childish exercise. For whom did she intend it? There was no one to receive it, really—

"I want to go to my room," she said sullenly, refusing to respond to my arguments and looking over the somber shelves as if concealed ears lurked among the pages of Pliny. So we paraded upstairs again, I nearly out of patience until Elaine drew me into her floral bower and whispered desperately at me the moment the broad door closed on us.

"It's for *him*, don't you see, Amberleigh? Why must you make me spell out every letter for you? Do merely this one thing for me and I'll never ask another. I always used to leave notes there. In the boat. It was our favourite posting place. And Devora never knew. In the *Argonaut*. Please."

"Elaine, you're confusing me so—all right, I'll try. What harm can it do? But if *he's* here—are you sure he's here? That you haven't simply—conjured—him from somewhere only you know the paths of . . . ?"

Elaine dropped her light grey eyes to her hands and the note clutched in them, that I had tried to return to her. A tear pooled at the corner of her left eye.

"I want to try. To tell him. That we named him Michael. Perhaps he'll come. Perhaps he'll read it. I know he knows about the *Argonaut* . . . Shhhhh!"

With amazing duplicity, Elaine's defencelessness transformed into everydayness, leaving me to jam the little note up the cuff of my sleeve.

"Oh. Sorry to interrupt anything, ladies." It was Norah Chandler, hovering somehow hopefully at Elaine's bedchamber door. "I say, have either of you access to some purple thread? Perhaps Henrietta has a supply somewhere. I've been trying to repair this silly shirtwaist. I've got to get more wear out of it; I've only had it a few years."

Elaine and I exchanged glances. The purple silk waist that hung from Norah's hand was atrocious in both colour and cut— she'd do better carving it up for scarves or handkerchiefs.

"Let's see it," demanded Elaine, suddenly businesslike. Norah laid the pathetic thing out on the bed. An underarm seam had rent and pulled into a gaping hole. Elaine shook her fair head.

"Perhaps Henrietta or Devora's Etoile would have something in purple silk to mend it with, but, Norah, why don't you simply forget about it? It's really done in."

Norah sat down beside her worn shirtwaist. She stroked the fabric fondly before laying her small sewing kit and the heavy sewing shears beside it. "It's actually quite good fabric, you know," she intoned almost mournfully. "Ceylonese silk, as the Temple dancers wear. I had it made for me by a serjeant's wife in Bombay. I wore it for my wedding."

"You're fortunate the moths haven't got into it," I said into the awkward silence, and then realized my faux pas.

174

"I'd hoped I could make it more modish, you know," she said, bending her carelessly pinned-up hair over it so her face was hidden. Something in her voice made me wish myself a hundred miles away.

"But what's the bloody use?" Norah burst out. "What's to be modish for? They always have it their way, of course, and we women are left to patch things up and recut our lives and sew them together again all crooked." She caught up the shears in a passion and cut brutally into the plum-coloured silk, which flowed away from the blades in a long slash like the Red Sea parting before Moses.

"Oh, don't—" Elaine started, somehow repelled by the ferocity of Norah's gesture even though she'd advised the mutilation. Norah's scissors sheared off a great squarish piece from the back.

"Here," she said bitterly, waving it aloft. "If you're so fond of it, use it to dry your tears. You'll have need of it. They'll see to that, the bastards." She looked into our shocked eyes once, tossed the purple banner at Elaine and gathered up the remains of the waist and her shears under one arm. We watched the open door through which she had disappeared a silent minute or two.

"She's really embittered," said Elaine softly. "About her husband, I mean."

"Aren't you, sometimes?"

"No. I don't like to remember things—it makes my head feel tight." Her hand rubbed her forehead until it left a red place on her pale complexion. "But I've nothing against *him*. It was simply something that happened once a long, long time ago. Or it seems so. And I think I remember, it seems I remember that it was nice—oh, but don't ask me, it's best when I don't remember at all. If you make me remember you'll have to leave, Amberleigh, that's all there is to it." Elaine's thin hand had grasped me by the wrist and I wrenched free, suddenly seeing her as overwrought and threatening. It was the Evil Twin stepping forward to confuse me again—which was the Elaine I knew and which the one who puzzled me?

"Oh, I'm sorry, did I hurt you, Amberleigh?" Elaine's light grey eyes focused on my wrist and the white marks that faded from my flesh as she watched. "You see, if you'd merely take this note for me, it would be all right again. I get so restless sometimes," she complained, almost hurling herself at the window and fanning her long fingers on the pane. She spread her hands wide, like a drowning person.

"Sometimes I think I'd be better off leaving here, but then I see the sunlight glancing off the little lake and I look at the green of it all around me—the ground, the trees, the way it used to be and still is—and I can't go, I can't go." She wandered back to the bed and the purple square upon it. She got a pair of scissors from her tall China chest and began snipping off the square's edges in an even line. "Look, Norah practically butchered it. I'll straighten it out and then it'll be usable. For something. I can't tolerate to see things half-done. I like things finished."

"I'll take the note, Elaine," I said quietly to her back and the soft fair hair bowed over the cloth—so like and so unlike Norah's pose of a few minutes before. The graceful pompadour before me nodded once, in time to the slice of the scissors.

I left and went to my room and redid my hair and sewed on buttons all afternoon. I forgot the note up my sleeve—now that expression meant something!—until halfway through the dinner duck. I looked round the table. Sir George was speechlessly eating what little he did, Symes at his elbow to refill the constantly draining glass. We ladies were kept to our customary two glasses of wine. Devora was pale across the snowy linen, with two purple thumbprints under each eye. I assumed migraine and noted that she still toyed with her first glass of wine. Tranquil across from me sat Elaine. I wondered if I asked her about her urgent note right now, would she merely look up a bit puzzledly and ask "What?" in a voice clear as the consommé that began our meal?

Norah, I'd noticed, had twisted a plaid taffeta ribbon into her carelessly upswept hair. It balanced there, like an ill thought, and fooled no one with its rakish gaity. I wished Devlin were there; he'd add some spice to our stodgy courses. He'd drop something more between the duck and the savoury than his napkin. I smiled to imagine the St. Clare dinner table so revolutionized. Perhaps that's what the United Irishers meant—no more above and below the salt, no more salt for Irish wounds at all. I'd like to see my dinner companions transported to some fisherfolk's cottage—would they be so superior then?

"Where are you off to, Amberleigh?" Devora asked after dinner as I veered from the trodden path to the drawing room and turned for the stairs.

"I'm not feeling well, Lady St. Clare, I thought I'd spend the evening in my room. Resting."

Devora's brown eyes pinioned me briefly against the painted

176

panelling. "I hope it's not migraine, dear. Migraine can be very unsettling. Let us hope it is only La Grippe."

"I trust it isn't anything that serious, Lady St. Clare, but I think I will try not to overdo."

She nailed me to the panelling with one more bright brown look. "No. I doubt you would ever 'overdo,' Amberleigh."

As I walked up the half-lit staircase I glanced back. Devora was still standing at the foot of the stairs, one hand pressed to her temple and her eyes shut. She wove on her feet for a moment, then caught the handrail, straightened and walked on. The pain, I thought, must be terrific. Migraine enough to drive her out of her mind and into some hazy, not-quite-clear-world where things must tilt and tip. Poor Devora. I'd been hard on her. Perhaps she did only want the best for Elaine. Perhaps she deserved more consolation than Sir George could give her. And wanted only the best for Elaine.

And so did I. Which is why I bundled up in my Glen-plaid cape and took the servants' stairs past the kitchen and into the sharp fall air. I watched my breath form in the light that fell from the kitchen door swinging closed behind me. I felt for the note paper at my wrist. Gone! No, there. Merely turned around the sleeve and on the other side.

Quickly. Walk quickly over to the lake. Do the errand. Find the place to put it and walk back. It needn't even be totally dark by then. It was still quite light passing the yard and going around the stable. Once I stopped and glanced back at the house, dimly lit from this side. It was darkening faster than I'd anticipated, as if a giant candle snuffer were slowly capping Carnhaven for the night. I turned and walked more quickly along the edge of the woods, skirting the formal gardens and geometric paths through them. I would feel so conspicuous there.

My heart quickened and then beat to keep pace with my steps. The ground was hard; my steps crackled over sticks and forlorn little piles of wind-wafted leaves. Devlin wouldn't be frightened going through this countryside at evening. He'd done it before, with the United Irish. Perhaps they were even out here this night—the thought made me shiver under the warm wool that cloaked my gabardine. Too insubstantial for such a night. "On such a night as this . . ." That was the line of a poem, what poem? Memory evaded me. A noise. There, behind me to the left. What? A bog bogeyman? A quick brown fox going home from the hill? Tom, Tom, the piper's son, stole a pig and away he run . . . It was astounding what folderol went through one's mind when fear needed to be shoved away. I stumbled over my own hasty steps and deliberately slowed myself. My skirts rustled with the wind. Here, here was the place where I'd lost the sketches and Adrian had helped pick them up and told me—how long ago? A summer away. A lifetime, really. That soft summer day, picked up by the wind and whirled away like my sketches. Adrian whirled away like a sketch of a man. The glade seemed hostile and unhappy and I hurried through it. Now down the path to the lake. Now here, where Maisie Dillingham had paced in her summer pink organdy.

Dark already, the dark water lapping round the dock and the little boat. *Argonaut*. A brave name for so battered a boat. I must be brave. I cautiously made my way to the end of the dock and felt for the rowboat's mooring. Yes, tied safely and tautly. I could board her. I stepped inside, my stomach lurching as the boat bobbed a bit on the little waves.

I shut my eyes against the dark and felt my way forward. To the place Elaine had said, the hollow made for messages. Who would come here? Some figment of her past? Some ghostly brother with whom she used to play? Or a man, a man who really had been her lover. I almost doubted he existed. He had been forgotten, like the vague-eyed child who lolled on some unknown lap in the North. Perhaps he was a Londoner, her one-time lover, some leftover Lothario from Devora's last attempt at a season and a match for Elaine. It didn't matter, here I was—carrying secret notes in my sleeve, wrestling with fear on an unsteady, shoddy little rowboat on an Irish lake reputed to house a monster. Mrs. Willoughby, where are you? Where is your letter? Take me back to Boston and sanity and spinsterhood and the schoolroom. Elaine, it would have been best to have forgotten me too, to have left it all behind us at Miss Meachum's for the mothballs. What good would I do her now? Feeding into her futile fantasies.

Or were they? I wrested the note out of my cuff, a much harder job than slipping it in had been. Getting out of fixes was always more difficult than falling into them. What if Elaine really had a lurking lover—someone vague and mysterious and sinister. Perhaps I underestimated her, perhaps I was acting courier for an ill-meined, ill-meaning man who would still do Elaine harm. One of Norah Chandler's kind of men, perhaps a nobody who sought to prolong his tenuous St. Clare connection. By now I'd materialized sinister Gypsy lovers and hard-hearted Soho blackmailers. I reached to put the note in place and something cracked behind me. Like a shot. Like doom. The crack of doom. I whirled while crouching there in the boat bottom. The precious note fluttered from my fingers and over the side. I didn't care. I stared into the blackness. The still, opaque darkness. The line of saplings and underbrush back from the shore that looked woodsy and wild by day. It was a midnight mystery now and I was almost glad I couldn't see it.

I half-stood and scampered my way out of the boat. My knees were trembling as I stood on the jetty and my hands were moist. I edged off the dock, anxious to have no depth of black water behind me. Not even a few inches. '

Another crack, farther away. Should I speak? It didn't matter, I opened my throat to form a sound and whatever sound was starting there clung to my tongue and refused to exit. Someone there. It had to be. A someone. A who. Who? The Irish? Devlin? Or—Elaine? She was the only one who knew of my mission. Had she changed her chameleon mind, decided to take back her note, had she come to stop me? I needn't worry about that tiresome note after all, floating soggily along the shoreline now. I was not a bad emissary at all. She didn't want it left, that was it.

I stepped further out into the clear length of land between the wide water on one hand and the wildwood on the other. The devil and the deep blue sea. Caught between. But only Elaine. I'd have company back to Carnhaven. Good. Night fears had made me nervy. For a moment I questioned answering that crackle, that curious reticent presence who hovered behind a wall of wild grasses and saplings in the dark.

It had to be Elaine.

"Elaine, it's you, isn't it? You've come out for a walk, haven't you?"

It had to be Elaine.

CHAPTER NINETEEN

"ELAINE," I whispered. The soft lap of the lake was uninterrupted. "Elaine, it's all right, you can come out now." A step or two and I was on the pebbly lakeside. A sudden scrape and I whirled. Only the *Argonaut* brushing the dock. Eerie, how someplace so open and holidaylike in the day should become harsh and chilling by night. I heard a step and turned to find Elaine moving slowly from the shadow of the beeches. She was bundled up in a long cloak and walking strangely, as if she were injured.

"Why Elaine, here I am, what is it? What's so urgent that . . . Elaine? Why don't you answer?"

Still she came towards me, the soft brush of her cloak across the ground louder than her footsteps. She was walking almost stealthily and there was something about her, some twist or shadow of a movement that reminded me of someone— wounded. I had a quick thought of Devlin and the danger abroad at night and feared that she too must have been prey to some wandering band of patriots. Or soldiers.

"Oh, Elaine . . . here, let me help you."

Her hand reached for my arm and she tightened on it and almost bore me to the ground with her weight.

"Lovers," she whispered in a husky voice. "They're all gone now. All the lovers, all the beaux."

"Elaine, don't laugh like that, it's—unnerving. Are you remembering again, is that it? Please, you mustn't. It's not good for you. You must be as you were. We can't go on like this, keeping you from slipping back into something only you can recall. Come away to the house."

"No, we can't, can't go on like this. I've taken care of them all. All the lovers. And the loved. Except for you, Amberleigh, I haven't taken care of you. Poor Amberleigh." Her hand reached for my face in a kind of caress.

"Let go of me. Elaine! You know you frighten me when you're like this. Like the day on the lake. It's just a bad dream, truly. Let go!"

Her grip had tightened and I suddenly felt again as if there were fathoms and fathoms below us, as though I were suspended over some bottomless chasm and the fear was worse because it was not depths of dark waters I feared, but the murkiness of Elaine's memories, drawing me down and down.

"Elaine, I'm your friend. Come back to the house. Please, Elaine, are you hurt? Can you come?"

Her voice was still hoarse, her words wandering, incoherent. She was another person, the Evil Twin revealed to me on the lake.

"Friend?" she hissed. "I have no friend. None. Only lovers. I don't like—friends. I loathe friends. They cut you and step on you and trample your soul. They leave you for lovers. They all leave you for lovers.

"I had a baby once," she sobbed suddenly. "Just a little baby. But I gave it away for lovers. Always for lovers. You have a lover," Her voice was sharp, accusing. Something in it made my stomach knot, my breath stop.

"No, Elaine, that's a mistake. You know that's a mistake."

"I know, I know! You have a lover. I take care of my friends with lovers. I ease the pain. Pain's Ease, it should be the name of an herb. I am an herb, I take very good care of them. All of them. All of their lovers. Men are beasts!" she burst out venomously. "They walk on your soul and they leave the door open when they go."

Her voice was cracking and became almost a live thing in the dark. I drew away, folding my shawl around me to repress a shudder. She was not a . . . normal . . . thing that night.

"Those that walk with the beasts shall die like the beasts. Amberleigh, you keep a beast on a collar and chain. Oh, don't bother denying it. The others denied it but I showed them, I showed them before the very last. I showed them the beast. At the end . . ."

She was advancing on me and I turned to run a few steps down the lake shore, stopped and looked again. She was following me in a steady, businesslike manner that frightened me further; it was so unlike Elaine. It was all so unlike Elaine.

I plunged into the trees on the other side of the lakeside clearing. Darting under branches, slipping on twigs and leaves that carpeted the forest floor. Across, across the clearing, through the woods and out the Fairy Circle. Then I'd be on the road. It wasn't that late, just past sunset, someone would be on the road surely. A farmer, a cottager, a gameskeeper in search of twilight poachers. Someone. She was still behind me, I could hear her scrabbling across the ground, her heavy breathing. Or was it my own? No, I couldn't run to the road. Did I want anyone to see her like this? No, I'd lead her away, tire her. She was not strong. If I could keep her running, exhaust her, and lead her back . . . Lady St. Clare would have to know. It was rotten that she'd be in a position to permanently discredit her stepdaughter, but there it was. Elaine was utterly mad for the moment.

And coming closer. A stitch in my side made me gasp and almost stop but I reached the clearing, threw myself up the hill I knew so well from the day I had dragged Devlin up it and hurried along the bridle path at the top. Amazingly, Elaine ran right behind me. I'd hoped for time, to throw her off my trail, but she always remained close enough to hear the rustle as I passed. I could never lose her, any more than a fox could lose the hounds. A fox! That's what I needed, some place to go to ground, to hide in until Elaine was herself again. Lunge through the underbrush, run, run, keep running. A place to hide. A hiding place. Down the hill, so fast I thought I'd fall. Here I should lose her...No! Was she inhuman? Was she...?

"Elaine, let me go!" I was sobbing as she caught my hand from behind and whirled me around until we both fell in a heap on a ground littered with sticks and stones. "Elaine, you're not yourself, Elaine..."

A sudden flash of fire licked across my arm and my whole body shuddered. Dazed, I stopped moving and felt another cold-hot slice along my face. Something warm oozed down my cheek and wrist, for some reason a vision of Devlin in the underbrush flashed into my mind.

A knife. She had a knife.

I thrust her from me with a strength I had thought exhausted, with a surge of self-preservation that raged through my body like fire through a furnace. Already the pain was firing down my face and arm.

I stumbled to my feet and began running when I had thought myself beyond crawling. "Elaine, Elaine..." someone was whispering faintly. I think it was I.

Plunging through woods now, careless of the whip of branches, heedless of anything but careening over the next rise, down, under, across. Away. And always behind me the thud of her feet. A dull beat that rivalled my own heart.

Someone was sobbing. A shadow that seemed to run with me. I wished she'd be quiet, she'd betray my position. The hill ended in a dark bulk at its bottom. My dazed mind imagined deer, Druid and then troll. Troll. The bridge. It was the hulk of Shallowford Bridge. I lurched down towards it, then veered to the side, stumbling into the icy water up to my knees. I crouched behind a tall stand of reeds and froze. Like the hares trapped in the open on Carnhaven's lawns, foolishly standing stock still in broad daylight and hoping not to be noticed.

It was not daylight now.

I heard motion, an ugly sort of muttering with words that made no sense. The reeds to my left once bowed in the moon-light with a swish, as if a hand were probing them. Or a knife. Then it was still for a while. I dared not even shift the weight

182

from my aching ankles. I waited a long time, my hands clasping my arms and stifling the bloody flow from the line of fire on my arm. I slipped a little into the muddy bank. I didn't care. Everything was burning, burning away. It must be the sun, rising.

I awoke to the real sun slanting through the tree trunks, to cold and stiffness and someone saying "Dear God" and lifting me out of the water.

Somewhere there was another sun, a cool milky sun, melting and spreading in a pool over my head. I felt my neck tilted back, as if I were floating in water, but I couldn't feel water. Floating, floating under the milky sun.

I looked harder. Everything above me was white. I was puzzled. Had the sky gone pale? Had I . . . The white sky resolved itself into a familiar shape and substance. A canopy, a gauzy canopy on a bed. I turned my head and found my cheek on smooth, cool linen. A low fire burned along my face and arm. I lifted the arm experimentally—it was wrapped with something white. My motion started a flutter from the side of the room and a girl rustled over.

"Awake now, miss? Ah, yes, and it's been awhile. Would ye be wantin' me to pull the curtains or will ye be sleepin' a wee bit again? Now just ye stay there, and don't be thrashin' about or Mr. Hemlock'll have my cap for it. If you'll most faithfully swear not to stir so much as an eyelash, I'll be dartin' off to find the dear man like he said to do . . ."

The little maid with the white cap perched on her thick black hair shook her finger at me one last time and vanished.

Where was I? When was I? Or even worse, was I at all? Then I recalled the icy water lapping around my legs and the cold snaky caress of the reeds.

And I remembered Elaine. Dear God (that phrase again), dear God, what was to become of Elaine? What had become of her?

"You did right to call me immediately, Cathleen," came a deep voice from the hall. A moment later Hemlock bustled into the room.

"Hemlock, it is you? Then I must be—"

"At Shallowford, miss. Right in the Shallowford, in fact, if truth told, and in a sorry state, too. The gardener's boy found you at dawn and luckily I was up to see you properly taken care of. Now . . ." Hemlock drew up a chair, planted his hands on his knees and assumed a very stern expression.

"It looks like you won't be running to fever, thank the Lord, despite your dousing. Fortunate you are it was a clear Irish stream you took your nightly ablution in. In India, the water's so blo——er, so blasted, filthy a body dips so much as a finger in it and it's malaria for three months. Now don't jostle yourself, miss, it's all been attended to. The doctor from Glenverran's been by to examine your hurts. You've acquired a rather long gash on your arm—nothing serious the doctor says, though they all do, but in this case he's right. Won't affect movement. I've seen men in India refuse treatment for such a scratch so there's no cause for concern. And, ah, a smaller gash on your head. It'll take a while to heal but within a few months you'll never even know they were there."

I raised my left arm and looked with some wonder at the gauze that girdled it from wrist to elbow. The sleeve of the lawn nightdress had been cut open from shoulder to wrist.

"We'll be changing the bandages twice a day to keep it clean. Cathleen can do it for you but I'll want to see it from time to time. And you're to leave them alone between dressings."

Hemlock returned the chair to its place and prepared to take his leave. "And His Lordship will be wanting to talk with you. About just what occurred on his doorstep."

But I didn't want to talk to Lord Hugh, or to Captain Mayfair, or to anyone, about what had happened.

I was not to have my quizzing yet. I slept most of the day, chilled and still dazed by my night in Shallowford's muddy embrace. I was given nothing but broths and porridge and Kitty, as the dark-haired Cathleen preferred to be known, to attend me. By Tuesday I was allowed to sit up in a cast-off bedjacket with Chinese dragons and bats worked in maroon and blue satin whose former owner I couldn't even begin to imagine.

Shortly after I finished my midmorning onslaught of more gruel and tea laced with lemon and honey, Hemlock knocked and entered with uncharacteristic reserve.

"His Lordship wishes to know if you are ready to receive him," he enquired formally.

I sighed and set aside the last of the tea. The leaves in the cup's white bowl did not look fortuitous, although I was no expert reader of such signs. "I doubt I shall ever be ready to receive His Lordship," I told Hemlock, "but lay on, MacDuff." I adjusted the ribbons on the abominable bedjacket and folded my hands over the coverlet.

"Good morning, Miss Dunne, you're looking a bit more

cheerful than you did yesterday morning." Lord Hugh trailed Hemlock in briskly and immediately pulled up a chair to my bedside. It looked to be a lengthy interview.

"If you can say that," I replied dourly, "you should consider standing for Parliament. On the Prevarication Platform. But repartee is hardly your dish of 'tay,' so demand your explanations and let us avoid the commonplaces."

"I'm delighted to note that your experience doesn't seem to have... mellowed you." He couldn't resist having the last word under the arch of one raised eyebrow. "Very well," he went on, leaning back in the delicate little chair and extending his boot-clad legs before him. "I want to know what you were doing out the other evening, how you were injured, by whom and how you ended up enjoying the comforts of Shallowford."

"Why, how kind of you to enquire about my health. I'm doing very well, thank you, after nearly being slashed to death and drowning besides."

"I am omitting the amenities merely on your suggestion, Miss Dunne. And if you believe that a dose of tartness will distract me, you are mistaken. I want explanations, not girlish games."

"It seems to me that hopsitality under these circumstances hardly gives one licence to pry."

He stood up and set the chair aside in one motion.

"Very well, if you won't honour me with an explanation of these events, I'll have to call in Captain Mayfair. I had hoped to keep this affair quiet, for whatever it's about, it does neither of us nor the neighbourhood any advantage."

"No! No Captain Mayfair. I really don't care to have Captain Mayfair as a permanent witness to my folly. You say that this 'thing' could be hushed up—do you mean it?"

"Of course," he said, sitting again after turning the chair back to my bedside and straddling it. I felt more than ever in the witness box, but I weighed my choices and the serious look on Lord Hugh's face.

"Why do you give a fig about what happened to me?"

"I don't," he answered promptly. "But I have certain... interests... in the neighbourhood and I don't want them interfered with. I shall do a great deal to see that it is so, do you understand me?"

His eyes were as hard as obsidian. For the first time I noticed they were a peculiar hazel hue that could go as yellow as a cat's or as dark and distant as a storm cloud. It was the latter I was being honoured with at the moment. I could guess his concerns—Devora was more and more linked with his name. Sir George would not last forever and then the younger man could easily step into lordship of Carnhaven as well as having his current ample holdings. Tidy. How much would telling him even a smattering of truth do to hurt Elaine's cause? Had Devora told even him the truth about her stepdaughter? Elaine was the heir, though—would they not both like to see her declared incompetent, these lovebirds with larceny on their minds? Oh, they were both hateful and I should not tell him a thing.

"You're with the United Irish, aren't you?"

"No! That is," I improvised, "not seriously. I was merely carrying a message for...someone. And somehow someone knew about it and tried to intercept me, that's all.

"Quite a collection of 'somes.' You of course have no idea who attacked you. What became of the message?"

"It's gone. Truly it is. I must have lost it. I ran so, through the trees, by the Fairy Circle, you know...and down the path...till I came to the bridge. Then I couldn't run anymore and I hid."

"You were running away from the road, why?"

"Was I? Mercy, I had no notion of where I was running, I can assure you. Out alone in the dark like that with someone behind me—" The shudder with which I ended this pretty speech was not fabricated, for once more I felt the whip of pursuit along my back.

Hemlock, who'd been standing mutely by during all this, coughed reproachfully. I fear he was taken in by my theatrics, sweet man. Lord Hugh shot him an impatient glance, but backed his chair off a bit.

"And you 'lost' the note?"

I nodded innocently.

"Quite a tale." He got up and paced the room. "And who do you believe was pursuing you? Not one of the Irishers, you admit you were a courier for them. Captain Mayfair's men would hardly carry knives through the woods..."

"You'd be surprised what Captain Mayfair's men would do to a woman alone, sir; I beg you not to absolve them so utterly till you have some knowledge of them."

"Well, they wouldn't do it with knives, at any rate. What man would pursue a girl through open woods at night brandishing a knife? It sounds like a penny dreadful." His voice so dripped with scorn that I ached to confound him.

"It wasn't a man."

"Not a man?" He and Hemlock exchanged startled glances and Lord Hugh once again drew up to my bedside. "Would you have us believe that a woman traipsed after you through half of County Clare? With a knife? You must be mad!" he snorted.

"If I may suggest, m'Lord," said Hemlock, advancing to his master. "The face wound."

"What?"

"The face wound bespeaks a woman, m'Lord."

"Not always," said Lord Hugh opaquely. But they both bent their gaze to the side of my face. "You think it deliberate, then?" I reached my hand up to the great wad of gauze on my cheek.

"Face wound?" I asked with sinking heart. "Hemlock, you said that it was my head . . ." I'd simply assumed the bandage was over part of my face because it couldn't be attached to my hair. But as my fingers probed my cheek I found the answering ache that told me the knife had left its mark upon my face.

"It will heal, miss. Why I've seen men in my time . . ." He glanced at his master and trailed off the sentence.

Lord Hugh was lost in thought, his arms crossed upon his chest, seemingly unaware that his man was mired in trying to reassure me about scars in front of one who clearly would bear his to his grave.

"A woman." Lord Hugh appeared to be tasting the idea. "You're not lying about this, are you?"

I didn't deign to answer and I think he read the truth in my face. He paced silently a few more times around the room, then stopped abruptly at the foot of the bed.

"Who is your lover?"

I crimsoned from the top of the bedjacket to the roots of my red hair. Hemlock fairly hung his head at the indelicacy of the question.

"Are we back to prying, then?"

"My interest is academic," he replied coldly. "It might cast some light on the identity of your attacker; it might mean it had nothing to do with the rebels at all. All Glennverran knows your history, my girl; there's no use denying it. Did he come with you from America? Or was he always from here . . . ?"

"I'm sure I don't know how anything you're asking me can have a single thing to do with what happened. But it was a woman, that I know, because at first I thought she was . . . someone else."

"And you won't tell me who—"

"I have no lover! All of Ireland is not wide enough to hold a lover of mine. You must not expect everyone to be caught up in the sordid little intrigues you yourself indulge in. I am here to attend my friend, not to collect billet-doux and—and lovers!"

"It struck me that you were not unaware of the advantages of such collecting," he rejoined, stung at last, "at least when it came to something solid in distilled spirits."

"What an odious inference!" I said, for it was true. "You seem to think you have a helpless victim to insult at your will. I would as soon—hurl this vase at your heels as exchange another word with you."

I picked up a precious something from the bedside table in a tearing rage and made ready to throw the thing. "You had better leave me in peace," I threatened. "I have been through a terrible ordeal but you convince me there are worse."

Hemlock's sober face seemed pasted on as he viewed the scene, and I suppose I must have looked a sight, kneeling on the bed and waving the vase around while draped in the grotesque bedjacket. Lord Hugh simply cast his eyes at the ceiling and took, I thought, a too hasty leave, although he did his best to lounge out the door as if it were his idea. Hemlock winked at me as he drew it shut behind him.

All in all, I felt quite triumphant. Lord Hugh had been nicely diverted from the details of my disastrous outing and I doubted he would reflect long on the "note."

I examined my weapon before tabling it again. It was rather fine, a Chinese object, I think, and quite valuable. I was glad I hadn't needed it to make my point.

As soon as I made sure they were both gone, I slipped out of bed, still a bit wobbly, and made for the glass. It took some managing, but I was able to unveil the side of my face. It was a horrid slash along my temple, purple and black at the edges, the raw flesh oozing and damp. I felt suddenly ill at the sight of it—no wonder Hemlock had prated of "head wounds"; it was a terrible disfigurement and I would have cried, but it seemed too hopeless for that. Dunne the Governess wouldn't fade into the woodwork now. There was nothing for it but to rebandage my face and pray time would be kind at least.

Elaine, Elaine would never have done that to me. It had to have been someone else—the voice had been ragged, hoarse, it could have been anyone. Any woman. How fared Elaine, I wondered. How fared Amberleigh Dunne, I wondered more ironically. And how fared the wielder of the knife, that blank personage who pursued and cut and made the very reeds bow and dance attendance upon her, how fared she and who was she?

I was beginning to get a headache from it all and slid down into the soft linens.

It was midafternoon and Lady St. Clare was there when I awakened.

"I swear, Amberleigh, you must have ears like a cat. Here I was about to slip away without waking you and you open your eyes at the moment and catch me. It doesn't matter, I've decided not to take you back to Carnhaven today."

She was stunning in a grey melton suit furred with beaver. So very proper and stepmotherish that one would be an absolute ingrate to question her sincerity. But I did.

"Not back to Carnhaven?" I felt a stab of irrational worry. Was it Elaine they wished to keep me from? Or me from her? Or was there some purpose to keeping me in Lord Hugh's clutches? My head was beginning to ache again.

"No, my dear," she soothed. "You're much better off resting from your—ordeal—here, though what really happened I'm sure I can't puzzle out from Hugh's account." Her "really" called me a liar, but I was finding myself indifferent to what she thought of me.

"And Elaine, what of Elaine if I don't go back?"

"Oh, Amberleigh!" Her rippling laugh was like a length of lace unraveling from a spool, a pretty thing but manufactured. "Truly we hardly hired you to companion the girl every single hour! Elaine is fine, quite fine now. She seems to have forgotten...everything. And I want it that way, Amberleigh. Overmuch concern on your part could revive her memories. So perhaps you both should have a holiday from each other. I think we've decided well."

A knock on the door forestalled my protest. Lord Hugh entered, dressed as I'd never seen him, in riding breeches, boots and a heavy sweater.

"I'm having a carriage brought round for you and the girl, Devora, but why did you bring those bags over from Carnhaven?"

"They're some things for Amberleigh," she said, getting up and whirling her skirts to meet him. "I think it's better she stay here for a few days more."

"The devil you do!" I'd never seen him so angry. "I don't believe you're thinking, Devora. I don't want Shallowford cluttered up right now with a schoolgirl in recuperation and a gaggle of her friends traipsing between here and Carnhaven daily."

"Hugh." Devora's voice was commanding and pleading at one and the same syllable. "I detest inconveniencing you, but there are pressing reasons... have you ever known me to be a nuisance to you without reason?"

She had crossed close to him now and was looking up with her head tilted just the right amount to the side. His lips moved as if to reply. Instead he grasped her firmly by the elegant elbow and piloted her onto the little Gothic balcony outside the windows. I saw her hat nodding vehemently and Lord Hugh's unrelenting back. My opinion of the matter, it seemed, was not required. There was a low discussion, then Lord Hugh snorted something about "baggage"—a flattering reference to me, doubtless.

Back they came in a moment or two. "So," said Devora, smoothing on her brown kid gloves and heaving a little sigh of relief. "It is settled and Amberleigh is to stay." She bent gracefully to brush my cheek with her lips. "Then we'll see you at Carnhaven by and by, Amberleigh, dear. Now, not to worry, it's all arranged. You'll do much better here than jostling back to Carnhaven. Things are such an uproar there."

"Do you think she'll disfigure?" she murmured to Lord Hugh as she glided out the door. "It won't do much for her chances..."

Hemlock bustled in before I had long to dwell on her last words; he'd obviously been alerted that I was to be his charge.

"Oh, Hemlock, please don't bother so about me. You do nothing but tend to invalids nowadays."

"These times will make more than invalids, miss," he said grimly.

My recuperation was hardly one in the conventional sense. I spent my days rattling around Shallowford House in search of distraction. Lord Hugh had repaired to London for the week—as soon as my staying at Shallowford was settled he found urgent business elsewhere, something of a relief for me, but I was sorely pressed to entertain myself in the idle house. The library, with its shelf upon shelf of leather-bound lethargy, soon bored me, although I found some American books and Richard Burton's accounts of life in Arabia fascinating. There was not one good American dime novel, the very thing I needed to get my mind off what was possibly happening, or not happening, at Carnhaven.

Hemlock had been left behind to tend me, although that

only consisted of supervising my bandage change once a day. Each afternoon I took the opportunity to take a hand mirror and go to the window and examine my temple in the relentless daylight. Hemlock disapproved of my obsession, warning me it would take weeks and months for the scar to heal. But my daily inspection only revealed a line of ragged raw skin that both fascinated and repelled me. It didn't seem a part of me at all.

I was lost one evening in another of Burton's travel books, happily curled up in a large red leather chair in the library when Lord Hugh returned.

"So there you are," he said, shutting the door and advancing on me. "Well, it's settled with Devora. This time you are to go back to Carnhaven for certain. Tomorrow." He plucked the book from my hand without asking leave and scanned the title. "Burton?" He looked amused. I had the sinking feeling that Richard Burton was not considered genteel reading for young ladies. Or spinsters, since I was no longer that young and must remember it.

He sat on the arm of the chair opposite mine and, when I reached for my reading, withheld it. "Hemlock tells me you're in something of a decline," he said, looking at me sharply, as he would a horse with a lame foot, I'm sure.

"Hemlock shouldn't have told you anything of the kind. I'm doing perfectly well, thank you, and will be only too glad to depend no longer on your kind hospitality."

"Sarcasm is a weapon of the young," he said.

"Perhaps I should consider myself complimented?" I returned even more sarcastically. Lord Hugh looked at me steadily and without replying.

"Come here," he said finally, beckoning me to the window where the westering sun was already brushing the sky with pink watercolours. He turned me to face him in the alcove, then tipped up my chin and tilted the side of my face to the light. I flinched, but before I could regret the instinct I saw that he seemed not to have noticed and was scrutinizing my temple with the intensity of a connoisseur contemplating a disappointingly flawed gemstone.

"Will I live?" I asked flippantly.

"Possibly," said Lord Hugh, dropping his hand from my face. Then with an air of resolution he turned me from the window. "But I think you should see a—consulting surgeon. I know of just the one in London. I'll take you there tomorrow."

"But Lady St. Clare expects..."

"Lady St. Clare expects what I tell her to. I'll send over word of your delay. It won't mean much more than a few days. Be ready to leave early tomorrow if we're to catch the Channel crossing at noon. I shan't be in to dinner." And he left the library without another word, without saying why I should go to see his "consulting surgeon," or even who it was. There was something strange about the way he had dwelt on the words, as though he were making a jest for himself alone.

I had a long silent dinner in the empty dining room to consider the possibilities but ended, as usual, puzzled by Lord Hugh's unpredictabilities.

The journey to London did nothing for my uncertainty. It reminded me of my maiden voyage to Ireland, save that now I had an escort and Hemlock to purchase the passages, count baggage and attend to all the sordid details an independent woman must manage for herself. Lord Hugh was brusque and retired to cards in the salon on the Channel voyage. On the train he perused the newspapers and left me to watch our hasty progress from bucolic pastures to the wider-spreading web of factories, flats and commerce buildings that was London. Our carriage headed not for Harley Street, which surprised me, but for a well-tended residential area behind Belgravia. It was unlikely that any surgeon would be in his consulting rooms now that Big Ben was tolling seven o'clock.

We stopped at a brick town house and were ushered into a well-kept parlour by the butler. I could hardly keep myself from gaping, the room was so lined with rare and beautiful things, quite unlike the austere Georgian simplicity of Carnhaven.

There were jewelled eggs on gilded stands, velvet-covered boxes, porcelain figures of shepherdesses reclining with their shepherds in flowered and bowered profusion, golden cupids bearing candelabra, a japanned piano in one corner near the heavily draped windows and several florid paintings on the walls that were almost enough to make me blush.

"This is a *Viennese* surgeon," Lord Hugh said with a particularly wicked gleam in his eye as he noticed me eyeing the bric-a-brac. Indeed, I felt myself inside the whipped-cream heart of a very rich Viennese torte.

The doors suddenly were opened and a woman wafted into the room. "Hugh! How pleasant to see you. When did you come down? Surely town has no attractions for you this week? There's not a dinner party worth foregoing luncheon for—scandal seems to have packed and left for the season and I'm much too sensible to think that you've come merely to see me."

I'd never seen a woman quite like her. She was willowy and seemed to be floating in a shimmery gauze sort of thing. Her voice was thick with Viennese cream and the English words rolled off her tongue as if they'd been dipped in butter and bathed in sugar first.

"I've brought you a patient, Louisa," said Lord Hugh, indicating me sitting speechless upon the peach velvet pouf.

"Eh, who's this? The light is so dim I hardly saw the girl. Walters, the lights, please. We're not saving oil, you know." The butler, who had nothing like the reserve of Symes or Lord Hugh's, even cast his mistress a resentful look as he rapidly turned up the wicks and withdrew.

The light revealed a greater profusion of colour in the room, but the beautiful face of Louisa faded as the brighter glow played across her treasures to greater advantage. She was, I saw, more than forty.

I was surprised.

CHAPTER TWENTY

"WHAT DO you mean, 'patient,' Hugh? My services are hardly medical," the woman said, looking at him in an amused, expectant way. "Is this one of your little games?"

"Show her," he ordered me and, half dazed, I got up, walked over to her and pulled back the few strands of hair I had arranged over my scar. She frowned and recoiled slightly at the sight of my raw face. Then, leading me by the chin, she pulled me gently into the circle of one of the lamps.

"Yes? It is bad but soon enough will be better." We both looked at Lord Hugh for what was expected of us.

"Soon isn't good enough," he responded, checking his pocket watch with a kind of impatience. "I want to take her to dinner at Alcott's tomorrow, Louisa, and I thought it would be interesting to see what you could do with her by then."

"So? Yes, it would be intriguing. And how did this happen, little one?" She stroked my hair absent-mindedly, but her eyes were glittering with speculation.

"It doesn't matter, but I'm depending on you to make it seem as if it hadn't have happened." He stood up, clearly done with us. "I'll be by at seven. Send to Hemlock at my club if there's anything you require, Louisa." Lord Hugh was at the parlour door and seemed glad of it. But he turned to us before he left. "Louisa, tell no one I'm in town."

We were left to face each other, Louisa studying me in a way I couldn't fathom.

"You are good friend of Hugh?" she asked, leading me to the fire. The gaze she bent on my face came away unsatisfied. "No. Your . . . father, he is friend of Hugh?"

I shook my head. "My father is dead." It was the first time in many years I'd been called upon to say that and the words still went off in my brain like a pistol. For a moment the house in Eaton Square flashed past my mind with all its inhabitants of old and then it was gone.

"So, we put you to bed tonight and tomorrow we begin to make ready for Alcott's."

I was tired, as she had seen, and followed her docilely up a thickly carpeted staircase, down a dim hall and into a room as richly hung and plush with upholstery as her downstairs parlour. She rang a small pull by the fireplace and a middle-aged maid quickly appeared.

"Tilde, good. Always prompt, my dependable Tilde. We have a guest. Have Walters light the fire and you find a nightdress for her. Oh, and better to unpack her baggage tonight, else all will wrinkle."

Between the two of them I was undressed and bedded like a child, tucked under a feather comforter so high and light I went to sleep dreaming I'd been changed into a Viennese cream puff.

"Yes," I heard Madame Louisa's voice through mounds of cream, "sleep. We have a lot of work tomorrow."

I woke up, amazed I'd slept so soundly in a strange house, an unknown bed. It was the clink of Tilde's breakfast tray that aroused me, but before I could settle down to it, Madame Louisa had swept into the room, trailed by a blonde dustmop of a dog with a green bow above its wide olive-black eyes.

"No time for that now!" She clapped her hands at Tilde and the raw-boned maid moved with surprising grace. Madame Louisa took the room's center, giving commands with quick gestures of her small square hands. The flowing fur thing danced around her ankles and squeaked periodically. "Hush,

194

Eclair, my delight," she cooed to it before turning on us with stern words.

"You. Up and wash the face. Tilde, get her one of my morning wrappers. I've lured Horst to come this afternoon, but only by promising the moon with a chain on it, so we must be ready. Oh, and, Tilde, my coffee—I will be able to do nothing without my coffee."

Within minutes I had been ushered into her bedroom, installed on a carved chest at the foot of her lavishly draped satin bed and left to gawk while she and Tilde pawed through gown after gown from a nearby dressing room. Eclair clattered between us on her tiny nails.

Green satin, lavender taffeta, black peau de soie and yellow silk—the gowns Louisa whisked from her cupboard astounded me. I loved the first she produced till the second came. Then the next seemed the most beautiful in the wide world. How had she come by so many spectacular gowns?

But *my* choice was far from Louisa's mind.

"Green? Too predictable. We must not be predictable. Hugh would never forgive us. What you think, Tilde, lavender? With the complexion, very good. The hair, no. Black? Ah, yes, black is a colour for you, child. What is the so-strange name, Amber Leigh? Yes, black for you, but wait five years and then never go out without it. But what to do now?"

She disappeared into the dressing room once more, popped out looking triumphant and propelled me to the full-length glass to hold a lavish white lace frock up against me.

"Aha! Tilde, I knew we could find just the thing. And now we trim it—with what?"

Efficient Tilde—I could see why her mistress spoke her name with reverence—was already there with a basket of silk and velvet ribbons, taffetas and organdies in plaids and stripes and rainbow colors. There were ropes of pearls and brilliants. Gold braid and tiny net flowers with sparkling buds. Louisa probed the box with the delicacy of a surgeon, one eye upon me, one on the trims within. I stood useless, holding the gown up while she laid one rare and beautiful band after another across it. Finally, a roll of aqua velvet ribbon caught her eye.

"Yes, this is just the thing. Two falls at each shoulder I think, Tilde, one on the bustle and little ones on the hem in front. And a head piece also."

But first the gown must be fitted. Louisa sat and sipped her café au lait from a gilded cup (Eclair lapped the residue from

195

the saucer) while Tilde corseted me with little help from the subject.

"Tighter, tighter on the waist, Tilde. She'll never get into it unless we make it very tight. Too much country living, Amber Leigh, too many bacon and sausage."

But when the gown floated over my head, the waist was cleared with an inch to spare. "No matter, tonight we let her out half an inch. But no more."

They both tucked and pinned and pulled at me. They fitted my feet with white satin slippers that pinched. "But no matter," said Louisa.

When I was finally fitted, Louisa took one last look, then nodded. Her satisfaction ended suddenly.

"Ach," she intoned so tragically she might have been Duse playing Phaedra, "one more thing we need. Ah, I have it! Tilde, have this note taken to Hemlock at the Falstaff. We need a little more frosting for our cake."

Then the gown was whisked off my shoulders, I was slipped into my wrapper and given a croissant and café au lait. Tilde had vanished with the gown, a sewing box and an intent expression.

"It's a bathing for you now, and then we will have Horst—and the face—to do."

I wondered what there was "to do" on my face as I was led to a small wood-panelled room with a porcelain tub enclosed in a sort of closet and water that ran into it from pipes.

"Marvelous, yes?" beamed Louisa. "You can't think how nice it is. Tilde, her bath."

"I can bathe myself," I protested, one of the few times I could get in a word on my own behalf.

"Not like my Tilde can do it." And with that I was left to disrobe before Tilde, suffer a thorough scrubbing with an ample sponge and a final immersion in water so perfumed and oiled it made me feel guilty just for being there.

By early afternoon I was brought again before Louisa, who waited in her dressing room with the most amazing creature I had ever seen. He had a great taffy-coloured pompadour, a loose-sleeved shirt, no coat, a droopy tie around his neck and a long doleful face which grew even more somber upon viewing me.

"Yes, Horst, this is our little experiment. Sit, my dear, so Horst can see."

"Hmmmm," said Horst, running my still-damp hair through his fingers. He had long fingernails. I stiffened my neck until

I realized that my hair was what Horst was here to see to. I'd heard of men who did women's hair but had never expected to be the object of such a scandalous procedure.

"Crushingly difficult, Louisa. I can't do a thing without cutting. It'll have to go. All this mane. Chop it off. And had we world enough and time, the color should be taken down a bit, frankly. Yes, I see the problem here," he said, examining my face again. I was actually becoming hardened to these inspections and barely shrank at all. "That's why the cutting. But I definitely can do something for you," he drawled.

"Cutting? Louisa, I don't think . . ."

"Good," she snapped. "Then the cutting it is."

So half my good red half-Irish head of hair fell in tendrils upon my lap while Horst hummed something operatic to himself and snipped away at my forehead and temples. My neck was getting stiff, my feet were half asleep and I was perishing of hunger. Louisa's lively face was my only glass, and it was noncommittal. The curling iron came out next and dipped in and out somewhere above my eyes. I began to smell the distinct odor of singed hair.

Horst was finally dismissed, with much cheek-kissing between them, and I was led sheeplike to the full-length mirror. My hair rose in an imposing pompadour, but the front and sides were sheared and crimped to hang in little curls. I wasn't sure I liked it, but the scar was barely visible amid the froth of red fringe.

"Brilliant," said Louisa, "really brilliant. Horst is wrong about the colour, though. Don't pout, you will like it soon enough."

Again I was corseted and petticoated. Finally Louisa led me to her glittering dressing table, that I'd been eyeing all afternoon.

"But I don't paint, Louisa," I said doubtfully. "I don't think it's for me."

"It is for everyone, Liebchen, and especially for you right now." And she dipped her strong little fingers into a medley of fat glass pots and applied them to my face. After her ministrations my cheeks were pinker, my lips redder, my brows and lashes darker and my eyes brighter, for she dropped a clear liquid into each that burned for a moment.

"Always pinch your cheeks just before leaving your room. If you want more colour in your lips, bite them while you are alone. Keep the face taut, do not droop and always eyebrow up. You must think like a queen, eh?"

Being beautiful sounded more torturous than it was worth, but Louisa's commentary went on while she painted my new face. At length she pulled a large jar with coloured salve in it from a special drawer, drew back my newly fashionable frizz and applied the ointment to the ragged line of pink skin along my face. The scar faded as I watched. My eyes, amazed, met hers in the glass.

"You will not be so hasty about the fine art of 'painting' now?"

"No, Louisa. It's miraculous. I never dreamed it could disappear like that. It's truly marvelous."

"That's the good girl," she said.

So it was a new and an old me that was carefully fitted into the white lace gown, now trimmed with aqua loops.

"What is the matter, Amber Leigh? You do not look pleased."

"It . . . it has no sleeves. I am not used to gowns with no sleeves."

"Nonsense. There's sleeve enough."

I surveyed my bare arms. Except for two meagre inches of lace that swept from the bodice and across my upper arms, I was utterly denuded.

"And the bodice, it's so . . . well, it didn't fit this way this afternoon," I lamented, eyeing the décolletage with regret.

"Of course not, why else you think I had Tilde work all afternoon to alter it? This is no time for an attack of false modesty, you are being fashionable! Besides, we haven't got the gloves on yet. Gloves will make the difference. Oh, and here—this too will dress you a bit more." Louisa unwrapped a small box that was lying on a tray. "Yes, very nice. Hugh has chosen well," she said, pulling a choker with two rows of pearls centering on a huge square-cut aquamarine from the box.

She hastily fastened it about my throat, helped me into long white gloves and led me to the looking-glass. The daylight was dimming as night descended on the city. Somewhere in all the lamp-lit rooms other women approached their mirrors for a last look at their labours. But one of them was a tall slender woman whose neck and shoulders gleamed against the glow of a white gown, whose throat was clasped with a glittering jewel and whose auburn hair was mounted on her head like a crown.

"Well?" said Louisa.

I shook my head, half dazed. The glittering creature in the glass shook her head as well. I lifted my gloved arms slightly;

the ghost in the glass met my gesture.

"It's hard to believe it's me, I mean, I. You *are* a surgeon, Louisa."

She looked perplexed at my tribute, but smiled a satisfied smile. "And the hair, it is so right. You see, Tilde, Horst has pulled the curls forward on the head, like a hat tilted rakishly. You remember it. It will be the style soon, Amber Leigh. And you will debut it. At Alcott's."

"Louisa, this is enough. Do I have to go anywhere as well? What is this 'Alcott's'?"

"You hear, Tilde, there are still innocents left in this weary world." Louisa looked shocked at my ignorance. "Alcott's is merely the most soignée, chic, how you say...smart... place in London. A place the people worth watching go to be watched by other people worth watching. For dinner, after the theatre, the opera..."

"A public restaurant? No, really, I couldn't. I've never dined in public before, I'm sure it's really not proper. For me to go with Lord Hugh would be, well, a scandal. We don't do that in Boston. Or Glennverran. Louisa, don't ask me."

But she simply regarded me with those chocolate torte eyes, the look that said, "A whole day of my life I give to make you beautiful and this is how you repay me."

So I meekly listened to her last instructions as I was outfitted, like a soldier going to the front, with a white satin reticule for a kit and dabs of Essence d'Gardenia for ammunition.

"Now, listen carefully, my Amber Leigh. Eat a touch of everything but all of nothing. Lightly on the wines, my child; you are there to be seen, not to make one, to prove that one scratch does not mar the glass, eh?"

I could have pointed out that I had proof enough, that there was no need to parade myself before the world. But then, I supposed Lord Hugh, having delivered me over to this magician of his, wished to test the illusion. The thought made me nervous.

"Hurry, Tilde." There was an edge in Louisa's voice. "It's nearly seven and Hugh will be here any moment. Ach, a wrap, we have no wrap...Tilde, get me the white capelet, the lamb with marabou...no time, bring it along after. Hugh is here."

She captured my wrist before I barely had time to catch up the ample train and follow her down the hall. At the top of the stairs she left me to billow down ahead of me. I hung back, suddenly feeling ridiculous.

"Hugh! Hugh!" I heard her voice waft upwards like an excited child's on Christmas morning. "You must see. It is a miracle."

Being regarded as a "miracle" didn't help the surprise package on the stairs trying to descend without tripping over her train or spraining an ankle in the too-tight slippers. But it was better than being regarded as a governess and the thought of the long grey days of the rest of my life was enough to bring out the Duse lurking in me. I forced my gloved hand, which had been clutching the polished walnut railing, to slip lightly down its smooth length. I stopped peering anxiously at the steps and raised my head. If one must suffer for beauty, well, breaking one's neck was a quicker way than most. I thought of the hackneys, those burnished high-stepping beasts hitched to the most elegant carriages in London. My head rose higher, my shoulders set back and I felt for the first time I truly lived up to the image of me in the glass.

I would not make a fool of myself in front of Lord Hugh. I would be a smashing triumph. I would be a Devora for a day. I would make all the peasants in my peasantish background proud of me. Indeed I would, if only there weren't this fluttering in my stomach and this tautness starting in the back of my neck.

Lord Hugh and Louisa waited at the newel post, conversing softly. I wished I could quietly turn and disappear back to the landing.

But it was too late.

"Here she is." Louisa pinioned me with her voice. Like a butterfly on velvet. Lord Hugh, looking stern in evening dress, turned to view the specimen and as he saw me his face absolutely froze, expressionless. I faltered, suddenly sure the paint had melted to drip over my features, my hair had fallen into snarls, the gown had dissolved into rags.

There was a quick flurry of fur past my feet and a bouncing wave of blonde hair surged down the staircase to the hall.

"Why, Eclair, you naughty, naughty girl! You've ruined our Miss Amber Leigh's entrance, you coquette." Louisa swept the little dog up in her arms and beamed on the rest of my descent.

"Excellent, Louisa, your charge is almost presentable." Lord Hugh took a frothy capelet from the waiting Tilde and draped it over my all-too-undraped shoulders, formally presenting me with his arm. I took it reluctantly, rueing the day—yesterday—when I'd ever agreed to this mad outing to the city.

Lord Hugh handed me expertly into a hansom carriage, hired, I noticed, but of first quality. The little carriage lanterns flickered in the plush-lined interior. I was suddenly panicky. What had I been thinking of, to be rattling off alone with a man who was no better than a stranger and very likely much worse than he should be? But he cast himself into the seat opposite and paid very little attention to me.

In a very short while the carriage stopped and I was handed out before a door lit by blazing lanterns and patrolled by a man in a greatcoat.

"Evenin', m'Lord," said this stout soul, opening the doors for us. I glided through with my heart in my throat and surely about to burst the pearl choker and send beads scattering all over the elegant black-and-white marbled foyer floor. A majordomo was at my elbow, Louisa's capelet was whisked off my shoulders before the pang of regret I felt at the loss of its protective presence had even made itself felt.

"Will the Godolphin Room be satisfactory, m'Lord?" came another accommodating voice from behind me. I hardly cared to turn and see what other attendant our progress had gathered.

"No, Nevins. I think the Regency Room tonight, by the fire if you can."

"Most certainly, m'Lord." And I flowed into procession behind Nevins at a tap from Lord Hugh on my elbow. The train trailed behind me with that satisfactory heavy feel only good dressmaking can give. I kept my eyebrows arched à la Louisa and my head high according to advice on another matter from someone less versed in fashion. Nevins nimbly threaded his way between a number of pink linen-covered round tables, half occupied by several exceedingly wealthy-looking individuals, and through an arch into a room dadoed with cherrywood, with green brocade wall covering above.

Lord Hugh seated me at a small table near a crackling fireplace. I tucked my reticule to the side of my glittering table setting and began working the gloves off through the small pearl-buttoned slits at the wrist. It was a matter that required my total attention if I were not to begin flailing wildly with my elbows. Another formally attired serving man came round while I was so engaged and Lord Hugh gave instructions for dinner, rattling off a lot of French dishes so fast that despite Miss Prue's noblest efforts my schoolgirl French could hardly decipher it. But I believed I picked up the phrase for calf brains.

My gloves finally disposed of and the surreptitious glances

I took around the largely vacant room done, I looked at Lord Hugh. He was tasting a white wine another man held ready. After his nod my glass was filled and we were left to confront each other across the pink linen and the hyacinth-and-baby's-breath centerpiece.

"Have you never eaten out?" he enquired, much in the way I would have said "Have you never read?" to an Oxford scholar.

"No," I said shortly, still not sure I approved of the entire proceedings. He laughed lightly and I sipped the wine. It was better than anything I'd ever tasted; I had all I could do to remember Louisa's instruction to eat little and drink next to nothing.

"And in—was it Philadelphia—in that city did they have no public restaurants?"

"Boston. None that I would care to go to in my position."

"Yes. You were governess there?"

"Yes. Or at least I attended the children. Whether I governed them at all is a matter of some question."

"You were not a good taskmistress?"

"Oh, I could lay down the law, but American children are quite independent, you know. No kowtowing to Miss for the sake of it, only if it will gain them something. Practical little beasts, I suppose."

"I'm surprised you find such willfulness a fault. But you hadn't planned on playing instructress, had you?"

"No, I hadn't planned on anything, that was the entire problem. When Father...died, I found no amount of planning could have changed things at any rate. There was no money." I looked directly at him as I said this; if he had a remark to make he decided against it.

"And your father, he was an importer, was he not? I recall a Dunne in Bradstreet Square who had some rather lovely things—crystal and such fripperies."

"Yes, Father mainly brought in things from Scotland and Ireland, the linens and laces, the glass, the wools and whiskies..."

"Ah, now there's a piece of goods worth importing. Whatever else one may say about Ireland, one certainly can't fault her whiskey."

"I have not had the pleasure," I replied somewhat stiffly, though Father had never been abstemious and I'd secretly been burning to sample the drink the gentlemen retired to over their cigars.

The soup arrived and conversation ceased while I sized up

the place setting and finally found the proper spoon among the ten or so pieces of silver laid out before me.

It was a murky, boglike broth with some small black things floating in it that I thought it better not to enquire about. But its flavour was delightfully subtle and I played with the unhappy thought that they were probably only mushrooms and likely poisonous at that.

Lord Hugh attended to his soup in an all-engrossing way. I watched the firelight play across his clear-cut features and wondered why he'd had such sudden mercy on me when he'd been in a fair way to being hateful and humiliating at every turn. Where did he acquire the scar that was so distinctive? I rapidly flicked my eyes over it; usually in conversation with Lord Hugh one looked everywhere but there. It was not long, but deep, and marred a set of features that would have done Lord Byron credit, albeit a bit more stubborn. A bitter thing to bear when one was healthy, wealthy and handsome otherwise.

Faces were strange things, I thought, looking at the lean line of Lord Hugh's clean-shaven jaw. Now that was a sinister angle if I ever saw one. Devlin, with his shock of black hair and closely trimmed black beard, should have looked menacing but he seemed as jaunty and friendly as a puppy. It was a face you trusted while its owner infuriated you.

But Lord Hugh was constructed along the lines of a greyhound, that aloof aristocratic hound, all sleekness and no rough edges. It was a face whose eyes one seldom met, but then again perhaps that was the scar. Even Adrian, who'd been quite good-looking enough for any one man, had relaxed into an endearing sort of crinkle now and again. It was one reason I—almost—lost my heart to him. But I couldn't see Lord Hugh crinkling if his life depended upon it. No, there was some reason he'd invited me along on this masquerade and it would be a dry day along Galway Bay before he should use me to whatever purpose he had.

He glanced up, caught me studying him, and his eyes narrowed slightly. I had the presence to look schoolgirlish and flustered and quickly return to my soup.

"Your father died recently?"

"A few years ago."

"And the importing business?"

"Dissolved."

"You have no other relations?"

"Virtually none. My mother died soon after I was born and,

well, Father had dozens of shirttail cousins parading through, but none of them stayed long or returned again. At any rate, I never saw enough of them to know them well."

"And your mother, was she Irish also?"

"Oh, no, Mother was as Anglo-Saxon as Alfred the Great. No, Father was the only outlander among us. I don't suppose it was easy, living in an England that condescended to one's race and probably getting no thanks from his relations for turning Anglophile."

"But you know nothing of your mother's relations?"

I was tiring of this catechism in place of conversation and decided to add some spice to it as our first course arrived.

"You seem extremely interested in my antecedents," I observed. "Or is it my pedigree?"

He was half obscured by a plate of steaming something the waiter was placing before him as I uttered this last, but I saw a flush creep lightly along his cheekbones. Something had struck home. He tapped the fork once on the linen with a kind of frustration.

"I am most anxious for you to try this next dish, Miss Dunne," he said with startling solicitation, changing the subject. "For one who has inhabited the North American coastal states, it should be a rare treat."

I forked the soggy mess on the Sèvres china and tried a steaming forkful.

"It's quite a rarity here of course," he continued, watching me. "One seldom finds eel prepared as well outside of Paris. Such a delicate flavor, don't you think? I believe you'd better have some wine, you look a bit done in. A true rarity, as I said, though there are actually those squeamish enough to object to the source of such a dish. Foolish of them, don't you think?"

"Not at all," I replied when I had stopped coughing. "I can't imagine anyone choosing to consume the mashed . . . body . . . of a perfectly harmless sea creature. It was not very sporting of you not to forewarn me. I hardly think it is friendly of you, Lord Hugh." It was the first time I had addressed him by his Christian name and I imbued it with all the ice I could muster for so short a syllable.

"Come now, my dear Amberleigh," he responded even more solicitously, "you hardly tasted the dish, and were you not overconcerned with its constitution I daresay you'd find it a delightful blend of sauce and seasonings."

"Thank you, no. Louisa said I was to exercise caution and

eat very little or I should devour myself out of house and gown."

"Louisa is a very good instructress," he said in such a curiously flat tone that I looked sharply at him. He was halfway through the disgusting eel and showed no sign of stopping. I nearly choked again, resorting to a good many more swallows of wine than I'm sure Louisa would have approved.

How revolting of him to have actually ordered the mess—I suppose surprises like this were "one of the little games" to which Louisa had referred. I wondered what other "little games" to which he was addicted. Then again, I didn't want to wonder at all. He was my only escort for the evening.

"Did you like America?"

"I daresay I never thought of it in terms of liking it or not. It was the place where I was able to procure employment and, yes, I rather liked the idea of travelling, of living somewhere else, somewhere foreign."

"And was it?"

"Not really. Everybody in Boston was trying desperately to pretend they were like everybody else—in London or Paris." He laughed at that and I found myself warming to an analysis of Boston and my years there.

"It's incredible how the Americans, having loosed themselves from Britain, now spend half their days copying English customs and manners and dress. Truly, I couldn't fathom it.

"Mrs. Willoughby was an agreeable enough lady with manners as unfurled as her several chins, but she would have given half her life and her passion for chocolate-coated cherries for a title, I swear. And since she couldn't have one, she acted as if she did until poor Mr. Willoughby dived into his account books directly on coming home from the office. If aristocracy doesn't attract them, money surely does, and I never saw so much of it wasted."

Lord Hugh was openly laughing now and I felt a bit ashamed of holding up a mirror, and an unkind one at that, to people in whose home I had lived.

"But they were not bad people; they were very warm and kind, actually. I laughed at the way they tiptoed round their servants so that there was some question as to who was serving whom, but I never heard them say an unkind word before a one of them." I was silent a moment. "I've seen a lot of that at Carnhaven."

"Carnhaven is not typical," said Lord Hugh.

"Isn't it? I think it may well be. It's not merely because

I've Irish blood in me, that counts for naught. I think myself English and I am, anyone's arguments to the contrary. It's simply cruel to see the way these people are treated and despised openly. They are good, honest people. But somehow we English come into their land and the Irish are nothing but bugs to be crushed under our overprivileged feet."

"You've been talking politics with Devlin Quade, I take it."

"I haven't been discussing 'politics' with anyone. I am simply concerned to see people treated like cattle. It embarrasses me. It is not kind."

"What you say reminds me of India. Now there you would see people treated like cattle. And cattle treated like people, for that matter, for they have sacred cows there that no one may tamper with under great peril, though an entire village be starving. Now there is a land fit to raise your indignation, Miss Dunne. It's a pity you didn't see it."

"It's a greater pity that it didn't raise your indignation, Mr. Davenant," I snapped, dropping his title like a gauntlet.

But he merely looked amused.

"Doubtless you are one of these avid Home Rulers then? I beg you to keep your voice if not your sentiments down; such shades of opinion would not do well here."

I glanced around, startled to find the room had filled during our conversation, if anything that teetered upon the brink of argument could be called that. Most of the tables were occupied by twos and threes of gentlemen in evening dress. But at least two others were given over to couples and I breathed a sigh of relief at seeing the women looked quite respectable. Or if they weren't, at least they wore it well.

Another plate had come and gone almost untasted before the fowl was brought and this I tackled with all the appetite that fasting brought on.

"You haven't answered me. Do you think Home Rule should serve Ireland any better?"

"I wonder why you trouble yourself with my opinion. I am only an ignorant female." And I returned to the squab with redoubled fervour. It was a beastly bird to manage and I quite took my aggressions out on its innocent bone structure.

"Simply because I am an intelligent man doesn't mean that I might not be interested in what ignorant females are thinking." And he smiled. Blast him. I should give him a plan to make his privilege shrivel.

"It's quite clear to me that if after four hundred years you

206

cannot convince a conquered people to remain that way that one might as well turn them loose. Would you keep a horse you could not ride? Of course not."

"Many men do," he interjected cynically, but I ignored the insinuation and rushed on.

"These people—and truth to tell I've come to know them at all only in the time I've been at Carnhaven, but I swear I know them better than most lifelong British residents—these people were not meant to be half-citizens, forbidden to read or write by the townships, to speak their own tongue, to have their land divided into barren patches that hardly feed the animal yard, much less the household. Their cottages should be their own, the landlords should be dislanded or whatever one would do and we high-minded British should leave the place in peace."

"And if we left, what do you think would become of your sketchpad cottages then? Ireland is no garden land, no Eden, though the Irish would have you believe it was. On the whole the crops it produces are miserly and its manufactured products scanty. Government is more than fine phrases and a matter of putting the yoke on people, as you'd call it in your innocent altruism. It's bringing industry to the farmlands, developing the local areas, keeping the books and keeping the damn country going. They'd slide into the Atlantic without Mother England grasping their coattails!"

"You're speaking from privilege, because you've never had to know adversity, what it's like to earn your own—eel—or to fight your own battles, and if you think that Ireland can be kept down much longer you're not looking at her people and you're not looking at your own weaknesses."

I must have been glaring by then, for my hands were fists on the immaculate linen. Lord Hugh looked fairly ruffled himself, but he didn't answer me.

"Well, I am looking at Miss Dunne," he said finally in a calmer tone, "and I believe she'd better look at herself in a glass."

I sat back in my chair, suddenly aware that I was hardly the picture of cool elegance I was dressed to be while grasping my knife and fork like weapons and pounding their handles into the cloth to make a point. I relinquished them to my plate.

"I believe you'll find a retiring room beyond that curtain," said Lord Hugh, indicating a green brocade fall behind us. I took my cue, gathered up the flimsy reticule and retreated to the doorway.

There was a waiting room beyond, with no attendant. I approached myself in one of the several mirrors set round the room. My colour was very high; no need of amplification from Madame Louisa's harefoot tucked into my reticule by Tilde, ever efficient. I hadn't thought I'd been that earnest in my conversational efforts; but then we'd been sitting rather near the fire.

There was a small ewer and basin with a number of embroidered towels by it on a stand. I wet a cloth and applied it to my cheeks and face. I leaned my forehead against the glass. It felt cool.

Why had I come? Lord Hugh was playing deep and I'd been foolish to think myself a match for him. He had learned more of me in the last two hours than anyone at Carnhaven knew after several months. And what did I know of him? Nothing beyond the facade he cared to present me. More and more I became convinced that Elaine stood in very real danger from such as he.

I saw the curtain swag in the mirror and heard the light chatter of a woman's voice— "... something new for him ... where do you suppose he found her, that astonishing hair ..." I turned to find two women from a table across the room entering my refuge. They stopped talking abruptly. Eyes cast down, we politely edged passed each other and I returned refreshed to the green room and the pink linen field of honour.

Lord Hugh had obviously arrived at the same conclusions as I. He seated me most solicitously and directed the conversation into his Indian adventures, which truly sounded half made-up, they were that exotic. I'd always believed India to be a story concocted by Mr. Kipling and the soldiers who served there to pass the time.

"Do you mind if I smoke?" Lord Hugh asked during a lull. I imagine I should have minded, but I supposed there was no other room to withdraw to and acquiesced. He slipped a flat silver case from a breast pocket and extracted the slimmest and smallest cigar I'd ever seen. It was a dark cylinder of tobacco and I knew instantly it was a cigarette but I'd never seen one before in my limited life.

I watched fascinated as he lit the thing and exhaled a blue stream of smoke through his nose. I'd never seen anyone perform that trick with a cigar. It was perhaps the most astonishing event of the entire evening from my standpoint, but Lord Hugh seemed totally unaware of how *outré* I found his habit.

He leaned back in his chair and drummed his well-manicured fingers on the pink linen as he smoked and regarded me through his yellow eyes.

"At least this evening has been a *succès d'estime*," he finally pronounced, taking a sip from the brandy at his elbow. A single glass of wine was obviously considered liquor enough for a lady, for the only thing at my elbow was air.

"What do you mean?" I asked.

Before he could reply, his eyes suddenly shifted past me and he stood to extend a hand to someone behind me.

"Trevor," he said, "I half expected to hear of you from Bombay by now."

"Hugh." The other man glanced down at me and I didn't care for either his look or his looks. He was of medium height, with silky fair hair smoothed back and a small pale mustache. He must have been past fifty, for his face, though pleasant enough, sagged here and there in little pockets. His expression was arrogant and arrogantly he sized me up while he talked with Lord Hugh, his watery eyes darting from my aquamarine necklace to my red hair to my fashionable décolletage. Most especially to my décolletage. I felt my colour rising as inevitably as the tide.

"No, I postponed that venture." He turned again and fixed me with his downward glance. This time I met his gaze, as noncommitally as I could, but I met it. I would not flutter my eyes down like a schoolgirl.

"And your charming companion?" He turned for an introduction.

"She is from the country," said Lord Hugh imperturbably.

"One of your Irish finds, Hugh? None of us can fathom why you hide yourself away in that bog-ridden backwater. Unless you unearth such jewels as these . . ."

He held his hand out for mine on this gallantry, but I resolved to withhold it. Before I could make a point of it, I heard a satin slither to my right.

"My reticule," I cried, dismayed to see it on the floor. Lord Hugh and the waiter made a dive for it, the waiter coming up with the trophy and handing it triumphantly to me. It seemed to me that Lord Hugh had been quite near my bag before it fell.

"At any rate, I mustn't dally. Come round when you're not burdened with such vivacious company. We'll talk." The man called Trevor flicked me once with angry eyes, bowed to Lord Hugh and wove his way through the little tables and out.

"Blessed be the peacemakers," breathed Lord Hugh to himself. "I'd rather not have Selden to contend with just now, so perhaps you could manage a smile and a nod as we leave. Or would that be too compromising for a lady of your moral standards?" he hissed as he drew back my chair. I flushed, reminded once more that I was a fallen women in certain circles.

Luck had it, as he had anticipated, that we caught up to Trevor Selden in the foyer. I liked his looks even less under the brighter glow of the chandelier. He was just accepting his stick and hat as I had my capelet slipped onto my shoulders by the attentive manservant. I nodded regally to the worm and bestowed my most dazzling smile upon him. His interest rekindled startlingly—he stood more upright, regarded me significantly, bowed again to Lord Hugh and departed mollified.

"You see, honey is more attractive than gall."

"Only if one wishes to lure vipers," I said.

"That is one viper I most urgently wish to pacify. Thank you for your assistance, it's almost the only thing that would satisfy the man."

"He looks dissolute," I observed as he handed me into the waiting carriage.

"He is. And he probably thinks the same of you."

"Why should you care about mollycoddling such a revolting man?" I asked, suddenly realizing that of all things I expected from Lord Hugh, reticence was not one of them. In the half-light of the carriage lamps he looked a bit uncomfortable. "Lay it to my avocation," he said mysteriously and in a way that brooked no more questions.

The carriage lurched around a corner without warning and we were hurled up and down again at such a jolt that my double strand of pearls clicked together like castanets. A quick touch from my fingers assured me of their safety.

"You like that trinket?" asked Lord Hugh.

"A bit," I said, not caring to appear too enamoured of anything I owed to him.

"Odd what women respond to," he mused. "If you want more of those," he said, nodding to the pearls, "you'd better be kinder to the Seldens of the world."

My fears of seduction revived instantly.

"I would be as happy with glass," I said stiffly.

"And if you could not afford glass?"

"Then berries."

He laughed then, so heartily it frightened me, for I didn't see a jest.

"Here," he said, "if you don't want to exchange pearls for berries immediately, they'd better be untangled."

I turned my head and felt a catch as the cape tripped upon the clasp. Lord Hugh leaned across the seat and began working at the pearls. My first instinct was to lean away, but I only turned my head to give him a better chance at it. This was how a hare in a trap would feel when the gamesman came to take him, I was convinced, not sure whether Lord Hugh intended to throttle me or kiss me, both actions I considered him fully capable of.

But he merely untangled the pearls and sat back, striking his white gloves against his hand absently. I rather felt like a prize horse who'd been trotted out into the ring to win ribbons for his master and then allowed to run behind the carriage on the way home once the thing was done.

And, I thought, if I'd been such a shocking success, I certainly didn't think boredom was the emotion I would inspire in the male breast. But Lord Hugh was hardly typical.

For a moment I wished Adrian could be sitting opposite me. I almost saw his burnished brown hair shining in the lantern light, felt his special, warm and somehow—tingly—gaze upon me.

"You look splendid, Amberleigh," he'd say. "I had no idea you were such a beauty. I've been a fool, Amberleigh, not to see that you were meant for me. I never really believed what they said . . ."

"Didn't you?" I would reply with aloof elegance. "It's a pity you never really knew me, Adrian, it could have been so, so . . ." Perhaps I wouldn't toy with him, perhaps I'd take him back. As if I'd ever had him. Perhaps there was still some way . . .

"Dinner must do something for your disposition. Why the Mona Lisa smile?" Lord Hugh's remark broke the surface of my reverie as a stone shatters a still pond.

"Because I suspect we're at our journey's end," I snapped, grateful that a sudden forward and backward lurch of the springs bore out my words. As he handed me out he tried to bend his penetrating gaze on my face but I kept my head well down and was most engaged in managing my train and shaking out my skirts. It was humiliating to have been caught mooning like a schoolgirl by Lord Hugh and I resolved that it shouldn't happen again.

Inside the hall, faithful Tilde was waiting; she'd been curled up on the music-room sofa, but came at the sound of our knock,

211

she said, tenderly removing the marabou capelet.

"How did it go?" There was an anticipation I'd never expected to see on plain Tilde's face.

"Fair," said Lord Hugh, refusing to let her take his evening cloak and tossing it carelessly over a bench. "No, quite splendidly," he amended as Tilde's face fell. "You and Louisa can take full credit for your labours." He grinned, pinching her woebegone cheek. "You managed to fashion a silk purse after all. But she will tell you all about it, I'm sure. And is *she* . . ." He nodded towards the stairs and it was fascinating to hear how the same personal pronoun could take on such different accents, I noted to myself. Tilde had nodded in reply and Lord Hugh left us without a word to take the stairs with a peculiar kind of reluctant energy. The air crackled with that Something Is Up feeling, but a quick glance at stolid Tilde assured me I'd get no illumination from her.

"So it was a success?" she asked, already beginning to fuss at my folderols and examine my train for damage as I preceded her up the staircase. The upper hall was still. I heard no murmur of voices, though the thick oak doors would see to that in any event.

In my own room—I was fair developing a habit of playing musical bedrooms of late—Tilde expertly extracted me from my gown and underpinings. She was like no other servant I had encountered, for I noticed she never called me "miss."

"A success of sorts, I suppose," I finally assured her. "If you can call having a stitch in one's side and feet that feel half-amputated a success." I kicked off the beastly though beautiful slippers with relief. "But I believe I did look quite nice, quite— unflawed. Why, one man even gave me lewd looks . . ." I went to the glass, looking quite different now. This was surely one of Tilde's nightdresses; Louisa would never wear this practical Mother Hubbard of flannel. "But this . . ." I drew back the red fringe that was beginning to seem familiar and inspected the side of my face. ". . . this can be corrected. Erased. It truly amazes me."

"You looked—very nice," said Tilde briskly, evidently feeling that too much praise was spoiling, but I could tell she was proud of her efforts.

"It was nothing but a miracle and I'm very grateful to you and Madame Louisa for having worked it."

Tilde blushed, to my amazement. She ducked her head and edged to the door. "I'll help you pack in the morning," she said almost inaudibly as she fled down the hall.

People were so surprising. Here in this gingerbread house lived a woman with a face like a thistle and the sensibilities of a pansy. I was glad I'd specially thanked her.

I bounced into bed in better spirits. Tomorrow I could return to Carnhaven—and my problems with Elaine—almost my old self. I wondered why Elaine had been so distant from my thoughts lately when I should have been obsessed with her. I really hadn't been given time to puzzle out her riddle, but I would solve it when I returned.

And Adrian. I hadn't thought about him for a long time until I had conjured his presence in the carriage. He was probably in London now, perhaps not even too far from here. If I concentrated all my thoughts and sent them to him, if I called on him with all my will, could I reach him? I tried it, my mind speaking his name over and over. "Adrian... Adrian..." I stopped. What if it worked? I was startled to find I still had a tear for Adrian and Amberleigh and what might have been.

Tomorrow would be that delightful voyage across the Channel—I was looking forward to a little wind and water to clear my romantic head of cobwebs. Tomorrow I'd see Hemlock again—strange, I'd missed his cheerful presence after a week of sharing Shallowford with him. Hemlock was likely at the Falstaff Club now, loyally waiting up for his tardy master. A good many people awake and wondering in London tonight, I thought.

And Lord Hugh and Louisa, I wondered what they were about. There was something strange there. A knowing and a not knowing. There was another puzzle worth working had I the time.

I wondered why Lord Hugh never had anything done about his scar, it was evidently easier than one thought. At least I wouldn't have to worry about that; doubtless it would fade as Hemlock promised. I liked Hemlock; he had an honest, straightforward way about him and he refused to play games. Well, he had hedged about where my wound was, but I could hardly blame the man for that. But that was as good as over, wasn't it...?

I thought I was still thinking but something must have happened because the next thought I had was that it was morning.

CHAPTER TWENTY-ONE

I AWOKE with the sunlight filtering through the curtains and Madame Louisa drawn up to my bed on a boudoir chair. She was wearing a filmy dressing gown and looked fresh and lively. But even though she had sat with her back to the strong daylight, a habit of hers, I imagined, I could see the fine network of lines alongside her mouth and eyes. It was like seeing a stereopticon card clearly, then through the double image of the viewer—everything wavered a bit.

"I've had Tilde bring you the hot chocolate and a croissant—but that's merely because you had such a tiring evening yesterday. One mustn't overdo these things or one's figure goes and then who would want you, eh, Liebchen?"

"Nobody wants me at any rate," I answered a bit tartly as I ravenously broke and devoured the croissant and reached for another.

Madame tapped my wrist to stop me.

"That's not what I hear. Hugh and I had a long discussion of you last night. Now, don't look resentful, it's only natural that I should wonder how my protégé did. Hugh tells me that you were a triumph, that every eye at Alcott's was paying homage to your table."

I had the grace to blush.

"You don't know this city, Amber Leigh, but Hugh Davenant does. And he says you were a surprising success. Hugh isn't generally one to be surprised, at least by women. So I asked about you and he told me that your prospects were, shall we say . . . not good. How you came to stay with the St. Clares and, of course, your—indiscretion. Now, stay still and listen to me."

She rose and went slowly to the window before facing me again.

"You may have wondered in your—relatively—innocent country mind exactly how I fit into this great scheme of things. Some of the enlightened peers of England—and you'd be surprised how few there are nowadays—bring me their sons for . . . tutelage. You might call me a headmistress of sorts."

The irony in her smile as she said this seemed to turn back upon her and pierce her.

"It is not a bad arrangement. These Englishmen have a frightening ability to smother their most natural inclinations, while I, I found early in life that I had certain ... appetites ... that are not always acceptable in a woman, not even in Europe, which should know better. Never let anyone tell you, Amber Leigh, that a woman must regard her role in nature's scheme as duty. But I think you know that."

What could I tell her? She obviously accepted me as the stained country girl all Glennverran thought me to be. And I had not yet found a way to deny it without maligning Elaine.

"So it is a very fine arrangement, my dear," Madame Louisa went on, advancing to the side of the bed with a smile while I plucked nervously at the coverlet. "I have my parade of boys, my undergraduates, who really suit a woman of my temperament much more adequately than a man of fading powers or one distracted by the business of life. But don't mistake me; I'm not suggesting such a life for you."

She paused while I considered her words. Louisa bent her head to toy with her sash and I saw the sheen of grey starting to cloud the brown. I suddenly understood the relationship between her and Lord Hugh.

"And he, he was one of 'your boys,' was he not?" I demanded.

"One of the first," she said with a smile and a glance to the side that saw nothing. "Hugh was really a charming boy. And to have a brilliant career, you know, in foreign service. And then they sent him off to that wilderness they call a country, that England wouldn't know what to do with even if she won it by the blood of her young men. And he came back what they call a man, not charming at all anymore really. It was more than the scar—a scar would not have embittered the boy I knew."

I watched the gently shifting curtain shadow on the coverlet and we were silent.

"But they all leave me eventually, my boys."

"You ..."

"Yes, Amber Leigh, go on—we are being very frank, you know."

I loved her smile—it was gentle and wise and I couldn't think of her as a bad woman.

"You loved him, didn't you, I mean really loved him?"

"I loved all my boys," she said abruptly, standing up and moving away.

"But him more," I persisted. "It explains..."

"Nothing." Her voice was bleak. "No, I was older already when I began. I'm always older. And they cut their apron strings just as they do from their mamas. But I teach them to be good lovers, that is my contribution to the world. And God knows it needs it. There are wives and mistresses who would bless me for it.

"And that's why I speak to you of this, my Amber Leigh," she said, returning to grasp my hands for attention. "You are young and I see in you a rare lack of—of this silly British fear of love. If life offers no prospects worth considering, think of this. You could be what you were last evening—a woman sought after, admired. True, you are not quite a beauty, but you could pass for such properly attended. And you're bright, more than enough, to manage a dozen men. I could advise you—you would have a gay, glittering life."

I was speechless, a rarity for one with my Irish loquacity usually to the fore. "But what you propose is nothing more than my becoming a...a...Scarlet Woman!"

"Oh, for God's sake, you sound like Hugh." She put her hands to her head and whirled to the window. "I merely try to offer an opportunity in life to a—a homeless girl—" She paused a long time. "And I am lonely. You could live here with me. There is no one I can talk to, day after day."

I saw her then, her delicate profile hard-edged against the bright light—aging, waning, hoping to relive her girlhood in a younger woman.

"You say Lord Hugh didn't like the idea either?" I asked, wondering why his sense of morality should so suddenly resurrect.

"Oh, Hugh was terribly amused, he said I was dreaming dreams. That you're merely an 'experiment' and 'a vain, precocious little liar at that.' That he had never intended to play procurer of high-priced harlots." Her voice had gotten deeper and more bitter with every word.

"But," I said, forgetting my insults in her suffering, "he as much as called you a...a—"

"I know." She sighed. "Sometimes it's hard to remember what a charming boy he was. With Hugh nowadays, it's almost always hard. Well, he says he's taking you back this afternoon, so we must get you ready. But there's nothing to prevent you from taking the Channel back to me if you decide to try my world. Remember that, Amber Leigh. We'll write," she ordered crisply and with some of the Teutonic discipline back in her voice. "But you know," she said suddenly, sinking down beside me on the bed. "I think it's this"—she gently brushed my new curls aside from the scar—"that makes Hugh so unreasonable about you. But if it hadn't been for that, we'd have never met. So..."

Madame Louisa swished out of the room, soon sending Tilde to help me pack my new treasures—the gown, the slippers now slightly scuffed and the thing that meant the most to me, the large jar of the miraculous salve that hid scars. I could hardly believe I was meant to keep it all, but Tilde remorselessly saw it packed. The aquamarine and pearl necklace I held a moment in my hands before I slipped it in amongst the petticoats—I had ambivalent feelings about it. It was costly, but a mere bauble, a prop in a now-past play, to Lord Hugh. And it was just a taste of the life Louisa offered. I loved it for being rare and real and costly. And I hated it for being something I owed to Lord Hugh, who had become my momentary benefactor simply because he knew what it was like to be marked by someone else's hatred for life.

Some of Madame Louisa's paint still clung to my cheeks that morning. Either that or I was restless to be going home. Carnhaven seemed so remote; getting back to it was a goal I could face for the first time with some equanimity.

"Miss Dunne!" said Hemlock with a stunned look as I drifted into the hall while Lord Hugh made his farewell to my mentor. "You look as though you'd had a month in the country instead of a night in the city," he said bluntly, immediately remembering his place and folding his lips with self-reproach.

"It's reassuring to know some of our party are observant, Hemlock." I smiled as I drew on the tight kid gloves. "Perhaps it shall help us arrive at our destination efficiently." But I had forgotten what Hemlock's astonishment had reminded me of—my head still wore the efforts of the incredible Horst. A glance in the glass assured me that even Devora could not fail to notice the change. I looked much less the country mouse and more the city cat. Someone of whom account must be taken. It was incredible what appearances could do for one. I felt more commanding as well. As though I could stride back to Carnhaven and gather up the reins and teach Devora a step or two. This time I would crack the conundrum that was Elaine. Or I would leave and give the entire thing up.

Lord Hugh finally came through the hall, wordlessly gathering up Hemlock and me like attendant waves, and flowed into the hansom. Hemlock rode aloft with the driver but there was no conversation to overhear inside. The way to Waterloo Station was familiar, the street crowded with midday wagons and drays and some few carriages here and there.

I recalled the last time I had rattled to a London railway station; it had been following my father's funeral. I briefly wondered if it would have been possible to stop at his grave; but Lord Hugh's face did not look amenable to sentimental gestures this morning. I remembered how like a funeral procession my last carriage ride out of London had seemed. This day seemed gayer, brighter. There was a sting in the air that reddened cheeks and raised hearts. Hemlock's impeccable timing saw our party hustled from carriage through station to rail compartment before I'd had much time to analyze the glow in the late summer air.

Aboard ship on our extended Channel crossing, I escaped to the rail to consider it. Hemlock brought up my rear very shortly.

"You like the air, too?"

"On occasion, miss," he responded noncommitally.

"Then why are you hanging about looking awkward? You've not been ordered to guard me?"

The turned-down corners of his mouth confirmed my guess.

"Hemlock," I reproached.

"His Lordship feels that you are disaster-prone," he explained uncomfortably.

I considered the charge. It was true. What did Hemlock know of me save for the two highly unconventional entrances I'd made into his usually placid household? Once to demand accounting of a wounded man I'd been instrumental in bringing there. And again, wounded myself, found soggily soaking in the pleasant brook that babbled past his front door.

"You don't know what to make of me, do you, Hemlock?"

"I'm not sure it's my place to say, miss." His tone was proper but unenlightening.

"When would it be proper to say? If I were, say, Head Housekeeper at Shallowford, would you speak your mind to me then?"

"Hardly, miss. The Head Housekeeper is first in the establishment and despite my greater intimacy with the Master, I would hardly speak familiarly to her."

"Well, in my old role as governess then."

"It would not do for the valet to interfere in the doings of the children's education," he responded primly if hypothetically.

"Parlour maid, then," I suggested in exasperation.

"Well, yes, miss. That is to say, were you parlour maid I might feel it would not be beyond my place to address some personal opinions to you."

I laughed until a staid couple taking a deckside turn stopped to impale me on their bland gaze. "Oh, Hemlock, you're like every male in the world since Eden; you can't converse with a woman unless she's your social inferior. I'm sorry to learn that the man can be as defensive as the gentleman."

Hemlock turned the perfectly proper black bowler in his hands around once. His eyes instinctively glanced left, then right, and then—assured we were alone—he sighed.

"No, I don't know how to take you, miss. I'd say you were one of them modern ladies who smokes and rides motorcars, but I know that's not your style, as we say. But what should it matter what I think? I can't recall anyone enquiring before."

"Then you haven't been associating with the proper people, Hemlock. That is what comes of being in service to a barbarian. We all care what others think. And whether they wear starched linen or celluloid collars shouldn't make a whit of difference."

"Well, all I know is," said Hemlock, turning his hat in his hands as if he wished to wind it up and send it spinning into the blue, "that it don't make a whit of difference to me why ladies take their travels, though it might to some."

His eyes were bright with sincerity. It had cost him something to express his own opinion. I'd forgotten what else he knew of me, the whispers that circled from kitchen to kitchen in every big house in County Clare. I'd been thinking of myself as the decent little woman I was, not the soiled maiden reputation painted me as, otherwise I would have not been so frank with Hemlock. What could he think of me now, taunting him into relationship in such a forward way?

I blushed.

"Yes, I seem to be very well-travelled of late. I hope you don't think that this trip has been anything but—" I couldn't finish the humiliating sentence. I did care what people thought; I cared what Hemlock thought.

"Oh, no, miss. The wind isn't blowing that way at all. But I wonder why you'd come? He isn't beyond ridiculing a person in his own sharp way . . ." He stopped, guilty, I guessed, at having characterized his master so unprofessionally.

"I was ordered, Hemlock, that's why. Surely you can understand that. I had no idea...He told me he was taking me to a surgeon, I hardly had a chance to protest."

"Ah." Hemlock nodded. He seemed about to say something else but paused. The hat made another interminable round in his hands. "Are you certain you wouldn't like to go inside, miss? The wind's enough to knock the hat off one's head—"

I unsheathed a portion of my ten-inch-long hatpin for Hemlock's perusal and smiled. "I hardly think the wind's enough to disengage this. You can see I'm well-protected, from wind and whatever else might prowl the deck. So go back in; you're not made for crisp grey days at sea, I can tell that."

"It's India has been my ruin, miss. Made me homesick for humidity and hot sun." Hemlock grinned. "Well, if you're not minding it, I'll go in."

"And inform His Lordship that I'm positively fastened to the rail, so no one will have to be sending out search parties after we arrive, if you would be so good."

I turned back to the whipped grey seas and the endless horizon tipping and tilting in the distance. I continually forgot that I wore two faces for the world. The face Devora's scheming had laid over my own was a second skin to me. It must set everyone off; I must seem an incongruous sinner to some, with my Miss Meachum's innocence barely tarnished—with no patina of vice to overlay my sterling character.

And now I'd met a real tainted lady. A painted, tainted lady. It had been most improper of Lord Hugh to bring an unmarried lady like myself to such a place. But then, I was again discounting that mask of Devora's that marked me more than the small scar ever would. This trip had been as much a gesture of ridicule as of sympathy, I decided, as the wind whipped the new fringe back from my face. For once I did not feel like cringing behind my hair or my veil. But there was some sympathy at the heart of it, I believed that. More sympathy than even Adrian had shown to me over his careless shoulder the evening of the Carnhaven ball when he had drifted out of my life forever. How truly ironic. And Devora—Devora would not like that I had been singled out for escort to London. Perhaps she would even imagine the worst. Good. If I were to be hung for a sheep and a black one at that, I might as well have the satisfaction of knowing that it made someone miserable.

And Elaine. Was there anyone more miserable than Elaine? Why? Why did I so calmly accept the incredible fact that she'd had her illegitimate child with the lawless union that preceded it and still remained a question to answer? Perhaps I was accepting too much at Carnhaven as it appeared on the face of things. I must come there again as a stranger, probe its secrets as delicately as Madame Louisa delved in her ribbon basket and unearth whatever trail proved fruitful.

Something had happened there that had been the ruin of Elaine. I knew that. And Devora knew its name and would not speak it. Lord Hugh was as interested as I in Carnhaven's mysteries. Adrian was—merely someone I once knew and probably unconcerned with the events there. And the rest—Hemlock, Devlin, Norah Chandler, Mrs. Featherstone, for that matter—were unrelated to the central puzzle. Unless it had something to do with Devlin's United Irish. His face flitted before my mind, black-bearded and younger-looking than ever. But was it? Wasn't he another "face value" I was taking for granted?

Thinking of black beards, my eye wandered and caught the figure of just such a man leaning against the rail a few yards away. He had been staring directly at me. I quickly turned my glance aside to discourage such liberties, but something told me his eyes had done nothing of the sort. I could feel his eyes graze the side of my face. I peered in the opposite direction—nothing but abandoned rail and grey waves beyond, heaving rhythmically. I found a pretext for looking down and slid him another look of appraisal. Stiff, bearded profile, in his middle years, plain clothes, almost somber... and something familiar—but had he edged closer? I whirled suddenly and leaned my back against the railing. My heart pounded inside my travel cloak. There, the door to the main cabin—farther to my left than my deck partner was to my right. I scanned the open deck for the stuffy couple who had stared at my laughter. Gone. Probably driven away by the sight of a woman conversing openly with a man... Hemlock. I wished I'd let him stay. But I was being ridiculous. Why should I be anyone's victim? Blackbeard was merely a travelling tooth-powder sales representative. Or a dour Scottish parson on holiday. Anything but a danger to me.

My eyes flicked over him again. Again he was closer. He turned from the rail and wrested a pipe from a pouch, packing it carefully with tobacco. A pungent spiced aroma caught my nostrils just as his eyes once more netted mine. I stared fixedly at my shoe tips, visible under my blowing skirt. Perhaps he simply misconstrued my position, perhaps he was merely making eyes at a female travelling companion... I was imagining it all, just like a spinster to do such a thing. Create slightly sinister admirers to soothe her sense of rejection. I should be flattered really, not fluttered. Not allowing this moth in my throat to beat its wings against probability. I clutched the rail with one gloved hand and leaned away from it ever so gradually. My "escort" appeared not to have noticed. Quickly then, and I hoped silently, I dashed for the door and the cabin below. The metal handle was cold and slippery to touch; a gust of wind chose that moment to flatten the door shut, resisting my desperate clutching. Over my shoulder the bearded man strode towards me.

"Blast," I hissed to myself, feeling the door finally give suddenly and ricocheting inside the narrow stairway. My cheek came up short on wool broadcloth.

"Are you running the Steepledown or—"

There I was, sandwiched between Lord Hugh on the one hand, asking his interminable questions—I don't believe the man knew a simple declarative sentence—and the bearded menace without. But Blackbeard had resolved his sinister features into the perfectly ordinary face of a doctor of medicine or a clerk or someone quite respectable. He brushed by us with a nod and a tip of his sober-coloured hat to me.

"You always seem to have been running when I come across you," observed Lord Hugh. "Was it laps around the deck this time while carrying a message for the United Irish?"

"Any message I'd be sending now would have to be by semaphore," I glowered while adjusting my hat. "No, the wind was simply up and I decided to take refuge below, isn't that what they call it?"

"I was coming to retrieve you anyway. Hemlock had nothing better to do than play nanny, why didn't you let him?"

"Because I wanted to think."

"And that requires solitude?"

"Yes."

"You seem bent on playing the recluse, Miss Dunne, surely an unrewarding stance for one of your years. Come down the stairs; Hemlock's looking for a partner at whist."

Of course I would be consigned to playing parlour games with the servants, much as a tiresome child is farmed out to the help. I couldn't resist smiling; it was the way Mrs. Bowers dealt with me when I was nine and underfoot—"Off with you, Jenkins' lookin' for a game of cards, but don't you beat him now, you minx." Jenkins had been a good instructor; Hemlock

222

went down in the first few hands and quickly suggested rummy. I agreed; Jenkins had been a past master at rummy. The day I knew I could beat him was the day I knew I was too old for such diversions.

But it did help the dreary journey pass quickly. And I'd so hoped for a bright, brisk crossing—not this slogging through sullen seas. I glanced about the small salon. Lord Hugh was ensconced at an alcove table, immersed in sheaves of papers he drew from a portfolio. Blackbeard was sipping tea in time to the vessel's gentle roll and eyeing me steadily over the cup.

"It's your play, Miss Amberleigh, do you want the discard or not?"

Hemlock's impatient nudging drew my eyes back to the pasteboards fanned out in my hand. My gaze fastened on the jack of clubs, a rather dire-looking bearded fellow, now that I looked.

"No—I, I'll pass it by..."

"Hee-hee," crowed Hemlock, "that's me rummy then. This boy didn't spend all that time in the shade of Calcutta for nothing. I've won me first game." In his excitement, Hemlock's carefully schooled speech slipped a notch. I saw Lord Hugh raise a dark eyebrow from across the room. He jammed the papers back into his portfolio and ambled over to the baize-covered table on which my hat and the ruins of our cards reposed in equal disarray.

"Hemlock, I haven't heard you so elated since you won Bobby Baker's chestnut filly on the verandah of the regimental club in Calcutta."

"Aye, m'Lord, but you were winning her sire off His Almighty Earlship in the game room inside at the same time..."

Hemlock launched into another delighted cackle. I'd never heard his laugh and it startled me. Lord Hugh smiled indulgently. For the first time I could fathom Hemlock's loyalty to his master. It had been different then, a sort of camaraderie that overcame birth and station. All men, all soldiers—some officers and some merely enlisted men—sent off together to Mr. Kipling's land of blistering sun and ragged infidels. It was a kind of male unity that I could never bridge, that ran beneath all the daily ins and outs of the master and valet's relationship like an underground spring. It was a sort of intimacy. And it had nothing to do with one being master and one servant.

I gathered the cards up and laid out a simple Patience, well remembered from those endless afternoons at Twin Beeches.

My glance tested for Blackbeard and found him moved—to another alcove where he now smoked the pipe I'd seen him filling.

"You do crave solitude," said Lord Hugh, leaning over to view my construction and drawing up a chair. His position obstructed my view of Blackbeard; I couldn't tell whether purposefully or not.

"I'll play you a game if you're so skilled as to set Hemlock hooting at a win," he offered.

"I don't think I like your stakes," I said. No, that was a forward remark; I hadn't meant it that way. "Besides, I have no horses to wager." I swept up the cards and prepared to lay out the game again.

"We don't have to play for anything concrete."

"What do you want to play for," I snapped, "my virtue? Oh, that's right, I'd forgotten I don't have it anymore." The cards snapped down on the table in perfect rows, save that I was laying out eight instead of the customary seven.

"Perhaps you do still have—information?" His eyes remained on the cards, as if he were curious to discover how I should deal myself out of the corner I'd played myself into.

"What kind do you want? On the price of tea in China? The correct way to knot a jabot? What colours mix together to produce green? I have all sorts of information." I laid the pattern out for eight rows and heedlessly began playing the game. Actually, it didn't work out badly at that.

"No, you're so inventive, Miss Dunne," he said finally, lifting his eyes from the cards to mine, "that I doubt I could keep up with all the information for which you'd wager me. It was a thought."

Lord Hugh unwound himself from the game table and returned to the mysterious papers. For a moment I had a burning desire to do a little snooping. I had a clear view of Blackbeard again and he was still in a position to watch me—or our party. I finished out the Patience, eight rows and all. And I won.

Our landing was chilly, punctuated only by the calls of wheeling gulls above us. Hemlock saw us hastened from dock to hansom to train station to railway carriage. I lost my gloves somewhere along the way and Lord Hugh almost lost his portfolio once, I think. There was a great flurry and he and Hemlock deserted me to go off and enquire. They returned with Lord Hugh clutching the case under his arm.

"Let's board now," he said abruptly, pulling me from my station seat by the elbow and hurrying me along the tracks. He practically prodded me up the stairs of one carriage, then through two more and off the train. We crossed more tracks and finally mounted another carriage on a train facing the opposite direction to the first.

"What are you doing?" I turned on him when he had selected our compartment and Hemlock was storing the hand luggage. "I've lost my gloves and I think you've lost your senses, if not our way. However will my baggage catch up with us? We are going to County Clare, are we not? You're not planning another misrepresented journey to London, I hope—"

"Patience," he whispered, looking ironic. He pulled the blinds and shut the door. I began to feel distinctly hemmed in. Even Hemlock's presence didn't reassure me. I almost began to long for Blackbeard. For the first time it occurred to me that our party was being followed and that it might be to my benefit.

I sat down silently and mulled the situation over. My hands were like ice, from fear and the missing gloves. I'd said it previously to myself. Lord Hugh was a man of whom I knew nothing and likely much worse than he should be. The train had started with a jerk and I found my ruminations proceeding to the rhythm of the wheels.

Lord Hugh is a mys-ter-y. Could Blackbeard be a pro-tec-tor? Where are we go-ing? Could Blackbeard be a con-fi-dent? Lord Hugh is a mys-ter-y . . .

CHAPTER TWENTY-TWO

SOMEWHERE, FAR away, through a black narrow pool above my head, something was different. I struggled upwards against the dark oily water that covered me. My cheek came up against something cold and hard. Black, it was all black. My eyes probed the gloom ineffectively until a click behind me brought my head round. It was Hemlock, arms up, poised against a low light.

"Just me, miss, getting the baggage down."

I looked to the hard dark of the train window again and the frame which had pillowed my sleeping head. Beyond the black of nightfall I finally pieced out the outline of the little Glenn-verran station, the gleam of tracks gliding off into the lanterns' dim light. There was a hiss of steam and the steady chug of the locomotive engine as it pulsed on the track. We had stopped.

"We'll be late," I said suddenly, standing and promptly striking my head on the overhead rack.

"Here, miss, you'd better wait where you can't damage yourself. You've slept the entire day away and it looks like you'll do the same with the night."

Hemlock smiled and gently urged me by the elbow into the passage. I was dazed, still half asleep and wondering why. Save that I was unaccustomed to the late hours the Alcott Club had entailed the previous evening. I waited by the window facing the wild side of the village while Hemlock gathered the last of the hand luggage. Lord Hugh's portfolio was not among it.

"Where's—"

"His Lordship had an errand and left as soon as the train stopped. I'm to take you on to Carnhaven in the carriage."

Hemlock had managed to quick-step both me and the luggage down the little steps and onto the platform. There was night chill in the air and I pulled my travel cloak closer. But the carriage was there, black and quietly grand, with two dark horses blowing white mist from their nostrils into the lamplight like sorcerer's smoke.

Hemlock would have ridden atop with the coachman, but I insisted he share the interior. "It's cold, my good man, and you've said yourself I need something to keep me awake."

So we settled inside the commodious interior, ripe with leather smells, and rattled our way to Carnhaven on a set of very silken springs.

"How late is it, Hemlock?"

"Past ten, miss, from what my grandfather's watch tells me."

"It's a splendid timepiece. I wonder how I managed to drowse the entire trip away; you weren't feeding me green tea, were you, Hemlock, on shipboard?"

"Lord no, miss. But here's the House now, miss, they'll be waiting up for you no doubt. I believe His Lordship wired."

He escorted me to the door and into Symes' indifferent hands, with my modest pile of luggage mounded like a desert island on the cold grey-and-white foyer sea. Symes ignored the intrusion, leaving it for a houseboy to convey my modest equipage upstairs. Concealed aquamarine, it seemed, was no talisman for fine treatment with Symes. "They are at cards in the drawing room" he informed me icily.

I ran upstairs to tidy my clothes and refresh my face, patting my cheeks with Madame Louisa's rouged harefoot before going below again.

I opened the doors on a muffled conversation and found a foursome drawn up around one of the small card tables set by the French windows.

"Aaaaha! Here's another fourth for you, Devora. I'm folded. Never was any demn good without playin' for stakes—dammit, where's the whiskey, you haven't been bribing Symes to go slow again, you gels—?" Sir George's laugh was not humourous as he pushed his ample form away from the table and lurched to the bell pull on the farther wall.

"George, you don't even know Amberleigh will want to play after her journey." Devora expressed her annoyance by blowing an exasperated puff of air at the curl that drooped over her temple.

"Well, well, it's our pussycat back from London. And did you see the Queen?" Norah's eyes flicked knowingly to me above the cards she still held shaded from all eyes, though the hand was over.

But it was Elaine's face that riveted me that night. It had only been days since I'd seen her last, but she had thinned everywhere, like a fashion doll too small for her clothes. All that alabaster complexion had gone translucent and her harpist's hands were as taut as harpstrings themselves.

"My, Amberleigh, is it the light or have you done something to yourself? I barely recognized you. Say something, Elaine, don't simply sit mooning. You haven't been keeping track of anything lately."

"I've been keeping track of *that!*" flared Elaine, coming to life like a waxen taper suddenly lit. Her grey eyes struck sparks in the direction of her father, now accepting an oversized whiskey and soda from Symes' tray.

"You're not to interfere," returned Devora, sweeping up the cards. "It's your deal, Norah."

Cousin Norah spread cards face down before her, almost like a Tarot deck.

"It's late, I'm tired," I said, ready to excuse myself.

"Are you?" Devora's challenge was in the twist to her voice. "At least sit a moment and tell us what you did in London. It's so dull there now, I expect, with the Season just about to start. Nothing ever happens when everything is just about to."

"I thought you knew. I saw a . . . a specialist."

227

"And?"

"I shall recover, it seems."

Norah took a sudden interest in Devora's and my dialogue. "That's right, Amberleigh, you weren't just away on social calls these last days. What did you have exactly?" Norah's voice was nothing more than bright cheerful conventional enquiry, but she could have been the Lord High Executioner for the pall that settled over the table as she asked her question.

"A twisted—"

"...Broken..."

"Ankle," I finished up, ignoring Devora's foolish and unlikely injury. "It's so absolutely silly of me. I suppose you haven't heard. I was taking one of my twilight walks and slipped—on some filthy leaves. I'd forgotten the frost comes already and makes everything slick. It was fortunate I'd only twisted the foot. At first they thought it was broken."

I said the last sentence with a significant look at Devora. I suspected she wanted the truth of my injuries as veiled as I did. Norah had automatically dealt during my story and I picked up the cards despite myself. Well, I'd play a hand or two and then dissolve gracefully up to my room. When I wasn't arranging hearts and spades in suit, I was stealing glances at Elaine.

But she watched me openly.

"There's something different about you, Amberleigh, I can't for the life of me decide what. Are you thinner? I think you're thinner. But it's more than that. You—look—different."

"Maybe she's simply more—footloose?" suggested Devora with an impish smile and an intention to distract Elaine. Her jest brought a slow smile to Norah but not Elaine.

"No, it's something in her face," continued Elaine stubbornly. "I'm surprised you didn't notice it, Devora, you're always so good about faces..."

Devora clapped her cards together and snapped them on the table top. She didn't want my malady discussed any more than I. "We've all been up too late, I think. I, for one, am retiring. Play on if you wish." She was gone so abruptly that silence was the only hand left for the remainder to play.

"Elaine." Sir George had descended on our table again, almost as if Devora's absence drew him. He put a clumsy hand to Elaine's fair hair, but the low glass of whiskey slopped over the side and he straightened up to steady it. His eyes, roaming confusedly, fell on me.

"Thinner," he said, as a child who recognizes a word in an

adult conversation and thereupon pipes it every chance he gets. "Thinner." Sir George nodded sagely. "Don't want to lose too much meat, m'girl. Then the hunt's hardly worth the chase." He pinched my forearm through my sleeve with a crooked smile.

"Father!" cried Elaine, getting up and running from the room in humiliation. Sir George continued to leer at me confusedly. Leer it was, there was no escaping it. I looked at Norah and saw her eyes cast down but her mouth screwed up tight.

"I'd better go up," I said abruptly, backing away from my chair and the table and almost out of the room. "Good night," I muttered ambiguously to the pair still left at the gaming table and fled upstairs.

This time I had no wish to seek out Elaine's room.

"Why, what's the matter, Miss Amber? Up comes Miss Elaine as if the bog banshees were after 'er. Then 'ere comes you, as ruffled as Tom Tabby when Mrs. Featherstone's 'ad 'er broom to 'im. What's the fuss? 'Ere now, sit down, you don't look quite well yet, you don't. I was going to get some rosewater for Miss Elaine but you look a bit done in yerself."

"Done in, no, Henrietta—merely a bit tired of pretending not to see half of what goes on in this extraordinary house."

Henrietta's unruly eyebrows danced halfway up to her cap lace. I had started with gossiping words and I was hard put to end them.

"It's nothing—rather amusing really—if it weren't so pathetic. Don't tell Elaine, she feels it enough already. It's her father, Sir George—I simply couldn't believe it. He, well, he played too much the solicitous host with me to pass muster."

Henrietta nodded sagely, her interest instantly stiffled.

"It don't pass muster much with me, either, Miss Amber, you can be hapsolutely sure of that. And 'alf the time when 'e isn't 'arpin' on poor Bridget, 'e's pinchin' 'er bc'ind, 'e is."

"What did you say?"

"I says, 'e's been pinchin' 'er be'ind, 'e 'as."

I absorbed Henrietta's "h"-less statement. It was a rare blessing she seldom had to pronounce her own name, I thought. But I finally mastered her meaning.

"Well, it's best forgotten, I imagine. I really didn't intend to gossip about it. I was simply so startled . . ."

Henrietta left me to deliver her balm of rosewater to Elaine while I struggled out of my clothes as best as I could alone. It had been a long, long day. I recalled the two card games

I'd been drawn into. And smiled when I thought of innocent Hemlock trading deals with one who'd bankrupted Jenkins of his tobacco money years before. Hemlock wouldn't have won even one game, I thought, if Blackbeard hadn't distracted me. Were Cousin Norah and Sir George still sharing the uncomfortable comforts of the drawing room, I wondered. Now, that would be an odd pair. I heard a click in the hall and guessed that Norah's door had just answered that speculation.

How shattering for Elaine. I hardly wanted to face her. Her father—a drunkard, and worse, a lecher. At least he had distracted Elaine from the question of my face. Did she see something different in me because part of her knew it would be there, the scar? I picked up my wrapper and went next door. Elaine was neatly bedded, with Henrietta darting about to put her things away. Elaine said nothing to me until the wiry little maid darted herself out of the room.

"I didn't mean to make a scene," she said. "But you *do* look different. Except that I know what it is now. It's your hair, your hair is different, isn't it? Of course, that's what it is. I knew it was something. It was bothering me."

"There wasn't something else, Elaine? Something you expected to see and didn't?"

"What should I expect? I expected to see you again a good deal sooner. Why did you have to go and hurt yourself? I hated being alone here." Elaine moved restlessly over to her dressing table and sat down to brush through her fine golden hair. "Adrian was here. While you were gone. Did you know that?"

I couldn't help staring.

"No, I didn't. Was he here long?"

"A few days. She had invited him, of course, the moment she knew you wouldn't be coming back immediately." Elaine's narrow fingers wound a strand of hair around the ivory brush handle. Her grey eyes glittered at me in the glass. It was so like a moment at Miss Meachum's—and so unlike.

"I wish you weren't here!" Elaine burst out then. "I wish you hadn't seen that just now. It's so humiliating. Why can't you go away? Go away."

"Elaine. If you feel that way about me, I will. I've been planning to leave, you know—"

"Then perhaps you should. It'll be better for you away. I know it." She bounded back into bed and rolled herself up in the covers like a sulky child. Her last words came to me through the feather quilt. "So leave, it's the best thing for you, Amberleigh."

230

I stood there for a moment, suspended in time by surprise and disbelief. I'd expected seeing Elaine to exile the last suspicion about her from my mind. Instead, she was hostile and strange, very like the one who'd sought to harm me in the woods, who'd swept the reeds with a knife.

I turned down the lamps and withdrew through the door, dismissed like Henrietta, my duties over. The questions, the mysteries around Carnhaven were not such exciting stuff after all. They were tawdry problems I didn't want to unravel, mildewed skeins that led to dark damp places redolent of musk. Carnhaven was a mausoleum and I was night watchman. Let the skeletons up and dance. Norah Chandler was wrong. I didn't want to know where they lay. Most of all, I didn't want to entwine myself in their sharp embrace.

CHAPTER TWENTY-THREE

THE MORNING sky was a grey shawl flung across the hills and heath, pleated and noncommittal, fringed at the horizon by blue-black shadows.

I dressed and didn't stop to peek next door before going down for breakfast. Let her sleep, let them all sleep. Soon I'd be the only one awake at all in this godforsaken—I paused before my traditional place at the empty table, startled. A bright silver circle gleamed beside my plate, the only ray of light in the shadowed dining room.

A letter. For me. From somebody. Who? Why? I was afraid the ring of portrait people around the room would dart in and steal my prize. I reached for it but a rustle in the corridor made me drop my hand back.

Devora and Norah, companionably coming down to breakfast together. I dared not risk their curiosity, so I joined them in their procession past the sideboard.

Trays of steaming sausage and meat pies, tea and the acrid odor of coffee. Scones and biscuits and muffins hot and soft inside the linen—who wanted food when there was a letter to devour?

But we all sat round the table and they began eating as if they had noticed nothing extraordinary. I slid covetous glances at the strange handwriting on the envelope face. The return address, yes—the last word looked like "United States." And before it, could I ever forget the no-nonsense cursive letters that were my mailing address (for the few who would write me) for so many years—"Boston"?

Elaine came then, and "good mornings" bounced back and forth while she parallelled the sideboard and took up her place at table. Somehow she managed to avoid me with her general greetings. I couldn't help noting she took only porridge and scolded myself for an unrelenting nanny.

But my eyes still slid to the envelope Symes had delivered early that morning. At last, an answer from the Willoughbys. It lay like a snake beside my plate, but I dared not open the thick pale cream missive until I was alone. Cousin Norah seemed to be concentrating on her sausages and meat pie, but her oblique glance slithered in my direction a bit too often, I thought. Devora, too, while she seemed regally indifferent to my rare piece of mail . . . still, I didn't want her to know my plans or how soon I could be ready to execute them.

Elaine was idly tapping her spoon against her porridge bowl, her eyes vacant and half dreaming in the slats of light that slipped in through the shuttered windows.

I took one last dip of marmalade and finished the croissant I could never seem to face the day without.

"Well. I've a good deal of sketching planned and it looks to be a glorious day. I'd better run and get my kit together; Elaine, would you like to come along?"

"No, thank you, Amberleigh."

I most casually slipped the envelope off the table, holding it innocuously against my skirt. Their eyes watched me leave, all of them somehow bright and curious. But I must have imagined it; surely my activities were not of paramount interest to all three of them.

In my bedchamber I ripped open the envelope without bothering to break the seal. The thick paper fell out, several sheets. Odd, it was a different color and texture from the envelope . . .

"To whom it may concern: This is to recommend to you Miss Amberleigh Dunne, as depraved a governess as it has been my pleasure to employ. Her moral character is excessively weak; she has, in fact, indulged herself with lovers throughout her career and even the children may not be safe from her lascivious advances, for all I know . . ." It went on from there, descending into greater falsehoods, vulgarisms and the like until I fairly blushed to read it. On like that for three miserable pages. I cautiously examined the seal, which in my haste I had

232

left intact. There—was there a blurring of the imprint, as if it had been softened and lifted off whole? The post markings on the envelope were clearly genuine; Mrs. Willoughby had dispensed the requested recommendation, though tardily. But this was not it. This was the demented ravings of someone very unhappy. Someone half mad with unhappiness. Someone bound to spoil things for others.

I examined the hand, a large, bold stroke in black ink. It looked a woman's hand, despite the aggressiveness of the writing. What woman? Or could it be a man after all? How difficult would it be to intercept a letter? It had probably stood on the hall salver all morning before Symes brought it to the family's late breakfast table. And arrived the night before, for that matter.

Was it merely a malicious trick? Or did someone have a purpose in foiling my plans to leave? There was something childish and spiteful about the way it had been done. I reluctantly turned my thoughts to Elaine. She had been so alien, so able to spin her personality on its axis of late. Anyone capable of blocking out realization of her lover, that she had ever been pregnant . . . No, Elaine was hardly capable of such obscene scrawling. But did I really know of what Elaine was capable?

I was still mulling over the puzzle when I slipped out for an after-dinner stroll. They had all made sly references to my ability to turn my ankle and disappear for long periods of time on my ambles, but I ignored them. Nothing but a solitary pacing of long duration would help me sort out the oddments that cluttered my brain like unused trunks in an attic. In some compartment a long-forgotten remnant must be lingering, waiting to be dredged out and reexamined. And I was no longer afraid of the knife-wielder; something told me her campaign had shifted to other ground.

The lakeshore called me; there was no getting around that fact. Ever since Adrian . . . Adrian and the ghostly rowing party that still traced an invisible path across its light-duned surface. It seemed a doomed place. Even in broad summer sunlight, in the days of dappled leaf patterns on the shoreline waters, of oars dipping flatly across the small even waves, even then it had been unlucky.

"A monster," she had said lived there, that girl—what was her name? That stalklike house-guest creature, admirably shaped for foraging—cranelike—among the shallows of life. How typical, her name eluded me, as had any character she might have possessed. Where was she now, this no-competition-for-darling-Elaine person, sipping tea from Sèvres porcelain in some dimly chic London town house?

Nameless as she was to me now, she had more opportunity of seeing Adrian Carstairs than I had. Devora would see to that.

Monsters! They don't need damp, still, land-locked lakes for camouflage, you poor naive girl-in-flamingo-pink. They're happy enough paddling around in the bottomless murk we call souls. Ah, but that was being bitter. I took a turn and walked slowly in another direction, enjoying the fall mists rising from the ground like steam from some giant underground kettle. The beeches' bare branches, the massive oaks' lonely twinings somehow reminded me of the recent foot race between me and the unknown woman who hated—things. Elaine seemed centered on this spot. I glanced toward the *Argonaut*, slapping dully against the low little dock.

> Break, break, break,
> On thy cold gray stones, O Sea!
> But the tender grace of a day that is dead
> Will never come back to me.
>
> Will never come back to me, will never
> come back to me . . .

Tennyson made a fine fellow mourner. And what did I mourn? A fair-haired boy because he was no more than that? My fair-haired friend because she was more than she seemed?

I shivered—the sun had bobbled below the treetops and a grey sulphur sky loomed through their dark branches. The mist crawled slowly and I hugged the carnival-coloured paisley shawl, a gift awkwardly thrust upon me by the impulsive Norah, around my shoulders.

Hunching oneself against the chill only seemed to make it worse. I must get back to the house before dark was utterly descended, back for another spiritless evening in the St. Clare drawing room. And then to bed. Idleness did not become me, I decided then. I became maudlin, I began to imagine things—for there, yes, on the surface of the lake, wasn't there a black solid spot that hadn't been there a moment before?

I stepped lightly onto the wooden dock, almost afraid it might turn to paper under my feet and sink with me to unthinkable depths—there was that kind of damp, listless feel about the twilight. As if the entire world were a hole to fall into... It was all still, except for the rhythmic slap of the *Argonaut* by my feet. All the same, all still. But the black moved. It moved, smoothly, like some stately black swan from a German opera—like the barge that came from Avalon for Arthur. My eyes pierced the mist and sent daggers of disbelief through it. How large was it, how far, dear God, how did it move? A log—a long, lean black log, merely appearing to be smooth and shiny and sleekly wet in the distance, that was all.

I was stumbling backwards across the dock, my shoes tripping on roughened boards, my heels catching in knotholes. When one foot without warning stepped backwards and down the few inches onto the ground, a strange little noise escaped me. I did not "Oh!", I told myself firmly, gathering my shawl and my wits about me. Only Maisie Dillinghams "Ohed!"

I retreated farther from shore, feeling no triumph at recalling the name which had eluded me earlier. The nameless black shape that still glided before my eyes was more in need of my assigning a word to. Something smaller than its mass, but black as Hades still, protruded from the water. Something very like a neck.

"An' what be ye doin' here, macushla?"

The voice was as soft and Irish as the fog and it slithered round my throat like a noose. I whirled, speechless, to confront it. And found another amorphous shape against the beech clearing and the rapidly lowering night shadows. This shape was recognizably human, though, and more worth facing.

"Ye look as though a sea silkie'd come upon ye sleepin' to take ye off for his bride. Would ye like to live beneath the cold blue waters, Colleen, and plait seaweed all day?"

"No," was all I could say, fascinated by the unseen face that uttered what I could only construe as lyrical threats.

"No, ye've too much of the mortal in ye for that fate. An' if yer interested in remainin' mortal, stay away from the lake by night, will ye?"

There was a wheedling, sinister tone to the voice from the fog. It was one to be obeyed. I nodded, but strained to decipher the speaker's mystery. I saw the outlines, barely, of the typical tweed cap the men of Glennverran wore. Something about his voice teased me. There was a familiar cadence to it, despite the music-hall brogue.

"And the silkies, are they monsters?" I asked to elicit more of a clew from his voice.

"Not so much monsters as lonely. They'll come a-slinkin'

out o' the deeps on a night such as this, with the mist wrappin' 'em up to the tip o' their heads. They're mermen an' it's wives they seek, the silkies. Mortal wives to share the deep wi' 'em. An' they keep 'em many mortal years, bound by pearly chains from sunken ships and nets the fishermen leave on the broad black bottom."

"You warn me away, yet you tell me tales. What am I to believe?"

"Believe that the long lone path through yonder woods and back to the Great House is a safer place for ye this night than on this strand exchangin' questions wi' me, sister."

There was something sad and gentle in his voice. And I believed the warning more than when he'd spoken harshly. I shivered. Almost I wanted to say the name that came to mind. Almost I wanted to place him, catch him out. Devlin. Almost I said it. I knew it was Devlin, twisting his tongue around the old accents and warning me it was underground business afoot this night. I glanced once more towards the lake. The hulking shadow that moved was gone. My own private mystery. Had it ever been there?

"Hurry, if ye wish to avoid the great silkie climbin' slowly out o' the water behind ye; hurry, girl, if ye want to keep yer life yer own . . ."

This time his words ignited enough fear in me to send me scurrying up the footpath in flagrant retreat, like a little red hen flouncing through the barnyard, my shawl ends fluttering wings behind me.

I half-ran the entire way back, not stopping until safe inside the humming, warm kitchen—still feeling the branches' catch on my shawl fringe, the way little beads of perspiration evaporated on my forehead that ached from running through the chill.

I would be careful not to venture out too close to sunset again.

CHAPTER TWENTY-FOUR

"IF YOU want to know," said the grimy notepaper pinned to the battered doll resting lopsidedly on my pillow that evening, "Something of Great Importance about your Friend and her

236

Foundling, take yourself to Bridey's Well before Dark Tomorrow. It will be worth your While. A Friend."

A friend, was it? In the world's estimation, senders of anonymous letters were hardly friends. I studied the crooked grey penmanship. Done in lead pencil and one none too sharp. The writing was uneducated though the phrasing was not. But then many people often spoke more impressively than they wrote.

The well-worn doll worried me. I could take it to represent Elaine's infant. If so, did it mean that the baby was in no gentle hands?

Or even in hands not meant to have it? Kidnapping had not occurred to me until I picked up the limp plaything and examined it. An ordinary doll, not unlike the one that shared my trundle bed twenty years before. But it was worn, poor thing, with a cracked china face and lumpily stuffed arms and legs. I felt a sharp shiver as I held it. I'd heard of Negro cults that practiced magic upon small lifelike figures. For an instant I wondered if my holding the doll caused an infant to stir somewhere far away. To the North. I placed it sensibly down. Why shouldn't I be a bit unnerved? I didn't often converse with nameless watchers and receive unsigned notes delivered by such an uncommunicative messenger.

I sat on the coverlet and absently straightened the doll's rough hair. Devora hadn't thought of that. If someone knew of Elaine's secret, could carry off the child and threaten to harm it—or even simply reveal its relationship to the St. Clares—oh, Devora would be in a corner then. For a half-second I almost relished the havoc such an event would wreak upon Lady St. Clare's well-honed subterfuge.

But why me, why on earth should I be selected to parley for Elaine? Or was Elaine too unreliable? And Bridey's Well, near dark. That must mean the St. Bridget's Well Adrian and I had stumbled over on the ride of last summer. It was a villainous place to meet a stranger, possibly a malignant stranger. Or not a stranger? Someone known to me.

I turned the doll over and inspected the tiny buttons fastening her bedraggled pinafore. They were all there; that one caring touch reassured me. I sat her up in my bedside chair and she looked almost sprightly in the warm lamplight.

"All right, Thumbellina," I told the serious little figure before turning down the lamps. "I'll go to your rendezvous. Though I don't like it—from taking one of those impossible horses to meeting your anonymous owner."

I sighed and leaped into bed the moment the lamplight died, a habit to save my ankles from whatever ogre might lurk under the bed. Childhood habits die hard, I thought. And I wasn't far enough removed from childhood horrors to not dread a solitary ride to meet with an unknown person at Bridey's Well. I would be an utter fool to do it. I wondered what I would finally decide by the time twilight fell the next day. That thought, and its repercussions, circled round my head like gnats, until I was sure dawn was lightening the tall curtained windows.

Thumbellina's painted eyes were the first thing mine fell upon when I awoke. And I carried her blank stare with me all that day as I vacillated between going on that fool's errand and simply turning the entire problem over to Devora. As usual, common sense fell victim to my distrust of Devora.

The stableboys were at their evening tea when I slipped into the stable and paced the long row of stalls. A muscular bay whinnied and moved restlessly as I passed him. I inadvertently shied away from the big horse. They all looked alike, massive heads and shoulders brushing their stall sides as they milled to inspect the visitor. Which was Lady Jane? Which liquid brown eye was the only one I felt I could trust? Jester's stall had been marked but was empty. Time and disrepair had erased most of the other names . . . I turned and walked the row again, no longer treading as delicately in the dim lantern light as before; evidently the boys had cleaned out the stable before retiring to their coarse scones and strong tea. Or stronger stuff with which to drink it down.

"Lady?" My whisper hung on the crisp air as visibly as my breath. But there was a whinny down the row and I ran to the box that housed it. It was Lady Jane, I was sure. I opened the stall door and led her out by the rope halter that circled her velvety nose. Her hooves rang on the stone floor with an echo that made me edgy. Lady stood docilely while I hurried to the tack room and seized a harness and saddle, only remembering the blanket after I'd returned to her.

I'd seen horses saddled at least a hundred times in my life. It couldn't be particularly hard. My fingers were cold in the evening air and the stiff leather baffled me. Saddling her was simple. I adjusted the stirrup arbitrarily. Guessing would have to do, I'd no time for more.

Lady nickered and butted her head against my chest when it came time to bridle her. I eyed her uncertainly and gave her my best governess lecture.

"Now. We're going to be such a good horse. Such a co-operative horse. See, I've merely to take this piece of steel and put it in your mouth. So smile for me, Lady, and let me put it in. Come on, such a pretty girl, such a good girl. You know how it goes in better than I, so do something with it, please."

I cajoled and crooned to her, I held the bit up to her large square teeth and hoped. Nothing happened. With trepidation, I gently forced her mouth open with my hands, pulling the bit quickly to the back of her teeth when her jaw dropped. The steel finally slid into proper place against the natural channel between her teeth and the back of her mouth. I sighed relief and continued to whisper to her ears, which pricked and flattened like semaphores relaying a message I couldn't read. The struggle to get both ears under the bridle straps at the same time was like trying to wriggle one's fingers into a child's glove. "Oh, such a fine horse, so friendly. Come on, now, we're going for just a little ride. Only we two, so come along."

She followed me mildly enough down the stable floor and outside. I had to use the mounting block to get on her and even then split an underarm seam.

It was an early dark, I noticed, as I evened up the reins and took a last look around the yard. Carnhaven's kitchen windows winked yellowly at me across the cobblestones. At the very top of the sky, the smooth white clouds still reflected light. But the horizon towards which I headed Lady Jane was dark with premature night falling upon the land. Lady's hooves ticked out a slow pace until I was free of the yard. Then, fearing for time and that an early sunset would make me miss the note-writer, I gave her my heel. We trotted out along the dark country road and then up the rocky footpath towards the bluffs.

The higher we wound, the more I could see the westering sun, sliding into the sea behind a curtain of purple clouds that flung itself across half the horizon and reflected rosily off the clouds at the other side of the world behind me.

It was lonely, lonely, perched on Lady Jane's broad equine back. But it was a glorious scene; I'd never viewed a sunset from a place as made for it as the hard, high bluffs of County Clare. Nevertheless, at that moment I'd have gladly settled for a luridly tinted stereopticon picture of same. I felt like a dark, grim pilgrim in a land steeped with colour about to extinguish itself in one last explosion. My riding habit was warm black woollen stuff—sturdy enough for the November-to-March hunt. But I shivered on Lady Jane's back. Once I almost turned her and took the road back to Carnhaven and an ordinary County Clare evening. They had not even missed me by now.

But if I did things properly, they wouldn't have to miss me at all. I had laid my excuses out before them like so many breadcrumbs. Sewing, I'd said. Some hand work in my room. Not really feeling well, I'd said, may retire early, may simply slip away and not to worry . . . As if anyone at Carnhaven cared enough about me to worry.

No, not fair. Elaine would worry. Even though she wasn't built for it, even though she'd been hostile on the surface. About me, Elaine would worry. For a while.

Lady wound her way up the steadily ascending path. Even in twilight her feet picked out a way free of boulders. Finally I thought the crest was near—it was all so different than in daylight. Distances were deceptive. The line of rock above me hovered like some hunch-shouldered troll or misplaced leviathan of stone.

And no light. I'd not thought to take a lantern to guide me back. Miles of sparsely occupied countryside around me gave no communal hearthglow to add luminosity to the landscape. I was en route to a rendezvous with a possibly murderous stranger and I hadn't even equipped myself with light. I wasn't conscious of reining in Lady Jane, but the horse had stopped, almost sensing my uncertainty.

What stupidity. A person that slow-witted shouldn't be allowed out after dark. I should be tucked up in the schoolroom with the other children who frighten themselves with ordinary things by turning them into night fears. Brave girl, yes, pat the horse's neck, Amberleigh. Lady Jane isn't frightened. And she's only a horse. I slid off Lady Jane's back, determined to see it through. I was an emissary, after all, personally selected by the mysterious unknown anonymous correspondent. A blackmailer, a kidnapper worth his ransom didn't injure his emissary. Of course not.

I groped in the gathering dark for a rock strong enough to pinion Lady's reins while I walked further upwards and met— well, what or whom was to be met.

But I slipped then, sending a rain of small stones and larger rocks behind me, catching myself only by putting a palm to the ground and feeling it rake along some sharp outcroppings. My feet slid out from under me and a knee bent to the ground. Behind me, Lady snorted once and I saw her head loom nervously above me. With mincing steps her hind hooves retreated backwards and her forefeet pranced a bit as she sidestepped down the hillside.

"Lady! Don't leave me, Lady," I pled softly, feeling desperately among the sharp rocks for the slender leather ends of her reins. "Lady! Oh, Lady."

She had stopped finally, a sullen irregular shadow some thirty feet down the track. Behind her bulk, County Clare fell away into dim, dark regions as unfamiliar as doom. I took a few steps towards her, sending another stone shower towards her delicate ankles. She danced backwards again, finally stopping still further away.

In despair, I faced towards the summit, silhouetted now against a sky squeezed of all but the last rind of colour. It seemed better, brighter, there somehow, than on a fruitless chase down the rocky hillside. I sighed and turned to climb the last few feet towards St. Bridget's Well. When I last looked again, Lady Jane was picking her way down the path, blending into a landscape that swallowed her whole.

Hole. Dear God, it would take careful steps now. I remembered the horrible sinkholes that plunged to oblivion up here. It was fortunate I'd once been here, that time with Adrian, lucky that if I shut my eyes I could call up a day bright with sunlight and sentimental recollections. There was a pit here. More than a mere romantic pitfall. A shallow pit at the top of the track, then we had edged around a large rock and there, there where the little goatman had dropped down on us and urged us away, was the place called St. Bridget's Well. A round, dark, deep hole to Hell.

I slowly worked around what I judged to be the edge of the open place, my hands fetching up on sheer rock, and felt my way along it. I didn't trust these shadowy, lunging shapes against a pale sky. It was dim there, not pitch dark yet, but dim as a house at night with only the moonlight drifting through its windows. I didn't want to stub my toe on an ottoman, I wouldn't want to trip over a—

The world fell away and me with it. I left a scream behind me, echoing off the rock I had just been touching. My feet flailed into emptiness, my shoulder jolted along a hard, bruising surface. Falling, dear Lord, fall—I came down hard, still against rock, still standing almost upright, clutching a rock wall. Cautiously, I extended a foot behind me, expecting to fine another plummet into empty ells below me. No, ground. Uneven, rocky ground. I couldn't have fallen far. I stood motionless and tried to think, not daring yet to relinquish the rock, expecting it at any instant to melt into sand and trickle through my hands. Then I would float further and further and faster and faster down. No rabbit hole for this Alice. No little white rabbit. Late, it was too late. Oh, Lady, why did you leave me? My heart pattered against me, trapped between my body and the rock to which I clung. I thought it would leap up of its own will and make a dash for safety, like a hare before the hunter.

I began to cry—little, tardy sobs because I was too numb to tell where I was hurt, too scared to cry out loud. So I smothered my fear and myself against the only solid reality I had, the rock.

There was a patter, like the clicking of the small stones together when I had fallen. A dull steady patter, light as polite clapping in a distant hall. It was raining—gently, soothingly— a sweet soft chill Irish rain. I uncoiled enough courage to work my way around the pit's edge until I found a spot sheltered by an overhang. I sank back upon my heels and decided to wait. For whomever had sent the note. Or for morning.

I didn't have to wait long. A soft scuffle above me warned me that either hoof or boot was making its perilous way along the same ground that had been my downfall. For a moment I questioned the wisdom of calling out, but plain fear and common sense overruled caution.

"Please! Is there somebody there? I've fallen in—can't you get me out?"

Silence. The scuffle stopped. Then a shower of pebbles rained down past my face with the water. I cowered further against the rock.

"Amberleigh? Is that you?" The puzzlement in the voice matched my own disbelief. I leaned out from my shelter and jumped up toward the voice from the dark.

"Why, Devlin! It *is* you! What on earth—?"

"Aye, there's only one colleen in County Clare'd get herself into such a pickle . . . damn, I've got to get you out of here before—Here, d'ye see my hand? Lucky it is you've avoided the deeper holes—a slide right down to the Devil, they'd be." I heard a scraping against rocks and sounds of activity above me and turned my face up to the gentle rain with gratitude.

"Oh, Devlin, you don't know how relieved I am to hear your voice. Oh, it's a muddle, all right, and I'm half mud from it already, so don't lecture me, simply get me out if you can."

"You've the luck o' the Irish, lady, that I was slated to come by here tonight," I heard him say, and then his dark faceless silhouette heaved over the side of the rocky lip above me. It didn't seem too far and his hand, a paler blur than his body, stretched down towards me.

"Can ye grab onto my hand? If you can, I'll draw you up like a bucket of water from St. Bridget's Well—would ye were that light."

"If you get me out of this horrible cold wet place I won't care how many Irish insults you heap upon my head. Hurry, please, Devlin. There's someone else coming—"

"An' how'd you know that? Well, catch hold of my hand and cut the blather!"

I stretched until my fingers brushed flesh instead of rock. Devlin leaned further and I felt his hand inch down mine to catch hold of my wrist.

"It's a cold hand you're givin' me, Miss Dunne, me dear. And there'd better be a warm explanation of this or I'll drop ye back in the pit for a while. Now give me your other hand if you can—"

There was a hollow clap somewhere above us. I felt Devlin's hand tighten suddenly on mine, ringing my wrist with pain.

"Devlin! You're hurting me. Was it thunder, that far-off sound? It startled me." His fingers loosened and I felt my hand slip through the circle of safety he offered me.

"Devlin! We'll have to try again. Perhaps I can get higher along this rock." I inched my feet up the incline and stretched upwards again. His hand wasn't there. I turned my cheek to the damp rock to give myself a longer stretch and worked my straining fingers backwards and forwards in an arc. Once I brushed Devlin's fingers and his hand swung into gentle motion, stirred by my touch. I reached again to catch his hand, to stop that hideously suggestive limpness.

"Devlin. Answer me! It's not a game. It's never been a game. It's dark and wet and cold and I'm, I'm—Devlin!"

I found his fingers again and tried to grasp them. They slipped away limply. I felt suddenly like some playfully vicious kitten toying with its prey. Like something living and heedless playing with the ragged simulation of life. I sickened and dropped back down to the hard hollow of rock that seemed more a retreat than a snare now. "Devlin," I called once softly, but there was no answer. Only the rain pattering on the limestone, driving into the mud, running in rivulets down my face.

I hugged the side of the pit and waited. There was nothing to hear. Once I stretched up again and touched Devlin's knuckles. His hand was mortal cold.

A long time after I heard a scrabbling over the hard ground and lifted my head to listen again. Had Devlin——? There was a snuffling, then a piercing whine that sent chills through my already half-frozen body.

"Boru," I called, "Boru!" The great dog answered with a howl that rose up to the dark, shrouded skies and ricocheted off the rocks around us. For an instant my calling of his name and the brute's soul-shattering howls blended into a grotesque duet. I sank back to my knees and huddled, listening to the melancholy baying of a dog mourning his master. No, it was not true. Shortly after, there were other sounds—more scrabbling I heard again between the hound's unforgettable whining howls.

"Hssst, lads. There's been bloody dealin's here. Collar the beast."

I stood up, hopeful.

"Please. There's someone up there. Please, I must help Devlin, I'm afraid he's badly hurt, please!"

"St. Patrick protect us! Riley, get the woman out of that hole. Ach, it's Devlin Quade, all right. Clean through. From behind. Bring that lantern here, Barry. Aye, 'tis nothin' to be done."

Strong hands dragged me up the ragged rocks.

"The light, Riley. Ah, it's that woman up to the St. Clare's That Dunne girl. What are ye doin' here? What do ye know o' this?"

"Nothing, nothing. But where's Devlin? Is he all right? I think he was shot—that's what I heard, the crack of it, I heard it." I scrambled over to the dark form lying in an arc of lantern light by the pit's edge. They had rolled him over and away from the incline, but his arm still dangled, stiffly, over the pit.

"Oh, Devlin—no. He'll be all right. Surely he'll be all right! It was to help me he came—oh, it was not long ago, so he'll be all right! But help me get him out of the wet, it won't be doing him any good, the rain. We helped him before. He was so pale then, too; but we helped him. Here, get him away; they'll find him and I won't let them. I won't let them." I tugged at his arms, as I had that day on the hill by the Fairy Circle. But Devlin was somehow heavier. Dead weight.

"Barry, get the woman off him, we can't have this maulin' of the body. And the dog, collar the damn dog. There's someone will by payin' for this, damn them, damn them."

The man who spoke finally came over to me himself and lifted me by the arm.

"Here, girl, you can't be takin' on like this. Dead he is and dead he'll stay. I've already sent a runner to see if the blasted beast's bayin' has wakened the township, so the bloody militia can come and we'll have to scatter for our lives. But I'll be wantin' to talk wi' ye again about this—"

"Jack, Jack, hey, Jack," yelled a man who came running from around the rock outcropping. "There's horses a-comin', two or three by the sound of it."

"Damn hound," spit out Jack, dropping my arm and fading away with the rest of the men as if they had all been mist.

I dragged myself over to Boru, who still whimpered by his master, and put my arms around his damp rough neck. I kneeling there and he sitting, we were of a height. I reached out in the rain and touched Devlin's face. It was like caressing a rock.

I heard the soggy beat of the horses' hooves through the rain, heard them nicker as their riders dismounted, heard the boots sucking through the mud.

"I say, what's happening here? We heard the baying down to the barracks—"

A man knelt by me and shook my shoulder. Another man lit and brought over a travel lantern. By its weak light I saw a face I recognized.

"Well, what is it? What deviltry has been doing now?" asked Captain Mayfair impatiently. I found words circling far away and herded them into the circle I formed with the dog and the two newcomers.

"It is . . . Devlin. Devlin Quade," I said dully, indicating the still form before the pit. Captain Mayfair bent quickly over Devlin while Boru growled softly. But I held onto him and he offered no threat.

"Good God, I believe the man is dead. And who are you, miss, that sits by the side of a dead man?" The lantern light had not yet fallen fully upon me and I was dimly glad.

"Amberleigh Dunne. From Carnhaven. But Devlin's not—dead. If only you'll take him to a doctor. He's not dead."

The other man knelt by Devlin and touched his neck. He held the lantern up above us, but even in that dim light I recognized the scar.

"You've seen!" I appealed to him. "Hemlock can work wonders, you've seen it. You've said it. Hemlock could raise the dead. Take him to Hemlock."

"It's too late," said Lord Hugh. "This time it's too late," he said, getting up. As the light withdrew from Devlin's face I felt he was somehow taking the life away from Devlin.

"No, you can't give up on him! Before . . . before he was pale too. I won't let him die, I saved him before. It had to be worth something."

Captain Mayfair was holding me by the arms as the sobs overtook my speech and I drooped finally, too spent to speak again.

"I say, Hugh, this is damned awkward, but could you ride back to the barracks and get a detail for the body? I'll take the girl on to Carnhaven, I suppose, but I'll have to talk to her as soon as she gets her composure again."

He piloted me towards his patient horse and together they lifted me into the saddle. Captain Mayfair rode pillion, but of that journey I remember almost nothing.

CHAPTER TWENTY-FIVE

"ALL RIGHT, Miss Dunne, I want an explanation."

A day before I would have laughed at the notion of Captain Thaddeus Mayfair affecting me with anything more than a desire to giggle. Or blush at remembered implied indiscretions.

But he stood before me in the St. Clares' cold high hall parlour, less like someone out of Gilbert and Sullivan and more like a military interrogator who could very well have me interned should my explanations not satisfy that unimaginative mind of his.

He'd half-dragged me into the house, refusing any aid, and closeted me—soaking wet and dazed—in the formal, heel-cooling room reserved for unexpected callers.

"Explanation?" I couldn't help it; my teeth chattered and I felt the water drip slowly from my hem to the bare floor to form a clear fat little puddle that caught my gaze more than anything else in the room. It was so unreal; so absurd for me to be sitting there, dripping onto St. Clare parquet, while an equally absurd chocolate soldier with a ludicrous little mustache questioned me. Something had happened to me. One moment I was in the cold wet world outside and the next I was sitting dazzled in the lamplight, whitewashed by walls blazing with clean paint and ordinariness. I felt as if I had looked at the sun.

"I can't explain anything. I know nothing. I feel so tired. Heavy, Elaine said once. Yes, I feel heavy." My eyes caught the puddle at my feet again, as if it were a magic mirror in which I should read my future. I averted my eyes quickly and located Captain Mayfair's face again. How had he become so stern? He looked quite intimidating, he looked . . .

While I watched he gave me an exclamation of disgust and walked to the door, yanked it open and barked for a blanket and some brandy.

I accepted the blanket when it came—a heavy expanse of native wool that locked the damp against my body but somehow made me feel safer, as if civilization had wrapped its arms around me again after I had been somewhere not quite human. Somewhere cold, with driving slashes of rain that pinned me into a cower—a land of unyielding rock and rainstorm, where Druids still lit their great fires. Perhaps Druids had done it, sacrificed that hand that had hung above me like a stilled pendulum while I waited in the pit below. I'd read of things like that. In stories. Perhaps I'd mixed up things I'd read with things that had actually happened . . .

"Sit d-down, please." Captain Mayfair had recovered his stutter and his everyday manner. I looked up to see him shrunken, like a melodrama figure taking the final bow before the footlights and becoming ordinary again. "Why had you gone there? It was their meeting place, you know."

"Their meeting place? Whose?"

"The United Irish," he said with a sigh, bending down so his face verged on mine and I could see the two faint lines at the edges of his very young eyes.

Console yourself, Captain Mayfair, someday even you won't be young and unauthoritative anymore. What can so young an officer do in so old a land? Are you any match for Druids? They require human sacrifices, you know. No. My thoughts were running on raggedly. I mustn't let them. United Irish, he'd said. Their meeting place. Of course, Bridget's Well. St. Bridget's Well was a secret meeting place for the United Irish. It was why the other men'd come along later. Too much later. Devlin—

I looked up again at Captain Mayfair. His face wavered before me as if it were reflected in a very bad glass. I was all water, an entire mass of dripping, pooling water. I blinked and my vision became crystalline.

247

"Why had you gone to a United Irish meeting place? I can't quite credit you were one of them. They very seldom let a woman in on their plotting, although they'll let their petticoats hide the men's dirty work later. T-tell me."

"Oh no, I've nothing to do with that. It's that I—I often go there, I rode there once before in the summer, you know. The place—I have a fondness for it."

The note. I must never mention the tattered piece of paper that had brought me there. To mention it would bring up the entire question of Elaine's baby, everything. No, I had gone there because I had wanted to, that's all. Perhaps I should have admitted to the Irish charge. Then I would have had an excuse for being there. Slowly, my wits were gathering. The day I couldn't deceive a Captain Mayfair, no matter how wet or weary I was, would be a day I deserved catching out.

"A fondness for it?" His voice was incredulous.

"Yes. Of course. I went there once with an, an old beau. Last summer. I have a sentimental attachment to the place."

I sat up straighter and pulled the blanket tauter around my shoulders, like a shawl. I was the Czarina of all the Russias and this, this Cossack, was questioning me. I stared at him, dared him to quarrel with my reasons.

He shook his fair head once and for the first time I realized that he was as wet as I. His hands sketched a small open and closing gesture in the air; he turned and walked to the door, leaving a small alien puddle where he had been.

"Another time, Miss Dunne, then. I won't have any man dead under my jurisdiction and not know the reason why."

He didn't frighten me. I watched him turn and vanish behind the broad door like a bogey man. Good. I wanted to be alone with my prophetic puddle and my thoughts. I wasn't thinking clearly, something was not quite snapping into place in my mind. I was being like Elaine, I was—I bent my eyes to the pool of water at my feet. Somehow it reminded me of the enormity of the night's events. To sit dripping in the guest room like an out-of-time icicle . . . I shivered. I was so chilled, it would be the death of me for certain. Death. No, the word glanced off my brain like light off a mirror. The word streaked into a corner of the room, into a shadow, and lay in wait there.

The door opened again. It creaked. Or was it riding boots that had creaked? Had Captain Mayfair creaked? No, his boots were probably too well tended by the barracks' boy—Captain Mayfair only creaked verbally. I took in the figure poised in the doorway. It was black and looming against the bright hall light that gave me an impression of many lamps hastily assembled. It was Lord Hugh standing there and his face was as grim as retribution. No, this night's hurdles were not all to be as easy as Captain Mayfair. I had taken in a startled breath at his appearance and now I let it out slowly. He'd learn no more from me than Captain Mayfair had. By all the saints in Devlin's repertoire I swore that. Devlin. A chill curled round me and squeezed until I thought my arms would hardly hold the blanket around me. That other word stirred in the corner and whimpered to be let out. I caged it and bit my lip.

"I must know the truth this time," said Lord Hugh, shutting the door firmly behind him and turning to advance on me. "I don't mean to be unkind—"

"It must be a native talent, then," I interjected. He was wet and muddy from the riding and had neglected to divest himself of his crop. "If you'd put that down, perhaps I'd be more cooperative," I said, pointing to the whip. He seemed to see it for the first time and set it with a controlled movement on the table. He looked at me a moment, then went over to a decanter on the library table and poured himself a glass of the amber liquid therein, drinking it down in short intervals. He swirled the liquor in his glass and remained lost in thought, as though distracted in the course of some action. I thought he seemed tired.

"May I try some of that?" I inquired meekly after a bit.

"Be my guest," said Lord Hugh, not at all visibly shocked at my request. He picked up the decanter and another glass in one hand and deposited them on the table before my chair.

"Could you pour for me, please? I should lose my blanket if I tried myself."

He complied, a bit impatiently, and I picked up the glass, casting a quick glance to the door he had so dramatically shut. No witnesses. I took a medium swallow and nearly bit through the glass rim as the living fire stung my lips and spread through my mouth and throat.

Lord Hugh watched me from the chair opposite with his chin cupped in his hand.

"I've not tasted anything like it before," I gasped.

"No, there's nothing quite like it," said Lord Hugh, pouring himself another ample glass. My respect for him increased by leaps and bounds. I dipped my tongue once more into my brew and called it back hastily. It got no milder with time. Lord Hugh eased himself off the chair and onto the floor before the fire, stretching out his muddy boots to the tiling. The wet leather creaked and I continued my trials of the whiskey.

"Is this Irish whiskey then?"

"The best."

"It is strong."

"Yes."

My eyes circled the liquid in my glass warily. It was the colour of melted amber jewellery, like dissolved topaz. Amber like my name. I wondered if I could become liquid amber and flow into the glass and drink myself out of existence. There was something incestuous about the thought. I watched the fire flicker. For the first time I began to feel warmer, for the first time I could let my mind slip back to the scene by the bog-pit with some sort of detachment.

"Where did they take him?" I asked after a bit.

"To the barracks. And Father McManus ultimately."

"He's gone for good, isn't he? 'To the wars he's gone . . .'"

"He's dead and there's no kinder way to say it."

"Or crueler," I said but my voice broke and the tears came washing down and fell into the glass I held tight with both hands before my face. No sobs anymore. Merely tears, slipping their remorseless way across my cheeks, into my mouth, until the salt seasoned the fire on my tongue. It was a bitter cup I was sharing with Lord Hugh and the ghost of Devlin Quade.

His profile faced the fire; I don't think he had moved in several minutes. I was beginning to feel more and more detached as the tears faded and my clear vision resumed. The figure of Lord Hugh seemed to be drawing away into a little scene I viewed through a window. I took another sip. It didn't seem to sting so much this time.

Lord Hugh's glass was nearly empty, I noticed. But he half sat, half reclined there on his elbow swirling the little liquor left in the glass around and around.

"If you weren't so demanding, so—unbending—I might have been able to tell you more—the truth," I said finally.

"But I am," he replied harshly, getting up. "I'll leave now." He took one last swallow and paused for a moment before me with the glass in his hand.

"Thank you," I said, extending my hand, for I felt somehow that he had been the only one who had let me know that Devlin was dead. And he hadn't asked any of his questions at the last. He took my hand for a moment and looked at me in a steady, stunned sort of way.

"Damn Devlin Quade!" he abruptly burst out and he turned to harpoon the cut-crystal glass into the hearth, where it shattered into a glissando of glittering fragments with a sound that brought my heart to my throat, pounding wildly. He was at the door and out of it before my foggy mind could move from the fireplace to him again. There was a rustle in the hall, a flurry, and then Elaine flew through the door and to my side.

"Amberleigh, what's been happening, no one will tell me. And what did Lord Hugh do to you?"

"Nothing at all, Elaine," I said with some wonder. But what had I done to him?

"Well, you're coming directly upstairs with me now," she said almost regally. "That awful Captain Mayfair—all spit and sputter—what was he thinking of, talking to you like that? You're wet through. And then Lord Hugh! What is happening, Amberleigh? Something is, I can feel it. They think everything goes over my head . . . You're coming upstairs. Henrietta! Help me with her."

Supported by Elaine and Henrietta, who had appeared at Elaine's summons—and trailing the soggy blanket like a graceless train—I was ushered past a pinch-faced Devora and a scarlet-visaged Sir George, called by my escapade from a night of quiet tippling in the study doubtless. Symes' sober face loomed above me also during that quick and thankfully confused sweep through hall and up stairway. Even Cousin Norah's avid eyes and blowsy pompadour haloed the servants' countenances peering almost shamelessly from the pantry door.

I was deposited in my bed and bundled up to the nose by Henrietta.

"Now you be still under these cov'rings, Miss Amber, if you want to keep out the chill. And a 'ot toddy, Master said you should 'ave a 'ot toddy. So I'll fetch it and then we'll all go back to sleep."

Sir George recommending a course of treatment for me? I was touched that my plight had gravitated even into his abstracted consciousness. But all this bundling, all this bewildering activity, couldn't close the great gap in my heart whenever I thought of Devlin. Truly gone this time. The words made the connection in my mind but had to span a chasm in my heart.

"Amberleigh." Elaine's fair hair haloed her in the lamplight as she sat on the bed's edge. For a confused moment I thought she was Cousin Norah. Henrietta had hurried back up bearing a pewter cup steaming with something strong and bracing. I turned away my head. The whiskey in the study had already blurred the hem of my mind; I didn't know if I dared let the fabric unravel totally. But Henrietta's hand was steady and insistent. The metallic rim clicked unpleasantly against my teeth and I succumbed. A spicy golden flame licked at my lips and danced through my body.

"Now go to bed, Henrietta. I'll stay up a bit with Amberleigh." Henrietta waltzed from the room, gladly enough I gathered through my daze; Elaine sighed heavily and turned to face me.

"Now, tell me, tell me what happened. And before you're too flummoxed by Father's 'medicine.'" She drew the cup away as insistently as Henrietta had extended it. Her eyes glistened like those of a schoolmate eager for gossip. I realized then that she knew very little about the night's doings, other than that I was the center of some scandalous storm or other.

"Devora's simply ashen. She'd been cooped up in her boudoir with another headache all evening, of course, so she couldn't tell me anything important about what happened to you—oh, no, my dear, she was simply too, too tired. But you're not too tired, Amberleigh. So you tell me. Please. I don't like not being told things, something bad always happens when I'm not told things," she said with a peculiar tone in her voice that woke me up a bit.

I shook off the toddy in a twinkling at this reprise of an Elaine who had a dangerous side and I pulled myself up against the pillows.

"They say a man was shot tonight, Amberleigh. And that you were near when it happened. Was it one of the United Irishers? I *knew* there was a nest of them here. But nobody'd listen to me, of course. Tell me what happened, Amberleigh, don't simply stare at me so strangely—"

"Elaine, it's true I was nearby. I was right there when he was shot. And it was somebody we—knew. Elaine, it was Devlin."

Something opened and closed in her face, something with a certain slow precision, like the lazy fan of a butterfly's wings. She stood up, her face clear as crystal to me in the unnatural midnight light of three lit lamps. Her fingers stretched out, as if she sought balance. And she swayed on her feet with her eyes closed, the lids glistening lavender in the unnatural light.

"Elaine. It's awful news, but—Elaine. Elaine." I lowered my voice to a whisper. She seemed almost mesmerized. I wished I had that strange doctor here with me to tell me what to do with her. I clasped her hands. They were icy, lifeless, as Devlin's had been...

"Elaine."

"They—killed—him. Like before. She—killed—him."

Each word tumbled out with its own peculiar emphasis, on a little pant, as if she were fighting for the air to expel them. I'd never witnessed anyone having hysterics, but I feared the oversight was about to be remedied.

"Elaine." All the authority I could put in my voice couldn't seem to penetrate the bell jar of emotion around her.

"I knew it would happen eventually. She couldn't let it go . . . it's my fault, my fault, my fault!"

"Shhh, don't shriek so; you'll wake the house and then Devora will come . . ." Her stepmother's name quieted her instantly.

"Yes," she hissed, suddenly secretive and sinking onto the bed to clasp my wrists. "We must be quiet about this. Or Devora will come. We mustn't let Devora know that we know."

"What do we know, Elaine?" I kept my voice as soothing as dusting powder.

"How they died. Both of them now. Both dead. I—I can't stand it anymore, Amberleigh, I can't stand it—" I wrested her hands away from her head, afraid in the desperate way she clutched at it she might begin tearing her hair in her distraction. Elaine was on the threshold of some tremendous emotional crisis. With only me to pull her through. If at all. At least she had no difficulty accepting the reality of Devlin's death.

Now that, that was hard for me. It was all too easy for my "practical and sensible" mind to play conjuring tricks with time. "Merely four hours ago," I would remind myself by looking at the clock, "we were both alive on the limestone. Merely seven hours ago, I was rattling around Carnhaven and Devlin was down in the village or walking in the woods"— unaware that the hot, hard impact of a bullet waited for him on the brink of the limestone sink hole. But Elaine didn't seem to need to play games with the hours, to ask who or why . . . she seemed to know.

"Elaine, Devlin was a member of the United Irish—"

"Oh, that." Her voice fell into casual disdain. "All Glennverran knew that. You don't think that's why he's dead, Amberleigh?"

"I thought—"

"No, you can't hide from it this time. It's her work, just as it was before."

"Who is 'she'?" As softly as I approached the question, it was not enough to lull Elaine into response.

"Her name? No, I can't say her name. Are you mad? If I said her name aloud, then she'd know we were talking about her. She'd know everything we're saying. I must never say her name."

"But that's nonsense, Elaine. People can't hear one's thoughts. The entire house is asleep, there's no one about but us. Who do you think might hear?"

"She can. She's very—soft. She comes softly and no one knows she's there. But she is. And she hears. And sees. And then—"

She broke into sobs again. I let her spend herself while I considered who "she" might be. Elaine often talked of Devora as "she", but somehow I thought this "she" was someone else again. There was not only hatred in the way Elaine intoned that single syllable—there was something approaching awe. As if "she" were somehow above the normal laws of nature. And the fancy that this "she" could read one's thoughts if one once mentioned her name aloud—now that was a childish superstition worthy of a nine-year-old's ghost and goblin-ridden imagination, not a grown woman's. Perhaps that was Elaine's trouble—she'd never really grown up beyond goblins.

"I should have been there when he died." Elaine lifted her tear-soaked face from the comforter. "But of course I'd been kept away. She saw to that. Devora barely let me come back in time for the funeral. She wanted us apart. She was jealous, because we had been so close. She'll never know anybody that well. And he lived, for a while. After. But I didn't get back in time. He was cold dead by then. So cold."

It was her brother of whom she talked. Not Devlin. Devlin had mysteriously melted into a boy who had died almost a decade ago. The boy of whom Devlin had told me that day at the abbey. Jason. The dare-devil. Jason. The brother.

"She killed him!" Her voice rose into that register that grated on my nerves. I shook her by the shoulders a little.

"Elaine. Elaine, stop talking like that. You can't know that. It must have been an accident. I've heard about it. The velocipede . . . I've been on a runaway bicycle myself. It's so easy to whirl straight for an obstacle . . ."

"Not him. He could ride the wind, anything with four hooves. Or two wheels. We three had such fun together. We couldn't keep up with him, Devlin and I. But we tried. And now there's only I. Left. Only I. I knew she'd take care of him. I knew it . . . Devora came then. With her newly mono-

254

grammed linens from London. 'S' she had on them, before she even came here. 'She-Devil,' it must have meant. That's her crest. Snake... Oh, Amberleigh. I feel so heartsick. I feel so ill. As if I'd just recalled something frightful—what was I saying. What shall we do without Devlin?"

It was the Elaine I knew speaking and the change was so chameleonlike that for a moment I lost contact with her. I wanted to ask more questions of that other Elaine. She frightened me, but she was my oracle for the mysteries here at Carnhaven, my Ariadne against the Minotaur. I had only to unwind her words, find the thread of truth within them and follow it. But I couldn't grudge my Elaine her normal grief for a childhood friend forever lost.

"Don't you want to go back to bed now, Elaine? It's late. And there's nothing to be done."

"No. Nothing to be done. Oh, Amberleigh. If you weren't here. If you weren't you, I don't know what I should do... I can't say I didn't know that we'd find him someday, twisted. It was all preordained. From before. But I never dreamed then that Devlin, too—she must have done it. It's the only possible thing—

"She saw it instantly. When she came from London. And she didn't like it. Jealous, she always was jealous. We were so close. In everything. Unnatural, she called it. I'll never forget. It was in Devora's new suite—suite, the entire west wing. It was still being done over. Rose and grey. So chic. So her. She called me in, away from Miss and away from him. It was cool there, like the inside of a champagne bucket. All ice and cold mist and little drops of light that glittered. The curtains were new-hung and drawn.

"She sat there and told me it was unnatural. That I would have to be sent away. That I was never to speak to a living soul about it. That I was evil, that we were evil. She would take care of that immediately, she said. And she would see me married to a proper earl. That I'd better keep my secrets to myself, that Father'd be no help to me. And she said she could handle Jason, that someone ought to have handled him a long time ago...

"So I was sent to Miss Meachum's. And had barely been gone a half term before they called me back. For his funeral. I knew then she'd killed him. But it wasn't so wrong, what we did. It seemed so natural—I don't understand. Do you understand? I'll never understand. I simply want to forget about it. That's all. Forget. I do that so well. I should have never—with Devlin. But for one moment I thought he was—I'm so confused. They are dead, aren't they? Why else would I feel so heavy? Take me to bed, Amberleigh; I'm so sleepy."

CHAPTER TWENTY-SIX

I AWOKE the next morning thinking of Queen Hatchetsup. Oh, that wasn't her real name; that had been the way we Meachumites had characterized that queer Egyptian polysyllabic name to pass our periodic history examinations. It hadn't worked. The nickname lingered and the reality slid back into ancient history where it belonged.

But today I thought of her. Why?

Of course. "Did Hatchet sup on Brother Mouse? Where did the Queen construct her house?" That was the rhyme we had concocted to remember the story. Hatchetsup had wed her own brother—Thutmose, wasn't it?—wed him and soon he was dead and Hatchetsup was Queen. The Egyptians did that sort of thing. We'd all giggled over the idea of one's marrying one's brother. I most of all since I'd never had one. The incident took on a certain eeriness now. I tried to picture Elaine's face at that long-ago moment. She'd been in the little group clustered over the provocative history book. But all I could evoke was a patch of periwinkle blue pinafore—what she'd been wearing that day. What expression her face had worn had not been of enough interest to me to register even a presentiment of the future.

She had married her brother and murdered him, the bearded lady the history book called Queen Hatshetsup, that had been it. What about Elaine? The Queen had donned the ceremonial beard of Egypt, called herself a man and heir apparent and had taken the throne. Wasn't Elaine sole heir now? Didn't she stand to inherit Carnhaven alone?

They were horrible speculations and I shoved them aside. I'd think of something else. I didn't want to know... And had Devlin been another brother to her? Someone who had invaded her intimacy too much and therefore had to die? Or did he die because she had to forget something that wouldn't be forgotten?

No, I wouldn't think of it. Not now. I'd think of something else, some other problem. Lord knows there were enough of them to ponder. Henrietta came in as I lay there running the night's events through my numbed mind again.

"I'm not sneakin' up on you, miss. It's just that the lamb next door is sleepin' like Judgement Day wouldn't wake her, so I've been tiptoein' about all mornin'. Can I get you a biscuit or the like for breakfast?"

"No—yes. I suppose I'd better have something and I don't feel like facing the sideboard downstairs yet."

"My, you look a bit done in yourself, Miss Amber. I 'ear there was 'orrible events up to the 'eath last night. Mr. O'Rourke from the stables was in the kitchen at daybreak, and 'e swears that a 'orrible 'ound was a-'owlin' the night through and 'e saw a pack in full cry runnin' against the dawn. A ghost pack, 'e claims. There's been a man done in, I 'eard, so you'd better mind yourself if you're goin' to be takin' any of those sketchin' outin's of yourn."

Poor Boru, certainly the "'orrible 'ound that was a-'owlin'!" Henrietta almost made the entire thing seem unreal, a country comedy on which the curtain would fall. And then all the actors would rise and take their bows. All save Devlin.

"'Ere, Miss Amber. You be shiverin' and there's not a window cracked—you'd better dress, then." There was no arguing with Henrietta the Practical. I prowled through the cupboard with sparse interest.

"What's the weather to be, Henrietta?"

"Most fair today. Wee Jack from the stables says the dew is liftin' already. You needn't dress awful warm."

Then it would be a good day for a walk—without knowing what I planned to do yet, I pulled a yellow tucked gown I had worn not so long before in happier circumstances from the rest. It was like a handful of sunshine.

"Ah, that'll be brighter, Miss Amber. You look more yourself already. I'll bring your tray in a twinkle, but first I'll peep in on our girl."

So Elaine was sleeping. I could well believe it, for I was certain that our—talk—of last night had exorcised any demons that still tormented her. It was as if she finally realized what had happened to her. And then forgot it. But how much could one forget the tragedies that dogged one? Could she dismiss her set of lovers any more easily than I could relinquish a man who meant nothing more to me than friendship entailed? Or had he been more to me than that?

Oh, it was a heart-sinking tangle, with trust the passage price to any answer. And I had very little of that rare commodity to give; I was locked in lies and innuendoes others had woven around me. I couldn't even be certain that Elaine hadn't—in her madness, it's true, but nevertheless real—I couldn't be certain hers hadn't been the hand with the knife, the evil presence that seemed to strike down those I'd cared for. Or we had cared for, for Elaine had lost two. Both Jason and Devlin. Two lover-brothers. And I had no lovers to lose.

It was unaccountable that death had stalked both of her illicit lovers—the wages of sin? But I couldn't believe Elaine guilty as others would; she was like some china-headed doll used for other people's games.

Other people's games. It was all other people's games. Devora using me to mask Elaine's shame, Lord Hugh using Devora to mask whatever he wanted to mask . . . and what had he been doing at the barracks with Captain Mayfair, that they both had come so quickly last night? Now there was a thought that merited further exploration. It was true, they both had come riding up, together. Both of them at the ready. I recalled their muddy boots, the heavy clothing they wore, fit for a long, wet night out on the moors. That tore it; I'd have to find out.

I didn't even wait for Henrietta's promised tray or take a hat, but slipped down the hall and the back stairs, across the garden and to the Fairy Circle.

The clearing was still as I crossed it, and deserted under the morning sun, as if even the wildlife forebore to set foot upon it unless they had to. An eerie place and now suddenly a threatening one—for I saw the pale white ghost of Devlin's hand, there, near the underbrush. It had all been for naught, that frantic struggle up the embankment I now scaled with ease. And here, here Lord Hugh had taken Devlin away on Blackbriar to be tended by Hemlock. Dear Hemlock. At least Lord Hugh had not betrayed his trust on that occasion. Perhaps I could tell him a bit of what I knew and he would then explain the puzzlements of which only he understood the workings.

I cut through the narrow bridle path and stopped at the top of the hill that curved down to the broad road, Shallowford Bridge and the tree-dappled walls of the House itself.

It was here I had nearly failed in my flight from the knife-wielder, was it only two weeks ago? But it was more than that that made me pause to contemplate the beech trees and reconsider my course. Lord Hugh was a conundrum, a mys-ter-y. Dare I really trust him? Did I want to? Did he trust me? Did

I even want to see him again? Indecision was ever one of my flaws.

"He's not to home." The voice came from behind me. I whirled to confront a rough-clothed man emerging from the woods.

"Don't ye be frightened, miss, I'm not lookin' for trouble. I'm but a watcher," he said grimly.

This self-proclaimed watcher wore a seamed and leathery face. If I were to cast him in a country drama, it would have been as the primitive coastal fisherman or perhaps the wily poacher. My last guess may have been closer, for his clumsy brogues had given not a creak as he had approached me and there was something of the hunter in the narrow glint of his grey eyes.

While his attention focused on me with almost frightening intensity, I had the impression that he simultaneously was aware of every scuttle and scurry in the underbrush, that should he need to, he could turn and vanish into the veiling trees as totally as a deer.

"You're the girl up to Carnhaven." The way his lips curled on "Carnhaven" made me almost afraid to own it. "Devlin's friend. I want a word wi' ye."

I couldn't have left if I had wanted to do so; he blocked the way back and somehow I saw no point in trying Shallowford. I believed that he knew the comings and goings of its occupants well enough.

"Why were ye out there wi' him?" he asked brusquely. I must have appeared startled by the suddenness of his question, for he went on almost apologetically. "The other ev'nin'. When we found him. And you. What know ye of this one's doin's?" His head jerked in the direction of Shallowford. "Ye'd better tell me, Colleen. I don't savour roughness on women but I want answers . . ." He shifted his weight and pulled the rifle that had stood almost innocently against a stump next to his leg. It looked like a cane.

"You're Jack," I said abruptly, remembering his voice at last.

"Aye."

"Then you know—well, Devlin was with you, your party. I had been—invited to that place. But I fell into the pit. And then Devlin came—I don't know why he was there or how he happened by just then. But Devlin came. And he was helping me out of the pit when, when—"

"But why were *you* there, girl? There was no reason for you to be there. Unless ye were one o' us. Or them. It was a meetin' and no one had business there but us. That's why Devlin was there. But why he came early I don't know, I swear by St. Bridget. So tell me true, girl, what brought that terrible ruin to the countryside last night?"

"Oh, I don't know! Wouldn't I tell you if I could? Don't I miss Devlin as much as any of you? I got a note, about something that meant a great deal to a friend of mine, on a purely personal matter. It was foolish to go; the note was—suspicious. But I did go. And slipped into the pit. And then there was Devlin...and then Devlin wasn't there anymore. He was a good friend. I would never betray him, you must believe that!"

Jack rubbed the three days' stubble upon his pointed chin, his eyes so narrow in skepticism they almost disappeared.

"An' what about that one?" he asked again, indicating Shallowford. "I still haven't figured that one out, no more than one knows why a cat crosses one road and not another. Why go you to that one?"

"I—I thought he might know something about the entire puzzle. But now I think that I may have been mistaken. Or if not, that I might not want to know what he knows."

Jack laughed, a high, wheezing sort of sound that startled me. "Sure, if that's the logical way in which ye ponder out a puzzle—'I don't know if I want to know if he knows what he might know'—no wonder you're a bit pixilated about the happenin's." He chortled again, as a man does who seldom finds humour to set him off. But his face resumed its seamed seriousness shortly.

"These are dread times, girl; and none for curious tabbies to be nosin' about tomcat's doin's...It's me guess you've done no harm to us or our cause, save by overmuch curiosity. But it killed the pussycat, missy, and I be doubtin' you've got enough lives in ye still to be insertin' yourself into our affairs." Having delivered himself of this cheerful homily, he turned to go.

"Wait! About Devlin. When will the—interment—be?"

"Tomorrow. 'Bout ten. Churchyard down to the village. You'll be comin', will ye?"

"I don't know. I can hardly believe he's gone, though, that he won't come swinging around a corner, whistling as he did..."

"Aye, he's gone for sure, girl, and a good man he was for us. Gone like a thousand lads before, who were all burnin' to

260

see the bloody English beaten from our shore. It's a bloody little island an' I'm not simply swearin'." He picked up the rifle and turned again to leave, taking several steps before stopping. He spoke without turning back to face me. "The wake's tonight. At his mother's cottage, off the Limerick road behind the village. If ye want to come, you'll see how we mourn our dead."

"I don't know, it might be viewed as—I wouldn't want to intrude . . ."

"Whether it be an intrusion or not, well, that stands or falls on how ye feel, don't it, Colleen?"

And he was gone into the shadow of the trees so quickly I wondered for a moment if I'd been conversing with a Leprechaun. I stood shivering in the shadow of the path, somehow rooted, afraid to go forward or back.

"Devlin." I said his name on a half-sob and it felt better to hear it there, fading into the leaves and sky, as if he were still existing somewhere, were still real. I remembered the hard grasp of his hand. I was the last living thing he had touched. It was for me he had leaned down into the pit to become prey to the phantom that haunted these moors and woods. With knife, with gun. But I feared no enemy as much as I dreaded the aching knot that tied my emotions into a cat's-cradle, a bitter kind of grief that I could not categorize.

I excused myself from dinner with the family that evening and, donning the appropriately black riding habit, took a virtually unnoticed exit from the House through the kitchen. Henrietta and Norah were sharing a cup of tea around the big kitchen table, but I escaped with a nod and no explanation. I had noticed a grim grey shadow beneath my bedroom window and when I stepped out the door, Boru came slowly over to me.

"Mrs. Featherstone."

The bulky cook, red-eyed and sober, came to the threshold at my call.

"It's Boru. Devlin's dog. He seems to have adopted me. Could you find some scraps for him from time to time so he's fed? I really don't know what else to do with him."

"Bless yer heart, sure I can. But if he's got anything like Devlin's appetite it'll be a job—" She seemed on the verge of snivels again, so I let Boru into the kitchen and myself out. If there was anything I didn't need on my way to Devlin's house, it was a mate for my misery.

The stableboy saddled Lady Jane in a minute or two—I

hadn't asked leave to take her but didn't see how anyone could object—and we started down the road. "Behind the village off the Limerick road." There were dozens of little cottages nestled round about the village, each equipped with a thatched roof and a cat on the sill. And usually a small but glorious rose garden. "Sketchpad scenes," or something like that, Lord Hugh had called them, implying that the skeleton of poverty lay beneath all that perishable prettiness.

I shouldn't have tried to come, I told myself as Lady Jane's sure hooves picked the way along the rough country road. Perhaps I couldn't find the cottage, perhaps it would get pitch dark and I would be lost. Or worse, perhaps I should find the place and be unwelcome. I'd been only in the Great Houses; cottages were local colour for my sketchpad. For one with such poor prospects, I suddenly realized I managed to travel in elevated circles. What would Devora think if she could see me plodding along on Elaine's blooded mare towards a mere tenant's cottage? The thought kept me going.

I had no difficulty finding it after all. A figure here, then there, off the road and on the road, converged on an inescapable point—a whitewashed stone house precisely where Jack had said it would be. My fellow travellers were predominantly old women hooded with black shawls. They marched steadily and grimly on, taking no notice of the marvelous sight of a mourner on horseback. They all walked. Sometimes a barefoot trio or quartet of children scampered silently alongside a figure too bent to be their mother. I began to dread those bent figures. I began to wonder what they carried for heads on those stooped shoulders. I felt as if I were being swept along in a procession of something very abnormal, of silent ghouls perhaps, on the way to watch a young man's soul in passing. I'd heard of wakes, briefly, from Father.

"Bishops don't like it," he'd barked once. "So it's one custom I'll drink to." And he had laughed an ironic laugh, strange from so quiet a man. But Father had been a confirmed anticleric, I understood that now. I also knew that the Roman hierarchy was attempting to snuff out the practise of wakes, perhaps because the custom drew on wells of pagan superstition. Or just plain whiskey well passed around.

I tied Lady to a beech fifty paces from the cottage and walked the rest of the way, unwillingly joined by my road mates into a sort of procession. I'd left my derby hooked over the saddle pommel, but took the black veil from the band as a scarf.

We women wound our way to the narrow door, around which a group of men stood in talk. I saw one raise and silhouette a bottle of something against the twilight sky; he drank and passed it on. One murmured as I brushed by, but Jack's voice came out of the dusk. "It's all right, Barry."

I didn't even turn to look at him, but melted across the low stoop with the others.

A small, crowded but somehow warm place. I looked up to homely wooden rafters, around to a crowd of strange faces, mostly women's. One draped her shawl over her shoulders and I saw her face was as young as mine.

"In here, miss."

She drew me apart from the crowd and into another room. I was grateful for her guidance. The next room was smaller than the other. And unoccupied. Save for the cot, the narrow low cot against the whitewashed wall. I saw it and my breath came in with a sort of gulp. The girl next to me put out an arm and I gripped it.

"You're new to the custom?"

I nodded. I hadn't quite known what to expect. But not this—Devlin laid out in a white robe on a cot draped in white linen. A cross joined his hands across his chest, his hands wound round with a string of large wooden beads, a rosary. His face was as pale marble as the Dover cliffs. And as hard. The light from a cluster of candles on a table at the cot's foot danced in his features—it almost appeared to imbue them with life . . . there, did an eyelash flutter, the corner of his mouth, did it twitch? A finger—? No, he was still. As still as anyone could ever be. Truly dead. No kinder or crueler way to put it.

"Am I . . . ? Is it customary . . ." My voice seemed broken and hollow in a room too tiny for echoes.

"You can stay to kneel and say a prayer," the girl answered. "Then come back to the kitchen. There may be others comin'," she mentioned, stepping through the doorway.

Kneel and say a prayer. I hadn't done so since a mere child at Mrs. Bowers' behest. But I did it then, anxious to meet the manner of their custom, to insult them in no way. My position gave me a clear view of Devlin's face. I kept my eyes on the wide wooden floor boards for a moment before I looked again. He resembled an alabaster monk, a figure from some medieval romance. Or even King Arthur on the way to Avalon. Wasn't that what Avalon was all about? A serene life after the wounds and warpage of a certain amount of time on earth? But Devlin's time had been too brief, had been unnaturally—cut. I didn't even know how old he had been. And those songs, the simple melodies with the lilting Gaelic words he'd been collecting—who would sing them now? This minstrel boy's strings had been rent assunder, too. County Clare's one faithful harp had been stilled. And the cause in whose clandestine army he had enlisted? A chimera also. A thing fought for centuries to no good purpose. I didn't understand it, any of it. And I didn't want to stay there, in that bare little room with only marbled flesh for company. I should never have come.

I made my way through the low doorway and paused on the threshold, looking for a quick way to fade from the kitchen and into the bracing evening air. I'd have to run the gantlet of men alone, but even that was better than the horrible stifling atmosphere I felt at that moment inside. Out. I must get out. The girl who had guided me earlier intercepted me halfway across the room.

"Would ye be wantin' a cup of tay? And to meet the boy's mother?"

It was too audible an invitation to ignore. I thanked her, was handed a heavy white porcelain cup brimming with a black liquid and escorted to a woman who sat beside a rough table piled with foodstuffs, from the neighbours, probably. She was rocking just imperceptibly.

"How do you do?" I said softly. "I'm Amberleigh Dunne. From Carnhaven. Devlin . . . I . . . we were friends."

"Friends?" she said dully after a long moment. "Aye, friends he had. Always a good one wi' friends. The oldest isn't always the warmest. Likely to leave for America, or want ye off the farm as soon as he's wed. Devlin'd never leave. Or marry. He was for me and for the land. And for us." Her voice vibrated on the word "us" like a harp string. I knew then this was a mother willing to lose a child to a cause called liberty or Home Rule or whatever names one could give it. It was in her bones to want it—this thing called freedom—and it frightened me. In her place I should be calling down curses on men and causes. This is what Devlin had wanted me to be a part of, this blind sacrificial single-mindedness, this—inhuman—hope of a future linked to no other nation. I could never do that. Poor Devlin, all those words wasted on me; words, and not much time left to him though he didn't know it. If Father was leery of clerics, I was leery of causes. Particularly if pain and anguish were their only recompense.

"I'm sorry. I'll miss him."

She smiled up at me then. For a mere split second, the eyes

buried in her broad cheekbones and many crows'-feet grew brilliant and blue. She was, I realized, perhaps only ten or so years older than Devora. Twenty years ago she had been my age, she had been . . .

"Miss him? Oh, yes, he was one to be missed. His shadow will run wi' me all my life. But first I'll know how he was taken from me. That Jack Reilly has promised me." She leaned urgently forward, as if for the first time placing me. "Do ye know?" I met those eyes and wished I could feed her an answer to quiet that feverish ugly need. I shook my head. She sank back with her appetite for an answer still unsatisfied. I edged away towards the door.

"First the husband, now this," said my guide softly. "And still Maureen'd send all her boys to war, down to the ones in skirts, if the United Irish'd have 'em. Don't be worryin' about her; she'll survive. We Irishwomen have been doin' it through worse times than these. Now, you're out of it 'fore the keenin' starts. Safe journey to ye."

I thanked her and brushed out the door, past the softly muttering circle of men whose voices stilled as I passed. "Good night, miss," called a bold one after me, with a certain unpleasant raillery. But the "hushes" that followed that outburst gave me less fear for myself than had the Queen's own. I untied Lady, mounted her awkwardly and tied on my hat again, anxious to make Carnhaven stableyard before complete darkness fell.

Devlin, I think, would have laughed at my retreat. Devlin would have laughed at a lot of things I found deadly serious, including his own wake, it occurred to me. I smiled to myself for the first time since that nightmare on the limestone bluffs. Devlin was still alive wherever the thought of him brought a smile. I sang softly all the way back.

> "Sheilagh, dark Sheilagh, what is it that
> you're seeing?
> What is it that you're seeing,
> That you're seeing in the fire?
> 'I see a lad that loves me,
> And I see a lad that leaves me,
> And a third lad, a Shadow Lad
> And he's the lad that grieves me . . .'"

It might have been the epitaph Devlin himself had selected for our friendship. The lad that leaves and the Shadow Lad that grieves . . . But the one who should be grieved was Elaine. Save that she seemed to have done with grieving and passed on to a new kind of life. That ability to separate herself from unhappiness, from the way things were, it was not a normal facility. Perhaps I should be thinking less about the dead and more about my friend Elaine, who still might need me. I patted Lady Jane's satin neck as we came into the yard and whispered into her ear as I dismounted. "You've been a good horse and looked after me. Now perhaps I'll have to look after your mistress."

CHAPTER TWENTY-SEVEN

BUT THE dead are not as easy to dismiss as that. The next day I donned a gloomy mood with my funereal blacks—my own this time, not borrowed of Elaine. I told her where I was going, but she only nodded with solemn grey eyes and asked no questions. Devlin's burial.

Devora caught me up in the hall to offer the dogcart, which I refused. She barred my way, dressed in white-and-grey-striped silk, and told me how she would have had a wreath sent to the churchyard, but that under the circumstances it seemed inappropriate . . . Her tapered fingers jabbed nervously at her pompadour and her brown eyes fluttered from my face like a butterfly from pursuit. In her way, Devora mourned Devlin too.

I was glad to walk, garbed in lusterless black, through a world of green gone grim. The woods surrounded me with their living, leafy lushness; the woodland creatures chattered and chirped my way to the open space surrounding the village and the lone whitewashed spire of the little Catholic church. A knot of villagers lay tied across the green of the little churchyard. I walked down the last rise and made for the small clearing where grey stones dotted the green with more than natural regularity. Save for that macabre symmetry, it might have been one more County Clare field riddled with rocks the earth had spit back at the sky.

At the gate I hesitated. I didn't recognize anyone from the previous night. They were all simple folk, dressed in coarse linens and wools. The old women in their kerchiefs and shawls, the young as plainly attired. The men were over to the side, shuffling and muttering and turning their caps round and round in their gnarled hands. I'd never seen men with hands like that, hands fashioned from wresting their livelihood from the ground. It made me feel superfluous.

Their Mass had just ended; several men came carrying the wooden coffin out the door, with Father McManus in a white surplice and purple stole following. Two small boys, their tousled hair as black as coal and their steady faces as white as worry, preceded him. I melted behind the women to hear the sonorous Latin syllables fall upon the mean wooden box. It was rougher even than Father's sorry coffin. I suddenly realized that I had stood before at a graveside confused and unhappy. It was sad that this man I'd known but a few months should grieve me more deeply with his death than my father, but it was the truth of it. I half expected Devlin to lunge out of the still box, to announce that it had been some sort of ruse, some mistake. But the soft Latin murmur continued. The wind rifled through the shawls shadowing the women ahead of me and across my brow. It was over sooner than I'd thought. And the meagre procession left, then the men—stopping at the grave one by one to throw a handful of dirt within. Then the dirt began to be shoveled in with that sharp thump that is like no other sound in the world, whether in a field outside London or on rocky green Irish ground. The women made their last pauses, his mother kneeling to say several "Ave Marías" over the heedless box vanishing under the earthen burden it bore. I stayed till last, afraid to come near them in their grief. I was an outsider. Almost a curiosity-seeker, I felt.

The hole filled up amazingly quickly. What had been a wound in the earth was merely one more significant mound after the gravemen's labours. My memory bored through six feet of loose dirt and rock to picture Devlin as I'd last seen him. At the wake, peaceful and young, with a face of carved ivory. I imagined his eyes open and blazing blue. What would he say to me, if those lips could move, what last words were there for him? He had not even been allowed a farewell speech, he who loved to twist his tongue up with words, to tie the language in knots and smooth it out again. He'd come, in part, to collect the lore of an older people. And he'd gone again before half the work had been done. And the old lived on to mourn.

> "The minstrel boy to the war has gone
> In the ranks of death you'll find him . . ."

Rank death, that makes even blue eyes lose their glimmer. Useless. And useless to question.

I turned to collect Boru, who had loped tardily behind me all the way from Carnhaven. I hadn't had the heart to turn him back. The rangy dog was stretched out behind a monument no taller than he was. This was no churchyard full of archangels in flight or reclining lambs in Abraham's bosom. No, merely simple slabs of stone. I walked slowly back up the hill, reading the names—McGillicuddy, Ryan, McCafferty, Kelly . . .

Once, while I eked out a half-chipped-off date with my eyes downcast, I had the strangest sensation of being watched. Right at the back of my bowed neck, as if that spot were as naked to someone's gaze as it would be to the axeman. I lifted my head so quickly that Boru followed my motion with his own. All still green silence tinged with grey. Save for the fresh earth mounded there . . . fool! Did I expect Devlin to come leaping out from behind a headstone, eager to declare the entire thing a prank? I glanced at Boru, sniffing the air with his broad black nose in an interested but uninvolved manner. No, Boru would give a cry to wake these dead if he scented his master about. Morbid. I was growing morbid. It had started with Elaine's confinement in that desolate place—my nerves weren't what they had been and a violent death did nothing to steady them. That was all.

I turned to trudge up the hill and towards the blurred line of young trees edging the wood to Carnhaven. It was mid-morning. The birds were twittering as if their lives depended on serenading Devlin with the last of his lyrics. Boru was beside me; the church and sacred ground behind me.

And yet . . . and yet. I didn't fancy the sharp lean lines of those young trees, so like a fence. There was something shrouded about those woods, something veiled within them. Patches of morning mist still scudded across the ground. Wisps drifted upwards and clung to the stark branches, almost like raiment hanging daintily from some weird sister's limbs . . .

And there was someone there. Some watcher. I knew it.

It was not a case for speculation, it was not my imagination taking the bit in its teeth. There simply was someone there.

"Boru." The great dog halted obediently at the catch of my hand on his thick neck hair. "The road. We'll take the road today, Boru," I said softly and confidently to my only companion. "Not the woods today, Boru."

I had to coax him from the myriad scents and small scurryings that waited his mad chases and snufflings in the hills and hollows under the trees. He followed me on a sharp turn towards the road and we came back to Carnhaven the long, weary way around. But I didn't feel watched after that.

"Here, Boru, Mrs. Featherstone will feed you, you ravenous beast, you," I whispered as I let him into the kitchen and took the corridor to the front of the house.

This was the way Devlin had led me so easily that first day when I'd come uncertain and new to Carnhaven. Now I knew its twists too well. I felt I'd always glided through Carnhaven's halls and along its walls, as if I were immured here and would remain here the rest of my days—fading, like Norah, into the feel of the place, losing myself in its largeness and simply learning to be a part of it—

"Oh! Symes! How you startled me."

"Startled you, miss? I'm sorry, miss. I was merely going to the kitchen to see to the wine cellar." Somehow Symes explaining his movements made me feel as if I should be accounting for mine—for my idiocy, rather, in lobbing around the front hall door and into his well-rigged front like a tennis ball into a net.

"I've been seeing to Boru and—"

For once the impeccable Symes interrupted me.

"Oh, the dog. Yes, I see, miss. Well, I was about to bring this to you." Symes yawed and glided towards the console table, picking up a small silver salver and holding it out for my inspection. The way he had said "this" made me expect to see a snake coiled upon its shining surface.

"It was hand-delivered an hour ago," Symes said rebukingly, implying that had I been where I ought, I would have had it ages sooner.

A square white envelope, addressed to me. Perhaps it was a snake after all; there was a certain sinuosity to the hand. A strange hand; I'd never seen that writing before. I could feel the thick smooth wax of the seal on the envelope's underside. I traced its impression before I turned it over. It was a "D."

CHAPTER TWENTY-EIGHT

I SO seldom received mail that I stood for a moment studying the envelope before I opened it. And delivered by messenger. Symes, fairly twitching in anticipation, was forced to withdraw with a disappointed simper upon his formal face.

It was plain white stationery, but heavy. I finally slit the seal with my jet hatpin from the somber straw I'd worn for Devlin's funeral. The note was from Lord Hugh and it was very brusque.

"I would be gratified by your presence for dinner. Eight o'clock tomorrow. Hugh Davenant." More like a royal command than an invitation. I thought I knew what he wanted. Not my presence, but information. His appetite for information was increasing by the day. And the handwriting, brash in the blackness of the ink, but precise and graceful too. It was not the handwriting I had expected of him. But look where Devora's bashful backward script had led me not so long ago. It was unwise to trust to intangibles like handwriting, I decided.

To go or not to go. I debated, rereading the brief message and taking new offence at its tone. Gratified indeed! "His Lordship would be gratified by the honour of your presence at your beheading. Prithee don't draw back."

Well, I wasn't afraid of him. Not overmuch, anyway. I went upstairs and unearthed the serviceable stationery I used— cream anonymity for a person who existed between two worlds.

I, too, penned a brief message. "I shall be—prompt. Amberleigh Dunne," I scrawled in my most aggressive hand. No "delighted," no "happy," merely "prompt." And I rang for Henrietta to take it down to the boy for delivery. Her black skirt had barely whisked out of sight around the corner before I wished it back. Too late. One would have to stand or fall with one's impulses.

It wasn't until dinner that night in the long somber dining room that I had to face the music.

"I received an intriguing letter in the post today," Devora remarked dreamily over the vichyssoise. Elaine tensed, I could sense her tightness across the table; Devora had a way of shattering dreams with that voice—others' if not her own.

"It was from Adrian," she said, suddenly lively, and looking directly at me. "It seems the family brewery, or whatever one calls that sort of place, needs his personal attention again and he begged leave to call upon me. Us." She smiled most particularly at me on the last word. "I shall, of course, invite him to dine and stay the night tomorrow. You should like that, shouldn't you, Amberleigh?" Her voice was as light and as sharp as a hatpin. My mind flew back to the note.

"It doesn't matter whether I like it or not, Lady St. Clare," I replied evenly. "I shan't be here tomorrow evening."

"Not be here? But why, if I may enquire, my dear? Where else would you be?"

"I'm to dine at Shallowford."

Her face, calculated in its calm cruelty, froze for a mere instant, and I saw what she would be like old and without her powder and paint. She dropped her gaze and circled her spoon meditatively through the soup. It made an unpleasant sound.

"To dine at Shallowford . . . Well, you must give my regards to Lord Hugh. I'm sure Adrian will be—desolate to have missed you. I doubt he can spare more than a day on—us."

"It is a pity," I said, meaning it more than she could detect. "It never rains but it pours."

Elaine suddenly kicked at me under the table. I took in a gulp of air, and as the faces turned to me, mumbled, "The soup, it's hot."

Elaine was almost hysterical across from me at the idea of cold potato soup being overwarm.

"Elaine, stop that giggling, child!" Lady St. Clare's voice was hard. "One would think you were still a schoolgirl and not a woman full-grown and—" She clearly had been about to allude to Elaine's disgrace but checked herself, more on the servants' account than her stepdaughter's. Elaine didn't even shrink. She'd been like that of late, almost too impervious to pain, like someone numbed.

"I shall be here," Elaine announced. "To entertain Adrian, I mean, since Amberleigh won't be here. Adrian and I get along very well, so you needn't worry, Devora, about boring him for dinner. I'm sure we two will manage quite well at dinner, Devora."

"Aaaah! Take the demn potatoes away," bellowed Sir George abruptly. He'd been drinking his wine rapidly and had taken little interest in his dinner-table repartee. "If that Carstairs fellow is coming again, Devora, you'll have to play hostess

271

alone. I'm promised for cards with the Squire and he's into me for too demn many pounds for me to play fop at one of your fancy dinners."

Sir George heaved himself out of his chair, frowned away the attentive servant who leaned forward to aid him and lurched out of the room. "Symes, a whiskey in my study," he ordered before quite disappearing around the door.

At times like these I became almost embarrassed for Devora. I stole a glance at her; her face was as clean and etched as the head of Medusa confronting Theseus on the hall statue.

"He must eat!" burst out Elaine. "He's not hardly eaten again. It's your duty to see that he eats, Devora. You could do something about it."

"Elaine, you had better attend to your dinner and be silent or more than one St. Clare shall fast tonight."

"Oh, yes, it's easy for you to speak to me like that. But one day if he—becomes himself again, it's not me that'll be sent from table."

Elaine's face was crimson with rage. Her hands were trembling and I watched in fascination as a spark of something very like rebellion dawned in her thin face.

"Elaine's not herself, Lady St. Clare, but she's right. I don't know how much longer a man can exist on—"

"And you, you keep out of it! You're here on sufferance, miss. And for her sake only at that."

"Am I indeed? I thought there were reasons deeper than that." She ignored my thrust and turned toward Elaine, who still clutched her soup spoon much as a soldier holds a bayonet against a cannon ball.

"I've done all I could for you, young miss. Burying myself for months on end in this miserable—" She searched for the worst epithet she knew—"farm country! I've played duenna and chaperone till I felt seventy years old, I swear. But little good it did me and—" She suddenly realized servants were present and some of her former restraint resurrected. "At any rate, I don't want recriminations from you. Or your companion." She fairly spat the last word in my direction and left the table abruptly, almost overturning her chair with her train. A serving girl ran to balance it.

"Oh, you've done it now, Amberleigh," said Elaine in a low triumphant voice. "It's your dining at Shallowford that's set her off. I daresay she'll get one of her headaches out of this and will be out of our hair for the evening. Let's finish dinner and then I want to talk with you. In my room." She darted a cautionary glance at silent Norah, sipping soup almost primly at her end of the now-almost-deserted table.

After dinner Elaine bundled me off to her room, demanding an accounting of my invitation and speculating madly all the while.

"Oh, it's so delightfully galling for her, Amberleigh. She'd thought she'd hooked him utterly, you see. And up comes an invitation for you to dine. Alone."

"That's what worries me. I mean, I'm not sure it's proper, that's all."

"Not proper? Of course, it's not proper. That's what so exciting about it. Oh, Devora, your head must surely be throbbing by now."

"Elaine, you can't hate her that much?"

"Oh, can't I? Indeed I can. I've had a lot of time to learn. Father was never, well, paternal. But he didn't drink whiskey like wine and he wasn't simply an irritable—lump—till she came. I can't forgive her. Ever. Sometimes I could kill her. For what she did to us. She made me go away from him, she kept us apart. And then I never saw him again. Ever. Ever."

Sir George may have become a changed man while Elaine languished at Miss Meachum's, but I doubted that his personality had turned so completely Elaine could feel that her former father was lost to her forever. One had to be careful of melodramatic overstatement with Elaine. So I soothed her and petted her and took a false interest in my outing to Shallowford. Elaine was certainly more entranced with the idea than I was. But perhaps her enthusiasm helped me quell that little doubt that lurked stubbornly at the pit of my stomach.

"What are you going to wear? You've got to wear something, something Devora-ish!"

So a search began through my motley wardrobe. We soon discovered that I had nothing suitable to don for a tête-à-tête with the Rake of Shallowford.

"Truly, Elaine, I don't care what I wear. If you'd read the invitation you'd know that I could come in rags, for all it mattered—"

"This afternoon gown is really splendid on you, Amberleigh, but it's simply not appropriate for evening—what about this one, the white lace?"

The white lace. No, somehow I did not want to go to Shallowford in Madame Louisa's borrowed gown. I wanted to go on my own terms, armed with my own clothing and girded with my own sense of self, not as some fashion doll

273

dressed to prove a point. I was tired of being manipulated to other people's images of me.

"Here, Elaine, this will do. It's moire taffeta, quite the right fabric for evening. And black—a bit formal but—"

"It's so stiff, Amberleigh, with that high collar. You'll look like a dressed-up governess."

"Perhaps that's what I am."

Elaine studied the gown. It had very elegant lines, a trim waist and a cool sweep of skirt, not to mention cunningly tucked leg-o'-mutton sleeves. But it wasn't attractive enough for her by half, I could see that.

"At least let me give it to Henrietta to freshen for you. And a bit more trimming—something sedate in black velvet, I assure you, will help it out. You haven't had the benefit of a London Season, Amberleigh, I've had six. I shall do right by you." And she whisked the gown from me with an imperiousness that amused me so much I let her go. At least she no longer dwelt on Devora.

Devora herself neither appeared the rest of that evening nor the next day. Her maid brought breakfast and luncheon on a tray to her boudoir, casting stormy looks at Elaine and myself whenever we crossed her path in the hall.

Twelve times that day I must have vacillated between telling Lord Hugh the total truth and a nest of absolute lies. I must have rehearsed a dozen half-truths in my head and by midafternoon I was absolutely flummoxed. Sometimes I thought things in such a state of mistrust and despair at Carnhaven that I believed only truth could help the muddle. At other moments, I pictured betraying Elaine and I simply couldn't see her exposed to the barrage of criticism the world had aimed at me.

Elaine, oblivious to my dilemma, organized the day for me, like a nanny sending her favourite nursling off to tea.

"Here, Amberleigh, Henrietta has just finished the gown. It's six o'clock, so you'd better try it on."

"But what have you two done to it? There's something horribly wrong!"

"I've merely had it made a bit more—soignée. You'll see; here, let me hook you, but Henrietta is coming along and insists on seeing." Oh, she made it more soignée all right. The fox had instructed Henrietta to remove the entire yoke, so an extremely sedate afternoon gown became an off-the-shoulder evening dress.

"Now, Amberleigh, you know the sort of thing Devora wears—and my idea did work, you look like an actress!"

274

"I don't want to look like an actress, Elaine! I've never seen anyone—well, wear a décolletage with long sleeves..."

"I know what you look like. You look like a queen. Like Mary, Queen of Scots. It's so perfect with your white skin and red hair, do wear it!"

Well, Mary, Queen of Scots, had been beheaded. Perhaps the gown was appropriate. And it was more suitable for a dinner invitation now, however perfunctory.

"I'll find some of my grandmother's Whitby jet—or no, here's a scrap of black velvet ribbon, try it around your neck— yes, very nice." And didn't the ladies of the French Revolution wear red velvet ribbons around their necks in a cynical attempt to suggest the mark of the guillotine? At least mine was black.

"I wish you really would care more about your appearance, Amberleigh, it's really quite important. Sometimes I think you'd half prefer to slink around like Cousin Norah, all tatters and dragging petticoats... There. Henrietta will help you with your hair. And please use a touch of paint. And the hare's foot!"

Elaine shut the door before her last instruction had barely cleared the threshold. I could barely believe her light-heartedness. And Devlin dead but, what, seventy-eight hours? No, two days. What would Devlin say if he saw me now, I asked the unquestionably Thespian figure in the glass. Ah, Red, he'd say, it's a fine sight ye are, but what's goin' on in that head of yours? Have ye a thought for anything beyond tomorrow and what's to become of ye? Have ye ever wondered what's to become of these farmers and cottagers and fisherfolk who are your people?

But they weren't my people. Devlin thought a mere accident of birth, of nationality, made one a patriot. Always harping on me to become devoted to something in which I had no interest. Always singing his song, the one about the minstrel boy—oh, how faithfully he'd harp on "one faithful harp shall praise them," these fallen Irishmen of endless battles and futile rebellion.

"My love's an arbutus on the borders of Lean,
So slender and shapely in her girdle of green..."

I was humming another of his songs. And stopped. One thing for Ireland whatever her political failings, I thought as I leaned into the glass, the dew-drenched mornings certainly had a silken effect upon one's complexion. Even the scar seemed to be slipping off my face like a bad dream sliding away when one is waking. Someone had done that to me. Some woman. Elaine, if she had, must have struck from that other part of her personality; I couldn't conceive of the Elaine who had connived at dressing me turning her sewing shears upon me.

Devora? No, that aristocratic hand turned to daggers and drama? But her headaches, which left her isolated and unaccounted for in her room for hours at a time. And her jealousy. She was madly jealous, I had seen that last night at dinner. Companion, she had hissed. Hating me, taunting me with Adrian and hating me for a dinner invitation to Shallowford. She had thought she had the upper hand. Until the whip had descended.

And Adrian. I'd have thought he'd have evaded Carnhaven like a dose of salts until I was safely removed. What brought him back? I almost wished I was descending the stairs now to float into dinner with Adrian. But the carriage, ordered efficiently by Elaine, was waiting. Henrietta stood by with my black lamb cape and net veil and the die was cast. Or perhaps, some of the cast might die.

I quietly descended the staircase after a final blown kiss from Elaine watching from her doorway. Perhaps Adrian would be near the hall or in the study, perhaps he'd hear me pass and come out—but the house was silent and I smoothly settled into the carriage without a glimpse of him. I was vaguely melancholy. But I had never been escorted about in such style since coming to Carnhaven. If it were a tumbrel I was riding in, it was an elegant one. The coachman handed me out at Shallowford, which somehow looked much more antique and sinister by night, and knocked at the archaically arched door. I was then handed over to the still-expressionless butler, who unwrapped me with exquisite indifference and led me to the library. Lord Hugh waited within.

It was familiar ground, that strange-ceilinged room with its great plaster cones sweeping down like some sultan's seraglio draperies and the cathedrally arched wooden bookshelves, balconies and railings. For all its size it had an intimate air, even a conspiratorial one.

"You are indeed prompt," said Lord Hugh, showing me to a red leather Morris chair that crouched gracelessly by the fire. I would never learn to love these modern designs. "May I offer you some before-dinner sherry? I've had the table set up in here; the dining room is rather large for just the two of us to rattle our forks in."

"I didn't know it was to be a fork-rattling occasion."

"It needn't be if you would table your knife for a moment."

He stepped over to the wall to ring for the butler and I sunk back a bit in the red monstrosity, seeing for the first time the small round table installed on the balcony near a reading alcove. It did look rather charming. Lord Hugh was not looking terribly uncivilized; he was wearing an elegant, cutaway suit edged in black velvet. At least our modes matched, if not our moods.

"You look—different," he said, handing me the sherry in a delicately etched glass after the butler had withdrawn.

"Is that compliment or criticism?"

"I don't think it's either," he said thoughtfully. "I rarely indulge in excesses of either stripe."

"Nor I in seeking them," I replied evenly.

"Did I imply you did? If so, I beg your pardon."

A silence fell then and Lord Hugh began to look restive. It was all so absurd, at least at Alcott's there had been some social fabric surrounding us to help us weave a conversation together. But now I felt wary, and somehow frustrated and restless. Lord Hugh extracted the slender silver case from his breast pocket and asked my permission to smoke. I acquiesced and again watched fascinated as the ritual progressed to the blue smoke stage.

"I wasn't certain you'd come," he said abruptly.

"Why not? You implied once that I was not particular about whose hospitality I sought, surely you wouldn't expect me to turn discriminating at this late date?"

"If I had wanted a fencing partner for dinner I'd have asked one."

"What did you expect? I know very well why I was summoned here." He raised a hand in protest but I rushed on. "It's information you want, all having to do with the filthy little connivings going on around the entire village. I've never seen a countryside so riddled with plots and marplots. It's revolting and I wish everyone would come right out with—things, instead of assuming things or taking other people's words on—things . . ." I hadn't meant to speak quite so impassionedly and paused to take a sip of sherry, its mellow sting calming my tongue before I said more than I cared to.

"So it's forthrightness you favour at the moment. Very well. Yes. It's information I want. And if I'd had enough of it

277

earlier, Devlin Quade might not now be mouldering in St. Stephen's yard and a dozen more like him soon to join him. Is that frank enough for you, Miss Dunne?"

I had never shuddered before, but I did then, as his words hit me with almost physical force. Lord Hugh stood by the mantle sipping his sherry and watching me impassively, like a chess player an opponent.

"You! You speak as if it were my fault for not confiding in you. Why should I? 'Miss Dunne this and Miss Dunne that'—it's clear you've disliked me from the moment we met and I'm perfectly happy to return your sentiments. Besides, how could you have changed anything? It's not fair to lay Devlin's death at my feet merely because, because . . . it's not fair. And you're one to talk. You were only interested in paying court to Devora, in worming your way into Carnhaven. And wasn't Devlin nothing but trouble to you when he came here wounded? You made that plain. Confide in you! No, you didn't want your affairs upset by such ragged goings-on as a revolution, oh no. But to really change something in this miserable moth-eaten land, to actually take a role in this bloody little drama called Ireland—no, I think you wanted to remain offstage and unbloodied—"

I suddenly realized I was describing myself as much as him and stopped dead, while the words hung in the air between us. I was speaking with Devlin's voice, as he would have to me, had he been so harsh.

Then Lord Hugh mercifully broke the silence, speaking so candidly I was surprised. "I, too, have a stake in this land—and, no, I don't mean merely a monetary one. I think something can be done. It was a very near thing that Home Rule didn't pass six years ago. A very near thing. If Parnell hadn't discredited himself by meddling with O'Shea's wife . . . A political settlement could solve the strife, could stop this wasteful killing and—is there something you want?"

"More sherry, please," I said, holding up my glass. My insight had been a blow. I hardly heard what he was saying. I *had* been indifferent just as Devlin had said, in his teasing way. And now here was Lord Hugh speaking solemnly and sincerely about Home Rule and political settlements and I was at sea, feeling marooned and like a hypocrite.

"I'm sorry," he said. "I did not invite you here tonight to upset you. But I had hoped some matters could be settled. Everywhere I turned at Carnhaven, you were there. At first I thought you might be a courier from America bringing money for arms—it's not so ridiculous, there's a strong tie between the emigrants and those still here. I even had you followed on the trip North, thinking there was a possible importation of arms by sea scheduled. But when your destination was reported—on the other hand, it made a damn good cover."

It was as if he were thinking out loud, reciting the ifs and whys of my behaviour like a jury weighing evidence, a judge rendering a verdict. Would Amberleigh Dunne be found wanting? Or not? Or simply "Not Proven," the most damning indictment of all.

"You had me followed? Why should you go to such lengths?" I asked half incredulously. "Even if you have some altruistic interest in the country itself, which I find incredible in an Englishman, to follow us North, to spy upon us, to— why, you *are* a spy!"

He set the glass down on the carved wooden mantle with such emphasis that the sherry tilted wildly from one rim to another. I watched it blankly, like a child entranced by a paperweight with falling snow in it.

"Spy is not a word I care to hear in my house."

"There are words I prefer not to hear myself, but that stops no one from using them," I responded with some heat. "Why else would you even care about my doings?"

He walked away from me, then stopped.

"It's been a game to me," he said in the bitter tones of self-examination. "A nice gentlemanly diversion under the guise of diplomacy. 'Davenant, you've a place in Clare. Looks to be a nest of rebels. Take a look around up there. Nothing major in the works. Merely keep an eye on things...' That's how it started. And they were quite right, something is going on down here. Enough to get Quade killed."

Guilt. Oh, I recognized its soggy, slimy coils around the throat, the self-examination on which every point began 'If I had' or 'But for me...' and ended, always, with Delvin's face live and vivid in the space behind my eyes. I shut them but the face remained.

Lord Hugh came over to me, kneeling before the red chair. He captured my wrists, forcing me to look him directly in the eyes.

"Listen," he said intently. "I don't know who or what you are, but this game is too deep for you. It's not even a game and I think you know that well enough now. I need the truth from you. At any cost. Tell me."

His eyes were earnest. So Eve must have been persuaded

to taste apples. Only I was his Tree of All Knowledge . . . or was I?

"What do you take me for? Why do you think I am privy to any special information? Do I strike you as an agent, a master spy? Really, m'Lord, you're being absurd!"

"I don't know what you are. That's why I'm asking. You may simply be another village maiden caught out by the combination of a tryst and nine months . . ." I turned my head away but he put his hand up to my chin and forced me to regard him again. "Or you may be an overzealous supporter of the United Irish, sacrificing your reputation to camouflage courier activities. Or you may even be an extremely clever Irish agent, bent on fomenting an ugly series of incidents in our quiet little county. In any case, you aren't leaving here tonight until I know the truth."

"And what shall you do, pray?" I cried angrily, breaking away from him. "Is there a dungeon in this Gothic pile of yours? Someplace convenient where the servants shouldn't hear my screams? I can very well credit it. Before I would tell you so much as my grandmother's middle name, I must know why your interest in these matters is so all-consuming."

During my pacing I had come to rest at his abandoned sherry glass. I took a quick sip from it, but it didn't quiet the agitation that rippled through me. Perhaps he *could* torture me, certainly the Morris chair was uncomfortable enough to give a good start to it. I rested an elbow on the low mantle and cradled my aching forehead on my hand. "You're quite right. There are things that I know. But believe me, they only relate to personal matters. There are also reasons why I can tell no living soul about them."

"Well, I'm not about to offer my life to become privy to your secrets," Lord Hugh intoned ironically. He had followed me about the room, but at a distance. "You look like Bernhardt, just there," he said, not unsympathetically, "in one of her more tragic tragedies. Tell me, you'll feel better for it."

"Shall I?" I said bitterly. For I knew then that somewhere in the past two minutes the last fence had been cleared. I would tell him, simply because I was too weary not to. "But if any harm comes to anyone from what I tell you, I shall kill you," I added fiercely.

"That was more like Duse," he said coolly, sitting gracefully in the Morris chair.

"You forever accuse me of acting a part," I flared, "and

yet you're the busiest stage-manager in Glennverran. Perhaps you'll tell me your interest in such hand-dirtying ventures as politics, m'Lord."

"Academic, really. I don't suppose it'll hurt to tell you I'm on assignment for the Home Office, to prevent just the kind of bloodshed you got a taste of on the moors. After the Phoenix Park murders, the political johnnies are more interested in prevention than they used to be. That's all I'm at liberty to tell you. You'll have to take the rest on trust."

Trust. Oh, there was a fearful lack of trust. Trust the man who browbeat me, who ridiculed me, who was johnny-on-the-spot when Devlin died? But I was weary with muddling my way alone through the tangle. I sat in the opposite Morris chair and clutched my reclaimed sherry as a talisman.

"What do you want to know?"

"Your trip North," he said, leaning forward intently with a shadow of triumph in his light eyes. I was too drained to care.

". . . Was what it was rumoured to be and nothing more. An out-of-the-way spot to bear an inconvenient child."

"You became—pregnant—in America?" His voice was somehow subdued, husky.

"I don't see what that has to do—"

"You said you'd answer."

"Very well. No, I did *not* become—pregnant—in America."

"You were here then and only pretended to come from America?"

"No. I did not become pregnant here, either. I have never been—pregnant." I took a long draught of the sherry while a lengthy pause prevailed. What I had hung onto for months, the false impression I had allowed to be woven about me before the whole world, suddenly was rended like a summer cobweb. I kept my eyes cast down, more shamed by my admission of innocence somehow than I would have been by guilt. The room was absolutely silent a moment longer. Then Lord Hugh leaped to his feet.

"Of course, Elaine St. Clare—and all these months, no one ever dreamed or questioned . . ." I said nothing. "Elaine St. Clare . . ."

"If you tell anyone, if Elaine suffers in any way from this . . ." But he waved me silent, still playing with the shock of the facts.

"I'd simply assumed—"

"It was a natural assumption."

"Elaine St. Clare, a bit of sea mist that one can't even imagine—of course they would think it was you. And you did nothing to stop them."

"What could I do? Hire a town crier to make the rounds shouting, 'It was Elaine St. Clare'? Is that how I'm to serve a friend?"

"It's incredible," he said, looking at me as if he'd never seen me before. "I'm not often fooled by women. I could have sworn you were no virgin."

I was not too fatigued to muster a flush. "You make it sound like a flaw. And besides, I merely said I had never been pregnant. I didn't lay claim to anything else." Why I was compelled to appear wordly-wise with Lord Hugh I hadn't analysed, but at any rate my intimations didn't work. He merely shook his head.

"My dear Miss Dunne," he said, for once sounding as if meant it, "you are remarkable. Would I had such a friend." He refilled my sherry and began pacing in a businesslike way. "So it was poor Elaine . . . and you protected her because—But how could she let you assume the blame for her act?"

"Elaine hardly knew what she was. It was all so . . . so foreign to her that she seemed to blot out the entire thing once it was done with. She remembered again a bit, recently," I added. He didn't have to know about Jason and Devlin. That was truly personal. "But it slipped away again. You know how Elaine can be. I couldn't expose her to the kind of cruelty public knowledge of it would draw. Devora was hard enough on her—"

"Devora? Do I detect her fine Italian hand in this? You didn't simply come to Carnhaven and volunteer for the role of red herring, did you?"

"I'm not that noble," I said ironically.

"You surprise me. Here, let us have dinner. We can finish it up over something soothing." He led me to the table and seated me. The sunset was turning the horizon incarnadine and a line of grey cloud edged with brilliant copper slashed across the sky like a scar.

"Don't droop so," he urged softly across the immaculate linen as the butler and the serving men entered with the wine and the first course. "You make me feel quite the brute."

Now that he had twisted my story out of me, he seemed sorry to have heard it. Well, he should feel unworthy; it was a sordid tale and could have no bearing on his interests.

"Would it help if I told you something nice, such as you look stunning?"

"You're only saying it to put me into good humour," I said, sipping the wine—white this time—rather more thoroughly than Louisa would have approved.

"What can I say?" he asked once the servants had retreated. "I've had no right to be worrying at you, but I thought—see here, it may still have some bearing on things. What about the woman who followed you in the woods and cut you? Or is that another misapprehension?"

"No, that was true enough. Save that I had no note, I wasn't acting as courier for anyone. I thought at the time it might have been Elaine. She babbled about lovers in a husky voice, that woman, and with Elaine's condition . . . and she knew where I was so I assumed—But now I think it was someone else."

"So you make assumptions also," he said quietly.

I cast up my eyes from the plate and quickly scanned his face. He was looking very serious and I noticed how his features sharpened as his expression grew more worried. Something bothered me. I realized then that I did not want Lord Hugh shamefaced and troubled. I wanted his arrogant old self back. With that I could deal. But now, we seemed to have become two different people, both of them much more uncomfortable with whom to live.

I ate lightly—because my appetite was in retreat—and drank rather more wine than I usually would. A pleasant sort of lassitude stole over me during that largely silent dinner. Lord Hugh was so abstracted he barely noticed me, and I—I seemed not to care about things as I had before. After dinner I took my wine glass and made my way to the Morris chair, sinking back into its depths as if it were an old friend, and extending both my arms over the leather sides. I felt like Ophelia, floating.

"I fear I've asked too much of you," said Lord Hugh, standing perplexed and rather nervous before me.

"Why?" I enquired lazily, and took another sip of the dessert port. I studied the scarlet glow in the glass. It was like a rich ruby drop of blood. I felt as though some tremendous weight had been drawn off me, like a wet cloak on a bitter fall day. I had not realized how inhuman carrying a secret made one feel. It was almost as if I'd transferred the onus to Lord Hugh. He seemed to grow more agitated as I relaxed.

He abruptly walked over to me and took the wine glass from my hand, helping me to my feet.

"No more of this, I've got to get you back to Carnhaven before it grows too late or you become too—foxed—to manage it."

"Why? With my reputation, surely there's no haste?" I laughed, throwing my head back as I did so and finding that the room suddenly lurched. I straightened my gaze and shook my head, but Lord Hugh still had to support me lightly. "I do believe I have had rather too much wine," I said, trying to crush an imperious desire to giggle.

"Good Lord," said Lord Hugh.

"Self-praise?" I asked archly.

He was supporting me as lightly as a ballet dancer balances his partner and looking more appalled by the minute.

"Listen," he said seriously, but I confess his seriousness seemed to dissipate through my light little fog. "I truly didn't intend for this to happen. It must have been a horrible strain for you all these months and I don't blame you for despising me—but get a hold on yourself, Miss Dunne, I can't send you back to Carnhaven like this."

"Why not?" I seemed to be fond of whys in this state. "It will doubtless enhance your reputation as a Lothrar—Lothari . . . oh, as a lover," I said quite coquettishly, hooking my finger in his lapel buttonhole.

"Sit," said Lord Hugh, half carrying me back to the Morris chair. "Don't move. I'm going to ring for coffee."

He did so while I surveyed the room from inside my garnet glow. When he wasn't looking I retrieved the wine glass and had a good swallow. Immediately he leapt across the room and wrested it from me, once again escorting me to the chair.

"Poor Elaine," I intoned mournfully while we waited for the coffee. "She's not had an easy life. I shouldn't have said anything."

"I won't tell a soul on pain of death about her secret, so rest easy on that," he said. When the servant entered he asked for Hemlock, who came along shortly after, while I was engrossed in studying a large glass ball that stood on a table near my chair.

"Coffee, Hemlock, strong and plenty of it. And bring it yourself," I heard Lord Hugh say grimly. "Keep the servants out of it. Miss Dunne has had something of a shock," he explained.

Hemlock's wondering eyes ranged over to me arrayed across the Morris chair and grew as large as dinner plates. He vanished rapidly with a knowing look.

"No, no, no! I *won't* drink coffee! It's a heathen drink. Tea, now I might drink tea. Louisa gave me coffee oh lay. No, café au lait. That was quite all right. But I won't, won't drink it black," I said when the delicate cup reeking of the strong acrid scent was placed before me.

"Hemlock, thank you, you may go. All right, Miss Dunne. You are going to drink coffee and you are going to drink it until you beg for mercy in clear, unslurred, bell-like tones. Now come."

He brought the cup to my lips and forced me to take one sip, then another. By the end of half an hour I'd consumed at least three cups of the vile liquid.

"No more. I shall be ill, truly!"

"Now, we'll take a turn around the room. Come, up on your feet." He paraded me around the library for another half an hour.

"My goodness, I was a bit tipsy, wasn't I?" I asked when we passed the fireplace for the twentieth time. Lord Hugh dropped my arm and regarded me intently.

"Yes, that's better," he said, leading me over to the mantel. "You looked positively green for a while."

"It was the coffee," I asserted.

"No, it was more than that." He smiled. "I promise solemnly that I won't reveal anything you've said tonight. But we should talk again on this—I'm afraid we were diverted from our purpose." My, he was full of "ours" and "we's" all at once. "Are you better now?"

"Yes, thank you, I feel quite my old self," I replied.

"No dizziness? No more giggles?"

"Did I giggle? It was more of a light laugh, as I recall."

"Yes, you're quite, quite sober now. Aren't you?"

"Absolutely," I said, looking him straight in the eye. We faced each other in front of the fireplace.

"Good," he said with a most strange expression in his eyes. I'd never seen them look so dark without his being angry; it was as if he were a cat whose iris had exploded into night. "I want you to be sober for this." And he put his hands on my shoulders and leaned towards me. He's going to kiss me, I thought, wondering why I did nothing to stop him. I stood frozen. Time seemed to have held its breath. I felt this odd, mesmerizing pull to lift my face to his, but I fought it successfully. I kept my chin steadfastly level but he bent to meet my mouth anyway. Our eyes held, mine paralyzed, his with an expression I had never seen before, that made me suddenly breathless. Oh, Amberleigh Dunne, what have you done? His mouth matched mine and there was warmth, wet, a fire like whiskey between us.

When he finally drew back I remained absolutely still. Save for my still slightly parted lips and the quick way my bodice rose and fell, the entire episode might have been a dream. We were still standing close and our eyes still took each other's silent measure. He slowly reached up and untied the velvet ribbon at my throat, drawing it slowly around my neck before putting it in his pocket. I didn't ask him why he wanted it. I didn't ask him anything, though questions were all that I had in my mind. I simply stood there, absolutely sober, and regarded him.

"I'll have the carriage brought round to take you back to Carnhaven," he said calmly after a moment. And so he did, escorting me to the door, handing me in and saying nothing but "Good night, Miss Dunne," as the door shut upon me.

CHAPTER TWENTY-NINE

CARNHAVEN WAS almost totally dark when the carriage drew up before it. I wasn't used to seeing it like this—remote, shaded, almost alien. But perhaps its facade reflected only my own interior upheaval. I felt like a Cinderella whose fur slipper was lost in translation, whose lost footwear came back as crystal. Something was the same and not the same. But at least I had not been beheaded—at least I think it was still there and in one piece, although a tiny throbbing at the back of my neck was beginning to drum on my consciousness.

I glided up the stone stairs subdued. Symes admitted me wordlessly and gestured to the staircase, lit by the flickering gaslight on the newel post. The white-painted rungs made a dancing pattern on the walls; going up those stairs would be like running a ghostly gamut of whirling shadow figures. I paused at their foot, long enough to hear the creak of a hinge in operation. A moment later a small draught tickled the back of my neck. I wished Boru weren't down in the flagstoned kitchen. I even wished Lord Hugh were here and would have paid another kiss for the privilege. I was afraid to turn and confront whatever had caused the small stirring—afraid it might be no one. Afraid it might be a woman. With a knife...

"Amberleigh..."

The whisper was low and vibrant and somehow familiar. I turned, startled by the swish of my skirts across the floor in the silence.

"Amberleigh..." It was almost unreal, the way the voice skimmed along the hard marble of the foyer and curled up to my ears. Like fog, it enveloped me and drew me to the library door. My footsteps were crashing in the quiet house, but Symes had long since glided out of sight and no one came to stop me. I pushed the door—ajar—a bit wider.

"Adrian!" I'd forgotten that he was here. He drew me into the dim room quickly and shut the door. I felt almost claustrophobic for an instant. Until I remembered that it was only Adrian. The fire was almost out and only one lamp burned softly on a Hepplewhite table.

"You look half-frozen, come over here." Adrian led me to the feeble embers. "You're white as a ghost...I'm sorry if I startled you, but I wanted to speak with you and I was afraid I wouldn't catch you in the morning."

"No, we don't seem likely to meet—in the morning," I couldn't help remarking a little bitterly, remembering the ball. He seemed to miss my overtone.

"You're looking splendid, Amberleigh. Simply splendid." The lamp glow dusted his hair with honey colour, his not-as-bright-as-Devlin's blue eyes seemed softer, easier to look into than they had before. He spoke in half-tones, afraid perhaps that the house should hear us, but I was surprised at the small spark of triumph I felt to be closeted in cosy corners again with Adrian Carstairs.

"Splendid," he said again, as if that were the safest word in his repertoire. It was hard to imagine glib Adrian pressed for verbal spells.

"You surprise me," I said frankly. "I never expected to see you again."

He glanced down and sat across from me on the Queen Anne armchair before the fire. "No, I don't suppose you did. I certainly didn't expect to see you again. I was disappointed to find you not in."

"Were you really? Oh, come, no game is so serious that one expects to retire the pieces for keeps. I suspect you were very glad to return me to my box here at Carnhaven; that kind of chess can be very costly, can't it? You were rather closer to checkmate than you thought." I slipped off my black tulle scarf and folded it across my lap. The jet spangles that bestrewed it caught the firelight and danced before my eyes. Adrian seemed a long way off; a far, faint figure from a faded tintype. "There's always Maisie Dillingham."

"Anger is a sign of life, at least," he responded, leaning into the light to rest his arms upon his knees. He was wearing a very smart suit and vest of grey melton. I could see him at meetings of the board, at the opera, at the right charity balls down through the string of years that stretched before him like so many sausages. He would grow stout and drink too much and crinkle at young girls from very old professions in his dotage. He would buy a coat of arms and a family tree and own a shooting lodge in Scotland. He would subscribe to the right charities and the wrong newspapers. He would see his sons in Parliament and his daughters in marriage to all the respectability left in Britain. He would be very successful and he would probably even marry me if I worked it correctly.

Was my future vision so awful? He sat across from me, natty now, trim, not too terribly dull, with still a weakness for Milton among his Middle Class virtues and vices. I could do worse. Elaine St. Clare could do worse. Who was I to quibble about a missed beat in a conversation, a misunderstanding . . . a too-quick turn on a heel. He was back, possibly contrite, and I didn't want him. I think.

"Devora said you'd gone over to Davenant's place."

"Devora is, as usual, scrupulously truthful."

"You oughtn't to do that. I've no right to meddle, I suppose, but you've got to be careful of your reputation—"

I laughed then. "Oh, Adrian, why? If I recall, it was you who was being careful of my 'reputation.' What have you decided, that I'm not so degenerate after all, that there's many a slip 'twixt the cup and the lip and that my cup hardly runneth over? Have you no Milton to quote me—Elegy for a Fallen Woman Forgiven?"

"Oh, for God's sake," he said irritably, getting up to pace into the shadows. "You women always dramatize things so. I don't give a damn about your past. Not really. That's what I discovered when I stopped to think about it. No reason for me to be—stuffy—about it."

"And if I were to tell you that it was not true, suppose I could satisfy you with an explanation—?"

"But it's of no account, don't you see? You don't have to

produce explanations for me . . . I've really been naive about this. As if you were some porcelain dainty that mustn't get your skirts dirty—it's not as if we're considering a lifelong liaison. I'd been acting St. George and the dragon and there was nothing to slay. You could come back with me. To London. There are dozens of pretty little houses that would suit you. It's better than rotting at Carnhaven and escorting Elaine into senility the rest of your life—"

"You will have to put things plainer for me. I'm afraid I'm not accustomed to being up so late; it muddles my brain."

I kept my eyes on the scarf, made of the net they call illusion. I folded it and smoothed it. I understood him all too well—he was offering me the life Louisa foretold for me. I could pass from one of them to the other, gently handed on about the circle until I grew too old and then perhaps they would all go together and pay for a retirement cottage somewhere discreet like Wales. It was easier than one thought to become a fallen woman, I mused. And why not? It was a practical enough solution to the pestering question of my whereabouts next month or next year. I could become clever at flattering them, at searching out their weaknesses and buttressing them.

Louisa was right; I could be very good at it. And the righteous anger I believed would sweep me away from any contemplation of such a life, where was it? How could I sit here and mechanically pleat my scarf and consider such a step as calmly as I mulled over the trim for my new fall suit? Devora had brought me to this. No illusions, no Adrian Carstairs to be swept away by my beauty, my brains, my sweet dispostion, and offer his hand and heart to the humble goose girl. These things could be handled so much more smoothly these enlightened days.

He circled round again in front of the fireplace, having extended the most honourless part of his offer from the darker reaches of the room.

"I thought," I said, and for some reason there was no life in my voice, "that I should be glad to see you again."

"What is it?" he demanded. "You haven't gone and done anything foolish with Davenant?" The sharpness of his tone told me both what he meant by foolish and what he would do about it. His offer would be politely voided.

"It was a political interview," I said ironically.

"Do you always dress so for political interviews? I must investigate your party."

"Lord Hugh hasn't the slightest interest in me, and I wish you'd stop making mountains out of molehills. Is that any way to make unconventional proposals?"

"You're taking it badly; I knew you would." He walked up to me and drew me up to face him. "All right, don't look at me, but listen. I don't do this every day, you know. In fact, I've never done this before—oh, it was fun enough to flirt with all those winning young ladies and yet keep them at arm's length. I became rather good at it. But it doesn't seem to be working with you. I rather missed you, you know. Oh, it surprised me, too. Blast it," he shook me a little and I felt the scarf slip out of my hands. "I'll even marry you if I must."

The ultimate sacrifice. I looked at him then, amazed. He already looked sorry he had said it. His hands on my shoulders pulled me closer and he kissed me briefly, awkwardly on the mouth. Well, and why not? I was evidently irresistible tonight.

"Why do you make me feel like a schoolboy?" he asked, dropping his hands in exasperation. "I'm usually rather better at this, you know. I wait up for you like a child for the Sugar Plum Fairy and I come away feeling I've caught the Red Queen." He plunged his hands in his pockets dolefully and regarded the embers crackling into extinction on the hearth.

"Adrian. Please. It's too much drama for me. Take your exit and we'll try another rehearsal some other day. I don't know how I feel about you. But I was angry"—he turned to protest—"I was very angry for what you seem able to believe of me and I don't think there's much point in going over it anymore. You don't understand me, no matter how much I intrigue you, and I would be very unhappy in the role you offer me. Now please, let me go upstairs."

He moved to stop me, to say something else, and I saw the frown lines etched between his light brows. He looked very handsome in the half-light, very boyish. I felt old and emptied and extremely tired. I went upstairs, welcoming the flickering shadows for their mesmeric effect. I think I needed a good night's sleep.

Adrian had come to the foot of the stairs to watch me ascend. I heard his tentative steps but I didn't look back. This Eurydice was happy enough to return to her prison, if that was what Carnhaven was to me. The hall was unlit and I skimmed along the walls, finding my door by touch. Somewhere in the house there was a weak little creak. It sounded like I felt. I shut the door behind me and sank with relief upon the testered bed, feeling the taffeta skirt billow up around me like a great balloon. I realized that I was quite uncomfortable, that the whalebone in my corset dug into my flesh and the pins in my hair into my head. But I was too fatigued to move and disrobe.

The emotions tumbled around inside me like pins in a box, each pricking at my comfort, my security. There was meanness—a sharp stab of triumph to have Adrian back and begging. A sort of feminine sense of power that I imagine spurred more than one Greek tragedy. Life was so unfair for a woman. To be so dependent on what *he* would do, on whether *he* would think of one, or write the vital letter or even bow when one passed in the street—but revenge, no, that led to nothing but illusory gratification.

And Lord Hugh, who'd also laid hands upon me that night. It was strange, I'd always found him unbending, unable to accommodate himself to me. Yet it was Adrian—endearing, crinkly Adrian—who had stood there stiffly insulting me in a dozen different ways and too blind to see it. Perhaps it was because for the first time he had really cared for the object of his game. Or had I simply been too easily satisfied when he abandoned me; did he want me more demanding so he could again cut loose and prove that women were merely overmuch ballast for a well-rigged man-about-town?

It was terribly puzzling. I felt bitter still and more than puzzled. And Elaine. Elaine's secret was no longer mine. A pin of fear pricked against my stomach as I sloughed off the taffeta and began struggling with the corset laces in the dark. If he told—but no, it was only gossip and I didn't think Lord Hugh, whatever else his faults, gave a fig for country gossip. He'd said he was on assignment for—what—the Home Office? I sat down on the bed again, overwhelmed. It hadn't really sunk in, what he'd said. So he'd told me something he wished hidden. It was an equal exchange of information. And it helped explain his interest in Carnhaven, in my doings, in Elaine's mystery. But what assignment? Devlin. Could he have had something to do with Devlin's betrayal, something he'd not told me about? I remembered the glass crashing into the fireplace the night Devlin died; was it the casting away of guilt?

CHAPTER THIRTY

I AWOKE early, but forced myself to lie in bed until sleep wafted over me despite the bright daylight floating in at the windows. If I lay abed long enough, I knew, Adrian would be on his way to the station and as removed from my life as I wished him to be. It was hard to sleep, that morning; despite myself my ears strained for the faint slap of horses' hooves on pavement. In my drowsy mind, a phantom dogcart circled endlessly in the drive, endlessly collecting a smartly-suited figure that would embark and disappear only to repeat the process as another sliver of sound slipped through the windows. I stayed there until all the morning mutters had died away, until Adrian had to be well gone. If only I could send Lord Hugh packing as well, I thought, when I finally crawled out from under the comforter.

But the Lord of Shallowford was not as simple to dismiss as the late great Emperor of the Ephemeral. When I found the breakfast sideboard already cleared, I went to Feather for sustenance.

"There's a boy been waitin' for you in the yard" was the information she extended me with my croissant and apricot marmalade. I ventured outside, still nibbling, and did indeed find a fine freckled fellow of about thirteen, lingering near Norah's Opal, who played with a doll on a little bench. The boy's eyes lighted on me and he came over somewhat reluctantly, his nose already wrinkling with the scent of an unwelcome task upon it.

"Miss Dunne?" The formal address came oddly from as rough-and-tumble a visage as his, but I answered gravely.

"Yes, indeed, but how did you know?"

"Master said you'd match me own." The lad ran a hand through his stiff copper curls.

"Oh, he did, did he? Then I needn't ask who your master is, for in the taking of liberties there's none in County Clare to match him."

"Aye." The boy grinned, friendlier now that my speech had instinctively fallen into more local forms of expression. "I've a message for ye, Miss Dunne, an' I'm to deliver it as set down." He thrust his grimy hands in his breech pockets and rattled off the words he'd memorized.

"His Lordship wishes to extend his compliments and the suggestions that you resume your interrupted tête-à-tête with him this morning at Shallowford Bridge, if you would be so kind, Miss Dunne." How typical. To send a Machiavellian message interlarded with French phrasing in such a rough envelope.

"And did His Lordship, your master, deign to mention a time for this rendezvous?"

The boy's eyes squinted at yet another Frenchified mode of expression, but then he clung to the obvious part of my question.

"'Leven, miss. Though I'm not sure that it ain't past that already, an' it not bein' my fault entirely—" The rebuking look he gave me for keeping him waiting in the yard while his message grew cold was heated. It reminded me of Devlin, that sudden kindling of indignation in this boy. I wanted to put my arm around his shoulders and tell him not to fret so seriously at life. But thirteen was the beginning of manhood for these Irish boys, especially in such times, and I couldn't breech that fierce line of independence in him.

"Come in," I said instead, "Mrs. Featherstone will have a scone for you." His brow was thunderous at the thought of crossing St. Clare threshold. "It's only the kitchen, young sir—surely an Irishman can step across such a stoop without collaborating?"

He sent me a fast look, probably for surmising his difficulty, "You'll like Mrs. Featherstone. Devlin got on with her famously and she's no doubt lonely for the sound of a brogue, hmmmm?"

Something dawned in his brown eyes like a vigil light before a stone saint. "Aye, Devlin Quade. Ye knew him, mum? I saw him about the place and on the roads; he was a wily one, wasn't he, mum? Goin' about singin' like the village fool and all the while fightin' for the Cause. Till they killed him for it."

I thought I saw a new saint being assumed into the local litany and the vision chilled me.

"He *was* a fool, young man," I said sharply, though the very words hurt me. "He's dead. If that's the price of your Cause, it's a high one."

The boy's eyes smouldered with disagreement, but he said nothing. I saw he had decided that I would not be one to trust, despite my having known Devlin. I felt bereft again. But would Devlin have wanted his name to set these children afire with fierce words and fictitious notions of bravery and causes for yet another generation? I thought not. He had been a bard at heart, Devlin had, precisely the kind of "village fool" happy to make melody his life's work. In another place, he would have been a poet, plain and simple, I think. Here they wanted to make a saint of him, and he was too good for that.

We went inside and the boy made Feather's uneasy acquaintance. She plied him with what sweets she had on hand, a rare treat for one from the cottages. I checked the kitchen clock—it was nearly teatime. If I intended to honour Lord Hugh's invitation to parley, I should be on my way.

"I'm going up for a hat," I announced to the solemnly munching twosome at the work table. And fled, knowing how astounded Devora would have been at my new-found diligence in dressing. But for some reason that morning I did want a hat—a nice, wide-brimmed one that would shade my face. I unearthed a straw leghorn and clapped it carelessly on my head. A glimpse of myself in the glass made me pause. No, it really didn't sit well on my pompadour—I hastily pulled the pins out of my hair until it fell loosely around my shoulders. I had donned a sprightly gown of cream and violet-flowered organdy that morning. I regretted it in view of my new plans. It was too grand, too dainty for a woodsy walk. I would almost look as though I had preened for the occasion. I wanted to change it, but was trapped by my own determination not to spend a moment's bother in tailoring any part of myself to Lord Hugh or what he might think or how things would appear.

Well, if I looked like a stage shepherdess—all rosebuds and broad brim—that wasn't my concern. Why should I dress down for him? But I did look exceptionally charming in the glass; it was a pity I had no one of any consequence on whom to expend it. I gathered up my sketchbook, dear reliable pretext for everything, and then dropped it again. I did look a touch pale in the mirror. Too wan. People would wonder if I were ill and what I was doing tramping about the woods. Merely a touch of the hare's foot, merely a spot of colour—there. Better. Louisa would have been proud of me.

I whirled out the door with my petticoats frothing at the edge of the organdy, clattered down the stairs and emerged breathless into the yard. Opal still played in the sullen fall sunshine, solemnly serving tea from leaves to her expressionless charge. The boy also lingered nearby, hands in his pockets and his eyes on Opal's exotic profile—a carmel cameo fixed with twin black pools like coffee in two clean cup ovals for eyes. Her delicate beauty caught me for a moment, just as it had snared the Irish boy. I saw him say something to her and she glanced up with a smile. Childish country courtships—I was glad I was of an age and sensibility to be unsusceptible to such foolishness. Dunne the Governess would never have to worry about that!

But I did have to worry about meeting Lord Hugh like this, in the woods. Another hand-delivered message to stir suspicion and rumour. It smacked of a rendezvous. And after the other evening, well, I simply didn't want to give him the impression . . .

There was no one by the bridge when I arrived, so I set down my sketchpad on the stone rail with my hat atop it. The sun sifting through the trees, warmed its hands on my head. In the distance I could see sheep grazing by the ruined abbey, whose hulk just broke the horizon. I had not been there since that talk with Devlin. I doubted I should ever want to go there again. I leaned my elbows on the stone lightly, hoping no dirt should cling to my pale sleeves, and looked over into the lightly gurgling water just below. It flowed fast but smoothly, with few stones to slow it. The reeds along the bottom extended like a phalanx of green snakes. One would never guess how cold that pretty little stream could be. I shivered.

"Tuppence for your thoughts."

Lord Hugh was striding up the road in riding breeches and jacket incongruously cast on over a sweater.

"I thought it was a penny would buy thoughts," I pointed out as he came abreast.

"But yours are worth twice the price, I'm beginning to discover," he replied banteringly.

"Yes, my thoughts are costly. I'm not sure you'd care to share them."

He leaned on the wall and joined my unseeing gaze into the Shallowford without answering. But share thoughts I must, for there was a mystery here in these bird-chirping woods and green, green lanes. And a greater one out on the limestone rocks, where great holes to hell pockmarked the landscape. And there was the greatest mystery of all in the human wills that strived here. She with the knife, Elaine—if they were not one and the same—and Lord Hugh. Devlin's mystery had been the simplest to solve. An enthusiastic boy, loving his land and dying for it. Or had he? Who had let that vicious bullet loose to slice through his body and silence it forever?

"May I offer you a seat?" asked Lord Hugh, abruptly turning and lifting me by the waist to sit upon the bridge wall. For a moment I clutched at his arms, afraid I should fall once more into that chill water. But the wall was wide and the feeling passed. "There's something you haven't told me about the night on the moor," he said. "I can tell. The night we found you."

No, I hadn't told him about the note regarding Elaine's baby. It had apparently been as senseless, as misdirected as that ugly letter of recommendation supposedly come from the Willoughbys. So I did, while he frowned in concentration.

"But did you know why Devlin came there, how he happened to find me? There was to be a meeting of the United Irish that night."

Lord Hugh's eyes narrowed suddenly. "So that's one of their spots. Don't look alarmed, you haven't given anything away. They'll not return to it with half the barracks having been there."

"But, but Devlin was early, for the other men didn't come for a long time—after. A long time. I don't know why Devlin was early. If it hadn't have been for Boru tagging along as usual—perhaps nobody would have noticed anything was wrong."

"You've adopted him, I see," said Lord Hugh, nodding to the other side of the bridge. I looked over in surprise and saw Boru sitting patiently just across the bridge. And I had most strictly instructed him not to follow me. "Boru!" I scolded reproachfully. He lay down slowly and cradled his mournful eyes on his paws, looking for the world like a delinquent pup instead of the largest, fiercest hound in County Clare. I laughed then, for the first time since we had lost Devlin.

"Let him stay; he fancies himself my protector, you know."

"It strikes me you're in need of one," said Lord Hugh. Some chord in his voice seemed to me overintimate. He must be corrected as to the previous night's proceedings.

I picked up my hat to draw his steady hazel gaze from my face and pulled the violet ribbons through my fingers. "We are here to solve puzzles, Lord Hugh," I said severely. "Not to enact pastoral poetry. I wish to be certain that you are not labouring under any—misapprehension—concerning me because I do not wish to engage in any sort of—flirtation. But I'm sure such incidents are merely second nature to you, so—"

"Oh, I assure you it was nothing personal," he interrupted with mocking in his voice.

"Well . . . good," I said. "I think it only right that we should understand each other."

"Do we?" he said, riveting me with his gaze.

"I think so. It's clear that your major interest lies elsewhere. With Devora," I added, challenging him to deny it.

"Ah, Devora." He laughed then and for some reason my breath seemed to catch in my throat. I wanted very much to know what he thought of Devora.

"Devora is long past but a pretence of—how shall I put it delicately enough for you, Miss Dunne?" he went on even more mockingly. "A pretence of—friendship." His voice caressed the word friendship so ironically that its meaning was entirely clear. "Sir George and his country manners of both bed and board long ago convinced Devora that drawing room and garden pleasantries were all the tribute she needed."

"So you provide them?"

"If I hadn't, someone else would have. Perhaps Carstairs. Don't worry yourself about Devora—don't you know by now that she is more than capable of taking care of herself? And I needed her, she was my key to Carnhaven, where I'm still certain a lot of this—activity—somehow originates. Devora was my key."

"And now you've found another," I said bitterly. He was very adept at manipulating women. At turning them like keys to open to him whatever he wanted open. Too good at it. Wasn't I sitting here on Shallowford Bridge with the man, half the time afraid of falling into the stream and half the time afraid of falling in love with him?

It was the first time the thought had openly crossed my mind. Every sound seemed to stop as I examined the idea. I heard no birds, no rush of water, just a pounding in my neck as the blood flooded to my face. I kept my eyes glued to the hat brim, which I discovered I was rolling in my fingers, no very good way to treat Italian straw.

". . . you've been used that way too often of late to believe me, I suppose," he was saying. "But I only want to help you. I see you are troubled . . ." He put his hands on mine to quiet them and I felt panic welling in me. It was as if the Shallowford were quietly rising to engulf me; in a moment I should be happily drowning . . .

"You! You see nothing!" I violently wrenched my hands

away. "You're such a—a womanizer, but you know nothing of women at all! I shouldn't care for your help," I went on brutally, "if it's the kind of solace you extend to poor Louisa, who cares for you deeply and whom you treat like—like an old family retainer beneath all that social cleverness."

"Louisa?" He stepped back a bit and in the shade it seemed his face had paled. He looked puzzled and I realized, with a sinking heart, that he had never known she was in love with him. "What do you know of Louisa?" There was a hard tone in his voice; for the first time that morning I dreaded the water behind me and him before me.

"Let's walk," he said abruptly, pulling me down by the wrist so roughly that Boru growled and raised his shaggy head. Lord Hugh appeared not to have noticed it as I fell in step behind him somewhat breathlessly. Finally he seemed to remember me again and slowed his stride.

"What do you know of Louisa?" he repeated in a calmer voice, dropping my wrist.

"I know what role she plays in 'this great scheme of things.'" Somehow her words for it still seemed the only graceful way to say it.

"How?"

"She told me."

"At the same time she confessed her undying love for me, no doubt."

His words were disbelieving, bitter. I sensed I had waded into waters too deep for me, but there was no retracing my steps. He had taken the little bridle path and we were labouring up the incline slowly. Boru brought up the rear, I could hear his reassuring clumsy padding behind me. Lord Hugh looked as if he could strangle someone. I fear it was I.

"She didn't tell me in so many words," I replied, suddenly shy about transmitting a message received by intuition. "Do you think a woman—like that—has no feelings, that she lives the life she does without wondering every day when it will seem insupportable to her? She is not as young as she was. She is lonely. And she—" I couldn't say "love," the word wouldn't pass my lips— "cares for you a great deal. But you, you can come and go with that sort of careless lordliness of yours . . . how can you be so cruel?"

He stopped to hold back a thin whip of branch for me to pass. His face was white and etched. Somehow the scar near his left eye leapt into ugly relief.

"I'm sorry I brought you to Louisa. I'm sorry you had to

298

hear about the—custom, of which she is part. It is an ugly practise, suitable for safeguarding the daughters of Mayfair and Belgravia, I suppose, and bringing them like lilies to the marriage market, but an ugly practise that does great harm. How can I treat Louisa so, you ask? And I believed I was doing her a kindness. Most of them won't have anything to do with her, you know, once they're past a certain age. I could never quite—leave her—like that."

We had arrived at the Fairy Circle. There seemed to be no spot in County Clare I could go where the ghost of Devlin Quade did not lie in wait for me. But he was far from my thoughts on this occasion. I sat on the ancient log where I had first tried my hand at watercolours. My sketchpad and hat still lay on Shallowford Bridge, I recalled idly. Lord Hugh spoke as if somehow constrained to. He did not look at me very often.

"She couldn't have been more than thirty then," he began softly. "And she looked twenty. And I, I was an idealistic boy. A dreamer. I thought her the most beautiful thing I'd ever seen. I couldn't believe this exquisitely sophisticated creature could take even a passing interest in me.

"These things are handled very subtly, you understand," he said, turning to me. I couldn't meet his eyes for more than a second and dropped mine quickly. "No, I thought it was all happening—naturally. Which, in a way, it was. She accepts her—assignments—one at a time, of course. So I had no intimation that it was a serial sort of thing. A nice tidy business arrangement."

I didn't want to hear. I knew what the next part of the story would be. He had fallen in love with her. Committed the only real sin that mattered in such circles. He had fallen in love with not only a woman most unsuited to him, but one whose affections had been bought and paid for by every worldly father of good family in his circle.

"It was wretched puppy love, of course. I was but eighteen and down from Oxford. I don't know if Father ever knew which way the wind blew, but when I made my usual threats to join up for a little military adventure in India, he didn't dissuade me as he usually did . . . I wanted to make a name for myself, you see, become independent so . . . so things would settle my way. I didn't want to leave her, but I was not unaware how a uniform can age a man. I went in as an officer, of course. That, too, was bought by my family connections.

"It wasn't until I got to India that I heard about her. From the others, reminiscing over their warm whiskey and sodas on the club verandah at Rangoon. Luckily, I had not been so foolish as to confide my expectations to anyone."

He paused then and there were no words in the world I could say into the silence. The sun was warm for fall, uncomfortably so, but I couldn't move to seek the shade. It must have been so in India. Remorseless sun. Remorseless self-examination. No wonder he'd aimed those cutting remarks about my character at me; I must have seemed another compromised woman fighting to appear to be something else. What distrust it must have bred in him.

"That's how I acquired this." I'd never seen or heard him allude to his scar before, but now he touched a finger to it. "But even a hero's death was denied me, though not through any flaw in my recklessness. Of course, Mother had me back when she got wind of it, and gave Father hell for letting me go in the first place. I didn't care. I was no longer eager for Indian adventures. Hemlock is the only benefit I derived from the whole bloody episode."

And yet he had gone back to her. Casually, of course, on his terms, but probably the only one of the lot who did not bandy her name over their brandies when their dull wives of good family had retired to the drawing room after dinner.

And he had not married, it must be these ten years. No doubt London debutantes looked fairly flat to him after a menu of Louisa's concoction. She was an amazing woman, this siren who could win another woman over in twenty-four hours. She could never really have him again, of course, save in small superficial snatches. And that was sad, for she had loved him, too, although it had probably never occurred to her that he had returned the emotion and even intended to honour it. She never would have presumed that much. Not a woman in her position.

"I find confessing the follies of one's youth a not very favourite pursuit, Miss Dunne. No doubt you, too, find it a bore," he said, plucking a long grass from beneath our feet and chewing on it meditatively. "But things needed clearing up. And I recall taxing you rather closely in the not-too-distant past. Shall we call it even?" he asked lightly, the old look back in his eyes.

"Yes," I agreed. "I too have done foolish things. And more recently than you," I added ruefully.

"But you were not in love."

"No." I found my own blade of grass and tasted it to hide the blush that would surge to my face. It tasted sweet, but sour.

"Shall we return to present conundrums, then?"

"Yes," I said meekly, very angry with myself for having uncovered stories whose end I did not want to know.

There was a silence then; I must either suffer it or break it.

"Elaine . . ."

"Yes, what about Elaine?"

I very nearly had blurted out her relationship to Devlin. That was a secret truly too sacred to share. I shouldn't even have told him the truth of Elaine's confinement . . . "Elaine felt that Devlin wasn't killed because of the Home Rule to-do. She seemed to think it was someone else. The woman who chased me in the woods."

"Her again? Are you certain you didn't invent her for convenience's sake sometime when you were trying to juggle stories?"

"I didn't invent this." He didn't like me to allude to my scar, I saw the aversion in his face. But he frowned and considered the mysterious "Her."

"Could it have been a man? A man's voice in a whisper? There's a Captain Moonlight or two about these nights, you know, killing cattle or firing buildings, all in the name of mischief and Home Rule. One of these hot-tempered country boys might think it a lark to run the woods in disguise. Nothing creates a sense of drama like a revolution."

"I suppose it could have been a man, it was really all frightfully confusing. But I was able to break away from her—or him—that night. Is it likely a man intent on stopping me would have lost his chance?"

"Well, you're not exactly a wee wisp of a girl; he might not have expected any resistance. And some of these Irishers are wiry fellows—"

"It won't work. It was a woman, no man could feign what she said, that frustrated feminity—I can't tell you, you'd have to have heard it. She hated men. Not in so many words, but terribly, to her soul."

"I didn't think there were any women who hated men."

"A conceited lot you are."

"No, I mean deep down, whether the woman be a Suffragist or a nun or a—governess—I don't think there's a woman who really and truly hates men on principle. There's usually a reason. And she usually began by loving a man. Or men."

"But that would make us all eligible for—her. It could be—".

"Elaine," he said brutally.

"Or Devora," I rejoined.

"Or even—Mrs. Featherstone," he added to make peace.

"I'm surprised you exempt me."

"You're the principal witness to her existence . . . oh, I see. No, you've less hatred in you than any woman I've known."

"Then you don't know me," I said, suddenly aware of all the mean little triumphs I'd enjoyed at Devora's expense recently. And Elaine could hate, too. Elaine hated Devora, I'd seen that. And Devora, could she . . . ?

"What are you thinking of, I can see the benefit of the doubt forming."

"Devora." I gave him a level gaze. "Perhaps you can account for her whereabouts at the critical times."

He shook his head.

"But why Devlin? Devlin was the most—out-and-out—lovable person in County Clare. Who would kill Devlin? Why? What had he done to anyone? Elaine—liked him. Even Devora melted for him. He flattered Mrs. Featherstone and took plain Cousin Norah for a waltz around the room. Tell me, who? Why?"

His face had closed to me, like a four-o'clock in the afternoon. "Then it must be the rebels," he said stubbornly. "Why, Devlin Quade was a lieutenant. Next to Jack Reilly and Barry O'Day, he knew more than anyone else what was up. And something is up, I'm 'spy' enough to have learned that. Perhaps that's why he's dead now; perhaps they turned on their own."

"Or perhaps one of yours—"

"No, the soldiers are all accounted for. And I—" he turned his yellow eyes on me and drilled me with them—"plead innocent."

I held his gaze for a moment. It had occurred to me that the shadow of guilt might follow him. Not through any direct action perhaps, but through something else, some information dropped to the wrong party. No, he was too careful for that. I nodded and he seemed satisfied.

"I go over and over it," he went on. "I think it's a killer. That's what my instincts tell me. A ruthless, bloody killer with some reason for shooting Devlin, perhaps even for pursuing you with cloak and dagger. You've been safe since? Nothing—untoward—has happened?"

"No . . . nothing like that."

"What?"

"What do you mean?"

"You thought of something just then."

"The letter. Of recommendation. It was odd, but it could have been some practical joke, it's nothing. I'd written to my former employers in America for a letter of recommendation. So I could leave Carnhaven. After Elaine was settled. And it came, from Boston, with the postmark and everything. But Mrs. Willoughby would have never written what it said. It was—evil, filthy, what a half-grown child who'd peeked into some scandalous book would parrot. About me."

Lord Hugh's attention had been circling the clearing's edge; I was a bit put out that my difficult recital had so halfhearted an audience. But he turned to me in midsentence.

"Perhaps you'd find it more comfortable on the ground." He had me by the elbow and sitting on the grass with my back against the log before I could even shape my customary "But—"

"No fauna," he said quickly, noticing my uneasy eyeing of the damp patch of ground in the log's shadow behind my back. "I should tell you," he added, smiling pleasantly, "that we're being watched." He stretched out like a cat on a carpet and lay his head in my lap. It was heavy. "If you could hum something bucolic in A-flat I would be quite comfortable." He was smiling and had closed his eyes like a contented tabby.

"If someone *is* watching us, aren't you a rather passive target?"

"Oh, I doubt we're in immediate danger. It's simply better not to let anyone know that we're discussing the United Irish connection at Carnhaven. We can discuss other topics, you know," he said, flashing his eyes open at me.

"Who do you suppose it is—the United Irish? And why should they care if we talk—although that man was very interested in your comings and goings... And mine."

"What man?"

"In the woods. I was walking over—by Shallowford one day. Just after, you know—Devlin. And a man was watching your house. Said you were gone. And wanted to know what I was doing about the vicinity."

"Then we're giving him his answer," he said, putting up a knee and lolling the other leg across it as if he were settled for a good long siege of lap-laying.

"What if it's someone from the other side? Such as Captain Mayfair?"

"That's all right. He knows about us." He grinned.

"I believe you're making up the entire thing because you're too lazy to sit up decently—" The flutter of something moving beyond the underbrush ended my sentence. Someone *was* out

303

there. Someone shadowy and elusive. I caught my breath in a kind of panic. I knew the Circle held its secrets. I had not thought until now that they might be fatal ones.

"If you could manage to stroke my fevered brow, it would aid the illusion," Lord Hugh suggested sweetly, with a sort of aesthetic detachment.

His eyes laughed up at mine. I'd never seen him looking so handsome, his dark hair falling away from the temples where the brush of grey seemed almost an artist's humanizing conceit on a too-perfect portrait; his teeth white, even, disgustingly healthy. His forehead furrowed when he looked up at me and the artist in me wanted to smooth out the wrinkles; they roughened too pretty a page. It occurred to me that he'd never seemed so masculine as now, gamboling like a kitten across my lap.

There was an essential difference between men and women, something irrevocable. A mystery that showed its face most, perhaps, when the armour was off and the moat bridged. He loved mocking, flaunting the conventions that bound me. Adrian had delighted in that sort of thing, too. Men built the walls around women, then laughed and tried to tear them down. Was it merely some flirtatious form of man-woman banter, played at since Paradise was lost? Or were they right? Conventions abounded, he had said, to protect the daughters of Mayfair and Belgravia. Perhaps the daughters of Eve had been caught in too wide a net. Did that first woman fret because she wore no hat or gloves in the forest, much less because a man lay across her lap? Wasn't that the more natural scheme compared to drawing-room dalliances and tea-table temptations?

He was still watching me and I realized my thoughts had led me far afield from the Fairy Circle. And from both sets of eyes that watched me. I shivered a bit at the tiger in paradise.

"What—?" I had to ask as his eyes in their setting crinkled, fractured into a hundred tiny lines.

"My fevered brow," he repeated, pointing.

"The only thing that's fevered your brow is coming up with such idiocy," I said in my smartest governess snap.

For I didn't want to touch him. It would be like breaking the surface of some still pond, roiling the waters to no avail. Like taking a painting and fingering it when the oils were still wet...Always pushing to the ultimate limits of convention, always daring one to step out of bonds, over the line. And then, well, then one would be disqualified from the match. Abandoned on the sidelines to be retrieved by someone who played the game less and less by the rules. He was daring me to roquet him. I thought back to that innocent croquet game on Carnhaven lawn, when I'd first really seen him for any time at all. He'd had no reservations about playing the game to the hilt. And the chance I'd had, to make a bold move, to match him roquet for roquet. I'd avoided it. I'd taken the safer way. And the truth was I had done so because I hadn't wanted to touch him then, either, via croquet mallet or by hand. I had so much to lose.

He had plucked another of those sweet-sour long grasses and was engaged in peeling it idly. Half vacantly, I reached down and with a fingernail traced a light line alongside his left temple, just above the line of the scar he'd told me of that morning.

He caught my hand as if I were an attacker and looked up at me again. "You haven't lost your sting," he said, his eyes searching mine with a kind of pain and a kind of triumph.

I didn't know why I had done it. All his delving eyes could read in my expression was troubled waters. He sat up beside me and I noticed he was breathing quickly, shallowly, like a wild thing disturbed in its lair. His fingers still circled my wrist, so lightly they felt like a bracelet. I felt as if I had run a long way, exhausted. There was a tightness in my chest that seemed to be choking me. I wished he'd let me go, that I could shake free of him. Him and his scars and my scars—

"Perhaps you needed it," I said, looking at him cautiously through my lashes, on which, for some reason, tears trembled.

He sighed then, as if he'd been holding his breath for a long time. And helped me to my feet. "Our watcher is gone anyway, I think. We can resume our talk. And our walk."

I stood in my Fairy Circle, that I had named and painted and fought for life in, like an alien. He stood a mere two feet and an entire world away. If he touched me I thought I should shatter and if he didn't I thought I should cry.

"I—I can't really. I've told you everything I know. I've got to get back to Carnhaven. Really. I've told you everything."

"Yes, this time I think you have," he said gravely.

I didn't quite look at him, but shook out my skirts. "So. I hope it helps—things. That we can be free of all this, this confusion . . ." I trailed out of the clearing with my words. It wasn't even until I was halfway through the woods that I remembered the watcher. I stopped and put my hand on a young beech shoot. It felt real and sturdy, there in the dappling daylight. It *was* daylight. It *was* a real world. Nothing had happened in the clearing. No watcher had emerged to threaten us. It was the danger, the tension, that had me so frightened, my heart beating so—nothing had happened in the clearing.

I paused a few minutes to brush the grasses off my skirt and shake the cobwebs off my brain. I must use what I had learned from Lord Hugh, not shy away from it because, because—A killer, he thought. No cause, no nationalism, merely plain killing. A killer loose and free to kill again. And someone from Carnhaven. He believed that, I could tell.

A boy, with enough skin between the freckles that fretworked his face to flush pink from exertion, caught me up at Carnhaven yard.

"Miss, oh, miss," he called from a quarter mile away as if his skin depended on it, waving something above his head. I waited, amused, while Cousin Norah peered out the kitchen door to see the ruckus. He stumbled up to me, breathless but relieved.

"You be Miss Dunne, I think. Master said to give you this for sure." Between pants he smoothed and handed me my sketchpad and hat.

"Thank you—I'd forgotten these on..." I caught Norah's narrow eyes from the door. "...on a sketching jaunt. But haven't I seen someone very like you before?"

"Me brother." The boy grinned. "Kevin. He's out to the peat now."

"Well, it's a great effort you've made to deliver them and I've not a crown on me—"

"'Tis all right, miss," said the boy, flushing even pinker to his prominent ears. "I'm promised a chicken for me mum." He ducked his head awkwardly and took off at a jog across the yard.

I strolled towards the house, tucking the disordered pages together and ruefully inspecting the slight curl to the hat brim. I noticed a cockade of shamrocks, what we English would call clover, slipped behind the band and couldn't help smiling. It was the sort of thing Devlin would have done, though Lord Hugh's motives were more ironic. I glanced up to see Norah staring pointedly at the green cluster, her lips curling slightly with distaste. I'd thought her passionate in defense of Home Rule; it struck me odd that she'd object to an Irish insignia, however insignificant.

I turned the hat in my hands, unwilling to have my posy wilted by that basilisk stare of hers. I knew what she'd say. She was too coarse, too crude to leave my little floral offering alone. Just like a man, she'd say; inexpensive gestures and they'll have the hide off you later for it. I brushed past her in the doorway, holding the hat well away from her. I didn't want to hear what one woman who'd been disillusioned would have to say to me. I knew her tune well enough. I took the cool back stairs at a light run and retreated to my room. She'd been made a fool of, but that didn't mean I had to be. Always assuming things, always suspecting liaisons where there were none. Just like Devora. That smug superior know-it-all—

I had wrenched the gathering of greens from my hatband and stood there puzzled by what to do with them. No small vase around the room. They were growing limp from my hand's heat, I should have to decide soon. I hovered over the basket—grist for the upstairs maid to retrieve and throw out? I thought of pressing them in my volume of Tennyson and promptly blushed. Good heavens, girl, get your head on straight, it's only a handful of wild leaves . . . I settling on tucking them into my broad belt band, a fashion I'd seen but never imitated. I tried the effect in the long glass. Charming—but it was as if he had touched me when I fixed them at my waist, as if he were there with a hand around me—Lord love a duck, I said to myself, to the flushed figure in the mirror with a bouquet of clover in her belt—you're in love with him. I was, I had been for longer than I cared to think.

Breathless, but that was from the stairs, I went over to the window overlooking the terrace. I needed a broader perspective. The world stretched before me in so much limpid damp green rolling hill and woodland. And a chimney, there, that was Shallowford. My fingers stretched to touch that spire through the glass and I leaned my burning cheek against the pane. My chin rested uncomfortably on a mullion strip, but a little reality was strengthening.

"Damn," I hissed against the glass, happy to hear my voice and the expletive slide off into the empty room. It was so—bloody, that was the only word strong enough—so *bloody* predictable. It was what I'd unknowingly ran from during all my days at Carnhaven. A dozen, a hundred women before me, no, a thousand, had probably done the same stupid thing. What a filthy mess. The key adoring the hand that turned her. Oh, Elaine, to be in your light-and-shadow world for a while, to imagine things are not as they are—

When? No wonder he'd played off me in that teasing way of his. He'd seen what I didn't . . . no, I won't blush. Why waste a perfectly genuine, well-earned blush on an empty room? On oneself? And yet, if I didn't think this way, if I didn't lash myself with hard strands of reality, well, I could start riding this tide of elation, of excitement, that threatened to wash me inside out. I could conjure him if I wanted to, a presence that looked like life, the closeness of him. I could go back to the Fairy Circle now and lavish tender care upon that most unfevered brow. And before, too paralyzed to move, to pretend caress, I had reached out to touch the tenderest part of him. Stung him, he'd said. Did he know I moved out of compassion because love was still sheathed in me? That the scar which allied us drew my hand only because no matter how much he could hate it, I could love it more?

Why should he know any of it? Or even care? He would laugh at my sentimentality perhaps. I would, with a calmer head. And still I summoned him in my mind's eye, even when I told myself it was no use. When he said this. When he did that. How he'd arched an eyebrow. How he'd looked at me. When he kissed me, only last night— It wasn't good enough. I wanted to see him again. Now. And then I'd do my utmost to pretend that nothing had happened, to watch his every breath all the while pretending to be absorbed in his conversation.

I could never see him again. He'd know. They'd all know. Norah's narrow-eyed speculation, Devora's scent for such changes, Elaine's blundering emotional accuracy at times. I had finally managed to make an utter and complete fool of myself. Hugh Davenant. Lord Hugh Davenant. Hugh. What was he? I tried to break him down into so many separate words and gestures and looks and impulses. But it didn't work. I could get no perspective on the man. He was Him. No more, and God help the working girl, no less.

I pressed the clover in my Tennyson after all. Someday, I thought, when I am old and grey and more sensible, they will no doubt amuse me. Now the sight of them simply broke my heart. Recommendation or no, I'd have to leave Carnhaven now. Before the governess' most ungovernable feelings made life more miserable than it would be leaving here, leaving home, leaving him.

CHAPTER THIRTY-ONE

I HEARD the chatter of distant voices, washing over me like soft waves from a dream. I floated in the feeling until my mind grew impatient and began to pick out their identities. Norah's raucous laugh. A murmur for Elaine. Sharp little bursts from Devora. Breakfast on the terrace. It was a fine day already, an Indian-summer day, we should have called it in Boston. I could feel it in the sun-warmed air that wafted through my open window.

A basso joined the string trio outside my window, and curious, I slid off the high bed and went to the curtains. It was amusing to peer down upon their sun-washed heads. Elaine's fair halo flitting about the half-moon of linen-clothed table I could see beyond the terrace canopy. I heard the hearty laugh again and guessed that Norah sat too near the house to be visible. A pale-blue-chiffoned arm reached for the teapot; that could only be Devora. The deep murmur came again—Adrian? Back from the South and stopping over again despite my presence?

The object of my speculation strolled over to the balustrade with a white cup filled with something black. Coffee. I looked almost directly down on Lord Hugh. All I could see was the top of his thick chestnut hair, the Norfolk tweeds, the white cup. What on earth was he doing here at this hour? A glance at the little ormolu clock told me it was later than I usually rose, but still, he had never come over this casually previously—and but a few days after our discussion in the Circle . . .

Feminine laughter tinkled up towards me with the sound of silver striking saucers. He was probably being charming, damn him. I looked down again, leaning forward to see the group. Lord Hugh was sitting on a stone bench, one elbow resting on the carved stone balustrade, sipping coffee as if he belonged there. He took a draught then, tilting his head back. I watched, fascinated, until I realized his eyes might find me spying from my window. I drew back quickly, my heart beating an unpleasant little mazurka against my chest.

I wanted to look again, I wanted to go through the floor,

I wanted to be in Outer Mongolia. A few days ago I thought I wanted to see him again more than anything in the world. I didn't. I couldn't. But I had to go down, I couldn't hide behind my curtains like a piece of awkward statuary in a museum alcove. They would expect me soon, they would think it odd if I never turned up. They were unconsciously waiting for me. I perused the cupboard, unthinkingly looking for something to play off well against pale blue—idiot! I selected my plainest black skirt, my most-starched white shirtwaist. "Governish-ish," Elaine would have called it. Well I needed a governess to teach this silly shallow person in my head a lesson or two before someone else did it more harshly.

Schoolgirl infatuation, I thought viciously, pulling my hair into an unbecoming knot at the back of my neck. Better to have gone off to Adrian's uncomplicated kind of blundering fondness . . . I hurried down and teetered on the threshold of the open French windows a moment before anyone noticed me.

"Ah, here's Amberleigh."

"'Morning, Lady St. Clare. And company." I managed to flick my eyes so noncommittally around the terrace that they stopped at no one. No man. I could have been addressing a convention of chairs and balustrades.

"Hmmmm, try Feather's cheese pie, it's heavenly." Norah smiled one of her rare open smiles as she handed me a plate with a thick wedge of the aforesaid delicacy.

"Thank you, Norah."

"You slept so late, Amberleigh, I thought we'd never see you this morning. You must have been having delightful dreams."

I could have strangled Elaine and hung her on the line to dry. "I rarely dream, but I had a good sleep," I replied.

"The sleep of the innocent." Devora directed her stiletto remark to me, but she was looking towards Lord Hugh.

He wisely said nothing as I observed him stealthily through my lashes and the pretence of being absorbed in a forkful of cheese pie for which I had absolutely no appetite.

"This *is* savoury," I said to Norah.

"Yes, isn't it? I really think Feather has outdone herself. Of course, I'm an absolute victim when it comes to food. I'm getting so round," she said carelessly, pulling at her waistband, "that people ask me when I'm due." She broke into a high-pitched wild laugh.

Utter silence greeted this remark. I examined my cheese pie, Devora her nails and Lord Hugh his boots. Only Elaine,

310

bless her, took the comment at face value.

"I don't think you look fat, Norah. You've such spindly little arms, you don't look fat at all."

I noticed with surprise that Norah was right, she was thickening about the middle. She was also wearing a skirt and waist very similar to mine. I suddenly glanced to Lord Hugh, wondering if he had noticed the Tweedledee and Tweedledum of the pair of us. He was looking away, rather bored. I felt a pair of eyes on me and instantly turned towards Devora.

"We shall all grow fat if we don't get up and be about doing something," she said abruptly, her frank gaze of dislike never leaving my face. "Will you accompany me to the village, Hugh? The pair need the exercise and I've a shawl only Mrs. McGuillicuddy has a needle fine enough to mend. A Spanish shawl, I snagged it on the terrace . . ."

"Not today, Devora," he said in a final indifferent sort of way that should have cut me like a crop had he used that tone to me. The slight didn't glance off Devora, but it didn't slash her either.

"You're really becoming quite a lazy beast, Hugh," she said calmly and glided into the house.

"Elaine, perhaps you'd like to take a sketching expedition today," I said, standing up. "It's so fine."

"I don't think so, Amberleigh," she said, being aggravatingly thick-headed. "I'll simply stay here and sit on the terrace."

I sat again and brewed myself a cup of tea. Lord Hugh ambled over to the table with his empty cup.

"More coffee?" asked Norah with rare solicitation, leaning over to grasp the silver pot and pour for him with something like real grace.

Everyone was conspiring to keep me trapped upon the terrace. I could simply excuse myself and go in, of course, but somehow that seemed cowardly. Aggravating man, simply sitting there looking like the resident tomcat calmly waiting for the pigeons to disperse so he could bag his sparrow! I discovered I had brewed my tea a bitter brown and drowned it in an uncustomary dollop of fresh cream to take the taste away.

Norah sat back in her wicker armchair, swinging her slipper-clad feet and sipping tea. Elaine erected an edifice of sugar cubes. Lord Hugh sipped on interminably. And I drank bitter tea.

"I think, Miss Dunne," he said so suddenly that all three

of us started, "that a turn on the lawns would do you more good than that tea." He had walked over and stood ready to pull back my chair. There was nothing to do but acquiesce.

"You are a relatively transparent spy," I couldn't help remarking as we walked away from the ghastly terrace. "Shan't they wonder why you seek my company?"

"I shouldn't doubt it," he returned, and I could feel his eyes critically surveying my costume. I stopped and faced him.

"Is something the matter? Is there something you wish to say to me?"

How could I be so snappish at the pair of lazy hazel eyes I finally met for the first time that morning? I had thought his eyes golden, like a cat's, but they were a very human hazel after all. I noticed again the strand of grey at his temples, as if a light brush had left a heavy mark. I had stopped looking snappish, I realized, and was undoubtably looking something else. I corrected the oversight.

"Is there something of which you disapprove?" I asked again in a challenging way. "Pray tell me and I'll consider correcting it."

"And the Irish are supposed to have such a pretty way with speech."

"I'm only half Irish, or is that what bothers you?"

"You know what bothers me," he said a bit angrily, catching my elbow.

"Let go of me. I'm sick of your bullying and your teasing and your mysteries and your games. I'm going back to the house."

He didn't release me but stood there looking almost hurt. I felt an immediate pang for my words. Oh, it was hard to be sensible when one liked what was bad for one.

"What's happened to you?" he asked. And I couldn't answer.

"I want a word with you, surely you can spare that much of yourself," he said then, steering me into the boxwood maze.

"No. I don't want to have one word with you or twenty. It won't do any good. You always—"

"I always what?" We were into the maze and out of sight of anyone on the terrace.

"I don't know, but you always do it. Well, is it questions about Elaine this time? Any little detail you want confirmed? Some tidbit for Captain Mayfair perhaps?"

He laughed, a rich, easy laugh that made me even angrier.

"My word, you're the spitting image of Cousin Norah this

morning. Does she give you lessons? Or does that sort of thing come naturally to spinsters?"

My breath drew in. "I would say how dare you speak to me like that, but I know the answer. Does it disturb you that there are spinsters in the world who have eluded being made an accessory to some man's existence? Norah's no spinster, she left a husband in Calcutta, a rotter worth leaving. At least she had the sense to do something about it, not moon around like a lovelorn Elaine and let happen to her what may. There's no Lancelot in my future and I'm glad of it."

"What's happened to you? Something's happened to you since—" He grasped my arms. I shrugged his hands off again and again as he tried to catch hold of me; I was like a bird beating free of a cage.

"You're stupid," I was horrified to find myself saying. "You don't know anything. You're the stupidest man on earth."

I broke free and dashed around a corner of boxwood and around again, through short little lanes that ended in cul-de-sacs. I faced these dead ends with a throbbing fear. I had to get away. I didn't want him to find me, touch me. Finally I came upon a well-clipped square with a small stone bench. I sat on it and clasped my hands together on my lap until the knuckles were as white as the small statue of a nymph that coyly reclined near my bench.

"Amberleigh. Amberleigh." My name sounded foreign in his voice. It was a soft call.

At least he wasn't shouting for me, inviting the world to hear our—whatever. Well, I wouldn't let him find me, I'd work my way out of the maze and back to the house. If I kept away from him, it would all subside. Yesterday I'd felt so on top of it all and today—I rose and made my way cautiously around another corner.

The maze was labyrinthine. If I weren't careful I'd find myself back in Lord Hugh's—clutches, that was the word. I turned again. And again. He had stopped calling my name, so I couldn't tell if he had left or . . . He had wanted to know what had happened to me. What if I told him, told him that I—but did I? And did he think something more had happened to me than a mere change of mood? Perhaps he thought I had learned something, something damaging to him. Was there—evidence—here at Carnhaven against him, is that why he stalked its occupants so carefully? I wouldn't be betrayed by what could very well be false feelings. I didn't have to take his word on his Home Office work; after all, I distrusted it on nearly everything else... Where was the exit, why hadn't I looked at the way when we had come in?

I rounded another corner and faced the nymph again. Her stone lips seemed a little more mockingly upturned. Turn, that is what I would have to do. And return. How? How? I didn't remember. I'd been thinking, watching myself, not the way. In love with him? How could I be in love with him? It had been my imagination the other day. I—disliked him. Yes, that was it. And he was dangerous to me. He'd come and taken the light away from Devlin... Left again? Wasn't that the same way as before...? The sun is bright, it's not even noon, I can't be lost in a hundred-foot-square boxwood maze in the middle of Carnhaven lawn. I can't starve, I'll have to get out ultimately... but why this unreasoning panic, this fear, this urge to stop and scream...?

The boxwood loomed high and close on either side of me, hunching its shoulders like a row of giant trolls forbidding me exit. I took another turning, right this time, and faced another blank cul-de-sac. I whirled and retraced the path, so quickly that some twigs caught against my sleeve and snapped. Another turn brought me, stunned, to a stop. There was a wide square, planted and paved with a fountain and three small stone benches. It was the heart of the maze, where Devora walked with her lovers. Where she had walked with—him.

I turned—now I could get out, it had to be simple from here, from the heart of things... I rounded a corner and another corner, fighting the sobs that fluttered in my throat. It had to be simple now. A last lunge brought me perplexed to a U-shaped alley, as paved and planted and fountained as the other spot—was this the center of the maze, then?

I wheeled again, into Lord Hugh looming like a tweed statue behind me. A sob—half relief, half redoubled fear—escaped my throat.

"You're frightened half to death," he said, "for God's sake, why?" And he clasped me to him, pushing my face against his rough-coated shoulder, his hand buried in my hair. I shut my eyes against the boxwood hedge and relented from my resistance, clinging to him and afraid to open my eyes, afraid that I might be embracing the demon lover of the boxwood, a statue come to life.

His fingers began scribing soft circles on the nape of my neck, reminding me of my vulnerability. I turned my head to challenge his advantage and met his mouth coming towards mine. It was not like the other time, the before-the-fire-drawn-out-fire of a long soft kiss. His mouth was hard and rough on mine, asking something, demanding something I couldn't name. Leaning away only brought him closer. He was intent on me, and my flutterings to escape only made him impatient, as if I were a knot that wouldn't untie and he only had a moment in which to do it.

I was frightened, frightened by the way he held me to him, so that even through the starched tucks of my shirtwaist I could feel the press of his bone buttons against my body; frightened by the unhurried way he caught my right hand pushing him away and imprisoned it behind me, as if any protest I could make mattered for nothing... I would not be used this way. I... would... not... be... My left hand came up and without thinking I shaped my fingers into a claw and brought them up to his left temple. I raked my nails across his face just once, not really hard enough to break the skin, just a firm, long reminder of my resistance.

He froze immediately and his mouth drew back from mine. His eyes were dark. I thought again I had been wrong about their being a human hazel after all. He held me still for an instant and then he said quite composedly, "You're right. You're absolutely right. You can find your own way out of anything."

And he turned on his heel and left me to the maze. And my terror of the maze. I almost called out his name. Once. Almost. "Hugh," I almost called. But it sounded foreign to my mind. He was foreign to my mind.

I started crying then, stifled, sorry-for-myself sobs. I made my way to the little bench and smothered myself until I was certain no one was near; then I let my cries escalate to little whimpers that still wouldn't endanger discovery. I really longed to have a good bawl; but Carnhaven had no place for that. I would have to save my sobs for later when I could afford them, treasure my unshed saltwater as elderly ladies collect their tears in slender bottles at funerals to preserve their grief and remind themselves that they have had it.

After a while I felt very calm. I stood up, aware for the first time that clouds had crept in from the sea and the day was turning drab. I left the little garden and from thereon took the least likely turning. I came out of the maze as easily as if I knew it.

Boru was sitting on his shaggy haunches by the entrance. Poor Boru, always tagging along too late. Where had he been when I had needed him to growl warning? Someday he'd make his entrance on cue . . . I patted his head and he fell into step behind me up the expanse of lawn. I still felt sad, lost somehow. Sorry. I felt that if I turned my head just a bit, that if I let the corner of my eye catch the space behind me, I should see Devlin walking up the lawn behind me, wheeling the bicycle alongside him, whistling softly.

> "A lad that loves me
> A lad that leaves me
> And a third lad, a Shadow Lad,
> And that's the lad that grieves me . . ."

I stopped and faced the phantom that followed me—empty air. I even cast my eyes down in search of the tyre track across Devora's tended lawn. Nothing.

Children. They had all been children so long ago. Elaine. And Devlin. And Jason. And we three had been children, too. Devlin and Elaine and I, playing dangerous games with half of County Clare as our nursery. What had been between my two friends—no more than a childish, simple, easy yearning? Not like—Devlin never knew of the child that should have made him put away the things of a child. The war toys. Devlin died a child. And Elaine would live a child through all the cloudy Carnhaven years before her.

I left Boru at the kitchen gate and went inside. Time had dispersed all the others. I spent the day in my room mending my clothes. Henrietta could have done it, but plying the needle gave me peace. I thought about everything all through dinner and the quiet evening in the drawing room. I finally went to the library where I unearthed a Mrs. Somebody's novel and then dreamed over the printing all evening.

That night when I pulled down my covers, I found the disembodied head of the messenger doll resting peacefully on my pillow. Children. With childish tricks. I tossed it aside without much thought. If only my head could rest as quietly on that pillow. And it was strange, odd; I thought about Hugh Davenant a good deal that night. I found the small, raised place inside my lip where his kisses had marked me and explored it contemplatively with my fingers. It burned a bit when I did that and made me feel as if I were blushing from the outside in.

Three days later I got a note from him. Very brief. It said, "I'm sorry. I behaved abominably." It was postmarked London.

CHAPTER THIRTY-TWO

THE NEXT week dragged intolerably. Everyone seemed to be watching me for something. Elaine's grey eyes set whenever my glance caught hers. Devora remained uncharacteristically quiet, as if waiting for me to breech the silence with some revelation. Norah smiled at me, more friendly than she'd ever been, as if she sensed my new kinship to her.

For wasn't that what I was doing too? Running from a man, a monster of method and madness, who took everything you had too lightly. Norah was right. They were a dangerous breed.

By the time his letter arrived—note, really, and brisk, arrogant even in apology—I had half convinced myself he was Satan himself, masquerading on earth to lure maidens to their destruction. My stomach did a queer sort of two-step when I saw the handwriting on the envelope. I recognized it now. But I found nothing inside to change my mind or ease my disquiet.

Breakfast became the grimmest part of the day, with my Three Weird Sisters assembled each morning to silently interrogate my future. Whither thou goest, Amberleigh? The question hung in their eyes if not on their lips. And I couldn't answer them.

A week after the scene in the maze, I came down to find a letter superimposed over the shining silver platter by my place. This time they were all ahead of me and six eyes watched me as I picked up the missive with its violet ink and lacy hand. It was a fat little epistle and a glance at its contents riveted the word "Hugh" on my brain. I folded it again quickly.

"It's from a London acquaintance," I explained with a certain amount of truth. "It's so long and chatty I really don't want to be rude . . . I'll read it later."

"Pray don't let us stop you," urged Devora. "I'm sure we could stand something chatty. Lord knows you haven't been of late. Not since—"

"Yes, Amberleigh, what has it been with you? Cat caught your tongue? Or something else?"

I chose to ignore Norah's outright curiosity. But I couldn't ignore the blush that crept over my cheeks under their cross-examination. Elaine said nothing. She merely looked up from her plate once with her light grey eyes and shook her head almost imperceptibly.

After breakfast, of which I did not eat very much, I pocketed my letter and made my way out to the lawn. I debated going to the abbey or the boxwood to read it, but I felt the boxwood too disaster-prone. Finally I set out across the lawn and made for the Fairy Circle.

A red fox bolted at my approach and waved his tail in farewell as much as defiance. The great fir tree was as aloof and noncommittal as ever. Perhaps I shouldn't have come here. I had the impression of eyes all around me—Devlin's eyes, desperate in the underbrush. Soldier's eyes, narrow with speculation and a kind of greed that still gave me shivers. Hazel eyes, gold with glints, lazy hazel eyes too knowing . . .

Knowing what? I sat once again upon the heavy log, feeling foolishly sentimental about the gesture. And I opened Louisa's letter. I smiled over the salutation—"Dear little Amberly . . ." Only Louisa could think of me as little, only Louisa could make a misspelling seem an improvement.

"I promised to write you—and I am still oh-so-interested in your progress, shall we say?—you English like such things put more delicately than a realist like myself can manage it. Have you thought more of coming to my London and turning the town on its ear, as they say? Or is it nose? Oh, these expressions will destroy me yet!

"You must study German, little one, and then we can have delicious discussions of all that happens with no one to hear us.

"You are a neighbour of our most mysterious Hugh, n'est-ce pas? Forgive my French, I always wish to discuss intrigue in any language but this so-clumsy English. I am absolutely puzzled, the brain it will not take in what has happened. There is a lady there where you live, yes? A very fashionable lady, perhaps she is the reason for it. You must tell me, Liebchen. Not only to satisfy my most wicked curiosity, but it is important. Something is so wrong.

"I can speak freely to you, but you must promise to do my—detective work, would you not call it?—for me. Hugh has me so puzzled I can hardly speak of it. He came to town, to me, this week. To drink too much of my very good brandy, can you imagine it, and make very bad love to me. Hugh has never made very bad love to me—not since he was so downy-cheeked a young one, so I am puzzled by it. It is not that I do not expect to have very bad love made to me occasionally—ah, but you probably do not wish to hear of my wicked ways. But Hugh—so selfish, so soulless, it distresses me. Almost clumsy. I cannot understand, I taught him better than this. It is as if he had returned to being young and foolish so suddenly. You must watch for signs of what I say and tell me. And tell me of that lady. I fear something very bad is wrong.

"Do this for me, we are old friends, Hugh and I, and in ways you would not understand. But of course I can say nothing of this to him. Someday if you and I become true friends, I will tell you. Be brave, little duckling, and don't get your feathers wet again in the Shallowford."

Louisa's lapses into every language but English confused me. I sat there with the wind stirring the several violet-lined pages in my lap.

I didn't want to know that he had gone to London, that he had gone to make love to her, that he had changed, that he had made very bad love to her. I felt like crying and I felt like having somebody's head chopped off. The Salome in my heart envisioned the head at my feet with golden hazel eyes.

Beasts, all men were beasts. Now he'd gone and hurt Louisa, too. Save that Louisa sounded more concerned than hurt. Well, he had tried to make very bad love to me, only it hadn't worked. Perhaps Louisa was used to such things. I wasn't.

I stared at the Druid Tree, at its simple surviving solidity. But its trunk kept melting into four trunks, four posts, and I saw Louisa's elaborately testered bed again, the satin gleaming in dim candlelight. I saw him pressing Louisa to the linens, holding her as tightly as he had held me—no! I didn't care, I didn't. Why shouldn't he go to Louisa and London? I'd rejected him, hadn't I? I was right, he'd said, I could find my own way out of anything.

The Fairy Circle shrank to a vague brown-and-green blur before my eyes. I didn't want to know this about him. I didn't want to hear he'd been weak and foolish. Like a boy again. Louisa was right, it was very distressing—Hugh Davenant, angry and inconsiderate. Oh, he would be so furious with himself now. I cringed to think of the way he'd rake himself over the coals for such an impulse. And I had done it. Not "that very fashionable lady at Carnhaven," but that very unfashionable lady at Carnhaven.

And I'd been so cautious, so careful that no one should hurt me, that *he* shouldn't hurt me, that I'd never stopped to think that I might be capable of hurting him. It had all gone to Elaine. And Devlin. All my concern, my care, the softer things in me. All I'd given him was obsidian, a wall of carefulness. Something small, glittering and round glistened on the letter in my lap. Then Louisa's violet ink dissolved and ran in a little rivulet across the page. I, too, had made "very bad love."

I glanced again at the date in Louisa's almost miniaturized handwriting. Three days ago. Long enough for someone to leave London and travel back to Glennverran. Someone? Still I played games with myself. I pocketed the letter, almost wishing I had a secret place to hide it; I didn't like walking around with a piece of somebody's heart in my pocket. I toyed with leaving it tucked into the log on which I sat—but then it would be prey to every ground squirrel and casual lounger in the neighbourhood.

So I left it where it was, conscious of the telltale swell it made in the skirt pocket, and took the woodland path to Shallowford.

The house looked so still, so much the same, from the brow of the little hill where I paused. I almost had a feeling of going backwards in time, of coming on a mission to verify Devlin's safety. Devlin was beyond safety now. And still I came back to Shallowford.

I sighed and headed down the hill with no more thinking; it would be best to plunge myself into my next meeting with the lord of the manor with no preparation, no contemplation. No one seemed about and the knocker echoed dully against the heavy, timbered door. I waited a long while for the butler to answer. Almost I edged away from the threshold at the last moment, but a thump as the latch lifted held me to the spot and the uncurious gaze of the same man who had seen me come and go in states of high emotion was upon me again.

"I've come to see His Lordship," I said, unnecessarily I'm sure, since there was no one else in the household for me to call upon.

"His Lordship is out," returned the butler, Stevens, shortly.

"Do you mean that he hasn't returned from England yet? Or that he has and is not at home?"

Stevens sighed and opened the door wide enough to usher me in. Young women did not stand on doorsteps and enquire after the movements of young lordships in Stevens' well-regulated world. But I had stopped blushing for my irregularities of late, so I stepped smartly into the hall.

"It's really quite vital that I speak with him, Stevens," I emphasized.

"Very well, I'll have Hemlock looked up. Perhaps he can enlighten you as to His Lordship's whereabouts." The raised eyebrow that accompanied this speech left little doubt that in Hemlock's place Stevens would keep his information to himself.

I was shown into a parlour I'd never seen before, where I could peruse paintings of lily-pale medieval knights and languishing ladies in the new pre-Raphaelite manner while I waited Hemlock.

"Why, it's Miss Dunne." The warmth in Hemlock's voice surprised both of us. But I was glad to see his honest face.

"Hemlock, I'd forgotten how long it'd been since I last saw you. Have you recovered from that shuttlecock across the Irish Channel? I still weave a little at the thought of sea. But if you've returned, then he must have also."

A shadow darkened Hemlock's ruddy face. For a moment his expression reminded me of his master's.

"I did not attend His Lordship on the latest trip to London, miss," he said formally.

"Then he hasn't returned?"

"I didn't say that." He smiled. "Back he is and off again."

"Off again? Out of the country?"

"More like out *to* the country. But why do you want to see him so urgently?" Hemlock's questioning face suddenly collapsed into embarrassment. He had realized that his perfectly reasonable enquiry had been directed into a rather unreasonable situation. I refused to be derailed by mere awkwardness.

"It *is* urgent, Hemlock, I can't go into it. He left this morning? Was it something to do with the underground? The United Irish? Come, Hemlock, you and I both know what he's meddling in." I grew impatient with his too-stolid devotion to duty. It was as if some of Stevens' stuffiness had rubbed off on Hemlock's proper black coat as they passed each other too closely in the hall. "I won't betray him, for heaven's sake. I merely want to find him, I—" I broke off, realizing that I had been sounding too desperate. "He'll be back this afternoon then?" I said more quietly, taking a turn around the room to work out my nervousness.

"Yes, miss," replied Hemlock slowly. "Shall I tell him you called?"

"Of course tell him I called," I snapped. "You don't think

I came all the way over here for—for nothing?"

It came to me then that it could all be for nothing. I had taken a step, a step towards him, and he could very well simply back away and ignore it. Then I would be a solid-gold fool, with few in Glennverran who wouldn't have heard of it.

I jammed my hands in my pockets, feeling the paper of Louisa's letter crinkle under my fingers. "I'm going back to Carnhaven, Hemlock. Tell him."

I'd never ordered Hemlock to do anything before and he stiffened slightly at my tone. Then his brow furrowed and he said quietly, "I'll tell him, miss."

"Take care now," he added softly as he showed me out. And the puzzled glance I sent him at this unasked-for solicitation ricocheted off an understanding in his eyes that I found hard to meet.

I stomped back towards Carnhaven. I'd made a proper fool of myself this time, pounding on Shallowford's door in the early morning, demanding the master, ordering Hemlock about. Twigs snapped beneath my walking oxfords and I set my feet down more heavily, enjoying the crack as does a child who steps on thin layers of ice frosting the winter roads.

A new crackle joined my woodland percussion and I was startled but not surprised to see Jack Reilly ahead of me.

"'Mornin', miss," he said, tipping his cap and blocking my path with equal casualness.

"Good morning to you. And a fine morning it is for studying the migratory habits of the local wildlife, isn't it? Do *you* know where's he's gone?"

He didn't pretend not to know whom I meant.

"Aye, gone he is. And early, too. Who'd miss that black mount of his?"

"But why aren't you off too, then? Oh, you needn't pretend innocence. I know all about the Round-the-Mulberry-Bush games you statesmen have been playing. And I have reason to know that he wouldn't be hastening back to Glennverran right now unless an important parley, a negotiation, was arranged."

For once Reilly was on the defensive.

"What d'ye mean, Colleen? I'll not deny we've been keepin' a weather eye on the lad in yon house, but 'tis merely a precaution, ye might say. We Irish are a suspicious lot, for good reason, and we've a right to oversee our own. Or what should be."

"He's gone to meet with you, for heaven's sake, with your

men. What else would bring him back after . . . So what are you doing skulking around Shallowford as if it were a round of cheese and you a hungry mouse? The cat's on the road to parley, isn't he?"

"Meet wi' us? Why, we talked of it, but there was no meetin' today. We don't trust John Bull wi'out the light o' the moon to give us shadow."

"Not meeting with him? But Hemlock seemed so nobly secretive—it's obvious that if he's come back and gone out so quickly, it's only because something's . . . something . . ." I stopped talking while a chill of apprehension snaked its way across my arms.

"Here now, you're thinkin' again. And I get a strong feelin' that you know somewhat of what we wouldn't have you know. You keep your fine whiskers out o' our doin's, girl. Or there'll be hell to pay—"

"It may not be 'your doin's' at all, Jack Reilly, has that ever occurred to you?" I asked suddenly, looking at him intently. "And Devlin's death may have had nothing to do with Mother Country or Brother Rebels. Where do you meet now? If you were to parley with the English, where would it be? And someone from Carnhaven knows about it, don't they? Quick, be quick about it! Or do you want another Devlin rotting in Irish soil?"

"Meeting? We've changed it about. But why should I tell you, now, when the thing's about to come about that we waited for?" He seemed confused, but still wary.

"Don't you understand that I don't give a farthing for your secrets and your petty plots? You don't meet by the sinkholes on the sea now, do you? But it would have to be far enough for the taking of a horse . . ." I moved to pass him and he instinctively caught my arms. I shook myself loose so roughly it startled even him.

"You fool, you thought you'd been fomenting a revolution and you've been masking a killer. Devlin's dead because you've sheltered a murderer and now you can have more blood on your hands to no purpose. Perhaps it's all right if it's the blood of an Englishman."

His eyes turned slowly towards Shallowford and I nodded furiously at him.

"Now let me go—I've an idea, come along if you like."

I darted down the path, giving him only one glance over my shoulder. He was lost in thought, of no use to me until he made up his mind whether to jump with me or not. I tore down the Fairy Circle hill, twisting my ankle once and slowing while I half-hopped along. It felt better soon and I ran again, into Carnhaven stableyard.

"Quick, give me Jester," I shouted at a startled stableboy.

"Jester's out, miss," he responded hastily, caught up in my urgency. Jester out? Worse and worse. Jester had been out the night Devlin had died.

"Who took him?"

"I'm sure I don't know, miss. It was early and I was back forkin' hay—"

"Who's faster than Jester?"

"Why there's True Blue, miss, that old Sir George took to the Hunt in his better days. But he's a hard mouth and—"

"Saddle him. Straight. And be quick about it, for God's sake!"

The bewildered boy rushed to the tack room, coming out with the saddle so rapidly the stirrups swung about his head. In another two minutes he had the redoubtable True Blue, a rangy, well-muscled chestnut, standing before me with the reins trailing the ground.

I picked them up. "Well, give me a leg up. And hurry!"

I bounced lightly to True Blue's broad back and swung my leg over it boldly. The petticoats and skirt pulled up against my knees, but the open-mouthed stableboy had only a moment to absorb this astonishing sight, for I spurred True Blue once and the brute immediately broke into a smooth canter along the road. The grey ghost of Boru, slumbering in the yard, rose and watched me with some puzzlement.

Unhesitatingly I turned True Blue west. I had to be right. And True Blue had to be fast or it would be too late.

I kicked him again and he bore down into a hard, rolling gallop that almost sent me over his gleaming neck. I shamelessly twined my hands in his coarse mane, unbraided for the Hunt, thank God.

It was along this path I'd ridden with Adrian that day, when he'd doubted that many goats wandered into the rocky uplands near the coast. No, only killers came here, killers that rainy night when Devlin's lifeblood ran with the rain into the pit. I couldn't do anything then, why did I think I could be of use now? Why did I think—?

There was death in the sinkholes, death to the wild things that fell within them. And something wild that liked to kill. True Blue's shoulders were dark and damp with sweat but I kept him going up the narrow track as fast as I could.

Towards the top I saw Blackbriar's silhouette against the sky. I had been right. In my elation I reined in True Blue a bit and the huge horse slowed obediently.

Then I saw Jester, head bowed, nibbling at the wild grasses that sprouted between the rocks. His reins trailed the ground and he was lower from the summit than Blackbriar. Behind an outcropping of limestone.

I sighed. It could be merely a tryst that I was interrupting and if so then I'd happily sink into the pit and oblivion for interfering in it. But I didn't think so. I slid off True Blue's swelling side, landing badly on my ankle again, and took that last bit of rough trail to the plateau at a limping run.

Here, where Adrian and I had surveyed the sea and flirted so many eons ago. Nothing. I looked wildly around, hearing only the distant shriek of gulls. That was wrong. It was too quiet. I turned and ran further along the precipice.

CHAPTER THIRTY-THREE

I RAN, my heart trapped somewhere between my throat and stomach, to the limestone sinkhole where I had last seen Devlin alive. Where someone had fired a revolver into the rain and had left Devlin only a face to remember. She was not faceless to me any longer, that one. I knew whom to expect now. Now, when knowledge might be too late, when Lord Hugh had rushed to—but that was odd. The clearing surrounding the shallow pit was vacant. Silent. The sun was going into retreat behind a grey pall of cloud, but the light was bright, flat. St. Bridget's Well. It had been a long time since water had bubbled up through these dry, sea-stranded rocks . . . St. Bridget wish-me-well was more the phrase that rattled through my brain. Something, some indefinable urge, made me round the tall limestone outcropping and angle for the narrow pit blacker still than the one in which I'd spent half a night in my death watch with Devlin.

A man's body was lying near the well's edge, face down, and its look was so like Devlin's that I felt a double tear in my heart. But I knew it was not Devlin. I saw her then, her hair streaming out in drab yellow hanks, her dull-coloured skirts flying in the wind that whipped past us. We were on a bluff, a high bluff that overlooked the rocky lowlands leading to the sea. I saw the gulls, tiny spots, reeling out beyond her. She was labouring hard, trying to roll the figure to the pit's edge. She pried him over and I saw Lord Hugh's still profile. The breeze ruffled the short, grey-tinged locks at his temples.

"You've killed him! You vicious, bloody witch!" It was the battle cry of a Valkyrie and it came from me as I made for her in a rage that made me feel invincible. I could have torn her limb from limb, bone from bone, fed pieces of her to the gulls... She turned then, her grim brown eyes narrowing. There was a light in them worse than when she had railed against Britain, worse than when some piece of below-stairs gossip brought a malicious glow to her; it was the unholy glare of the fanatic shining from her eyes. The light of utter madness.

"Killed him? I hope so. It was easy, I waited up on yonder rock and cracked his stupid skull like a plover shell with this."

She waved the large stone in her hand with a certain ugly pride, like a craftsman his tool. But she still clung to her primitive weapon, perhaps because she wasn't certain he was dead, my mind considered with supernatural speed.

"Who wants him? Merely another vile English lord with no reason but privilege for taking up any space in this world! You don't surely care, do you, Amberleigh? You've gotten over those silly ideas. They're no good, all of them. Stupid selfish ugly beasts, fit only to be used and then..." She kicked lightly at him with her slipper-clad toe, her long face twisted with contempt.

In that one unguarded moment I was on her, tearing her away from her victim. He was lying terribly near the edge, I saw in the last second of clear vision I had before there was nothing but her wild eyes and foul breath, her heavy skirts and flying hair about me. It was like grappling with a demon out of legend, she was so beyond the human to me. I had her by two hanks of hair and we rolled upon the ground. It had not been that long ago that we two had contended before. But then she'd a knife. I grasped her wrist, the hand that held the rock, and spinning around, bit her as hard as I could. She gave a deep low cry of pain and surprise and the stone fell leadenly to the ground. But in my anxiety to disarm her, I had taken a weak position; she rolled me over with a facility that frightened me and pinned me beneath her, my one wrist bent painfully under my own body.

"So you do want him, eh, Amberleigh? That was ever your trouble. You'd have never made anything of yourself, merely another silly stupid girl running after anything that whistled for you. You should be grateful. I've saved you from yourself, though you shan't live long enough to enjoy it. Stay still. And listen to me. It will be the last you hear.

"Elaine—and you always suspected her, didn't you?—now she owes me double thanks. Though her mind's going, poor thing, and she's of little use to anybody. I'd thought I'd taken care of you with *him*. But I was wrong. *He* was not the one. A sorry mistake, for Devlin still had a role to play in the revolution. But I don't need any of them. Boys, playing at disruption and too stupid to let me more than run and fetch for them. And all the while, I was the one with the stomach for it . . . But I wasn't ready to lose Devlin yet. And it's your fault. You played the flirt with him in that disgusting way—"

I saw behind her mad reasoning. Devlin and I had never been more than friends—teasing, casual friends. I loved him as I would have loved a brother I had met only late in life. There had been no flirtation to see, she had twisted it all. Possibly because somewhere still in her perverse heart she had had hopes of Devlin for herself. Though with her loathing of men it was an attraction doomed to frustration. He had died because of me.

"We shall have our revolution, Amberleigh, and it shall be a bloody one, I promise you. Bombs and riots and street mobs . . . It's a pity you won't be there to see it. But I shall be there, every glorious minute. Stay still!" she ordered, slapping me hard across the face as I moved a bit under her.

For a moment the world reeled. Then my eyes fastened on her face again, an evil face, narrow and a nasty pink colour, marked with little pocks. She was a pestilence herself, a disease that ate unknowing upon those around her while they sought remedies elsewhere.

"Jason . . . !" I thought aloud, the notion hitting me for the first time. "Were you here when—?"

"Jason." She smiled slyly. "I'd just come from India then, you know. He was merely a boy, but he was rotten through. I saw how it was with them from the first. So did Devora, after I made sure she knew about it. We women always see more. It was Devora shipped Elaine off to school. But I took care of the main part of the problem. After."

"But you have been wrong. You've seen that. It wasn't necessary to kill Devlin. You could have been wrong about

Jason, surely no one could have known for certain. It was merely suspicion. And now, you needn't kill again. You're wrong about him, too. I care nothing for him, I made him go away. He can't harm you."

"Yes, I was wrong about Devlin . . . but not this time," she said viciously, sitting harder on me. "I saw the two of you going through the minuet that leads to making the beast with two backs. It's disgusting! Twisted. It will be a pleasure to send you to the pit with him. Or before him, rather."

Her hands tightened on the shirtwaist at my throat.

"I'm surprised you didn't invite me as a witness this time, as you did for Devlin, with one of your doll-delivered notes," I taunted her, as taunts seemed to be her language.

"No, for you this time, it was to be absolute nothing—vacuum. They'd never have found him. The authorities would have thought him vanished in some London fog. And you'd have always wondered. And hoped. I know you, Amberleigh. You would have hoped. I would have enjoyed seeing you hope, knowing him to be rotting to his ribs at the bottom of Bridey's Well . . . 'Full fathom five thy lover lies and these are pebbles that were his eyes . . .'"

It was Shakespeare, for a ludicrous moment my mind automatically searched out the source—"The Tempest." No! Why did one's mind always fly in six different, irrelevant directions when one needed it most? Norah was my target, I must aim all my energies at Norah.

"At least I would have hoped with some cause, Norah."

She caught the calmer calculation in my voice and wiped her hands roughly on her skirt. They moved horribly—kneading, washing each other, always working. I realized then that if they had not been directed at someone else, they would have been at Norah herself. Insight was slim salvation.

"Yes," I went on, "*I* would have had reason to think that he, and that Devlin, would want to see me again. That's what you can't stomach, Norah, because that 'husband' of yours—that you put about wants you back, wants to come here to collect you or kill you—he doesn't care at all, does he? He wouldn't cross the Strand to see you again, much less the Indian Ocean. It was all lies, all melodrama. You're merely another cast-off woman scorned. That's all."

She leaned back on her heels, her presence still pinning me to the ground, her hands wringing her skirt now.

"You! If I'd known you'd come here while I was at it, I'd

have brought the gun. The gun sufficed for Devlin. Or my scissors. You may recall my scissors. I'll shut your filthy mouth for good. You'd lie like that about me to other people. You have been, that's why they turn from me. Well, I don't care, I don't want to be 'liked,' that's too easy. Anybody can be liked. Even you. There's nothing in that."

She paused and pulled the next words from someplace inside herself where they'd never seen the light of day.

"And he would have come for me, too. It's quite a bond, don't you think, to be obsessed with me these twelve years? He couldn't let me go, he'd kill me if I tried to leave, you know. I'm the one has that. Not you. Not that snippet Elaine. I'd have fixed that honey-man, too—Adrian, all treacle and treachery—if either of you had given a fig for him. But I mustn't be distracted. I have work to do. And it helps the Cause, you know, two with one blow, you see? Oh, but you won't see for long, you won't carry around those wrong, hateful ideas about me much longer..."

With that she began dragging me rudely to the edge, I fighting all the time, but failing, for the struggle had loosed my hair and it whipped across my face with the breeze, half blinding me. Still I struggled, with quick kicks to her legs, foiled by the muffling of our heavy skirts. She was stronger than I, she was impelled by an unholy sense of mission. I was hampered by sanity and civilization and disbelief. It couldn't be happening this way, I thought, even as I fought to keep one patch of ground away from the edge. She had me half over, but I clung to her clothing like a butterfly to a leaf. She beat away my hands unmercifully and I felt a leg slip out over nothing. My stomach reeled with a wrenching jump.

"No, Norah," I could only whisper, "No!" Inch by inch, I slipped certainly over the precipice. I clung to whatever outcroppings of limestone I could, but my hands slipped away, scraped, always to the next lower jutting of rock. It was like being lost to quicksand, a slow, slow sink to oblivion. And all I saw when I looked up for deliverance was the eager face of Norah Chandler setting above me like some evil sun. It was to be the last sight on earth for me.

"What of Opal?" I cried weakly as I felt my body stretching out down along the rocks and growing heavy, too heavy to support much longer. "They'll know it was you and then what will become of Opal?"

"They're already after her, the stableboys, I see them leering in the yard," she muttered with a vicious light in her eyes. "I'll deal with them later. No, they won't know about me. Who's to tell? Not you!"

And she ground her sturdy oxfords brutally into my clinging fingers. My hands, already abraded grievously, gave way despite my desperate longing for life. In a split second I felt myself slipping away from the world. I felt unutterably sad and the scream was priming in my throat that would accompany me on my plummet to the pit below.

A hand out of nowhere seized my wrist as it was about to give way, a strong rock-hard hand with knuckles white as alabaster. "Hugh!" It was a cry of recognition and farewell.

"Hang on, for God's sake, hang on," he said between clenched teeth.

"I can't, oh, my dear, I can't! Give it up. I'll only take you with me. Give it up!"

And something more disturbed me, hanging there those long, luridly etched seconds. Once before I'd hung on a hand. I wanted him to release me now, for any moment I feared that clap from behind, that sudden sharp explosion of a gun. And he would dissolve into a red sunset above me and wash down on me like rain. I didn't want to plummet to my death knowing another Devlin lay limp above me. I didn't want her to win again.

Norah had drawn back at my eleventh-hour reprieve. Her wits gathered for another assault, she flew onto Hugh, pounding and kicking at him to make him relinquish his grip on me. He fended her off with one arm as best he could. And his eyes were demanding dark pools in a contorted face, pale, with a rivulet of red coursing its way across his brow.

"There've got to be footholds, Amberleigh, find them. If you can get some purchase—" He ducked as Norah lunged at him again, then he threw her back with a sudden thrust. His other hand came quickly down for mine.

"Now!" he said. "Climb now!"

I hugged that rock face as though it were a lover. I inched my body up it to help the steady pull from Hugh's hands above. But my own hands were bloody and slick, hot with fire, though that bothered me little then. His grip was slipping.

The sweat and tears poured down my face. Better to have gone over in one clean plunge. Better than this useless struggle . . . Hugh suddenly lurched backwards, pulling me upwards in a long swift motion that saw me all but over the cliff edge. I scrambled the rest of the way myself, chilled by even the suggestion of air beneath so much as my small toe.

Hugh cast one swift look at me and lurched to his knees. Norah was groggily propped against the rocks where he had hurled her, looking exactly like Thumbellina, the unkempt doll that had delivered my invitation to Devlin's death. She seemed like a rag doll with half the stuffing gone. And white, her face was white. But she staggered up and bared her unhealthy teeth. Ready to come for us again. Hugh met her and picked her up by the throat, as an eagle would gather a sheep. He shook her then wordlessly and like a rag doll she flapped in his grasp.

"No, Hugh! You'll kill her. She isn't worth it, she's mad—" I crawled to my knees and implored him to stop. It was ugly to see such anger. For the first time I saw Norah cower as he dropped her like carrion.

"You shan't better me," she said sullenly, backing away from us. "I've been too clever for all of you, had you chasing your tails like dogs, chasing each other. You're nothing but fools living in your safe, rose-petal-lined worlds while I, I hold the key to a way that will make this entire globe start spinning another way. A new revolution. You shan't take me for your courts and your witness boxes. I shall still have you in mine. And you will be found guilty! You shan't have me, not a one of your breed. I am better than you," she said with her lips curled, "you shall find that out."

Neither of us made a move to stop her retreat. We were too exhausted. It was enough that she was not thrusting her unnatural energy, her destruction, at us. I think in that moment we both could not have resisted another onslaught.

I heard a patter behind me and a strange yet familiar scuffling sound. Wildly, I felt the bluff top reel to another time. Patter. Scuffle. Falling. Hand. Devlin. Something large brushed by me with a bound. Devlin's dog. It was the great Irish wolfhound Boru. Not for two thousand years had his kind been bred to corner the wolf in vain. He had smelled my blood upon the rocks and some canine instinct arrowed him towards my tormentor. Perhaps he scented Devlin's death on her.

He bounded towards her and some sanity dawned in Norah's gimlet brown eyes. She shielded her hands and backed away into the air over St. Bridget's Well. The last of Boru's leap pushed her over the edge. He sat on the very brink, his shaggy head cocked, as her scream rang off the rocks for a long time, it seemed, before it ended.

Boru lumbered over to me and began licking my hands and face. It felt soothing and I hugged his shaggy grey head. "You tag-along, you're always late," I half laughed, half sobbed into his fur.

"The best way for her, really," said Hugh.

"Yes." It was odd, I felt as removed from her death as from that of a spider. Too much had happened, she had tried to break me too much for me to care about her miserable life. Or death.

"Are you all right?" Hugh's eyes were anxious as we both half-sat there on our elbows and took long gulping breaths of air. I nodded. Speaking seemed an intolerable effort. "And you?" I finally got out.

"No more than the sahibs managed," he said. "My God, she was a Tartar!

"Where does it hurt?" he asked then, surveying my bleeding hands and pushing Boru away. The big dog accepted rejection meekly and went to sniff the rock ledge where Norah had last stood.

"Everywhere." I managed what I thought was a weak smile.

"We'll go back to Shallowford," he said as if he expected no argument.

"Yes, thank heavens there's Hemlock to attend us. I'm becoming quite a regular patient of his."

"Hemlock," said Hugh, looking quite stern, "is not going to touch an inch of you. There are some things the master must reserve to himself." And he kissed my lips, already swelling from the biting my struggle with Norah had inflicted on them.

"Does it hurt?" he asked in a moment, suddenly considerate.

"Yes, but I don't mind. A little to the left would be better though."

And he complied most graciously.

CHAPTER THIRTY-FOUR

ELAINE AND I stood together on the platform, my baggage—grown slightly more mountainous since its first appearance there—surrounding us. It was a clear crisp day, and I didn't want to be cooped up in the little stone stationhouse somehow. Perhaps it reminded me overmuch of the chainstitch of events culminating in two deaths that had still hovered in the future when I'd sat there last.

Elaine stood beside me, subdued and nervously swinging her embroidered reticule against her smart blue gabardine skirt.

"I shall miss you, Amberleigh."

"It won't be forever. We'll still be back to Shallowford for the summer. And Dublin isn't a world away."

"No," she said reluctantly.

It reminded me so much of our parting days at Miss Meachum's. Elaine somehow reluctant to go to Carnhaven, I promising myself we'd see each other occasionally . . . but this time it would be as I wished it. It would be in my power now.

"You'll be a 'Lady,' Amberleigh." Elaine voiced my thought. "I'm merely an 'Honourable.'"

"You'll never be 'only' anything, Elaine."

I wanted to comfort her, to put my hands on her shoulders and tell her that life would look up for her soon—it had to. But my gloved hands were still almost useless. They'd been sorely injured by that desperate contention with Norah Chandler on the rocks; Hugh had been forced to surrender them to Hemlock's offices after all. The bruises, the scrapes on my body faded, though I still felt a bit stiff four days after, but my hands were delicate and many-jointed and not healing well. It was why we were hastening to London, delayed only by Hugh's straightening up details between Captain Mayfair and Jack Reilly. This time it was a genuine surgeon I was to see.

"And then it's to the chapel, m'dear, for a quick ceremony. We'll have to live in Dublin. Shall you mind it?"

I had protested vehemently. It was impossible, I told him. His relations would never accept me. He couldn't even consider marrying someone like me.

"I don't give a hang about my relations," he replied fiercely. So fiercely that I knew he did. And that reassured me. It would not be so hard if he honestly recognized the opposition that would attend our marriage. I hadn't fully agreed, but I'd stayed with him, "recuperating" at Shallowford. I couldn't imagine living anywhere again, where he was not. It was an advantage to have no reputation at all; then one could do as one pleased.

I hadn't seen much of Hugh at any rate. And I awaited our trip to London with a certain pleasurable impatience, that wanted to be almost abrupt with Elaine for standing between us. For she would see me off and Hugh had vanished with that intuitive sensitivity of his. Hemlock hovered discreetly in the background, for the first occasion in his professional life refusing to be invisible as long as his charge might need him.

"Devora's gone to London, too," Elaine said out of the

blue. "I think she'll stay there this time. It'd be too much to expect to be rid of her forever. But Father seems to be, well, coming back to his old self."

"And you, Elaine, how are you coming back?"

"Wonderfully, Amberleigh," she said, a smile lighting up her pale, calm face. She had quieted so much. That side of her nature seemed to have superseded the fevered vivacity I had known from school. She would never again be the overgay girl I had befriended at Miss Meachum's.

"You're sure, about being better?"

"Oh, yes." Her porcelain brow rippled into a frown and she dropped her voice to an almost inaudible pitch. "But sometimes I have such dreams, Amberleigh, they come out of the black and they are black . . . But it's always morning after. I try to remember that."

My own dreams were no longer the fields of wonder in which I had romped before the recent events. Sometimes I awoke feeling harried. Often I dreamt of falling down a long dark tunnel, like Alice down the rabbit hole, only this tunnel had no end at all. Sometimes a hand would reach out to heave me back to hard land. And often the face behind that hand was Devlin's.

"How is Opal?" I asked, for Elaine had taken the child under her wing.

"I call her Sara," she said abruptly. "It seems to fit her better, though she doesn't like it now. But she's a very bright little creature, and such a love of colour, Amberleigh! Henrietta is making over some of my old things for her and she's an absolute clothes horse, wants to change her ensemble three or four times a day!"

I was amused to hear Elaine sounding vaguely maternal. I could not picture her marrying—a man who combined brother and lover would not come again for her, I could see that. And that other one, that infant. It still haunted me to think of him, learning to crawl, to babble, at some cottage doorway in the North. Half Elaine, half Devlin; it seemed brutal to leave him there to strangers. But neither of his parents really existed anymore, one way or another. Perhaps these things were best left to the neat, cut-and-dried solutions people like Devora had resorted to since ancient times. At least he was not abandoned on the moor to die. I would keep track of him, though. Perhaps, if in the future there was a discreet way to further his education—there I was playing lady of the manor and fast and loose with Hugh's inheritance and we not even married yet!

Perhaps I would simply be his mistress. It was a fantasy that took me back to Madame Louisa's rooms. She fashioned good lovers, she had said. She said their wives, once and future, would bless her for her tutelage. I wondered now. Oh, I was certain there were a good many bad lovers about, cluttering up well-curtained bedchambers. I'd seen enough women tighten their lips when certain topics tiptoed through the conversation to know what they thought of their "marital duties." I wished I could ask Elaine. Things seemed to have gone naturally enough for her. Or unnaturally enough. But I had a reticence about prying into that part of her life—it was like picking off a scab to see how the wound is doing, self-defeating. But lovers, wasn't what made them good the quality of love that went into it? Not quantity. No practiced sort of Prussian know-how could substitute for that, one would think. I couldn't understand Hugh—for such a man-of-the-world he'd been remarkably restrained.

But he'd been busy, poor lamb, sending cables to the coast and meeting continually with Captain Mayfair—I'd thought they were allies—and even Jack Reilly. Somehow all the fun and fight had gone out of the Clare contingent of the United Irish after Devlin's death and Norah's use of them as camouflage for her muderous madness. Still, one would think that all the fascinating skullduggery in southern Ireland would run a poor second to one's intended bride.

I caught a dim glimpse of squared shoulders in a well-tailored Chesterfield through the station window over Elaine's shoulder. I felt suddenly hollow inside and anxious to be alone with him. I could have taken Elaine by her blue gabardine shoulders and heedlessly set her aside. It was appalling what steps undefined wants could make one consider. And that's where Norah had gone wrong. We weren't that different, I suppose, she and I—until it came time to deal with our desires.

Dear God, I hoped it wasn't too late for me, that I could be as easy and loving as, as—my eyes came back to Elaine, still talking at my absent reverie. Perhaps that childlike trust was the key, despite the fact that it had unlocked a Pandora's box for my friend. But that came from being given the keys too early in life. And I was reaching the age when all I might be left with *was* the keys. Ah, Hugh would handle it all for me—he would oil the tumblers, draw back the bolt, lift the latches . . . My mental metaphor was getting rather concrete. I felt a blush rise under the face veil of my smartest travelling hat. Poor Elaine, still so innocent somehow. I must not think the thoughts that were running through my wicked head before her.

"—it's a pity you can't take Boru, Amberleigh. But Mrs. Featherstone would be lost without a stray to feed . . . And he knows Carnhaven so well. We'll grow grey together, Boru and I—Have a wonderful journey, Amberleigh. And don't forget us!"

I embraced Elaine as I heard the distant huff and saw the puff of the bristling dark engine coming down the track. We stepped into the station to avoid the steam; Hugh joined us. Was it imagination, or did grey dust his thick hair more prominently now? If grey hairs were the only aftermath of our ordeal, I would be content.

The train trembled near the platform like a highly bred horse before the Hunt, its gilded green metal body glistening in the pale sunlight. Hemlock and the baggage had boarded. Hugh lifted me on board; my hands were too tender to grasp the brass rails. We settled into a grey-wool-upholstered compartment and smiled out the window at Elaine, who had emerged onto the platform again to wave good-bye despite the steam. I looked back a long while, until her slender figure slipped away amid a collage of green and stream. She looked like a figure in an Impressionist painting; for once I understood the artists' peculiar vision of the world. They saw it through a glass tearfully.

I turned round to watch the landscape with its saraband of sky, green grassy sweep and rocky cairns weave past the window. I rather hated to be leaving. It was a jumping-off point, a change that would see me forever different. I glanced over at Hugh. He seemed tired, and there were still a cut and bruise at his temple, but other than that, my mittened hands and our still-strained faces, a casual passenger would hardly mistake us for a pair who'd battled for their lives and seen a woman die a few days previously.

Was life that fragile—a sudden plummet through space, a hard little ball of lead hurtling through air—and life was there no longer? It seemed very real, that compartment and the certain comforting rock of the seats as we clicked along towards Dublin. Would it always be like this, the calm after the storm? I could picture it like that, Hugh and I riding off into time in perfect domestic harmony, forever ourselves as we were now, forever lulled by the steady knowledge that we were going to the same place—and yet it wouldn't be like that. This moment would melt and blend into so many other moments that if in a few years I tried desperately hard to recall it, if I tried even now to engrave it on my brain, it would be unreachable. Just as the moments at the precipice were receding to mere memories already.

But some memories were still questions requiring answers.

"Hugh, those two days you were gone almost every waking minute. After the thing on the cliff. Where were you, what was happening? I confess I was so drained I didn't care at the time," I asked suddenly.

He leaned back with a grimace and extracted one of his Turkish abominations, as I had begun to look upon his cigarettes. One must be in love when one can be so critical of another's habits.

"That, my darling naiad"—he never would let me forget my undignified dunking at his doorstep that long-ago May—"was a state secret so secret the Home Office didn't even let me in on it."

"So of course you won't tell me? I call that hard."

"So I will tell you. If word had gotten out about it, everybody'd been better off. It was the reason for the locals' plottings and connivings. And it was something worth busting their buttons about. A bloody underwater vessel—submarines, the technical johnnies call them. Putting around the lake with a steam engine as nice as you please. And the rebels got the damn thing towed overland and off the island before we caught them. So we never saw a bolt or a plate of the thing."

We rocked in silence a few minutes while I absorbed the news.

"I think *I* saw it once, Hugh."

"The devil you say! And on which of your midnight meanderings did you happen across this fabulous beast?"

He really wanted to hear about it, I could tell by the eager glint to his hazel eyes, the way they narrowed. In the entire affair, I think the thing Hugh regretted most was not glimpsing the mechanical monster that had haunted the lake.

"I don't recall precisely when I saw it. But I was by the lake at twilight. And I saw something big and black, gliding so smoothly, with a great hump on its back—"

"The conning tower, the blasted conning tower! Go on!"

"And it came towards me and I thought it was the lake monster, the great black thing that dwells in the deep. Then a long black line rose from it slowly, like a—"

"Like a gun? They didn't have a gun mounted, it's impossible!"

"Let me finish. And this long black thing arched up—on

a straight line, of course, because it had to be metal—but at the time I thought it must be flesh, and slimy flesh at that..."

Hugh impatiently watched my awkward hands etch my vision. "And then something dropped out, a little sign. And it said: 'Erin go bragh.'"

He sank back into the seat in utter disgust at my merriment.

"How much of the thing did you really see?" he asked ruefully.

"Only the outline. But why was it in our lake?"

"Testing purposes. In this case what one would paradoxically term a 'dry run.' It was built by a Clare schoolteacher who went to America to get the money for it. There are some who say this sort of thing will never work. But if it does, it'll mean millions. Think of how they could harry shipping in the Channel. What they could do in time of war... God, I hope they drown."

We were silent the remainder of the long journey over water and land, as exhausted in mind as our bodies had been on the lip of the pit after we'd beaten off mad Norah. It was late when we arrived at Hugh's London town house—I caught barely more than the sheen of dark wood in the gaslight as I was bustled upstairs to a room where a huge feather comforter waited as if meant for me alone.

In the morning I had to shake out my sadly wrinkled clothes myself. But there was a maid who lit the fire and showed me down to the breakfast room. Hugh was there, just finishing a breakfast of steak, eggs and marmaladed muffins. I took a muffin and nibbled it sparingly. My hands were still quite clumsy and it was an effort.

"Here," said Hugh, seeing my dilemma and throwing down his napkin, "we'd better play bird and nestling." But I didn't want to be fed, even from his hand...

"No! Hugh, the servants—"

"Shades of Mrs. Willoughby. And what has become of all that fine careless disregard for what the servants think?" he chided.

It was true. I'd seen the confused look the little maid had thrown me—ladies simply did not arrive by night at bachelor's London town houses.

"You're right. I do feel a bit clandestine."

"Then we shall remedy that. You're going to see Boswell for your hands today, and by week's end—I'm going to face

338

the music grandly and have the entire family down for dinner to meet you."

I was stunned. "Isn't that rather hitting them with the gauntlet?"

"Perhaps, but it's better than the word slithering its way back to them via the understairs," he said with a tight smile. "Don't worry. It's only so the family can't rail at me for marrying without telling them. You shall do fine. After all, you are a Leigh. And it's more important what you think of them rather than vice versa. We Davenants are never very good on first impressions. You loathed me at first, didn't you?"

"No," I protested, somehow embarrassed.

"You did, confess it."

"How do you know I don't loathe you now?"

"You're marrying me."

"But for your fortune."

The light in his eyes dampened; for a moment I thought I'd gone too far. The panic that welled inside of me swept away all concern with how his relations accepted me. He was angry at what I'd said, and suddenly the room seemed empty.

"It's what they must be thinking," I said softly, unwilling to retreat from the truth.

"If you wish to persist in these stiff-necked assumptions of yours—"

"Stiff-necked. It's what Adrian called me once."

"Adrian was a fool," he said shortly, watching me from under lowered lids. I did not disagree. "I am not. When I say you are stiff-necked you may believe me." A smile shadowed the corners of his mouth as he lit one of his post-meal cigarettes.

"Amberleigh, you simply must drop this foolish idea that you're somehow unworthy of such fortune. For one thing, it implies that I am gullible and I won't have anyone thinking that. Least of all you. It's not a good way to start the venture we propose." He crushed the cigarette prematurely out in a crystal tray. I watched the tiny ember flare into brief life after he abandoned it; then it faded to ash.

"What venture do we undertake, Hugh?" I had not meant my tone to be so serious, but it was.

"Happiness," he said, moving his light chair beside mine. "And sadness, too, I suppose. But it's happiness we're after, don't you ever forget that."

He gathered me to him and kissed me. The whole aristocratic cabal of Davenants vanished with that soft, sweet exchange between us. Damn the Davenants. We didn't need them, I thought fiercely, laying my head against his impeccably tailored shoulder. Weak words but strong feelings. At that moment I felt that time could mummify us forever in the breakfast room of Caroline Terrace, and I would be content.

"And what on earth did you mean by that Leigh gibberish?" I remembered suddenly, sitting upright.

"It's true. You do have a Leigh in your past."

"And what, pray, is 'a Leigh'?"

Hugh took out another cigarette and lingered aggravatingly over lighting it before he answered. "A distant cousin of mine, for one thing. You're the innocent product of a thirty-year-old scandal, of my distant cousin Marianna Leigh, in fact, 'dear Gwen's girl,' who upped and ran off with a certain dashin' Irishman..."

"Well." I sat back to take it in, as if being the product of something really scandalous rather than something only merely so were a feather in the cap of social standing. I suspected Hugh of inventing the entire relationship to placate me, for Father had hardly been what I would call dashing. But I remembered the spidery tracing on a locket courtesy of Mrs. Bowers' salvaging operations years before—"To M. from T." Marianna and Terrence. It fit.

"Then I must be 'of good family,' after all. How could you let me apologize for my unworthiness all this time if you knew?"

"The Leighs aren't that good." He grinned at me over a snake of curling blue smoke.

"But how did you discover the connection? Father never spoke of it, and my mother died so young."

He spread his hands wide and looked discomfitted. "I investigated your father's background when I was looking into the Carnhaven affair. And your role in it."

"And that's why all the London trips, even when you brought me—that time?"

Hugh nodded cautiously, as if uncertain how I would react to his delvings into the domestic circumstances at Eaton Square. I suddenly understood why. Perhaps "dear Gwen's girl, Marianna," had been riddled with bats in the belfry. Certainly Father hadn't exited this world in a manner to impress the Davenants with my suitability for kinship. Poor man, I was beginning to understand the impulse that could lead one to put a revolver to one's head...

"Then you know about my father, you are aware that

he . . . committed suicide." I said the word firmly. I hadn't meant to hide it from Hugh; I simply hadn't thought to mention it. My father's death seemed such a matter of history now. "It was a suicide."

"Perhaps," said Hugh reluctantly.

"What do you mean, 'perhaps'?"

"Your father was more than an importer of Irish linens and laces, Amberleigh. He exported quite a bit, too. It's one reason I thought you caught up in that Carnhaven nonsense. Terrence Dunne exported information, guns, ammunition, agents . . ."

"Are you saying that my father was a patriot?"

"I'm saying that he was a rebel," he corrected me with raised eyebrows. "Listen, Amberleigh. I have to tell you this." He took my hands. I'd discovered in our short intimacy that Hugh rarely made empty gestures, so I waited intently for his next words.

"Our Home Office was aware of his activities. Back then, in 'eighty-seven, right after Parnell's Home Rule thing went under, they were hypersensitive about an Irish uprising. It was also right after the Phoenix Park murders, and they would stop at nothing to stop the rebels. They put a lot of men on things like this. They may have put pressure on your father's trade to drive him into the open by ruining him financially. But as for his death—and I'm sorry, dear, but whether it was done by his own hand, or by the United Irish to cover the tracks of an exposed agent, or even by a zealot in our own ranks, it's been known to happen—we can never be sure."

I sat quietly for a moment. "Father a dashing Irishman who eloped with a pampered socialite, Father a Captain Moonlight?" My bewildered laughter must have puzzled Hugh. "I can't credit it. I hardly knew the man, to me he was a vague spider weaving webs over account books—and all the time . . ."

"All the time, he was an unconscionable rebel, like his daughter," said Hugh.

"I'll show you a rebel," I threatened, launching a mock attack at his throat, but his stiff collar foiled me.

"I surrender," said Hugh, laughing and turning in his retreat to pull me onto his lap and devour me as if I were apple marmalade. I giggled through his kisses, until they became so persuasive that we both elected to concentrate on the slow, sure fire we could build between us.

"Shipstead," I said suddenly, remembering the cruising butler and breaking my mouth away from Hugh's reluctantly. His eyes, cairngorm dark, regarded me with—not laziness—but a languid kind of content. Shipstead, I had just about decided, could jolly well be scandalized, when Hugh untangled me gently and sat back.

"I've got to visit the Home Office this morning, some loose ends to be neatly packaged. Hemlock will see you to Dr. Boswell's. I'm sorry, my dear, but I can't escort you."

And he was gone for the day. It all seemed rather anticlimatic. I, too, abandoned my napkin, in ruder spirits, I'm afraid, and wandered into the passage. I wasn't needed till mid-morning and I wasn't certain what to do with myself until then. I was being unreasonable, of course. Hugh had a great deal to do. I wandered up to my room and began attending to the clothes still trapped in the trunks at the foot of my bed. The room's decor was uninspired, all needlepoint seatcovers and tapestry, obviously intended for only the most casual of overnight guests. I was beginning to feel a bit displaced. Even the routine visit to the doctor was but an interruption in a dispirited day.

And so, to combat my odd ennui, I dressed most splendidly for dinner and Hugh's return, barely in time without a personal maid, it turned out. And my unruly Irish head wasn't perfectly arranged, even though my hands were rapidly regaining their dexterity. A slightly asymmetrical pompadour was Norah's legacy to me this night. I think it would have pleased her.

Hugh and I shared a before-dinner sherry; I remembered our dinner à deux at Shallowford library and its somewhat unconventional ending. Hugh came over to inspect the aquamarine and pearl necklace I had donned with rather more affection than the last, and first, occasion on which I'd worn it.

"Are you certain you want to wear that?"

"What's the matter with it?" My hand flew to my throat; I was certain it had been transmuted to a chain of locusts around my neck.

"Perhaps this might do better," said Hugh with a smile edging his finely cut lips.

He slipped a small velvet pouch from his pocket and fished out something dark and bright at the same time. It was the black velvet ribbon Elaine had insisted I wear to dinner at Shallowford, the one he'd taken from me after he'd kissed me the first time. But now it was mounted between a double row of matched diamonds, a pendant of emeralds and diamonds sparkling like dew on grass suspended from it.

"Hugh. It's—incredible! When—?"

It must have been en route to the jeweller's the following

342

morning to be ready now. It touched me unutterably, not for its worth, but for its faith. Faith in a moment's magic, that I had doubted for many moments since. He'd been sending off for jewels for me while I sat primly on Shallowford Bridge and told him I really didn't care to engage in a pointless flirtation. I added two more diamonds to my bauble at the thought.

"I'd better get it on you," Hugh said, "or you'll have the velvet soaked before it's even worn."

The necklace glittered in the glass like a thousand falling stars.

"Thank you, my dear," I said, giving him a salty kiss in return just before a scandalized Shipstead knocked to announce dinner.

I wore it for our wedding soon after, that necklace comprised of the most humble of materials, and the most precious. I wore it with my silver tissue wedding gown, a beautifully constructed thing with sleeves like lofty butterfly wings. I glittered as iridescently as some rare species, my markings laid out in seed pearls and silver braid.

It was to be "only family" in Hugh's sister's airy Belgrave Square drawing room. The Davenants hadn't been ogres, after all. When the wedding day actually arrived, I'd been kept upstairs and fussed over all morning. And no food. It reminded me of my ordeal in Madame Louisa's room. The thought gave me one sharp pinprick and then I dismissed her from my memory. I faced the glass while the maid fanned out my train for the last straight march down the hall, then down the stairs and through the flower-bestrewed arch and straight ahead, to Hugh.

Butterfly. Hadn't I once said 'moth'? Adrian. Butterflies live only a season—oh, but it was glorious to be gowned and glittering like a princess. And no scars. Hugh. I'd hardly seen him these last days. Not alone together since—now that was better, a "blushing" bride. I'd never looked so beautiful—between Louisa's lessons and a really first-rate dressmaker . . . No, not Louisa again. She'd had him so much longer than I, the first flower of his passion. I was jealous. How could he ever see me with the clouded, uncritical eyes of infatuation? But if I'd wanted infatuation, I should have taken Adrian and his pretty little house. I could have handled him.

Hugh, who was he? A stranger. Virtually. Bride fears, that's all. I didn't want to go downstairs. I didn't want to consign myself to him. Twelve forty-five. I wanted him. As Medea wanted Jason, enough to kill for, to commit the unthinkable.

Elaine. A pity she wasn't here. But we'd soon see her in

343

Dublin, where Hugh had a very refined sort of Home Office assignment. Nothing vulgar like espionage, but as an informal liaison for a new Anglo-Irish order. And I'd see we didn't create an anti-Irish English island like Carnhaven in our new home. We'd invite Irish poets, playwrights—rebels—to dine . . . We. Hugh. Me.

How did I get to the window? Now, I've messed my train. Well, Winifred will straighten it. Servants, I'll have servants now, my own household to run. Will I like it? It seems foreign. It seems decadent. The decadent Davenants. What would Devlin think? Why did they leave me alone? My forehead is hot. I'll get the vapours and topple like a half-consumed wedding cake if I don't take hold of myself.

Ten minutes. It's really a pretty clock. Is it correct? Yes, another carriage outside the window. It must be the Bishop. Is one more married when one is married by a Bishop? Hugh, I wish I could see Hugh. I could ask him, if it's all right, it it's . . . Hugh. Now there, my stomach did that strange sort of wiggle again. Butterflies. Butterflies for a butterfly.

Time for the gloves. My hands are moist. They won't go on—they were always so tight. "A lady always wears the tightest of gloves." I'll have to go down like a washerwoman, with fat wet hands and no gloves. "She couldn't fit into the glass glove, Your Highness, would you care to try another sister?" There, that's one. And I'll have to struggle out again for the ring part. Ring? Perhaps they'd forgotten the ring. No, not Hugh.

Three minutes. A cold, flat London day outside—grey sky and hard dirty snow on the square. Not a good omen. Omens, I don't need omens, I need smelling salts. I need Hugh.

And now, suddenly, Here and Now, managing the stairs in perfect time, in that peculiar stuttering gait reserved for state occasions like weddings. And executions. Music from somewhere. And familiar faces in unfamiliar finery gathered round the room, banks of white roses—winter roses—and greens. And the Bishop—not in full regalia, how relieving—waiting almost like a butler in black-and-white before the Georgian fireplace smothered in—more roses!

And Hugh there, at the wrong end of a pair of opera glasses. Waiting for me. I'd never seen him in full tails and white tie. He looks splendid, handsome, like a bridegroom.

And then he was beside me and I glanced at him—once, secretly. His face was as white and stiff and proper as his starched high collar. He was nervous! I put my hand through his arm and smiled. His hazel eyes caught mine. The Bishop droned. We appeared to listen attentively. We heard nothing, at least I didn't. I almost forgot to work the recalcitrant glove off in time, but my finger was bare when it was time for Hugh to slip the wedding ring on my hand. Something green and gold glided home to my third finger, left hand. More droning by the Bishop. It was done.

Ceremony broke ranks. Faces clustered near to congratulate us. I looked at my finger, with its unfamiliar bulky circlet of gold. I'd forgotten to ask about the ring. It was a great, square-cut emerald.

"Hugh, it's gorgeous. However did you think of it? I've always loved emeralds."

"Well, green is your color." He smiled, delighted in my delight. "But be careful of it; the stone is fragile." He patted my hand with its new ring and was swept away into the group of guests.

"Oh, do let me see!" I surrendered my hand to a growing circle of admirers. "Flawless," they pronounced with something green like envy tinging their voices.

It was odd how conscious I became of that sudden alien circlet of gold and green. "Fragile," Hugh had said, looking concerned, for I'm certain that glittering green rectangle of rock had cost enough to intimidate even a Davenant.

"You look like the lady with the withered hand," Hugh teased in the carriage en route to Waterloo Station. It was true, I was cradling my suede-gloved hand as if it were injured. "At any rate," Hugh went on under the brim of his bowler, "If the Davenants are ever hard up, we can always send you out to beg—it's really rather pathetic, you look like a bird with a broken wing, darling," he said, smiling and putting his arms around me.

"Hugh, the coachman." I protested, aware of shops and passersby flowing past our conveyance's open sides.

"Devil take the coachman." Hugh lifted my face veil with one hand and caught me even closer with the other. He kissed me there in the corner of the hansom cab that everyone used to get hither and yon, he kissed me until I would have asserted that there was no place in the world better for it than the cramped hard leather of a hansom cab rattling over cobblestones with jolts that threatened to part our lips but never did.

"You seem to have forgotten about safeguarding your ring," Hugh noted as we rounded a corner and my hand rapped smartly against the carriage side.

"The Devil take my ring," I said, lifting my face for another guided tour of gratification. But Hugh held me away and mocked me.

"You swear with such feeling," he said, smiling. "I must say, that's the first thing I found indispensable about you."

"You didn't! When? When did you hear me—?"

"That day in the clearing, when you carted Quade up the hill to my feet."

Mention of Devlin flitted across my face like a raven's shadow, but I turned to racking my brains to recall the borrowed curses I'd used to goad myself up the hill. "Oh, you didn't actually *hear* me? I never thought all this time that you had heard me."

"I most certainly did. You're quite right, the British soldiery are bloody bastards and they'd be proud to admit to it. But take your hands away from your mouth, Mrs., I'm not through."

"Oh yes, you are. And I'm no mere 'Mrs.,' sir. I'll have you know I'm a proper 'Lady' now so I shall have to insist on your behaving like a gentleman the rest of the ride."

"How boring," said Hugh, untangling me. And just in time, for the cabman drew up a moment later before the dark stone pile that was the station.

And so we were off on another round of trains and ships and trains, off to countryside clattering past a window and waves bouncing us gently across the Irish Sea and yet another rattling ride through true green Irish countryside. This time our train chugged north to the capital city of Dublin. It was a short journey—no time for His Lordship to disarrange face veils— and even in the privacy of the carriage, the view outside the windows enchanted me more than my bridegroom's face.

"It seems such a large city. And so Georgian. I don't know why I didn't expect to see red brick and white pediments again. I shan't miss Carnhaven hardly at all."

"I'm glad," said Hugh drily, looking a bit put out that a city could put his bride in raptures and himself in the background. "Hemlock had gone on ahead to set things right. I hope he has attended to everything..." Hugh frowned and checked his pocket watch.

It was the second time I'd seen him check a pocket watch. He did it so beautifully, looking down his perfect straight nose, the two tiny lines between his dark brows as symmetrical as a railroad track. He was beautiful and I mustn't ever let him know it, or he'd be insufferable. Even the scar had faded into something familiar. I wondered why I had ever imagined it made him look dangerous. Or rakish. It was dashing.

The carriage turned a final corner and stopped. My attention slid off Hugh's face to the scene outside—a lovely length of red brick row houses sitting primly behind small gardens fenced by black wrought iron. Our house in Dublin. It had a yellow door between two classic pillars. Behind the facade we found a splendid entry hall tiled in black and white.

"It's lovely, Hugh. I shall be happy here, I know it." The fanlight above the door cast an uneven illumination on our faces. Hugh's, I noticed for the first time, was looking as I had never seen it, a bit embarrassed in a pleased sort of way.

"Your wedding present is in here," he said, opening a door to one of the front parlours. At first I glanced around bewildered from the settee to the chandelier, the lowboy, side chairs and there, in the corner near the bowed windows, the piano.

"But, it's, it's *my* piano! My piano from Eaton Square. However did you get it?" I advanced on its familiar bulk, ran my hands over the polished rosewood, caressed the gash in the music rack where Pumpkin, the great orange tomcat, had knocked the candleholder when I was ten.

"Hugh, tell me. Don't just look insufferably pleased with yourself. Where on earth did you find it?"

"Hampshire."

"Hampshire?"

"In a country parsonage, where it was played only six days of the week excepting Sunday by the parson's light-fingered spouse. She was persuaded to part with it after a sizable donation to the county beautification fund."

"But how did you know . . . ?"

"A certain talkative Mrs. Bowers. I traced her when I was looking into Eaton Square. She gave me a detailed account of the last days there—"

"Down to the 'crows,' I suppose."

I took off my hat and gloves and began playing a few notes. It was fresh-tuned, but it had been a long while since I had touched that piano. The keys pressed smoothly into place, my hands began to take on their old sureness and the chords I played echoed pleasantly in the quiet room.

Strange, the roundabout travels people and things made. It was back again, this lost piece of my self. And there were other lost pieces that could never be returned, not by all the wealth and will Hugh Davenant possessed.

My father. And my mother. My mother who had been "a

Leigh.' A woman of good family who had married beneath her. Married who, Terrence Dunne, that quiet colourless man I knew as my father? What had he been then that she had left her family for him? That was why Mrs. Bowers had never told me of her—it would have been a tale of bitterness and early death and disaffection. We had been truly cast off, Father and I. And the only link to it all was the name my mother had given me. Amberleigh. Leigh. Amberleigh Dunne.

"I rather think I have married a rebel," remarked Hugh with a smile in his voice.

I looked up at him, startled. He was leaning across the piano, watching me play. Puzzled, I listened to my own meanderings across the ivory keys. It was the sad, sad strains of "The Minstrel Boy."

> ". . . to the war has gone,
> In the ranks of death you'll find him,
> His father's sword he has girded on,
> And his wild harp slung behind him;
> "'Land of Song,' said the warrior bard,
> "Tho all the world betray thee,
> One sword at least thy rights shall guard
> One faithful harp shall praise thee!"

I was celebrating the legacy of Terrence Dunne and Devlin Quade. Both dead, both died of a cause, a fatal dose of love of country. I hardly knew either of them, really; but Devlin had been right. I was one of them as surely as my hair came out red or as I loved Hugh Davenant.

"No," I said to Hugh, shutting the piano, "a patriot."